NINA'S STORY

by

William J. Millman

SB
Sunset Beach Press

SB

Sunset Beach Press

Manufactured in the United States of America

Cover painting: William J. Millman

ISBN: 978-0692615027

To Nina

Prologue

I am old now. My eyes don't see as well as they once did, my hands tremble as I write. My memory is as skittish as a new-born colt. But I remember the distant past as if it were yesterday.

One of my earliest memories is the smell of smoke: acrid, choking, lung-searing smoke. The smell of burning flesh and dying dreams overlaid with screams of horror, both human and beast. Little did I know that this memory would foresage my entire life. But then again, I was Ukrainian. What did I expect?

I was born during some of the darkest moments of the Great Patriotic War, my birth a *souvenir* of my father's infrequent visits home from the front lines. I don't remember those difficult times, but I do remember the War coming to an end when I was three. Despite the omnipresent shadow of Stalin, we in the Ukrainian Soviet Socialist Republic thought – *hoped* is perhaps more accurate – that our lives would improve significantly after the horror of the Nazi war machine was finally dispatched. With the announcement of the end of hostilities in May 1945, every peasant in every village from Lviv to Donetsk, from Kyiv to Simferopol, dug up hidden potatoes and made backyard vodka to celebrate. Every vodka-swilling couple looked forward to a brighter future. My parents were one of them.

By 1949 I was seven years old, the middle daughter of Volodymyr Levchenko, a peasant farmer, and his Western Ukrainian wife, Anna. The years after the War were difficult for all Europeans, but none more so than for those of us who had been caught between two massive war machines: Germany on the one side, and the Soviet Union on the other. In Ukraine, the War had revealed seismic faults in Ukrainian society. Some of our people fought with the

Germans in hopes of banishing the Communists from our country forever. Others saw the Soviet forces as our saviors, the only barrier to utter domination by the Nazi hordes. My father joined with the Germans at the outset of the War, but was outraged and sickened by the horrific slaughter of our own people at Khatyn and the massacre of tens of thousands of ethnic Poles in Galicia by the OUN. In 1944 he switched allegiance to the Red Army, although his earlier affiliation caused the Soviets to view him with considerable distrust. That distrust would come back to haunt us all.

In the days immediately following the War, the Soviets were so focused on rebuilding their own territory and securing lands acquired at the end of a bayonet that they gave relatively little attention to those of us in the outlying Republics. As long as we produced food for Moscow and Leningrad and kept our opinions to ourselves, they were willing to turn a blind eye to the dissension that boiled just under the surface. But then came the food shortages of 1946-47.

Extreme drought combined with the devastation of war resulted in food production in Ukraine, Moldavia and central Russia that was less than half what it had been at the start of the war. Stalin thought the peasants were exaggerating the problems to force special treatment from the Communist regime. So he continued to export grain even as our people starved. I was too young to remember those times, but I've heard the stories: of people eating grass and leaves and boiled leather. Tens of thousands, hundreds of thousands of people dying.

What I do remember is the forced collectiv-ization that followed. The Soviets sent teams of party faithful to organize kolkhozes – titular collective farms in which group ownership existed on paper only. Peasants like my parents were required to work 150 days a year for Mother Russia (or more accurately, for the glorious Soviet regime), while boys

12-16 worked 50 days. They were paid roughly eight rubles for a kilogram of rye that sold in Moscow for over 300 rubles. As you might imagine, many Ukrainian farmers did not support the collectivization. Those who did not were prevented from raising food for themselves and their families, or deported, or killed.

It was into this nightmare that I was born and came of age.

Chapter 1

The night was bitterly cold, with the frigid north wind blowing dust through cracks in the walls and ceiling that filtered down like powdered sugar, the wind howling as if the night itself sensed the horrors to come. I was asleep in the small room I shared with my two sisters, all of us arranged head to toe on a simple wooden shelf lined with straw. We cuddled close together for warmth, but nothing could alleviate our hunger. There had been no rain for months; the rich dark earth of our village had turned to baked clay, then to dust. The crops failed one by one until soon there was not even enough grain or vegetables to meet the quotas set by Stalin, let alone enough for us to eat. But that did not stop the Twenty-five Thousanders, the shock brigades of city workers sent to the countryside to collect grain that didn't exist.

I awoke to the screams of our neighbors and the smell of smoke.

"Stay where you are!" my father yelled to us all. "Do not go outside!"

No sooner had he ordered us to stay than I heard the front door open and slam shut. I knew he'd gone to help.

"What is it Momma?" our youngest sister, Yerva, only three years old, asked with a quivering voice.

"The Twenty-five Thousand," she whispered. "They have come."

We had all heard stories of the forced collectivization teams. Poor, uneducated city workers sent to enforce Stalin's impossible demands for more and more food from peasant farmers like those in our village. After years of drought there was no way to produce the grain, potatoes, pigs, goats and other foodstuffs that the General Secretary demanded – not if we wanted to keep any food for ourselves. Stalin did not care. He needed food to maintain order in the larger cities and to earn hard foreign currency by selling overseas. So the Soviets exported grain while those of us in the south – Russian, Ukrainian and Moldovan – starved.

We could see flames flickering in the distance, casting horrible shadows on the mud walls of our hut. The shapes of men – many men – dashed and wove through the orange glow like specters in the fires of hell. Angry voices and shrieks echoed through the village. None of us said a word as we watched our world burn.

Just minutes after Papa left, the thatch roof of our neighbor's hut burst into flame, illuminating the night and warming the glass in the windows where all of us crowded together to witness a spectacle we had never thought to see: citizens of the Soviet Union killing other citizens for food that didn't exist. My oldest sister, Julija, was close friends with Katya, one of our neighbors' daughters, and when she saw their home explode in flame she could not remain still a moment longer. Dressed only in a cotton night shirt, she ran for the front door with hatred in her eyes, intent on helping her friend and repelling the attackers. But just as she pulled the door open, my mother grabbed her by the arm and yanked her back inside.

"I must go!" Julija shouted. "They will die!"

"You will stay here!" Mama ordered her, her hand locked on Julija's wrist.

Julija pulled and twisted, trying to wrench her arm free, but Mama held on with a determination and strength that belied her small stature. Finally, when my sister would not – could not – surrender to the reality she faced, Mama drew her arm back and slapped Julija across the face with a fury that shocked us all.

"You cannot save them! You can only die," Mama said, addressing my sister's angry expression with a pained tranquility that Julija could not challenge. Instead, she collapsed on the earthen floor, her tears staining my mother's nightgown. We all rushed to her side to hold her and convince ourselves that the nightmare would soon end. But it was hours before the shouts and screams finally subsided, hours before we dared to remove the hand-hewn board that secured our front door. Papa had not yet returned and, despite our protestations, Mama decided to go look for him. The orange glow of burning huts still visible in the distance, the four of us refused to stay there alone. So we all went together, huddled behind Mama like chicks behind a mother hen.

We walked slowly through what had been our village, home to 400 farmers and their families. Like so many Ukrainian villages, the simple thatched-roof huts had been surrounded by flowering plants of every size and hue imaginable, a vibrant splash of color in the dominant greens and browns of a farming community.

This night the dominant color was black. Hut after hut stood gutted, the roofs destroyed, the white-washed clay walls smeared with soot. From the outside we saw that our own home had barely escaped the fate of so many others: flames had licked at the walls and singed the thatch closest to our neighbors. There but for the Grace of God...

Other families wandered the dirt streets, their eyes wide, numb with disbelief.

"Have you seen my Volodymyr?" Mama asked everyone we came upon.

"I saw him fighting the fires," one man said.

"At Igor's house," another added. "But that was hours ago."

We walked on, the heavy odor of smoke and death swirling in the night breeze. As time passed I became more and more frightened, fearful not only of a return of the attackers, but increasingly afraid for Papa. Where was he? The further we walked, the more death and destruction we witnessed, the more the coiled snake of despair wrapped itself around my stomach and squeezed. I could hardly breathe, and not just from the smoke.

When we at last made our way to the ruined remains of the Rodchenkos' home, we found more than a dozen men and women stretched out on the ground surrounding the smoldering remains. Many wore torn cloth bandages on their heads and arms and hands. Several were covered entirely with sheets and blankets.

"Have you seen my Volodymyr?" Mama asked the exhausted group. I held one of her hands tightly while Yerva grasped the other.

One man I knew, whose children I'd played with, turned to us, his face blackened, his head wrapped in sooty pieces of cloth.

"There," he said, as if the effort to pronounce that one word was all he could manage. He stuck out his chin in the direction of a body that lay just a few meters from us, a body covered in a stained white sheet.

Mama did not cry out, did not fall to the ground or beat her breast. Instead, she hugged Yerva and me to her side and then, leaving us in Julija's custody, walked alone to where the ghostly figure lay unmoving in the burnt and trampled grass.

"Where is Mama going?" Yerva asked, but Julija put a finger to her lips and we all three stood and watched in silence as Mama knelt beside the supine figure and gently pulled back the sheet. In the darkness we could not see what she saw, but we all heard her gasp, a throaty cry of pain, and saw her shoulders shake as she mumbled words of prayer.

"Is Mama crying?" Yerva whispered.

I looked up at Julija and when I saw the tears rolling silently down her face, I knew. I began to cry, and then Yerva joined in as well even though she was too young to understand why. As Mama stood, a neighbor woman went to her side and put her arms around Mama's shoulders.

"He was a good man, Anna," she said, loud enough so that we heard. "The bastards cut him down when he tried to save the house."

"What will we do now?" Mama asked weakly.

"Your children need you."

Mama looked back at us, wiped her tears with the back of her hand, and nodded.

"Yes, of course."

"We will help, all of us. We won't forget," the woman said.

Mama gave the woman's arm a squeeze and started back to where we stood. Yerva broke free and ran to her, and soon the four of us stood hugging and sobbing in the smoldering stench of that awful night.

*****

They did, of course. Forget.

For some weeks after the raid we received extra food from the hidden provisions held back from Stalin's shock troops. But too many villagers had been injured or killed in the raid. Too many stomachs were empty. Too many families had lost their men.

Mama had always worked in the fields, but for the most part only at harvest time when the rich land exploded into full bloom and required immediate attention. Now the main task at hand was to scratch enough food from the barren cracked earth to feed our small family. Some of our neighbors relied on their parents or siblings to help them through those nightmare years, but we had no living grandparents – they'd died in or just after the War, and Mama was an only-child. Papa had a brother, but he had been badly injured in a German bombing and was in no position to help himself, let alone us.

Despite Mama's insistence that she was too young, Julija accompanied her out to the vast expanse of wilted, dying grain to try to harvest what they could before the Twenty-five Thousand, or some other band of urban brutes came back to seize what little remained of our crops. Mama left me with a neighbor to look after Yerva.

I don't remember that time very clearly. I was young, and constant hunger is the one sensation I still recall. That, and fear. We'd all heard the stories of villagers hung, or shot, or set afire by Soviet squads sent to uncover the meager stores of foodstuffs nearly every farmer had hidden in a cold cellar beneath a barn, or in the surrounding woods. I vaguely remember the arguments among village elders about the strategy we'd employ to survive the madness originating in Moscow.

"We must share with our fellow citizens," one elder would say.

"But our people will starve!" another would answer.

And so it would go, around and around the meeting place, voices and tempers flaring until even that effort was too much for their tired, starving bodies. Most meetings ended in sullen disagreement, neither side willing to concede yet neither so convinced they were willing to risk their lives – all our lives – on that certainty. So life dragged on, each day a painful shuffle to maintain some semblance of normalcy.

For us children, the debates of philosophy and political theory were just so much background noise. We played with dolls made of dried corn husks. We sang songs and listened to stories of the time of Czars and costume balls and palaces. We ran when we had the strength. Many of us – more so the older people from the village – just died.

As the elders knew they would, the collectivization teams returned. This time, however, they talked and negotiated instead of burning and killing, and a shaky truce took hold that allowed us to keep just enough food to stay alive while shipping the vast majority of our harvest north. For most of our neighbors, this was a time of relative prosperity. The rains came back, even if not quite so predictably as they once had. The quotas enforced by the Supreme Soviet more realistically matched our capacity to produce the grain and vegetables and livestock that fed our brother republics.

But without a man in our household, we were always at a disadvantage. Mama and Julija did their best, but they could never till or cut or haul as much as Papa did. And over time, our neighbors came to resent the extra help we required. It wasn't something that I, as a small child, noticed. But I heard my mother and some of the other widowed mothers discussing their plight when no one else was around. They shared tales of exasperated looks and sharp words from former friends. They wondered aloud how much longer they could depend on those *friends* for help. And finally, when the ostracism of our neighbors grew unbearable, they resolved to appeal to our regional soviet for assistance.

They weren't naïve or foolish. They knew full-well that their request would likely fall upon deaf ears. What they didn't expect was the vehement reaction their plea would engender.

The Volost Soviet was comprised of delegates from each of the local villages. It accepted public requests once a month, a town hall meeting at which everything from land rights to crop quotas to family disputes were aired and adjudicated. For whatever reason Mama brought all three of us sisters to the meeting, perhaps hoping to influence the Soviet by our youth and innocence.

Mama was not the only person asking for help – literally dozens of widowed women as well as many elderly persons crowded the large open room to petition the Executive Committee of the Volost. The three-person Committee – two men in their mid-fifties and a cold, pinched-lipped woman of forty or so – sat at a raised bench at the front of the room. A few wobbly chairs, not nearly enough to accommodate everyone in attendance, faced the Committee members. The majority of petitioners congregated in small groups behind the two rows of chairs, while many other waited in a long line outside the ramshackle building exchanging complaints and evaluating their chances. Some had come from quite a distance, two days or longer by cart. All bore the look of a people on the edge: hollow cheeks, tired, downcast eyes, and the bent stutter-step that seems to afflict people when they're pushed too hard, too far, for too long.

Mama and we three girls all waited inside with the other widows and a few old men from our village. It became evident very quickly that the Committee was not in a giving mood as the first few groups of villagers were summarily dismissed after a tongue-lashing for their 'deviant anti-societal behavior.' By the time we were called to appear before the three Volost representatives, my knees were already shaking in anticipation.

"Levchenko!" the woman member of the Executive Committee read from a long list, her voice a raspy cudgel that bludgeoned instead of invited. "Anna Levchenko!"

Mama led the three of us to the spot on the floor where petitioners made their case. Perhaps I saw her through biased eyes, but to me she seemed courageous and unafraid.

"What is your business for this Committee to consider?" the woman asked, just as she had to all those who'd gone before us. The eyes of her two fellow Committee members stared at us with so little pity or empathy I nearly burst out crying.

"My husband, Volodymyr Levchenko, died a few months ago trying to help a neighbor fight a fire that threatened to destroy his hut," Mama began. I heard a few sympathetic comments from our fellow petitioners.

"In what circumstances did this occur?" the man on the far left of the bench asked, his eyes narrowed to slits.

"The Twenty-five Thousand came to our village looking for grain," Mama said, her voice strong, "grain we did not have." A murmuring of voices sounded from other villagers behind us.

"Did you fulfill the quotas assigned by Moscow?" the other Committee member asked.

"We did not. We *could* not. You know the drought we have suffered. The grain and vegetables did not grow. We gave them all we could."

"And who made that decision?" the woman asked. "Your husband?"

"Among others," Mama said. "The local soviet informed the regional committee that the harvest would be much smaller this year."

"Who are *you* to inform?!" the woman shouted, spittle spraying the bench top. "You think you are above the proletariat? Your hunger is more important than theirs?"

"We cannot grow food if we are too weak from hunger to till the fields." Mama's voice was softer, but still insistent.

"You think only of yourselves!"

"That isn't true! My husband fought with our Patriotic Forces against the Nazi invaders and was wounded in battle! Many others in our village did the same."

"Didn't some also fight against the Motherland?" It was the man on the right. He didn't sound angry like the woman, but there was no warmth in his words.

"Some did, yes." Mama's voice was now nearly inaudible, even to us children holding tight to her skirt.

"And was one of them your husband?" the woman jabbed.

"Volodymyr was wounded defending our country!"

"Did your husband ever fight with the enemy forces?" the Committee member to our left asked, glancing down at a sheaf of papers in front of him.

"He fought with the Ukrainian Insurgent Army. He was a patriot!" Mama said, but her words began to sound desperate.

"He was a traitor!" the Committee woman announced, and a black murmur roiled through the waiting crowd. "He fought against our brave soldiers and died attempting to hide food from his fellow citizens!"

The people surrounding us began to mumble, nasty, hurtful words.

"That is not true!" Mama cried out, but it was clear to even me, as young as I was, that the crowd no longer supported our claim. One man just behind us called out, "Enough with these traitors! We do not have all day!" The voices that agreed with him were a minority, but large enough to make my stomach crawl with fright.

"Volodymyr Levchenko did fight with the RKKA," the quiet man to the right of the Committee said after raising his hand for quiet. "But only after he'd shamed himself by fighting with the partisans. We cannot forgive his treachery, nor forget his service. One moment."

He leaned in toward the other two members of the Executive Committee and the three whispered for nearly a minute. It was clear to us that the woman representative disagreed vehemently with something her fellow members suggested, but in the end it appeared she surrendered to their superior numbers.

"You will be granted one-half a veteran's stipend," the senior Committee Member announced.

"And you should be grateful for that!" the woman member interrupted. "Your husband probably killed Soviet citizens. We are sometimes too... lenient in our decisions."

She glared at the two men on either side of her, who ignored her.

Mama looked as if she would say something, but before she could open her mouth the Committee member on the right said, "Next!" and we were literally pushed out of the way by the villagers standing behind us.

I thought Mama would be happy, since the Committee had granted us a stipend, if only half the full amount. But what I didn't realize at the time was that even a full stipend was not nearly enough to feed a family of four. Half would barely keep us alive. I remember us pushing through the crowd, some of whom mumbled unkind words, and then reporting to a woman who copied information from Mama's internal passport. In moments it was all over and we were outside.

I looked up at my mother and saw the sadness and desperation in her face.

"Why are you sad, Mama?"

She looked down at me and forced a wistful smile.

"I'm not sad, кролик," she said, patting my hair with her hand. "I was just thinking about the past."

I soon learned that the only thing sadder than the past for a Ukrainian in the post-War Soviet Union was the future.

Chapter 2

If we had felt shunned in our tiny village before our trip to the Executive Committee, we were positively despised upon our return. Neighbors we thought were our friends refused to speak to us. Late one night, a thrown rock smashed a window in our hut. Even small children, our closest friends, would not, or could not spend time with us.

It was in school, however, that we most acutely felt our isolation. The village основная школа was a renovated barn holding three classrooms. The first, which I attended, taught classes 1-4 – for children aged 7-10. Julija had already graduated to intermediate school, while Yerva remained at home with Mama. The first day I returned to classes after coming back from our trip, I was so happy to be back in my home village I didn't notice the stares and muttered comments from my fellow students at first. I had accepted at face value that my closest friend, Dasha, was ill and could not go to school with me as she had nearly every day previously. It never crossed my mind she might be purposely avoiding me, despite the fact that Mama had warned Julija and me of the reaction we might expect from our trip to the Volost. Parents? Members of the local Soviet? Of course they might be upset with Papa's past. But their children? Our friends?

It was my teacher who set the tone for the entire class. On my first day back to school after our trip, I found that my desk had been moved to the back row and my position as one of the favored students in the class – perhaps *the* favored student – had suddenly evaporated.

"Miss Levchenko," Mrs. Comrade Dudyk intoned as I argued with the girl who sat where I'd been sitting for the first few months of the school year, "your place is in the back, with other offspring of traitors to our country."

"Yeh, Levchenko, go back there with the rest of the vermin," one of the bigger boys in the class, an ignorant bully who often mouthed the thinking of his equally ignorant parents, said as he yanked one of my braids. Several other students laughed. I saw some of my closest friends shrink down in their chairs and look away in embarrassment. Humiliated, but more angry than anything, I did as I was told. For the rest of the year I was essentially ignored, the teacher only calling my name to order me to empty wastebaskets or clean erasers, or on those rare occasions when she could use a mistake I'd made on an exam or paper to demonstrate to my classmates how the children of traitors were inferior citizens and unworthy of the beneficence of the Soviet state.

With none of our former friends allowed to play with us, my sisters and I learned to occupy ourselves with our own games and inventions. Oh, from time to time we were allowed to visit other *shamed* families, but for the most part all of us whose fathers and husbands had fought on the wrong side of history stayed to ourselves, unwilling to subject ourselves to the ridicule and abuse we'd find at the hands of other village children.

Don't misunderstand: I wasn't a sad child, moping through each day harboring hatred for my father, or my friends, or even the Soviet authorities whose actions fed the animosity we experienced from our neighbors. No, I came to look upon my Papa's experience as a Partisan as a badge of honor, a mark of integrity in a shameful society that publically embraced the Russian invaders while at the same time privately berating them. We were Ukrainian, not Soviet, and no matter the consequences, Mama made certain we never forgot our heritage.

And so it wasn't a surprise that the few friends we made, the few families with whom we had any interaction at all, were also Ukrainian nationalists. As we grew older and the memories of the Great Patriotic War and the political divides it engendered faded from memory – at least among the younger people in our village – my sisters and I came into contact with a larger circle of friends and acquaintances, many of whom moved to our oblast in the early and mid-Fifties. Gradually, as the rains returned and the cracked, thirsty landscape once again turned green and gold with fields of wheat and barley, and brilliant yellow with row upon row of towering sunflowers, laborers who'd fled to the cities of the north returned to the land they'd abandoned but that still called out to their souls.

It was during the wheat harvest of 1959, a month-long community effort that brought out every able-bodied person over the age of 12, when I first met Bogdan. That year had seen warm, sunny days alternate with extended gentle rains, resulting in a bumper crop larger than any we'd seen in the oblast for many years. Workers flooded into the area in mid-July as we readied the equipment and workers to attack the fields. Julija had married and she and her husband, Marko, were leaders in our village collective. Yerva was 14, I was 17, and we were excited about the upcoming harvest. It was the one time of the year when new faces were seen in the region, and in particular, new boys. Our isolation from much of village life had put a significant dent in our relationships with boys our own age, and the possibility that we might meet the man of our dreams helped overcome the dread of working long hours, day after day in the hot, dusty fields.

We had asked Julija to keep an eye out for any young men who might meet our requirements: handsome, intelligent, kind, strong, and preferably wealthy, or at least with good potential.

"Are you looking for a boyfriend or the son of a czar?" she'd joked when we'd made our demands known.

We knew it was unlikely we'd find a perfect man in the wheat fields of our oblast, but it didn't stop us from hoping.

I remember the first two weeks of the season as unbearably hot and incredibly busy. All of us from the village and wagonloads of laborers from other parts of the USSR pushed ourselves to bring in the grain before one bad storm could undo months of good growing weather.

My life changed on a Monday, another cloudless sunny day with a sky the color of lapis lazuli. My team had just taken a break from the exhausting work of scything hectares of golden Ukrainian grain. The twelve of us – ten women and two men – gathered together in the shade of a gnarled old tree, our faces dirt and sweat-traced from hours of cutting and gathering. I didn't see the two horse-drawn wagons arrive until I heard voices calling to us from the road to the west. When I looked up I saw two groups of itinerant laborers, most likely extended families from the look of them, being led to our location by Julija. At first I was just curious as to whom my older sister had been able to persuade to join our ranks, since competition for farmhands during harvest season was intense indeed. Every oblast in the region desperately wooed the traveling hands, oftentimes promising them food and shelter to persuade them to choose one team over another. Rarely, if ever, were the visitors told that their services would no longer be needed after the harvest, and their presence would be, at best, barely tolerated.

This group looked promising. A mix of young and old, men and women, their well-worn garb looked clean and functional, unlike some others who'd passed through just days earlier. It was probably unfair to judge an entire group by a first impression, but we all did it.

"Looks like they might know one end of the scythe from the other," one of the older women in our team said as we watched the fourteen new arrivals walk toward us. Julija led the way, followed closely by two older men, almost certainly the patriarchs of the families. Just behind, four younger men and three girls about my age stared inquisitively, with two woman herding three younger children at the back.

"I just hope they're workers and not talkers," another said.

"Unlike you," someone countered, and snickers swept across our team.

As we watched, the group approached somewhat shyly, with little chatter and no laughter.

"Look who I've found to help you," my sister called out.

"About time!" one of our two men answered, and everyone laughed, breaking some of the nervous tension.

"Good afternoon," the eldest of the two men at the head of the group called out when they were no more than a few meters from our resting place. Oleksiy, the eldest of our male comrades, rose languidly and shook hands with both the two older men.

"Welcome. You've come to work?"

From just behind their two leaders, a young man answered. "Not much of a place for a vacation, is it?" He was tall, thin, and good-looking in a fierce, almost angry sort of way. His curly black hair stood out from the sides of his cap and framed eyes nearly as blue as the sky above. I felt my heart flutter.

Their elder leader turned quickly, and for an instant it appeared he might slap the young man for his insolence. But he restrained himself, saying instead, "Hold your tongue, Bogdan!" The young man did as he was told, but his eyes burned with anger.

"Young people today feel they must make their opinions known," the elder said to Oleksiy with an irritated shake of his head.

"You are not the only ones to suffer the hubris of the young," Oleksiy said, glancing back at us with a sarcastic grin. "They think they know it all."

"Not all, only most," I said without thinking, and my cheeks immediately blossomed as our younger people laughed and the older villagers looked askance. Oleksiy ignored me, introducing himself to the newcomers.

Ivan and Yure were the two family heads. We'd meet the others as we worked.

From the very first I had my eyes on Bogdan. I used any excuse to work near him, any ploy to talk to him. Still, harvest is a busy, hot, tiring business and I didn't find many excuses during that first day until we completed our labor just before sunset. We'd all assembled near the carts that would haul our exhausted bodies back to the village, a kilometer or so away. I'd just finished adding my scythe to the stack and was talking with Yerva about how much we'd accomplished, when I noticed by little sister's eyebrows rising and falling in a most peculiar fashion.

"Are you all right?" I asked, assuming a horsefly had stung her or she was reacting to some allergy that had unexpectedly afflicted her.

"I'm…okay," she said with an exaggerated cadence and jerk of her head that made me realize she was signaling something. Only I had no clue what. I followed her rolled eyes and found Bogdan standing just a short distance away, his gaze seemingly riveted on *me!*

I was struck dumb. I tried to think of something clever, or at least not simple, to say, but my lips refused to move. Yerva noticed my distress and came to the rescue.

"So what did you think of your first day?" she asked with no hint of the devious undercurrent her question entailed.

"You people work hard," he said softly.

"The harvest won't wait. One big rainstorm and kaput! It's all ruined."

"Not much chance of that with workers like you two around. What's your name?" Even as he asked her, he looked at me.

"Yerva."

"And your friend?" He jutted his jaw in my direction.

"She's my sister."

"Can't she speak?" he asked with a hint of a smile and a twinkling in his eyes.

"I can speak, when I want," I said, sounding more severe than I'd intended.

"Ah. So do you want to speak now?"

"I might. Who's asking?"

He took a few steps closer to where we stood. "My name is Bogdan, Bogdan Kovalchuk. You?"

"Nina, Levchenko. We live here, in the village."

He nodded. "We… move a lot. With the harvest. We used to live in Markova, but there was no work for my father and so we packed up and came down here where the grain is better."

"Our father is dead," Yerva said, and I gave her a nasty look she ignored.

"Oh? The War?" So many people had died during the War that it was common to find families without a father. I probably could've lied. But I didn't.

"In the forced collectivization. He tried to save a neighbor's house."

"Ah," he said, looking both pensive and apologetic. "It was a bad time."

"Is your mother with you?" Yerva went on, undeterred, and I wanted to kill her.

He shook his head. "She died. In '50 – the famine."

I wanted to tell him how sorry I was that his mother had died, but just then Oleksiy called us all to the wagons.

"We've got to go," Yerva announced.

"Can I ride with you?" he asked.

"Of course!" my little sister answered before I could muster the courage, and for once I was happy with her unthinking brashness.

I felt the eyes of some of the other young girls on us as we walked to the wagons, and thought I heard a remark or two under their breaths when Bogdan helped me up into the back of our cart. He lifted me up as though I were nothing more than a sack of wheat.

"What about me?" Yerva complained.

"How could anyone ever forget you?" he said, and he tossed her up next to me with no visible effort.

We talked all the way back home. I learned that both wagonloads of itinerant workers would stay at a makeshift campground on the outskirts of the village, part of but distinctly separate from those of us who lived there. They planned to stay through the harvest season, but Bogdan seemed truly happy to be with us, working in the fields.

"Anything is better than traveling every day, sleeping under the trees in a forest every night. You girls don't know how lucky you are."

He was right. Like most people, I only saw what was wrong with my life. How my fellow villagers had shunned our family for so many years; how we'd grown up without Papa; how we had little hope for a future beyond the confines of our oblast, a life of field work, marriage at an early age, and an adult life of quiet desperation. Listening to his talk made me realize that we also had the few friends we'd made over the years, we had our faith, and we had each other.

"Will I see you again tomorrow?" Bogdan asked as Yerva and I climbed down from the cart in front of our hut.

"We'll be in the fields," I said, but with enough of a smile to show I hoped he would.

I didn't wait for the cart to pull away, but went straight for our front door. As I pressed the handle, however, I glanced back in the direction it had gone, and found Bogdan staring directly back at me. He dipped his head in recognition, which sent me scurrying with embarrassment into the house.

"Nina has a boyfriend!" Yerva yelled out as soon as we stepped into the hut.

I punched her in the arm. "Shut up!'

"Mama, Nina hit me," my sister moaned, making it sound as though I'd beaten her with a whip.

"Nina, don't hit your sister," Mama said as she juggled several pans on the stove. "And what's this about a boyfriend?" I had had several male friends over the years, but never a real boyfriend. I could hear the restrained interest in her voice.

"It's just a new boy who came with his family to work the fields," I said nonchalantly as I pulled off my dirt-caked boots.

"What's his name?"

"Bogdan."

"He's cute!" Yerva chipped in as she scurried out of my reach. "And I think he likes Nina."

I glared at her, but she just raised her eyebrows in a mocking taunt.

"Well that's all well and good," Mama said, "but right now you need to wash up and set the table. Go!"

As always we talked about our day in the field as we ate, but after several pointed attempts by Yerva, Mama insisted we stay away from further discussion of Bogdan. As the sun set in a blaze of reds and pinks and darkness crept into our little hut, I thought we'd moved past the subject and was feeling pretty relaxed as Yerva and I prepared for bed later that night. No sooner had we slipped under the covers and called out for Mama to come give us our goodnights, however, than I learned we hadn't even begun to move past it.

"You know," Mama began as she sat beside us on the narrow bed the two of us shared each night, "you girls are not children anymore," and both of us understood we were in for a lecture. "You, Nina, will be eighteen in four months, and you, Yerva, are nearly fifteen. There are *things* you need to know."

I restrained a groan. I knew from talking with some of the girls in my school that their mothers had already given them 'the lecture', and I'd been privy to all the secrets they'd learned. I felt the superiority that only a truly ignorant person can feel, and a superiority to my sister that must've been insufferable.

"When girls get to be your age, they have... wants, and needs, that they didn't feel when they were younger." She was struggling, and I didn't make it any easier for her.

"Yerva is probably too young to understand," I said, only partly in jest.

"I understand!" my sister disagreed. "She means boys. Like Bogggg-dan." She exaggerated the last and would've received a swat in response if Mama wasn't sitting right there.

"All right – that'll be enough of that. And yes, to some extent that means boys. I don't know what you've been taught about how babies are made..."

This time it was Yerva's turn to interrupt. "Mama! We live in a farm village. We see the animals doing it all the time. We're not stupid."

"Of course not," Mama said, sounding as much relieved as chagrinned. "But there's more to it than just the physical part. Sex is part of love, but it isn't everything. To a woman, romantic love and even companionship are just as important sometimes."

"You're getting old, Mama," Yerva said, and received a smiling tap to her head for her trouble.

"That may well be, but you two are still young. Very young. And you think you know more than you do. Boys look at sex... differently."

"How Mama?"

"Well, to them sex is sometimes... separate from love, or even like a game. They do it just for fun."

"I know some girls who do it for fun," I said before I could catch myself.

"Well I hope you're nót one of them!" Mama said, and I found myself burning red.

"Of course not!" Except for an occasional youthful kiss, my knowledge of human love up until that time derived from nothing more than observation and the incessant gossiping of my peers.

Mama glanced over at Yerva. "Don't look at me," she cried out. "I don't even like boys."

"Except for Vanko..." I said, taking more than a little pleasure from the opportunity to get back at her for her previous jabs.

"Who?" Mama asked.

"Nobody! She's just being a... pest!" Yerva said, glowering in my direction.

"You were talking about boys," I prodded.

"Yes. Well, the gist of it all is that I want both of you to promise me you will be careful, with boys, I mean. Getting pregnant at your age would be very difficult."

"Like Yerva said, we're not stupid. We know what boys want, and they're not going to get it until we see a wedding ring on our finger. Right, Yerva?"

"A big, golden ring!" she said with the enthusiasm of her age.

That seemed to appease our poor mother, but despite our pledge it wasn't to be quite that easy to avoid the guiles of the local boys. Especially one in particular.

Chapter 3

For several weeks that summer we all worked as a team: traveling to and from the fields together in our horse-drawn carts, cutting, gathering, threshing, winnowing and finally hauling the grain to the local mill for grinding, even spending the occasional meal together to celebrate the completion of a difficult task or an entire field. The weather that year was spectacular: warm sunny days with just enough breeze to keep us from melting into little puddles, and cool starlit nights ideal for sleeping.

Looking back, I suppose it was inevitable that Bogdan and I would get closer. From the first moment we'd set eyes on each other there'd been an undeniable attraction, a spark I had never felt before with any other boy. It was as if our meeting had been preordained, a magical moment beyond our control or knowledge. So it seemed.

But romance was a simple thing in our world, nothing of the formality and pomp you read about in books or see in the movies. Bogdan had neither the money nor the inclination to sweep me off my feet and take me with him to Paris, or even the largest town in the oblast. His inclinations were more toward a broad smile, a twinkle in his eye and just enough attention to reassure me that I was the only girl for him. Or at least the one he cared for most. Bogdan always had a bit of a wandering eye, though I can hardly blame a boy of eighteen for acting his age. In retrospect, perhaps he was also teasing me a bit, making sure I wasn't *too* confident of our friendship.

As the summer came to an end, the anticipation of finally finishing the harvest was tempered by the realization that Bogdan, and all the other visiting laborers, would be leaving once the work in the fields was done. All of us on our team came closer as our last days together drew to a close, but none more than Bogdan and I. It's not as though it happened all in one week, or even one month. It was a gradual thing, a friendship that deepened and then blossomed over time. The years have blurred many of the specifics, but I remember one afternoon as if it were yesterday.

We had finished our daily tasks and were waiting with our follow workers for the carts that would haul us back to the village. Bogdan and I sat off to one side, away from most of the others, in an unspoken arrangement that had developed over the many weeks we'd spent together. We were talking, about what I don't recall, when he unexpectedly took my hand in his.

"Let's not wait for the cart," he whispered, his expression eager and wild. "Let's walk back on our own."

Part of me heard my mother's warning sound a caution I understood full-well. But I was thinking with my heart just then, not my head, and the possibility excited me.

"All right," I said, and even that required an effort to keep my voice calm and controlled.

When we announced to the others we would be walking back together we received the kinds of catcalls and ribald comments we expected, along with measured words of advice from some of the older workers. We took them all in stride and started back toward the village hand in hand.

It was barely five minutes later when we saw the cart coming out from the village to pick up the team. We brushed aside the driver's offer of a ride and ignored his questioning looks. Ten minutes later the cart returned loaded with our fellow workers, and once more we were serenaded by their attempts at humor at our expense. We watched wordlessly as the cart moved off into the distance, the sound of taunts and joking replaced by the slow clip-clop of the tired old mare that pulled the cart under the urgings of her equally old and tired driver.

"They're such children," Bogdan said when they'd finally disappeared around a bend in the roadway. "You'd think they'd never seen a man and woman walk together before." *Man and woman.* The very words took my breath away. Were we, really, man and woman? I still saw myself as a schoolgirl, albeit a particularly intelligent and perceptive one.

"They're just having fun," I said, more to break the awkward silence than to make any particular point.

"Children," he muttered once again.

He took my hand in his once more and we walked past field after field of scythed wheat and rye, the stubble of the stalks swaying nearly imperceptibly in the cooling breeze. I don't know if my imagination has burnished the moment over the years, but it seems to me now that the sounds of birds and insects swirled about us in the golden light just before sunset, a choir of voices singing hosannas to our mutual devotion.

"I'm going to miss you," he said after long minutes watching the sun dip below the treetops.

"I'll miss you too," I said, and my voice nearly cracked as tears welled in my eyes.

"I've never known a girl like you. I wish... I wish my family could just stay here. Live in the village."

"That would be wonderful."

We knew that was unlikely, both because the Soviet authorities did not often permit internal migration without a pile of paperwork and because Bogdan's parents had brothers and sisters back in their own village, some 200 kilometers to the west. But we could dream.

We stopped as if at some unseen signal. "I won't leave you," he said, his voice suddenly as adult as I'd ever heard. "I'll find a way."

I don't know if I believed him, if I believed it was even possible. I know I wanted to believe.

When he leaned in toward me I froze with excitement and anticipation. When his lips touched mine a spark of emotion surged through my entire body. The next thing I knew, we were running hand in hand off the main road into a field bordered by a two or three meter hedge that shielded us from any passerby. We kissed again, and again, his hands fumbling with my buttons as I tore at his, the world suddenly condensed into just the space we inhabited. He lowered me gently but firmly to where our discarded clothing lay on the field grass as his hands began to touch me, grab, knead my body as no one had ever done before. I heard a gasp and a low moan, sounds that came from a place deep within me, and as his mouth moved down to my shoulders and then my breasts, my back arched with desire.

Before I realized what was happening, he was inside me. I gasped with pleasure and pain, but didn't push him away. I *wanted* him there. Wanted him more than I had ever wanted anything. I knew the potential consequences, knew that we should wait, but in that moment of ecstasy I didn't care, didn't have a moment of fear or hesitation.

When he had finished, he rolled onto his back and lay panting beside me like some great hunting dog after a long run. I watched him without a word, running a single finger down his chest and stomach as if to reassure myself that he was really there, that the moment itself was real.

"Wow," he said, staring up at the drifting clouds as if hypnotized. "I've never felt anything like that before."

"You've never... been with another girl?" I asked, both needing and dreading his answer.

"No! Of course not!" he said, turning to face me with a look so tender and caring I wanted to kiss him again right then and there. "You are the only one! Now, and forever."

And then we did kiss again.

When we separated, we stared into each other's eyes for what seemed like a very long time. The light began to fade and the evening air turned cool; I shivered.

"We should be getting back," I said half-heartedly.

"I suppose we should."

We gathered up our clothes in silence, partly in awe of what we'd just done, partly deep in thought of what it all meant. We turned away from each other to dress, suddenly shy.

"I wish it could be like this forever," I said as I pulled my shoelace tight.

I didn't know then that a wish come true could bring so much pain.

*****

When we got back home we snuck a quick peck of a kiss on the road outside before I ran into the house. I think I expected everyone would immediately see what I'd done, and I was both proud and anxious to see their reaction. But they didn't know.

"You're back late," Mama said as soon as I'd shut the door.

"What did you and Bogdan have to talk about that you couldn't ride back with us?" Yerva asked.

"Nothing much," I said. "Just felt like walking."

"Sure took your time. Could've walked to the next village by now," my sister persisted.

"Leave your sister alone," Mama ordered. "Wash up and set the table."

With that, the interrogation was over. To me, the entire order of the universe had changed. To them, it was time for dinner.

Ironically enough, my mother chose that very night to question me about my plans after graduating from school the following December. I had done well in school, and was on course to complete all of my studies a semester early. We had no money for university, but Mama was determined that I would be the first in our family to attend. School itself was paid for by the State, but books, and supplies, and even clothes were expensive and the government stipend would not cover it all. Too expensive for a single woman with two teenage daughters. Besides, I thought Bogdan might have something to say about my future, but I also thought that his family would want to keep him close-by as long as possible.

"I'm not sure," I answered. "Of course I'd love to attend university..."

"Then you should!" Mama said. "Where there's a will..."

"We can't afford it, Mama, you know that."

"We will find a way."

"Perhaps I will find a job and save enough money." It was unlikely that I could find a job there in the village that paid enough to put anything aside, but I was young and hopeful.

"I will pray for you," Mama said.

"Better if you find a job," Yerva whispered.

*****

I only saw Bogdan once more that summer. After days of waiting anxiously for his visit, I had begun to think he was sick or hurt when he showed up one night just before sundown, his face twisted in a tell-tale grimace of pain.

"My parents don't let me leave our camp," he explained after intercepting me on the road outside our hut. "I told them I wanted to marry you, but Father forbade it. He said I was too young, and the family needed my help until the girls are grown and off on their own."

"That's not fair!" I called out.

"Fair or not, the only way for us to be together is to run away." To my shocked reaction, he quickly continued. "I've thought it through. We can go to Kyiv, or Lviv. They'll never find us in such big cities, and we can both find work."

He looked so earnest, so hopeful, that I almost said yes right then and there. But my thoughts strayed to Mama and my little sister. Without my help they'd be trapped forever in the poverty of our little village, with no chance of a better life. I felt torn in two, my heart split down the middle. I struggled to think of a way to help them without sacrificing my own happiness.

"Tell them you want to stay here," I begged Bogdan. "You can work and send them money each month."

He shook his head sadly. "My father won't hear of it. I've tried everything I can think of. Our only hope is to run off together."

I don't know where I found the will, but I did. "I can't abandon Mama and Yerva. They need me even more than your parents need you."

His sullen silence was my answer.

A week later, despite all his protestations, Bogdan left our village with his family. I felt as though I'd been kicked in the stomach.

For days I moped around the house, unwilling to see friends, prepare for the upcoming school year, even help my mother.

"Are you sick?" Mama asked.

"Bogdan and his family went back home," Yerva answered when I stared blank-faced into nothingness.

"There will be other boys," Mama said, but I didn't believe her. There was only one, and he would live forever in my heart.

As days melted into weeks, the sharp sting of his departure faded into a dull throb and life resumed some semblance of normalcy. I did my chores, managed to chat with friends without breaking into tears, and even attended the first day of classes. But deep inside, my thoughts and feelings were all directed at Bogdan. It was as if my world were shrouded in a mist of despair – everything grey, lifeless, loveless. Mama made my favorite foods; my friends tried to cheer me up; even Yerva was marginally less annoying than usual. But no light penetrated that shroud. Nothing could lift my spirits. I was alive, but my life was over.

Weeks dissolved into months and I did not hear a word from Bogdan. I had given myself entirely to my studies, losing myself in the poetry of Shevchenko, the achingly beautiful landscapes of Soshenko. I lived through their art, since in my mind my world had died.

And then in December, just a few days before my graduation, my life changed forever. I was washing before school, my mind gratefully focused on the exams that consumed all my waking hours. I ran the washcloth across my breasts and winced, the unexpected pain awakening me from my dazed existence.

'What is this?' I remember thinking. I felt no particular cause for alarm.

I mentioned it to my mother in passing at breakfast that morning, and to my surprise her face reflected concern.

"When was your last cycle?" she asked.

Until she spoke, I hadn't really thought about it. I was not ever very regular, and so a missed week or even month hadn't worried me. Until then.

"I'm not certain. Maybe two, three months ago."

Mama's eyes opened wide. "Two or three months?! Ninichka, tell me the truth now, no lying to your mother: have you lain with a boy in that time?"

My cheeks burned, and with Yerva looking on wordlessly I nearly lied. But in the end, I couldn't.

"Just one time," I managed to mutter.

"Nina!" my little sister cried out, shocked.

"Was it Bogdan?" Mama asked calmly, showing none of Yerva's histrionics.

"Of course it was! Who else could it be?" I may have made a mistake, but I wasn't sleeping around.

"We'll need to get you to the doctor," Mama said. "Just to be sure."

"But it was just that one time!" I argued. Looking back, I was naïve and foolish to be sure, but at the time I was so frightened I'd have grasped at any excuse to make it untrue.

*****

The nearest doctor's office was in the oblast capital, some 60 kilometers from where we lived. Despite all the villages in the area, he was the only physician within a day's travel. All the appointments had already been claimed for weeks ahead when Mama first called, and for a while it looked like we might have to travel further afield to have me examined. But just a few days later they notified us that a patient had canceled, and scheduled my appointment for the following week. Mama had made Yerva promise not to say a word about my supposed *condition*, and I certainly wasn't saying anything to anyone. Mama had even made sure no one overheard her when she used the communal phone at the village administrative center. It wasn't so much that we would have faced punishment from the local soviet – they were not particularly interested in who bedded whom. But the Orthodox Church held surprising sway in our region, especially among the older folks, and Mama didn't want to subject us, or herself, to the ostracism the Church would've instigated.

So when the date of my appointment finally came around, Mama suggested to friends and neighbors that we were traveling to the capital to investigate possible university support for me. No one questioned the excuse, since everyone in the village knew full-well that the only way someone like me could attend was if I received help from the government, a family member, or the Church.

We left at dawn in the Yiraneks' cart. They lived just a few huts away from us and had been one of the few families in the village to support us through the difficult period after Papa died. Mr. Yiranek – Yuri – was an older man, old enough to be Mama's father. His wife, Sofiya, had prepared food for us when we'd had nothing to eat. On this cool fall morning, Yuri drove the two-horse team that pulled us toward my appointment. I remember my heart beating too fast, my hands shaking. On the one hand, I was excited that I might be carrying Bogdan's child. Even though I hadn't heard from him in months, I knew in my heart he still loved me and was prevented from communicating with me by his family. On the other, I was terrified I might have to give birth to and raise a fatherless child. I'd seen enough of that in the village. I didn't want my baby to suffer from my mistake.

We climbed down from the cart a good kilometer from the doctor's office, close by the oblast administrative center where we could apply for university assistance. As long as we were in the capital it only made sense to inquire, while at the same time it kept my secret from becoming common knowledge – at least for a time. Mama told Yuri that we'd meet him at four o'clock in the same spot, allowing him to spend the day running errands and visiting friends. We only stayed a short while at the administrative offices, just long enough to learn that I faced a difficult battle if I expected to attend university.

"Are you a member of the Party?" the fat, middle-aged woman behind the counter asked when we queried.

"She's just 17," Mama answered.

"Her father then?"

"Died during the War."

"Fought with the Soviet forces?"

"Yes." Mama didn't elaborate.

"You?"

"Me?"

Mama didn't understand the question.

"Are you a Party Member?"

"I've never been a political person."

The apparatchik scowled. "I take it that means 'no'."

"No, I'm not."

"Young Pioneer?" That was a youth group that attended camp during the summers and practiced mindless support of the Communist Party all year long.

"We are farmers," Mama interrupted. "We work during the summer. She has no time for camp."

"We must all make time to support the Marxist-Leninist Doctrine," she said in a bored, bureaucratic tone that suggested her heart wasn't in it. She looked at me and sighed. "All right. Fill this out and bring it back when you're done," she directed, handing me a form. "Next!"

I was disappointed and dejected when we left the counter, but Mama would have none of it.

"She didn't say no. Let's fill out the form and see what happens."

I felt as if I was wasting my time, but did as I was told. When I handed the completed form back to the woman at the counter I tried to force a pleasant smile, but I'm sure it came across more like a pained grimace.

"You will be contacted if your application is approved," the woman said with absolutely no emotion.

When we left the building it seemed to me as though my dream of attending university had been shattered. Our next stop might well bury the pieces of that dream.

The doctor's office was several blocks away, past stores and shops that were bigger and better stocked than anything we had in our little village. In retrospect it's funny that we all thought the capital to be a sophisticated city, a place of high culture and refined tastes. Compared to even a small city of today the capital was really nothing more than a rural crossroads, but to us it was the Paris of our world. For just a few minutes I forced myself to look at the ready-made dresses and hats in the windows and think of anything other than the woes that beset me, though I don't think I was particularly successful. I know that by the time we reached the office I was nearly shaking with dread.

I won't describe the cold, inhuman treatment I received from the staff at the clinic. They were Orthodox believers who thought unmarried women who became pregnant were the Devil's playthings, and acted accordingly. The Doctor, a rail-thin older man with grey hair and gold wire rim glasses, was much more gentle and understanding as he examined me in ways I'd never imagined, but not even the most sympathetic physician in the world could've cushioned the blow when he announced upon completing his examination, "There's no doubt. You're pregnant. I'd guess three months or so."

His words, though hardly unexpected, struck me like the kick of a mule. For just an instant I had trouble catching my breath. I must've turned as white as fresh-fallen snow because Mama took my arm and held on as though she was worried I'd collapse.

"Are you certain?" was all I could mouth.

"Quite." He studied me for a moment, his pale grey eyes staring into mine. "Congratulations!" he added after a short pause, "You're going to be a mother!" I think he knew I was conflicted, but chose to put the best face on a bad situation.

I stumbled out of the clinic into the busy street beyond in a complete daze. I knew Mama and Yerva were by my side, could feel them holding fast to my arms for support, but it was almost as if I were dreaming. As if a blanket had fallen over me and the sights and sounds of the city were somehow muted, indistinct. I was probably in shock.

In little more than an hour all my hopes and plans had been turned on their head. I had awakened that day as a young girl with unlimited dreams, but was now an unmarried mother-to-be, with no certain future, trapped in a snare of my own making. I wanted to cry.

Mama and Yerva tried their best to soothe my anxiety, and I acted the part of resigned daughter as best I could to try to soothe theirs. But in reality I was petrified, my stomach churning, hands quivering. Since Papa's death I had never faced a challenge anything like what I faced at that moment. In fact, as I thought about it in the cart heading home I realized I had lived my life in a protective cocoon, shielded from the vicissitudes of daily existence by my mother and a few understanding neighbors. Now it would be my turn – to shield *my* child. Was I up to it?

*****

I tried to resume my day-to-day activities back in the village, but it was easier said than done. I experienced morning sickness in all its glory, emptying my stomach nearly every morning for three weeks on end, and after that whenever a smell struck me the wrong way. Mama and Yerva kept my secret as we tried to work out a plan to get me out of the village before my pregnancy showed, so word of my *indiscretion* did not spread widely. There was the occasional comment about how pink and healthy my cheeks looked, or questions from girls my own age about whether I'd put on a few pounds. I ignored them all, feigning ignorance. But as three months became four, it became obvious to all of us that I needed to either leave my home or face the barrage of criticism and ill-will that only a small village could heap upon a woman in my situation.

The biggest problem, or at least my biggest worry, was Bogdan. I tried to send him several messages, letting him know he was soon to be a father. But my letters went unanswered and attempts at telephoning were unsuccessful. I didn't know why he hadn't responded, but I grew more and more convinced that I needed to find him and learn whether his love for me still existed, and if it extended to our child.

When I raised the idea of seeking him out, Mama was adamant in her opposition.

"You should not be traipsing all over the countryside looking for the man," she said. "You haven't received a single letter or call from him, and it's been more than four months. What kind of person would completely ignore the woman he loves?"

I didn't know the answer to her question, but I knew I needed to find out. So while I feigned acceptance of her edict, I planned in secret to go in search of the father of my child. I'd located the family home on a map: some 600 kilometers to the northwest. With any luck, I should've been able to hitchhike my way there in just a few days. So I squirreled away some basic foodstuffs and packed a small travel bag. One January morning, soon after Yerva had gone off to school and Mama had gone with some neighbors to a nearby village to shop for food, I stepped out into the street in front of my hut and set off to find Bogdan. I didn't know it then, but my life had just taken a drastic turn that would impact not only me, but my unborn child as well.

Chapter 4

That winter was one of the coldest we'd experienced in Ukraine in many years. Temperatures regularly dropped to twenty degrees below at night, and seldom climbed above zero even during the day. The snows came in mid-November and didn't let up the entire season. So when I set-off on my journey to find Bogdan, I was fighting not only my condition but the elements as well.

I'd dressed warmly and had triple-sealed my boots with mink oil to keep my feet dry, but nothing could stop the icy winds that cut through the thickest coat and gloves, pushing the drifts to heights of two meters and more. I didn't want anyone in the village to see me leave, so I trudged through knee-deep snow in the surrounding forest to bypass the town and begin in earnest my attempts to flag down a vehicle beyond the westernmost hut on the main road. I was somewhat confident I would find a ride sooner rather than later, since the road led to the regional capital and supply trucks plied that route regularly. But I hadn't accounted for the blowing snow and freezing temperatures.

Traffic was light that day, no more than half the normal flow. Eying the roadway for myself I wasn't surprised: the drifts so obscured the edges of the pavement that a moment's loss of concentration could easily send one of the heavily-laden trucks into a ditch, or worse. The cold was agonizing. I hadn't been in place for more than fifteen minutes when my fingertips began to ache. My cheeks and nose burned as if on fire. Every now and then a big old transport would rumble past, the sound of its diesel engine audible long before the truck itself came into view. For the first hour or so, not one stopped or even slowed to take a closer look.

I was beginning to think I'd made a bad mistake leaving home on such a frigid day and was debating whether to return to our hut and wait for a break in the weather, when the throaty rumble of an oncoming truck caught my attention. I took my stance, pulling my hood back from my face so they could see I was a woman, and waved my hand beseechingly to beg a ride. At first I thought the driver was going to roll past as the others had without a second glance, but when the large square-backed truck with canvas sides got to within twenty meters, I heard the welcomed sound of a downshift and saw the vehicle come slowly to a stop.

"Where you headed?" the driver – a man around 40 or so with a full beard showing flecks of grey and piercing blue eyes – asked from the rolled down window.

"Toward the capital," I answered.

"You're in luck – so am I. Hop in."

He leaned across and opened the passenger side door from inside and I pulled myself up into the cab with numb fingers that could just barely grasp the inside of the doorjamb. The warmth of the cab heater was heaven-sent, as feeling quickly returned to my fingers and toes.

"Nasty day to be out and about," the driver said.

"I need to get where I'm going," I answered, cautious yet encouraging.

"Must be important. My name is Mykhailo. You?"

He seemed pleasant enough, but whether it was my condition or my mother's constant admonitions to keep strangers at arm's length, I did not feel comfortable sharing my real information with such a new acquaintance.

"Katerina," I said, hoping the cold and wind-burn would disguise my reddening cheeks. "Thank you for stopping."

"Didn't want you freezing out there," he said jovially. "And besides, it's a long drive and a little conversation makes the time pass quicker."

I hadn't planned to tell him much about myself. In fact, I fully expected to invent most of what I revealed. But as the kilometers rolled past and he regaled me with endless details of his life story, I suppose I relaxed my guard and told him the bare outline of my current situation – minus the fact of my pregnancy.

"So you hope to find this man, Bogdan. And then what?" he asked when I paused.

"How do you mean?"

"I mean, what do you expect to happen if you find him? Will you marry?"

I had to admit to myself, if not to Mykhailo, that I really didn't know what to expect. I hoped Bogdan still felt about me the way I felt about him, but after all those months I certainly couldn't be sure.

"I don't know. I hope so, I guess."

"You guess?" he asked with a tone that told me he didn't approve. "You're traveling all that way, alone in a winter storm, and you don't know?"

Put like that, I suppose it sounded a bit strange. Even to me.

"Can we ever know what another person is feeling, or thinking?"

He shook his head with a wry smile. "How old are you?"

"Almost 18."

"I'd hate to be a man trying to tame you in a couple of years."

"You'd hate to try to *tame* me at any age," I said with just enough smile to let him know I wasn't planning on stabbing him as he drove.

"My mistake. I should've said trying to *understand* you."

We chatted amicably, about nothing the least bit inflammatory, for the next several hours, stopping only once to get some food at a small diner along the roadway. I felt warm and safe in his cab, but all good things must end. When we reached the capital he pulled off to the side of the road.

"I go into town from here. Want to come?"

I shook my head. "I need to get where I'm going. But thank you for the ride, and the company."

"My pleasure. Take care of yourself."

I'd nearly forgotten how frigid it was outside, but within minutes of leaving the caressing warmth of the truck I found my hands and feet once again turning to ice. Traffic on the far side of the capital was much sparser than what we'd seen in the east. It was as if all the grain and vegetables and farm animal trucks that flowed into the big city just disappeared once they'd off-loaded their cargo. Perhaps some of them only traveled at night. Perhaps the vast majority of farms were located in the eastern part of the oblast. In any case, the day was no warmer, the sun was dropping quickly into the slate gray evening sky in the west, and I still had another three or four hours of traveling before I'd reach the small town where Bogdan's family lived. I stomped my feet and tucked my bare hands up under my armpits from time to time to try to restore feeling to my poor fingertips, while the meager flow of traffic whizzed past me as if I didn't exist. After more than an hour of that, I began to almost wish I didn't – exist.

I was beginning to worry that perhaps I'd have to seek refuge for the night with some stranger living along the roadway, when finally the welcomed sound of downshifting gave me renewed confidence that I'd reach my destination before nightfall.

"Where to?" the young driver asked, rolling down the passenger side window. He was short and sharp-featured, with the clothing and haircut of a westerner from near the Polish border.

I told him the name of the village. He screwed up his face as if he'd smelled something unpleasant.

"Why?" he asked through his open window while I still stood in the freezing cold below.

"Why what? Why go there?"

"Have you ever been there? It is a very poor village. Bad crops for several years now."

Bogdan had already told me of the tribulations faced by the local farmers. The drought that had cut harvests back home in half had turned the rich farmland of Bogdan's village into a swirling dustbowl.

"I have friends there," I explained.

"There are a lot nicer places," the driver said, with a tone and attitude that probably should've made me question his motivation, except for the fact that my hands and feet were growing numb from the cold. "All right. Get in. I'm going right past there – to L'viv."

"Oh really?!" I asked, unable to keep the excitement and wonder from my voice as I climbed up into the cab. I'd always wanted to visit the big western Ukrainian city but had never had a reason, or the money, to do so.

"Why don't you come along?" he asked as the truck pulled back onto the highway and began to accelerate.

"To L'viv?" I asked. "I don't know anyone there."

"You'll know me," he said, his smile a bit too welcoming, his gaze a bit too presumptuous. I tried to keep my voice neutral even as I shifted closer to my door.

"Maybe in a few months," I lied.

"All right then."

We drove in silence for a few minutes as my discomfort grew. I began to wonder whether I had made a mistake; perhaps I should get out at the first opportunity. The cold gave me pause, however: maybe I was being too mistrustful. As the miles slid by he seemed innocent enough, lost in his own thoughts. As minutes became hours the warmth of the truck's heater and the hum of its tires slowly overcame my mistrust, and despite my best intentions I must have drifted off to sleep. I was dreaming of Bogdan and the shared joy we'd feel at our reunion, when I realized the sensuous touch I thought I'd imagined was all too real. In the smallest part of a second I realized that the truck had stopped moving and the driver's hand was inside my blouse, pawing at my breast!

I awakened with a verbal start and slapped at his hand.

He looked at me with more surprise than offense, and a leering smile spread across his face.

"Now now, Missy, no need to get like that. It's been a long, hard drive and you should be happy to pay me something for all those miles traveled."

I wanted to scream at him, to call him every vile name I could imagine, but I could smell the vodka and I knew he was bigger and stronger than me; the words stuck in my throat.

"What do you say, huh?" he continued, leaning tentatively in my direction as I backed against my door.

"Thank you for the lift, but I should be getting on my way," I said, but as I tried to open the door he grabbed ahold of my arm, hard.

"That's not very sharing, Comrade," he said sarcastically. "'To each according to their needs', isn't that what they say up north?"

When his other hand grabbed at the shoulder of my coat and tried to pull me toward him, I snapped. Without thinking, my fingernails gouged at his eyes, drawing bright red welts down both cheeks.

"Bitch!" he screamed, but before he could do anything more I flailed at the door handle and tumbled out into the snow below. Luckily it was deep enough to break my fall, though the drop did knock the wind from my lungs; I gulped the freezing cold air.

I wasn't sure if he would come after me or not, but I wasn't going to wait to find out. I scrambled to my feet and plowed through the knee deep snow until the parked truck was a hundred meters or more behind me.

I stopped to catch my breath and gasped aloud as the driver's side door opened. If he came after me I didn't know what I'd do. I quickly scanned the surroundings: nothing but snow and leafless trees. Nowhere to run. Nowhere to hide.

But he didn't step out. Instead he leaned from his seat and yelled back to me: "I hope you freeze to death, cyka!"

With that he slammed his door and put the truck into gear. As it rolled off into the gathering darkness, its red tail lights diminishing to tiny dots in the distance, I was actually tempted for just a moment to call out after him, beg his forgiveness. Give him what he wanted. But I couldn't.

As the red dots disappeared behind the black expanse of surrounding forest and the rumble of the diesel engine faded to just a whisper that finally blew away on the cold winter breeze, I realized that the rasps of my own breaths were the only sounds I could hear. That, and the pounding of my heart. I'd lived in the countryside my whole life, long enough to know that the closest human being might be many kilometers away, but the wolves and bears that inhabited the dense old-growth forests all around me might be much closer, close enough to smell my fear.

I felt that fear course through me. Felt its frigid fingers grab at my throat, twist my guts. But I forced myself to think of Bogdan, and our child, and with their faces in front of me I took first one step, then another and another, and began to walk down the narrow strip of icy roadway. I heard the cry of great night birds, the crackling of ice on branches high above me. But as the moon rose above the threatening black forest to illuminate the side walls of plowed snow that lined my way, the unthinking fear began to ease. My anger eventually overcame the dread, and for a time I trudged onward fueled by pure rage. *How could the bastard try to take advantage of a woman like that? And a pregnant one as well!*

But even rage burns to ash, and as the hours dragged by my energy and spirits flagged beneath the weight of my hopeless journey. The cold insidiously seeped through my clothing, through my skin and bone, to threaten the very heart of me. My eyes drooped and nearly shut, the pure white of the snow beckoning like the clean white sheets of a traveler's bed. It would be so easy to just lie down and close my eyes...

The shrill blast of an air horn startled me awake. I turned to see a lumber truck, laden with dozens of long, perfectly straight pine tree trunks, bearing down at me from behind. As if in a dream I waved my hand, at first languidly but then with urgency approaching panic. At first I thought he wasn't going to stop and I actually considered stepping in front of his path to force him to brake. But then slowly, almost imperceptibly, the long truck came to a shuddering stop.

"What are you doing way out here in the middle of nowhere?" the driver, an older man with a kind face half-hidden behind his long gray beard, asked with concern bordering on indignation. "You trying to freeze to death?"

I could barely form words. "Can I... get warm?" I asked through chattering teeth.

"Of course, of course!" he said, climbing down from his cab to help me up through the passenger door. "You must be half-frozen already."

I collapsed into the intoxicating warmth of the sheep hide that covered the truck's bench seat and struggled to make my body stop shaking. The driver climbed back into his seat and immediately reached out to take my hand. I jerked it back as if I'd been burnt, the memories of my last ride all too recent and painful.

"Just wanted to get some circulation back into it," he said gently.

I nodded, the words suddenly too much for my weary brain. He cautiously took my hand and rubbed it gently until the pins and needles of cold gave way to a wave of warming blood. I nearly groaned with pleasure.

"What *are* you doing out here?" he asked after a time. I looked up and saw his worried face studying my own.

"I'm traveling to meet my... fiancé," I stumbled. He showed no sign that he'd noticed.

"A bit late – and cold – for hitchhiking."

"I thought it would take less time."

He nodded, unwilling to judge me. "You're lucky I came along. It's supposed to drop to minus twenty tonight. Might have more snow."

"I *am* lucky. Thank you." Tears beaded-up in the corners of my eyes.

"Now now, let's have none of that," he said, pulling out a starched white handkerchief and handling it to me. "You're okay now. Where does this fiancé of yours live?"

I told him and he smiled. "You are *very* lucky. My route takes me right past there. With any luck, we'll be there soon after daybreak."

My tears swelled to a torrent. It was all too much.

When he put his arm around my shoulders I flinched, but then let him pull me into a protective embrace. He stank of sweat and diesel and tobacco, but also of kindness and care. I hadn't intended to say anything about the horror I'd just escaped, but the words appeared unbidden and poured forth in a stream of release. When I'd finished, he stroked my hair lightly.

"There's always a few bad apples," he said, "but most of us are good enough folk. A young girl like you needs to take care. It's not always easy to tell one from the other."

It was as if my Papa or grandfather were with me again. The sound of his words helped as much as his presence.

We finally set off on the final leg of my journey, and this time I stayed awake the entire time. Kliment, for that was his name, worked on a small collective farm in western Ukraine, not far from L'viv. He'd brought his livestock and produce to the Oblast instead of L'viv because the local soviet had declared the area a 'region of want', due in large part to the drought conditions we'd been facing. His wife of thirty years waited for him back home, along with a son, 28, and a daughter, 26, who was married with a 2-year old daughter herself. Kliment talked freely, with the an easy-going camaraderie I had rarely encountered other than with family and close friends. I, on the other hand, told him a greatly edited version of my own life, leaving out the details I thought might raise questions or concerns. I said nothing of my father's change of sides during the Great War, nor of the manner of his death. Kliment, to my great relief, didn't press me for further detail, but took what I gave him with a quiet understanding and show of interest that reassured my fears and quieted the inner voice that kept telling me the past would never die.

Just as he'd predicted, we arrived at Bogdan's small village just a few minutes after a glorious sunrise, a brilliant ball of fire rising into the clear piercingly blue sky that can only come just after a snowstorm. He offered to buy me breakfast at a small café attached to a petrol station, but I was eager to get to my destination.

"I can't thank you enough," I said as we parted ways in the station parking lot. "I'm not sure if I would've survived another day of that cold."

"You'd have survived," he said with reassuring smile. "You're tougher than you think."

In a way, those were just the words I needed to hear. I'd begun to question the entire trip, even my relationship with Bogdan. After all, it had been months since I'd seen him last, months without so much as a single letter to let me know he still thought of me. Yet I was determined to find out if the father of my child still loved me. And there was only one way to do that…

I got directions to the Kovalchuk farm from the petrol station manager. Fortunately, it was less than five kilometers to the north, and with the sun warming the early morning air I was confident I could walk there with no problem. I'd like to say that my confidence grew with each step I took, but that would be a lie. Thoughts of the best moments of our brief time together were interspersed with memories of sharp words and real or imagined slights, which in my nervous brain grew to frightening proportions. *'How will he react to the news that we're having a baby? Will he be pleased, or angry? What will his family think?'* The thoughts swirled in my head like a swarm of angry bees.

The countryside there in the west was noticeably different than where we lived, with more hills and less leafy trees. There were large herds of cattle and goats, but smaller fields of winter wheat. As I walked, I passed huts that were considerably larger than ours in the east, but also some that were smaller and less well-maintained. Every now and then I'd come upon another person or two walking along the same road, and when we exchanged greetings I couldn't help but notice that their accent was a bit strange, sounding more Polish than Ukrainian to my ear.

Two hours later I stood at the outskirts of the village where Bogdan lived. It was much as he'd described it: poor, small, but close-knit, as I learned when I stopped to ask directions to the Kovalchuk place at a small mud-walled hut.

An elderly woman, probably 60 or so, her face lined from many years tending her flocks and weeding her fields, answered my tentative knock.

"Good morning," she said as she opened the door in a colorful sweater and simple home-sewn skirt. I almost smiled at the pronunciation.

"Good morning. I was wondering if you could tell me how I'd find the Kovalchuk farm?"

She looked at me closely. "You're not from around here, are you?"

"I'm not. I'm from the east."

"Thought so. You have a funny accent."

I nearly exploded with indignation, but held my tongue. "It's a big country," I said instead.

"That it is. And you've traveled quite a bit of it to get here. What do you want of the Kovalchuks, if I may ask?"

"I met them when they came to our oblast this past summer for harvesting," I explained, feeling a need to be truthful with the woman but not quite willing to share more personal details.

The inquisitive look she gave me made me think she already knew why I was there, but I shook such foolishness from my head and smiled. "They invited me to come visit whenever I had the urge."

"In the middle of winter?"

"No time during the summer," I fudged. "Too busy with the crops and all."

"Ah. I know that well enough. As it turns out, you're quite near their place." She gave me meticulous directions that included a handful of landmarks as small as a painted mailbox. "You tell them Ruslana sends her regards."

I promised I would, and with a fresh-baked cookie to fuel my last kilometer or so, I set off with my heart pounding and my head awhirl. I can't tell you what those last few meters of countryside looked like – I have no recollection whatsoever. If someone can literally 'walk in a fog', that was me that chill morning so many years ago. My thoughts and emotions flooded every corner of my being. And when I finally saw the small, slightly decrepit farm house in the distance? I could barely draw a breath.

But I had come that far; I wasn't about to stop at the very doorstep of Bogdan's family home. I marshalled ever drop of strength I had left and marched up to the peeling blue front door. I knocked three times – three loud, perhaps overly-aggressive knocks.

Nothing. Not a sound came from within the hut, not even a single footstep. After all the build-up to my arrival, I felt a massive let-down that nearly brought tears to my eyes. I knocked again. And a third time.

Nothing. I suppose I couldn't quite believe it. I'd never really considered the possibility that I'd arrive to find no one home. After all, it was winter. The fields were frozen solid and covered with snow. Where were they?!

My mind spun: what if they'd gone to visit some family members elsewhere in Ukraine, or perhaps even Poland? What if they didn't return for days, or even weeks? I'd prepared for every eventuality except an empty house. Where would I go?

My knees felt weak and for just an instant threatened to buckle beneath the weight of my fears, when suddenly a familiar voice called out to me from a short distance down the dirt road that led to the hut.

"You there! Can I help you?"

I turned to face the unexpected sound with tears blurring my eyes.

"It's me! It's Nina!" I called out, my words heavy with emotion.

He didn't say a word. For a moment he stood as if frozen in place, and I must admit my fearful mind wondered if I'd made a terrible mistake. But then he broke into an all-out run, undeterred by the snow and ice underfoot. I stumbled in his direction half-blind with tears and half-numb with joy.

I don't know that I've ever felt so relieved as when he took me in his arms and showered my hair with kisses.

"My love, my darling," he muttered over and over as if he, too, couldn't believe I was there. I held on to him with all my strength and he nearly crushed me in his strong farmer's arms. When we each finally became convinced we weren't dreaming, he held me at arm's length with a silly smile on his face.

"What are you doing here?! Why didn't you let me know?" he asked.

I'd rehearsed my answer a thousand times, but now that it was time to explain I found it hard to annunciate. "I... I needed to be with you!" I cried out, and his smile widened even further. He took me inside the house where the blue and white tile stove gave off the most wonderful warmth, and took my coat and tiny bundle of clothes.

"I can't believe you're here!" he said.

"It was too long," I began with a tremor in my voice, but he put his finger to my lips.

"That time is over. We're together now."

He kissed me with a hunger that reflected my own, and in seconds his fingers were unbuttoning the front of my sweater. As much as I wanted him, I hesitated.

"What if they come?" I asked, putting my hand over his.

"They're all with my sister – she just had a baby. They won't be back for hours." His eyes were glassy with excitement.

"Boy or girl?" I asked.

He laughed. "Girl! Enough questions for now!" His fingers moved twice as fast and he kissed me so hard my lip bled. He pulled me into a tiny bedroom in back and eased me down onto the horsehair mattress that overlapped the edges of a narrow homemade bed. "I've dreamed of this."

Those minutes were some of the happiest of my entire life. His touch sent waves of pleasure throughout my body. His warmth filled me and sent me flying through space and time. I felt as if we were both part of something bigger, more important, our futures intertwined in a magical, spiritual way.

As we lay together afterwards, the only sound the crackling of burning logs in the stove, I decided to share with him our good news.

"I have a surprise," I said as he idly traced my jawline with one finger.

"Oh? Bigger than you yourself, here?"

"Bigger."

His tracing stopped. "Oh?"

I took his hand in mine and placed it on my stomach. "You are going to be a father."

There is a moment, an instant really, when you give someone that kind of news and you're not sure how they will react. I don't believe I ever consciously recognized my worry, but I knew full well that not all men – especially young men – are enthralled to learn their woman is pregnant. I probably held my breath. As it turned out, there was no need.

"You're pregnant?!" His eyes were wider than his smile, which spread from ear to ear.

"Four months," I said. "Are you happy?"

"Happy? I couldn't be happier!" he said, kissing me with a passion that verged on frenzy before jumping up out of bed, stark naked, and dancing around like some sort of Ukrainian leprechaun.

I laughed, and he laughed, and the two of us laughed together. It was a wondrous moment, one I'll never forget. If only we could've captured the joy of that moment and carried it forward in our lives. But life is never so simple, is it?

Chapter 5

Bogdan and I spent the rest of that day making plans. We had some disagreements, I must admit, but nothing we couldn't work out. We decided we'd find a place to live somewhere near Mama's, a place attached to a communal farm where we could live while Bogdan – and I when I was able – worked the land. It turned out he was eager to put some space between himself and his family, and I was just as eager to remain near Mama and Yerva (and Julija too, although she had her own life and rarely spent more than a few hours at a time with the rest of us.) The farmland was much better in our oblast, and so Bogdan would have greater opportunities to find work without the need to travel great distances.

We would be married, in the Orthodox Church, as soon as it could be arranged. I, of course, wanted my mother and sisters to attend the ceremony, so we needed to address the question of who would go where, but young and in love we were confident we could overcome any such *minor* obstacle. Our euphoric optimism lasted until just before sundown.

We were sitting in their small common room, sipping a steaming cup of tea and luxuriating in our happiness and limitless future, when the front door opened. His family had returned.

"Nina!" Bogdan's mother, Hanna, cried out as soon as she saw me. She rushed over and hugged and kissed me with unexpected zeal. "We weren't expecting you!"

Oksana, his sister, approached with a good deal more reserve. Three years older than Bogdan and still unmarried, she hadn't been overly enthusiastic about our budding friendship the summer before, and from the curious look on her face I could tell she wasn't entirely thrilled with my presence there now.

"Oksana, so good to see you again," I said, trying to start things off on a better foot.

"And you," she said, giving me a rudimentary hug and a peck on the cheek.

I was about to explain my reason for traveling so far in the dead of winter, when a hulking shadow filled the open doorway and Ivan Kovalchuk came in, stamping his feet to knock off the icy clods of snow that clung to his boots.

"Ivan," Hanna began immediately, her voice pitched a bit too high, a bit too cheerful, "look who's come for a visit! It's Nina Levchenko, from the summer."

The patriarch of the family took one look at me and turned to remove his coat without so much as a nod of recognition.

"What brings you so far from home in such awful weather?" he said as he stripped off the thick lambswool coat and a heavy flannel shirt beneath it. He stood in just a t-shirt, damp work pants and stocking feet.

"She brought us news!" Bogdan stepped forward to place himself between his father and me. "Wonderful news!"

Ivan's eyes narrowed. "What kind of news?"

"We're going to have a baby!" Bogdan shouted, nearly exploding with excitement. As I glanced around at the other members of his family, however, I didn't see the same enthusiasm. His mother looked stunned, his sister confused, and his father…

"Who's going to have a baby?" he growled.

"*We* are!" Bogdan continued, seemingly unaware of the reactions around him. He put his arm around my waist and pulled me close. "Nina and me!"

"And how do you expect to put food in that baby's mouth, and a roof over its head?" Ivan said, his tone even less enthused, if possible.

To his credit, Bogdan hesitated only a moment. He pulled himself to his full height and stared his father square in the eye. "We will find a way."

The icy silence that followed seemed to stretch far too long, but at last Hanna rushed to my side and gave me a warm hug. "Congratulations!" she said, and it was all I could do to avoid crying. "That *is* wonderful news." She directed the latter at her husband, who stood across the room with arms folded across his chest.

"Children having children. Don't expect me to raise it," he mumbled as he made his way to the stove.

"We won't, Mr. Levchenko," I said, my voice returning along with feeling in the rest of my body. "We will do whatever it takes."

"I'm sure you will, daughter," Hanna said, giving me another squeeze. I noticed Oksana wince. "This is very exciting, isn't it, Oksana?" her mother asked.

Oksana nodded as if in a dream.

"Come give Nina a hug!" Hanna directed, and her daughter broke free from whatever spell entranced her and came to do as she'd been asked. The hug was more a pat, her wish of happiness half-hearted, but at least she recognized our existence. Ivan stood rubbing warmth back into his hands by the ceramic stove, never casting so much as a glance in our direction.

Hanna whisked us over to the kitchen table where she poured us some tea and sat to hear "every bit of your story." Of course I didn't reveal 'every bit' of the story, but enough so she understood I'd been through quite a bit coming there to reunite with Bogdan. Oksana sat with us and listened without comment. Ivan continued to rub his hands and feign disinterest, close enough so he could overhear everything I said.

"So, have you two had any time to discuss your plans?" his mother asked when I'd finished my tale of woe.

I looked to Bogdan, and he to me.

"We're going to get married!" he said with a big grin.

"This house isn't big enough for small children," his father suggested from over by the stove, seemingly interested once more.

"We know that," Bogdan said without rancor. "We will get our own place."

"Here in the village?" Hanna asked. The hopefulness in her voice and expression made me feel a bit sorry for her. Just a bit.

"I don't think so," Bogdan answered carefully. "Nina's family has more space in their house while we look for our own, and besides, there will be more work out there."

"You're moving *there*?" Oksana said with a curl of the lip that left no doubt as to her opinion of the east.

I was growing tired of her superior attitude. "We are. It's so much prettier there, and friendlier," I said, stressing the last with perhaps too much emphasis.

"You'll be back. Those Easterners have never been overly welcoming of those from the west," his father growled.

"I thought they were very warm when we were there last harvest season," Hanna objected, but Ivan was having none of it.

"Of course! We saved their bacon. If we hadn't come along just when we did, half their grain would've spoiled in the field."

"I heard some of them calling us 'Polacks' when they thought we couldn't hear," Oksana chimed in.

"I'm sure they didn't mean it," her mother said.

"Mean it or not, that's what we plan to do," Bogdan spoke out. "We'll make the best of it."

He gave me a reassuring hug, meant as much for his father as for me.

"We'll help you as we can," Ivan relented, much of the gruffness gone from his voice now that he knew we didn't intend to move in with him and his family, "though it'll be small enough, I'm afraid."

"Thank you, Papa," Bogdan said. "Anything will be appreciated."

For a few moments no one knew what else to say, and so we all sat there in the kitchen trying to think of a line of conversation that wouldn't raise ire.

"Do you want a boy or a girl?" Oksana asked, breaking the awkward silence.

"I... I don't really care," I said. "As long as it's healthy."

"And doesn't cry too much," Bogdan said, and the little touch of humor seemed to break the tension of the moment. We went on to talk of our plans and they rehashed the high points of their trip to spend a few days with their daughter and the new addition to the family. It was a warm, encompassing time that promised happier times ahead.

If only promises were prophetic.

Chapter 6

After some discussion we were married in a tiny Orthodox chapel in Bogdan's village – compensation to his family for our planned move to the east. They never voiced their displeasure at our plans – at least not to me – but it was clear they'd hoped to have Bogdan in their midst for a good deal longer, especially with his parents getting older and less able to spend full twelve-hour days in the fields. Mama, Yerva, and Julija (with her husband) all came out for the ceremony, much to my delight. I can't say the two families came together with all the love and respect I might've hoped, but at least Mama and Hanna carried-on without overt rancor.

Our wedding day was somewhat awkward, what with both families feeling somewhat aggrieved, but after a few vodkas the barriers came down – at least a little. Bogdan and I spent our first night as 'man and wife' in a local inn, our two families having scraped together enough money to allow us the privacy of a bedroom separated by more than a hanging blanket from our in-laws, and I can say without a hint of a blush that we made good use of the precious space. If I hadn't been pregnant, I probably would've been after that night.

The next day we began the journey east. I seem to remember some talk of us spending a week or two with the Kovalchuks before moving to "those savage lands beyond the reach of civilization" as Oksana had declared after four too many vodkas, and I was open to the idea if not particularly enthusiastic. Bogdan, on the other hand, would hear nothing of it.

"We've begun a new life," he said as we lay in each other's arms that first night. "Let's get to it and make it a good one."

So, with a teary-eyed Hanna, a sullen Ivan, and a bored Oksana seeing us off, we all squeezed into our rickety old cart and began the long day's journey back home. In retrospect, it's amazing to look back and remember how hopeful and excited we were about the move and our future together. It's as if we viewed the world through a haze of romantic poppy-cock and youthful naiveté. We saw only the good in each other and our shared existence, none of the difficulties that inflict themselves upon every newlywed couple, let alone one with as little money as the two of us. "Love will see us through," became my motto. I accepted my husband's silence for acquiescence.

After good-intentioned initial conversation, Mama and my eldest sister gave up trying to draw Bogdan out into long philosophic discussions and fell back into the unthinking give-and-take that formed the backbone of our daily existence. Marko drove the cart, so it was left to Yerva to exchange pleasantries with Bogdan during the fourteen hour haul to our village. Luckily, Yerva was going through a stage where she was nearly as taciturn as my new husband, so I suppose it could be said they hit it off well – if hours of wordless companionship is considered successful interaction.

By the time we got home, we were all frozen, sun-burnt and exhausted. Bogdan and I had no reluctance to sharing the tiny space with other members of our newly extended family, especially since Julija and Marko continued on to their own house and Mama insisted we take the bigger bed. Part of me felt guilty at usurping her room, since her drooping eyelids and stooped posture spoke clearly enough of her road-weariness, but I knew she wanted to make Bogdan feel welcome as the new addition, so I gave-in to her insistence.

After that first night, Yerva *volunteered* to move her bed into the main room adjacent to the stove, claiming it was much warmer (if substantially less private.) Bogdan made short work of expanding my bed into a comfortable shelf for two, and for the next three weeks or so we stayed with Mama and my little sister as Bogdan looked for work and I looked for a place we could afford. It was a good time. Bogdan assumed his position of 'man of the house' easily enough, and Mama and Yerva seemed pleased to have us live with them, even if the hut was too small by half.

So when the local communal farm offered Bogdan regular work, and we moved soon thereafter to a small room above the most popular tavern in the village, I think they were genuinely sad to see us go. I know I had mixed feelings, feelings I kept to myself.

Those first months in our own room were happy ones as well. Bogdan settled in to his new job, and I was busy making plans for the arrival of our child even as I worked until I was seven months pregnant. Our life was simple, even Spartan, but we had a roof over our heads, enough food, and the promise of an exciting new world just ahead.

I visited my mother and sisters every week, and Bogdan exchanged the occasional letter with his family. He made a few new friends among his workmates, young men his own age who also were just starting their own families. Everything seemed to be going along just fine, until, that is, the eighth month of the pregnancy.

I remember it well. Too well. I was at home, sewing baby clothes and preparing Bogdan's dinner. He always came back from work at around six in the evening, unless it was harvest time when he might stay in the fields until sunset. During this season, however, six was the time I expected him. So when six o'clock came and went, I began to get nervous. Injuries were not uncommon on the farm, and with the nearest hospital over 20 kilometers away, I might not learn about a problem until long after it occurred. By seven I was pacing. By eight I decided to go downstairs and see if I could find any of his fellow workers to ask if they'd seen or heard from him.

By that point in the pregnancy my stomach extended so far out in front of me that I couldn't see my feet, but I waddled unsteadily down the narrow back stairs to the tavern below. I heard the merriment and music long before I pushed open the side door to the smoke-filled room. The tavern, a single room probably three or four times the size of our little apartment upstairs, was filled with farmhands and 'regulars', plus a handful of young town girls looking for a good time. I scanned the room, hoping to recognize one of the young men Bogdan worked the fields with. Instead, I found Bogdan himself, laughing and having a good old time, with one of those young girls from the village sitting all too close and looking all too enthralled with some tall tale he was drunkenly expounding.

He didn't see me at first, but one of his new-found friends did and tried to interrupt his story-telling. But Bogdan was having too much fun, and had had a few too many beers to allow anyone or anything to derail his runaway train of a tale. So he was completely unsuspecting when I stopped close by his side, my tummy extending out into his field of view moments before he realized the rest of me was there as well.

"Do you mind?!" he asked emphatically before glancing up to see who dared interfere with his drunken oration.

"I do," I said quietly, and out of the corner of my eye I saw a few of his 'audience' members wince in anticipation of what would come next.

At first, Bogdan was surprised and taken aback.

"Honey! What are you doing down here?" he asked, shoving the sweet young girl draped across his arm a respectful distance away.

"I was worried about you," I said, for I didn't know what else to say. "I thought something might have happened to you."

He looked up at me and blinked. "Me? No, nothing's happened to me! A few of us just decided to have a beer or two after work."

"I can see." Perhaps I was too stern, or perhaps not stern enough. I don't know. All I know is that I saw a change come over his face, an expression I had never seen from him before but would see all too often in the months and years that followed.

"Is it a crime for a hard-working man to have a beer with his friends every now and then?" he asked, his voice too loud, his face turning a dark shade of red.

"It's not. But I wish you'd told me so I didn't worry."

For just the briefest of moments a flicker of recognition, shame even, passed across his eyes. Then it was gone.

"No need to worry! I'm fine. We're all fine! Wanna beer?" I unconsciously put my hand on my stomach. "Oh, right," he said. "Not a good thing. Well then, have a seat and we'll order you a cup of tea, or lemonade."

Maybe I should have sat down. Maybe it would've made a difference. I don't know. I doubt it. In any case, I was tired, my feet were swollen and ached, and I was in no mood for tea or lemonade.

"I think I'll go upstairs and lie down," I said instead. "When will you be coming?"

At the last, his mood soured once again.

"When I'm done!" he snapped, and some of the others around the table recoiled. Not the young girl at his side, though. She smiled the vaguely self-congratulatory smirk that made me want to slap her face. I didn't though.

"If I'm asleep, please don't wake me. I've had a hard time sleeping these last few weeks," I said instead, and without waiting for his reply I went back up the back stairs, moving, if possible, even slower than before.

I tried not to stew over his drunken insensitivity, although clearing the table and putting away dishes did not occupy me near enough to take my mind off his cruelty. I even tried to justify his actions, telling myself *'he just needed to blow off some steam.'* But try as I would, I could not convince myself of his innocence and tears eventually found their way to my tired eyes. I fell asleep with images of his bloodshot eyes dancing in my dreams.

The next morning Bogdan was unapologetic, but he went out of his way to be helpful and quietly supportive. I suppose I was relieved, yet deep down a bit disappointed as well. I considered raising the issue at breakfast, to let him know that I had neither forgotten nor forgiven, but whether from fear or naiveté I kept my silence. Should I have confronted him? Would it have made a difference over the next weeks, months and years? Perhaps. More likely, it would have speeded the disintegration of our marriage. Which might not have been a bad thing.

*****

For a time our life slipped back into its old patterns and rhythms, though each of us tiptoed around the other with a sensitivity that bordered on neurosis. It was as if we each decided to place our lives in suspended animation until the baby came, an event we both ascribed magical powers to, as if the arrival of a child would salve all wounds and reinvigorate our struggling marriage. We weren't unhappy – at least I wasn't. But it wasn't real, in the sense that we spoke and acted like puppets playing out a script neither of us planned or understood.

I tried my best to lose myself in preparations for the birth. I traveled the short distance from our room to my family's house at least once a week, until my 35th week at which time all the jostling and bumps in the cart made me fear for the baby's well-being. Mama was wonderful through the whole episode, reassuring me ("Most men are pigs when we get big as a house with child. He'll come around."), giving me advice from her own experience, and just listening when I needed to vent my frustration – both with Bogdan and the interminable pregnancy. Yerva was so protective of me and vindictive at my husband's treatment that I eventually had to banish her from any discussion of my circumstances for fear she'd say something to Bogdan – if not hit him over the head with a shovel.

And so, in the early summer of 1960, I gave birth to my precious Kateryna. As luck would have it, I went into labor while Bogdan was in the fields and so depended on the barkeep in the tavern downstairs to call the midwife who delivered our little girl. I won't go into the actual delivery. Suffice it to say it was neither pleasant nor pain-free. But then again, what is in life?

By the time Bogdan returned home that evening, the midwife had cleaned up all signs of the ferocious battle that had taken place earlier in the day and Bogdan found me tucked neatly in bed, Kateryna asleep in my arms. The bartender told him what had happened, and I could hear him run up the stairs taking two steps at a time in his excitement. He burst into the room with no real sense of what he would find there, and was quickly chagrinned when he saw his sleeping daughter lying atop my stomach.

He tiptoed over to where we lay, his look a mix of surprise and disbelief.

"She's beautiful," he whispered after he'd stared wide-eyed for several seconds.

"And a quiet one," I said. "Hasn't cried or fussed a bit."

"May I touch her?"

"Of course you may! She's your daughter!"

I handed him up to her and he took her as if she were made of fine porcelain.

"Support her neck," I reminded him, and he quickly settled her into the crook of his arm.

"She's so small."

"She'll get bigger. Probably faster than we'd like."

I'll always remember the look in his eyes as he stared at Kateryna for the first time. It was probably the last time I was to see that look, or anything like it.

*****

The first weeks were hard. Perhaps I'd jinxed us by telling Bogdan how quiet our little daughter had been. She found her voice around Day Three and never let us forget her presence for the next six months or so. Of course, it wasn't her fault. She was a colicky little thing, her tummy always swollen, her screams originating not from boredom or self-absorption, but from pain. Unfortunately, knowing why she screamed didn't make the yells any less powerful or annoying. *I* could barely maintain my sanity after a few hours of that, and I was her mother. Bogdan... well, he was Bogdan.

The first night Kateryna announced her discomfort to the world, Bogdan was fast asleep, a few beers having lubricated his slide into unconsciousness. He awoke with a start.

"What is it? Is she sick?" He was genuinely anxious.

I held her over my shoulder and patted her back gently until a giant sour burp helped ease her torment.

"All that, for a bit of gas?" he said when she soon quieted and fell back to sleep in my arms.

"It's painful. And she doesn't understand."

"Well one thing I understand is that I won't be worth spit tomorrow if I don't get some sleep. See if you can keep her quiet." With that he rolled over and began snoring almost immediately.

I didn't blame him, exactly. I knew how hard he worked and how much he needed a good night's rest. But there was a bluntness, a lack of empathy that hurt. I shrugged it off and went back to sleep as well.

The next night was more of the same. Bogdan was curt to the point of impoliteness. The third night he ordered me from our bed and insisted I sleep on the couch and keep our daughter by my side so she would be less of a bother if she awoke in pain. I thought it might be just for the one night, so I acceded to his demands without much of a fight. But after three weeks of sleeping on the couch, and no change in sight, I had had enough.

"Bogdan, I think *you* should sleep on the couch tonight," I said one weekday evening. "My back is breaking from sleeping there so often."

"So whose back is more important to this family?" he answered, barely looking up from the newspaper that had become his refuge after dinner each night. "Yours or mine?"

"If we share the burden perhaps it won't bother either of us so much."

"Share the burden? I don't see you sharing the burden of earning money to buy us food, or to pay the electricity," he said with a sneer. "Just playing with the child every minute of the day."

"Playing?!" I couldn't believe my ears. "Do you have any idea what it's like to feed and bathe and watch and entertain a little baby? Do you?"

"If it's so hard, why don't you ask your mother to take the child during the week? Then you can earn some money too."

Kateryna was only a few months old! Did he really expect me to just drop her off at Mama's like a pet dog?

I bit my tongue, and he was sober enough to realize that my silence did not signify agreement and remained silent himself. For a couple of weeks I ignored the idea, continuing on with my daily routine as if he hadn't said a word. But then, just after the final big harvest, the commune manager informed all his workers that a drop in world grain prices had brought a commensurate reduction in the compensation the farm had received from the Central Soviet, resulting in lower wages for every worker.

Work was no longer an option for me, it was a necessity. I went to see Mama the very next day.

I was pretty confident she'd be willing to watch Kateryna while I worked, but nothing is certain until you ask.

"Of course!" she said without hesitation. "I can't think of anything I'd enjoy more."

While that was likely an exaggeration, I felt both relieved and content she'd so willingly agreed. After having spent three months with Kateryna, I knew all too well how needy she could be. I only hoped Mama still had the energy to deal with all her demands.

I was lucky to find a place with one of the harvesting teams almost immediately. In fact, I only interviewed the one time. Of course, it helped that Bogdan was working there as well, and the team manager, Dmitry, had known Papa.

"He was a good man," the manager said. "It was a shame the way he died."

"It was," I said. "I miss him every day."

"I'm sure. So, let's see. We have three teams in this region – which would you prefer?"

I was somewhat taken aback, but I disguised my surprise. "The one with my husband, of course."

I saw the slightest hint of a curious expression creep across his eyes, but I chalked it up to my own excitement. "Of course. You can start tomorrow?"

I could, and he hired me on the spot. I hurried home to tell Bogdan.

I assumed my husband would be thrilled to learn I'd secured another source of income, so his actual reaction came as something of a surprise.

"In *my* team?" he asked when I told him over dinner that night.

"Yes! Isn't it wonderful?!"

He hesitated just a split-second; not long, but long enough. "That's... great. When do you start?"

"Tomorrow!"

"So soon?"

At first I didn't understand. I thought I must've misheard him. "Why, yes. Is there something wrong with that?"

He was quick on his feet, I'll give him that much. "I just thought it might be better for your Mama if she had a couple of days to prepare her house."

I laughed, my initial concerns alleviated. "The house is so small it won't take her more than ten minutes to arrange things. Besides, Dmitry told me I could come in a bit late tomorrow. I'll help Mama get things in order before I report to the fields."

"Yes, that should be good then," he said before returning to his meal without a second thought. His nonchalance confused me. Hadn't he been the one to complain about the cut in his salary? Why was he so subdued?

My concerns were swept away by the need to prepare for my first day. I sent word to Mama that I'd be arriving in the morning with Kateryna, and received word back that she'd be eagerly awaiting our coming. Then I made lunch for both Bogdan and me, laid-out my clothing for the day, and arranged Kateryna's bottles, diapers, and all the rest for easy carrying. By the time nine o'clock came around, I was exhausted and fell asleep almost at once.

The next day brought even greater excitement. I must admit that as much as I loved spending time with our little girl, after three months I was looking forward to conversing with other adults. I hadn't said much of anything to anyone other than Mama and Yerva beyond 'hello' and 'goodbye' during all that time, since I rarely left our room and had few friends who would visit. The very thought of engaging someone my own age in thoughtful conversation motivated me even more than the extra money I'd bring in. Bogdan, on the other hand, was still quiet, if not sullen.

After a near-silent breakfast he grabbed his lunch and was about to set off when I stopped him.

"Aren't you going to kiss your daughter goodbye?"

He looked shocked, as though the thought had not crossed his mind.

"I…of course," he stumbled before hurrying to her crib and planting a loving kiss on her forehead. "See you there."

He pecked me on the cheek and rushed out of the room. At the time it didn't mean much to me, since he often seemed in a rush and my mind was mostly elsewhere. I finished my morning errands and bundled Kateryna up to take her outside.

I'd hired a neighbor to take me over to Mama's in his cart, and he was waiting for us when we came downstairs. The ride to Mama's house was painfully slow in the broken-down old cart, pulled by a horse who'd seen better days, but the distance was short and we arrived less than 30 minutes later. Mama and Yerva were waiting for us; my little sister ran out of the house to greet us.

"Nina! Let me see my little niece," she said after a quick hug, grabbing Kateryna gently and lifting her up for a viewing. Kateryna was still half-asleep and barely fidgeted, eliciting oohs and aahs from her glowing aunt.

"Aren't you so sweet!" she cooed as I dragged all the baby's clothes, toys and bottles into the tiny hut.

"There you are!" Mama greeted me just inside the door. I smelled fresh raisin babka and wished I could sit down and eat. Mama suggested the very same thing.

"No time," I explained. I unbagged all the accoutrements and displayed them for Mama, who waved them away with a flick of her hand.

"I know how to prepare a bottle and change a diaper," she said with a teasing smile. "How do you think you three girls got to be this age?"

"Thank you so much for doing this," I said, hugging her. "I'd like to stay home with her but…"

Mama wouldn't hear of it. "I can't think of anything we'd rather do," she said, turning to Yerva. "Isn't that right?"

Yerva was so involved with entertaining the rapidly-awakening Kateryna that she didn't hear a word we said.

"As you can see…" Mama added, turning back to me.

"Wait till she gets hungry, or wet," I hedged. "You might not be quite so happy then."

"Oh, nonsense. A little singing helps them develop their lungs."

"Then hers will be quite impressive," I muttered. "I'm sorry, I really have to run."

"Go, go!" Mama urged. "We'll have a wonderful day with the little one."

I couldn't express how much her words meant to me, how much they reassured me. I was already feeling more than a little guilty for abandoning my three-month old, but knowing I was leaving her with Mama and Yerva helped alleviate that pain. I rushed over to where my little sister was utterly captivated by her niece.

"You be good, Kateryna. Mama will be back before you know it," I said, bending to kiss her on each cheek.

"Are you *still* here?" Yerva asked with a smile.

In a second, I wasn't. My neighbor took me straight to the field where our team would be harvesting that day, arriving just as the sub-teams fanned out over their respective work areas. I thanked him and went directly in search of the team leader. Perhaps I'd arrived earlier than expected, or perhaps the argument had gone-on longer than they'd expected, but I walked right into a fierce shouting match between my Bogdan and... that same young girl from the tavern. Bogdan saw me just as I saw him, but the girl kept shouting for just a few seconds before he reacted and nodded in my direction. "But why does she have to work *here*!?" the girl was yelling, teary-eyed, before my husband's nod stopped her in mid-rant.

"There you are!" Bogdan said with all the sincerity he could muster. "How'd it go with your mother and Kateryna?"

The girl gave me a dirty look before she stomped off into the fields. It was a look that spoke more eloquently than any words. My suspicions were aroused immediately and Bogdan saw my reaction all too clearly.

"She doesn't like taking orders," he said following my gaze.

"Is that right? Surprised she still has a job, since so many of our young men don't."

"Her father's a Party member."

I nodded. Members of the Communist Party received special privileges and considerations. Always had, probably always would. But my intuition told me their disagreement was about more than that.

"I'm in the northwest sector," Bogdan said, whether to break the awkward silence or just to let me know, I'm not certain.

"I start in the southern zone. I imagine so Dmitry can keep an eye on me."

"Probably so. Well, see you later, I've got to go," he said as his team moved to climb aboard a cart for the kilometer trip to his section of the harvest field.

"Shall we have lunch together?" I called after him.

"Depends how long they give us!" he yelled back. "I'll come looking for you if there's time."

As I watched him walk away, my mind tried to accept what my heart rejected.

"Ready to get started?" Dmitry asked from just behind me.

All thoughts about my husband were swept away by a torrent of responsibilities and requirements at my new job. Our sub-team was divided up into three separate units: the harvesters (who cut the grain using either short single-handed blades or larger, two-handed scythes), the threshers (who bound the cut stalks into sheaths and then separated the grain from the stalks), and the winnowers (who separated the grain from the chaff and bagged the cleaned grain for transportation to the mill.) I was assigned to the latter group, since it required the least experience and the least body strength.

Dmitry knew I'd given birth just a few months before and was kind enough to start me out slowly. There were six other members of our group: five men and one other woman, a middle-aged mother of five whose powerful shoulders and forearms testified to the years of hard physical labor she'd endured. I knew from working summers in high school that women field hands could either be welcoming or, feeling threatened, cold and unkind. Luckily, Alina was not looking to find or keep a man and so had no motivation to see me as a threat. She was more of a mother figure, showing me techniques to save energy and using her sharp-edged tongue to keep those few men who were not at all put-off by the fact that I was a married mother of a young baby at bay when their interest shifted from good-natured ribbing to something less innocent. Luckily such occasions were relatively rare, as our team was not so big that rumors of impropriety couldn't easily sweep the entire field in a matter of hours.

Dmitry called for our lunchbreak a bit earlier than the team expected, quite probably because the hot mid-day sun was taking a good deal out of all of us, myself more than most. I sat with Alina and the other team members, sharing news about ourselves and our friends and families. We'd all grown up in the same oblast, and so we all knew many of the same people. The Party frowned upon gossiping in theory, but in reality we all hungered for news – good or bad – about familiar local characters. Men included. In fact, some of the men were worse gossipers than we women. Of course, Alina didn't really care much about what other people did, and I didn't have enough interaction with anyone other than my own family to garner the juicy tidbits that fed the shared interest. So I was only half-listening to their chatter, with most of my attention and an occasional glance cast in the direction Bogdan's team had taken earlier in the day.

Just a short time later I was more than a little surprised when Dmitry re-bagged his few remaining morsels of food and announced it was time to get back to work. I tried not to show my disappointment and walked to the nearest high point to casually scan the horizon for any sign of an approaching comrade.

"Expecting someone?" Alina said, coming up behind me so quietly I hadn't heard a footstep.

"Bogdan said he might join us for lunch, if they got enough time." I tried to keep the disappointment from my voice.

"This time of year it's more likely than not that Vladislav – that's his team leader – barely gave them enough time to eat and pee. Dmitry's a much nicer guy."

I wanted to believe, so much that I ignored the nagging voice in the back of my head that told me something was wrong. I was distracted for the remainder of the day, walking through my tasks as if in a dream. At the end of the day I took the cart ride to pick up Kateryna and then went home, where Bogdan was waiting. I tried to keep my mind occupied, but I couldn't avoid asking the questions that had been eating me up inside.

"So, did your team meet its goal today?" I asked when we sat down to eat.

"I think so. Vladislav didn't say anything, and knowing him he would've if we'd been short."

"But he didn't give you a lunch break?"

He looked up at me, suspicion in his eyes. "He did..." Then he realized why I'd asked. "Oh, yes, I'm sorry I couldn't get over to your sector. We only got fifteen minutes and there was no way I could get there and back again in that time."

"No, of course not," I said, and I left it at that – for the moment.

The following day, purely by chance, a comrade from Bogdan's team came over to our sector to borrow some harvest scythes. Dmitry had been instructing me on how he liked to have the grain bagged and stacked, so I was by his side when the laborer arrived.

"So, you're working in the northwest sector, are you?" I asked when Dmitry left to round-up the requested scythes. "You must know my husband: Bogdan Kovalchuk?"

His confusion was unmistakable.

"Bogdan? Is he married then? Didn't know."

"He is. We have a baby girl, just three months old," I found myself saying, though why I thought the man would care is beyond me.

"Ah." He nodded thoughtfully, but turned his gaze in the direction Dmitry had gone as if he couldn't wait for his return.

"You've got some very attractive women working in your team," I said after a long pause. At that, the field hand started and cleared his throat nervously.

"Yeh, well, I think perhaps I should go help Dmitry with those scythes," he mumbled. "I'll tell Bogdan I met you." He nodded in my direction, but without meeting my eyes. A flutter of unease rippled through my gut.

That night and in the days that followed I tried my best to maintain my composure and avoid the nagging harangues I'd witnessed many of our village wives inflict upon their husbands. I didn't *know* anything was wrong, and it wasn't fair of me to suspect my husband without anything more than a gut feeling. Still... I didn't sleep well and I could feel the pressure of my doubts eating away at me. I snapped at my fellow team members, once or twice at Dmitry, and even at Kateryna when she cried or fussed more than I might have hoped. What could I do?

I didn't want to burden Mama with my problems, particularly if they were imaginary, but I didn't have anyone else to talk to. So after a few days of this torment, when I was at her house collecting Kateryna, I sent Yerva off to buy some carrots so I could mash them for baby food and told my tale of woe to my poor mother.

"Has he been neglecting you?" she asked softly when I'd finished explaining my situation.

"No, I can't say he has. Nothing more than he has the last few months, anyway."

"It's hard those first few months. You're tired, you ache in your private parts – it's not like it was at the very beginning of the marriage."

I'm sure I blushed. Had Mama experienced something similar to what I was going through?

"No, it's not," I said. "Did you and Papa...?" I couldn't even finish the question.

Mama smiled. "Oh, we had our problems, like all couples do. But we worked them out."

"I don't know if I actually have a problem or not."

"Have you asked him?"

I'm sure my eyes bulged from my head. "Mama! I've seen what jealousy can do to a marriage. Remember the Popovychs who lived across the street? I can still remember lying in bed at night listening to her scold her husband. Eventually he just left. I don't want Kateryna to grow up without a father!"

Mama nodded sadly. "No, I suppose not. But you have to learn the truth. Just as jealousy destroys relationships, so does distrust. If you let your fears control your life, it won't be a happy one – for you, or your family."

I knew she was right. I knew I had to learn whether Bogdan was playing around with that girl, or not. But how?

*****

For the next few days I employed all the tried-and-true methods I'd heard of determining if a man is having an affair: I regularly looked for lipstick on his face and clothing; I surreptitiously checked his neck for bite marks; I sniffed his work shirts for any scent I didn't recognize. But try as I might, I found no definitive proof that Bogdan was anything but the loving husband and father he seemed to be.

So I went one step further. It was a night mid-week, Wednesday I believe. I told him I would be staying at Mama's for dinner after going there to pick up Kateryna, and so wouldn't be home until late. Part of me felt guilty for lying to him. But I couldn't stand the uncertainty a minute longer. I had to know.

I did go to Mama's, to see my daughter and talk with my mother and sister, but – as I had several times before – I decided to leave Kateryna there overnight so I could go about my business without worrying. I didn't explain why I was leaving her with her grandmother and aunt, but from Mama's comments and knowing looks, I surmised that she had a pretty good idea of what was happening.

"Be careful," Mama warned me softly when Yerva was off getting the baby ready for her bath. "A man is like a wild animal – most dangerous when he feels he's cornered."

I promised her I would and took the cart back toward our apartment. Instead of traveling all the way home, however, I got out about a kilometer away and walked the rest of the way. I told our neighbor I needed some fresh air; he had no reason to suspect anything different. I didn't go directly home, of course, but headed straight to the tavern downstairs from us. If there was one place where I thought I might find the evidence I both sought and feared, it was there.

The tavern was often crowded at that time of night, as the unmarried farmhands drank and socialized before concocting whatever meager supper they could manage, while the married workers came out after their dinners to get away from the wives and kids. I hid myself beneath a dark scarf that covered not only my hair but most of my face, making recognition in the dim light of the tavern all but impossible.

The heat, noise and smell of the room struck me forcefully as I slipped into the bar just behind a small group of young workers who'd apparently – from their slurred speech and wild eyes – spent some time at another drinking spot before coming to this one. Even if someone inside had glanced up at the group, they would've had trouble identifying me nestled among my newfound comrades, my scarf hooding my face. As soon as my eyes adjusted to the dim light I scanned the room from off to one side of the long and crowded bar. Just as the smoke and shadows hid my identity, however, they made it extremely difficult for me to recognize even familiar faces with any certainty.

So I walked. From table to table, stool to stool, I slipped quietly among the revelers, keeping my eyes down and being careful to do nothing to attract their attention. I felt my heart pound as I awaited either discovery or... heartbreak. But neither made their acquaintance with me. I began to feel a bit foolish as I completed a complete circuit of the room without seeing any sign of my husband... or his young 'friend.'

A couple of village men I knew only in passing called me over to join them for a drink, which only increased my embarrassment.

"No, thank you. There's a phone call for my husband," I lied. I'm sure they would've seen my ears turn red save for the smoky dimness of the tavern.

As quickly as I could without drawing additional attention, I made my way out of the room and started up the stairs to our apartment, sucking in deep breaths of fresh air to clear my lungs and my brain.

'What was I thinking? How could I suspect Bogdan just because I'd seen him talking to that girl once or twice?' I'd begun to chastise myself for my lack of trust, when a faint sound from the top of the stairs stopped me in mid-stride. At first I couldn't determine where it came from, but then it dawned on me. All my self-blame and chagrin disappeared in an instant. I ran up the last few steps and threw open the door. There, intertwined in a sweaty lovers' embrace on *our* bed, lay Bogdan and that girl.

"Nina!" he called out as soon as he caught his breath. The girl looked up at me with a bemused smile.

"You bastard!" I screamed, and with that ran from the room and slammed the door behind me.

I was already at the bottom of the steps when the door opened above me. "Nina, come back! I'm sorry!" his voice called out. I didn't stop, didn't even turn back to look. I was hurt, teary-eyed, and *angry*! How could he?!

At first I just ran, without direction or plan. I only knew I wanted to be as far from those two as possible. Slowly, as my adrenaline faded and my breath labored to keep up with my reckless flight, I eased my pace and pulled up in an alleyway several blocks away. I leaned over double to catch my breath, when suddenly tears erupted as I spewed my meal all over the pavement. By the time the shuddering that swept through my body stopped, I felt drained, exhausted both physically and mentally. I tried to think, but my thoughts scattered like chaff in the wind. There was just one place for me to go, one safe place in that whole terrible world. So I found a cart driver and went home. To Mama.

"My God, Nina, what is it?!" she asked as soon as she found me at her door.

I burst into tears once again as she wrapped me in her arms and drew me inside. It took several minutes for her to calm me enough so I could explain the entire vile situation.

"You poor thing," she repeated over and over, stroking my hair like when I was a child. Yerva sat across from us at the table, tears in her eyes, her lower lip quivering.

When I'd finally unburdened myself of every slight, real or perceived, that Bogdan had ever inflicted, when the first cup of tea had become two – and a cookie – only then did I catch my breath and stare silently at Mama, as if challenging her to make everything better.

"You can stay here with us tonight," she said softly.

"But what about tomorrow?" I wailed.

"Tomorrow you'll have to find him and talk this thing out." She said it so matter-of-factly I almost missed the import.

"Talk? With Bogdan?"

"You can't be serious, Mama!" Yerva admonished. "He's no good!"

"He cheated!" I cried out, my voice cracking.

"He's your husband," Mama said, her voice still unnaturally calm. "And the father of your child. Men do these kinds of things when their wives get pregnant."

I couldn't hold my tongue. "Did Papa?"

She shrugged ever so slightly. "No, at least not that I knew of. But your father was different."

"Of course. *He* wasn't a bastard!" Yerva continued, her face flushed, her eyes burning. "We should cut Bogdan's thing off!"

"Yerva!" Mama rebuked. "You will not talk that way!"

"Nina is your daughter!"

"And I'm your mother. What he did is inexcusable, but we will not stoop to his level. Understand?"

Yerva pouted but held her tongue.

"Good," Mama said. "Now, would you like another cup of tea?"

And just like that, the discussion was over. I stayed there that night, huddled close to Yerva like when we were kids. But we weren't children any longer. Our problems were real, the answers not so simple. Yerva kept up her whispered criticism of Bogdan until my eyes wouldn't stay open any longer. I dropped off into a fitful sleep, even my unconscious mind finding it difficult to easily accept a conversation with my husband the next day.

In the morning, we did not speak much about Bogdan. Instead, we talked about Kateryna and how quickly she was growing. Already she'd begun to look more like a real person and less like a baby. It was a safe topic, one which all of us could agree upon. But by the time the cart arrived to take me to the fields, my stomach was churning and all sorts of thoughts were whirling through my mind.

I'd decided to wait until my lunch break to confront him. I knew I wouldn't be able to eat much of anything, and having his team members as an audience helped insure he wouldn't shout, or worse. By the time the sun had climbed nearly straight overhead, I was in such a state I could barely fill a bag without dumping half the grain on the ground. A few of my team members asked if I was ill, and I feigned a summer cold.

I used the ten minutes it took the cart to take me to the field where Bogdan's team was working to rehearse my lines in my mind. I knew the confrontation was unlikely to go as I'd planned – when did it ever? – but the rehearsing helped ease my nerves, at least slightly. I asked the cart driver to wait, expecting our meeting to last no more than a few minutes.

Bogdan's team had already stopped for lunch by the time I arrived. I was relieved to see him eating with two of his male comrades, not the young woman I'd caught him with the night before. He jumped up when he saw me and came running over before I could get anywhere near his team members.

"Nina? Where have you been?! I've been looking all over for you!" he said, his expression so worried I could almost believe him. Except for the fact that my mother's house was the obvious place to look for me, and the one place he apparently had failed to consider.

"I spent the night at my mother's."

He grabbed me by both arms. "Look, I'm sorry. She means nothing to me. You and Kateryna mean everything."

I wanted to believe. I wanted to think it had been a drunken mistake. But I also wanted my say.

"How could you?!" I asked, keeping my voice just barely under control. The one thing I didn't want to do was cry. "How could you cheat with that... girl?"

"I... I was drunk. It'll never happen again. I already told her." He spit out the words rapid-fire, as if he'd rehearsed as well. "You see," he said, gesturing back toward his team eating their lunch, "she didn't even come to work today."

I scanned the workers and, sure enough, she wasn't among them. Somehow that small victory lifted my spirits, though I didn't want Bogdan to know.

"Did she quit?" I asked keeping my tone hard and sharp.

"I don't know," he said. "I haven't spoken to her since last night."

"And if she does come back? What then?"

"I'll ask the manager to reassign me to another team. Please, Nina. I'm begging you, come home."

Part of me wanted to tell him to go to hell, but part of me still loved him. And he was Kateryna's father.

"If this ever happens again..." I blustered, utterly unsure of what I would do if it did.

"It won't! I promise! I was a fool!"

I wavered. He looked so pathetic, so hurt.

"I'll think about it."

I started to turn when he stepped forward and grabbed me in a crushing hug that squeezed the very air from my lungs.

"Thank you, дорогий, thank you," he said, kissing my cheeks and eyes while he held on like a drowning man.

I almost gave in, almost returned his affection. But my anger and hurt still burned.

"Perhaps I'll see you at home," I said, pushing him away gently.

"Yes, yes, I'll see you there!" he called after me as I walked across the field to where the cart and driver waited.

I was numb. By the time I returned to my own team I had recovered somewhat, but apparently not so much that Alina couldn't tell something was wrong.

"What is it, what's happened?" she asked as I assumed my place next to her in the bagging operation.

"Nothing, just some personal issues," I lied, unwilling to share my shame with a co-worker.

"You look like you lost a friend."

"No, at least I hope not," I said.

Those words haunted me for the rest of the day.

*****

I spent over an hour talking with Mama and Yerva when I went to pick up Kateryna, explaining why I was giving Bogdan another chance. Mama was neither surprised nor distressed. Yerva, on the other hand, was outraged.

"After what he did, you're just going back there like nothing happened?!" she argued, her face distorted and red.

"He claims it was a drunken mistake and it won't happen again."

"The drinking, or the girls?"

"Both. Either. I don't know. I only know he's the father of my child and until now he's been a good husband."

"As far as you know."

At that, Mama came alive. "Yerva! That's quite enough! Doesn't your sister have enough pain without you inventing more?"

My sister hung her head, but I saw her eyes still smoldered. "I'm sorry," she said without much conviction. "I just don't see why you're being so easy on him."

For the first time I truly felt the two years difference in age between us. Yerva was a silly schoolgirl, her head filled with theories and fictional heroines. I was a married woman with a child. I had responsibilities I couldn't just run away from.

When I got home that night the first thing I saw was a bouquet sitting in a simple glass vase on the kitchen table.

Not wildflowers, but real purpose-grown blossoms arranged by a professional florist. I'd never received such a gift. It must've cost a fortune!

"Nina! I was beginning to worry!" Bogdan called out as he hurried to where I stood transfixed by the bouquet. He followed my eyes. "Do you like them?"

"They're... beautiful," I said, even as I struggled to maintain my anger.

"Beautiful flowers for my beautiful wife." He looked at me with such hopefulness that I felt my indignation seep out with a sigh.

"You shouldn't have," I managed to say.

"I wanted you to know how much you mean to me. You and Kateryna," he added, reaching down and taking her from my grasp. He kissed her on both cheeks and held her up high, eliciting an excited giggle from our tiny daughter. Despite my best efforts, my heart melted.

"She's as gorgeous as her mother," he said when he saw my expression soften.

"And you're full of it," I said with the best stern look I could muster.

Before I could react, he leaned in and kissed me full on the lips.

"I'm sorry," he said softly. "I was an ass."

I wanted to believe him. I wanted to believe he could change.

There was only one problem: I smelled beer on his breath and tasted it on his lips.

I hid my shock by turning to take off my coat. He was so involved in playing with Kateryna that he didn't notice my hurt look as I went to change out of my work clothes. He laughed and chatted with her, oblivious to my pain, while I hid my disappointment, and a tear, in the darkness of our bedroom.

Chapter 7

For a time, Bogdan was as good as his word. He came home right after work, played with Kateryna and took his turns feeding and changing her late at night, and generally reverted back to the man I'd fallen in love with and married. For a time I thought we'd overcome our difficulties and moved on.

For a time.

Kateryna was 14 months old when I succumbed to Bogdan's growing insistence that we have another child. After all, if we were going to give Kateryna a brother or sister, it made sense to do so while she was close enough in age to provide a playmate. It was not an easy decision for me; I had my doubts. I talked with Mama, and Yerva, and Alina, hoping to find a reason to tip the scales one way or the other.

"Are you kidding?!" Yerva said, reacting as if I'd asked her to marry Stalin. "You can't trust him!"

Mama was more practical. "Of course it would be wonderful to have a sibling for Kateryna, and another grandchild for me. But can you afford it? You'll miss at least a few months of work, and then you'll have to support two young babies at the same time. You know you'll be the one taking care of them most of the time. It won't be easy."

Alina, a single mother for many years, understood my dilemma most acutely. "How sure are you that Bogdan is going to be around? Is he going to do his part? Could you raise them by yourself if you had to? Would you want to?"

While I was busy weighing all the pros and cons, nature settled the issue for us. I became pregnant again. Not on purpose – at least not on my part. I thought I'd timed our relations to avoid the situation, but apparently my cycle was not completely predictable. In any case, Bogdan was ecstatic, and I was guardedly hopeful.

For the first seven months of the pregnancy he was an angel, helping me around the house, taking care of Kateryna when I felt poorly and Mama wasn't available, and staying clear of all the temptations that presented themselves. True to his word, he'd asked his team leader to transfer him to another harvest unit. His manager decided it would be better to transfer the girl, so he did. Bogdan told me of the move without rancor or blame, and I neither heard nor saw any further sign of her in his life.

I'd begun to think we'd weathered the storm, when once again fate took a hand. Or an arm, to be more accurate. One afternoon when I was nearly eight months pregnant, I heard heavy footstep on the stairs coming up to our apartment, well before I was expecting Bogdan to return from the fields. I opened the door to see who it was, and was shocked to see my husband supported under one arm by one of his team members, his other arm – his right – bandaged and held in place by a sling.

"My god! What happened?!" I cried out. His face was pale, his lips set in a pained sneer.

"He was disconnecting a plow blade from the nag that had been pulling it when it kicked him – broke his arm," his comrade replied when Bogdan hesitated.

"Come in, come in!" I stepped aside so they could make their way through the door. Bogdan half-collapsed in a kitchen chair.

He yelled so loudly I flinched.

"Does it hurt?" I asked, hurrying to his side.

"Yes, it goddamn hurts!" he said, his face distorted.

"The bone broke through the skin," his friend explained. "Doctor says it'll be six to eight weeks before he can use it."

"Six to eight weeks?" I said before I could stop myself. "That's terrible!"

It was worse than that. For the first few days Bogdan barely slept. In fact, he slept better propped up in a chair

during the day than in our bed. His arm pained him almost
constantly, and his mood was... well, bad. He snapped at
me, at visitors from his team, even at Kateryna. It **was**
terrible.

It quickly became obvious we did not have enough
savings to survive the two of us being unemployed, so I
suggested we ask Mama for a loan to get us through his
recuperation. He wouldn't hear of it. Instead, he sent word
to his family asking them for help. It took more than a week
to receive their response, and when word arrived it wasn't
what we'd hoped.

*'Harvest has been poor. Not enough jobs for all who need them.
We barely have enough for ourselves,'* his father had written.

We had no choice but to contact Mama. Or so I
thought.

"You will **not** ask her for help!" he roared when I
suggested it again. "I will find a way."

And so I waited. And waited. Two weeks into his
recovery I had nothing left in the kitchen to eat aside from
two heads of cabbage. I'd tried to raise the issue with him
several times, but he'd either refused to discuss it or
exploded in anger. So I decided on a different tack. I had a
long conversation with Mama and she readily agreed to
'loan' us some basic foodstuffs until the two of us could get
back out into the fields. I snuck them into the apartment by
secreting them in the bottom of the bag I used to carry
Kateryna's things when I took her for a visit to see her
grandmother. I was confident that Bogdan would never
snoop around in the kitchen, so he never knew just how
little food we had left.

Bogdan managed to persuade his team leader to request
an advance on his salary, but that covered less than a single
month's expenses. Somehow he convinced the tavern-owner
not to throw us out into the street. When I asked how, he
evaded answering until his patience ran thin.

"Mind your own business!" he'd screamed before tromping out the door. As if keeping a roof over our heads wasn't as much my business as his.

And so the weeks passed. I grew bigger and bigger, until just navigating the back stairs became a challenge. At first Bogdan spent most of his time in the apartment, repairing all the little defects we hadn't had time for when we both worked. But not even that apartment had limitless opportunities to stay busy. Eventually he found himself with nothing to do and the tiny room became even smaller.

He began to go out once or more a day, 'for a walk' he'd say. I had my doubts, my intuition raging, but there was little I could do or say to keep him at home. After only a few days of his wanderings, I once again smelled tobacco smoke and alcohol on his breath and clothing. He never seemed drunk, so to avoid arguments I kept quiet. Maybe the occasional beer was good for him. Maybe it allowed him to relax a little without his wife and child hanging all over him. Maybe I was just too tired and worried about the birth of our next child to care.

Whatever the reason, within the first month he was back to his drinking on a daily basis. There'd been no repeat of his earlier abuse, and no sign of the girl, so I crossed my fingers and hoped that the arrival of our child, or his return to work, would motivate him to forsake the daily visit downstairs.

He'd only been back working for two days when my contractions suddenly grew much stronger and ever-closer together. I sent a messenger to the fields even as I called the midwife. Despite all I'd heard from Mama about how the second birth was supposed to be so much easier than the first, my experience was much worse. Where Kateryna had seemed eager to escape the confines of my belly and make her appearance in this crazy world, Sasha seemed equally determined to stay inside me as long as possible.

Both Mama and Yerva stood beside me throughout the entire ordeal: eighteen hours of non-stop agony interspersed with short interludes of false hope. If I heard the midwife shout, "Push! Harder!" one more time, I thought I'd get up off the bed and strangle her. If I could – get up, that is.

From Julija's reaction when she stepped into the apartment, having come-by expecting to welcome our newborn little boy into the family, I must've looked quite the horror.

"My god, Nina! You're not still at it?"

"Can't... get... enough," I managed to pant through the waves of pain, my hair plastered to my face, my eyes scrunched shut so tightly I saw stars.

The rest was more of the same, over, and over, and over again. By the end, all four of us had tears streaming down our faces as Sasha finally made his appearance, his tiny face a terrifying shade of pale blue from the umbilical cord wrapped around his neck.

The midwife, by then my best friend and savior once more, quickly moved to cut the cord and unwrap it from his throat. To my great relief, he cried out loudly almost immediately and his face gradually assumed the distressed flush that signaled a healthy boy.

"There you are," the midwife said as she handed the washed and swaddled baby to me a short while later. "It was all worth it, wasn't it?"

While I considered how I'd answer, Yerva spoke up. "If that's what it's going to be like, I think I'll pass on the entire experience."

Julija laughed, Mama was shocked, and I had to bite my tongue to avoid agreeing with her.

"Perhaps you'll change your mind when you find the right man," I said instead.

She looked at me as if I'd grown a third head.

"How about you go downstairs to tell Bogdan he has a new son," Mama changed the subject.

"Why would I want to do something nice for him?"

"You're not," I interrupted. "You're doing it for me."

She pursed her lips in a pout that reminded me of how she'd looked when she hadn't gotten what she wanted as a young girl, but did as Mama asked.

"She has a point, you know," Julija said as soon as the door to the apartment closed behind Yerva.

"What's that?" I asked, suddenly feeling overpoweringly tired.

"He *has* been a bastard. What makes you think he can change?"

"Julija! Not you too!" Mama cried.

I held up one hand to stop the argument.

"Can I just enjoy this moment with my new son? For one day at least?"

Julija looked chastened; Mama nodded sagely.

Before I could say anything else, I heard familiar boots fly up the stairs.

"Let me see him!" Bogdan called out as he burst through the door. "Where is my son?!"

He came to my bed and grabbed little Sasha and all his blankets from my arms.

"Careful!" I warned. But he was too excited, too proud. He held the tiny newborn up in the air and planted a big kiss on his forehead.

"He's beautiful!" he announced loudly. "Just like his mother," he added as an afterthought.

"He has his father's eyes."

He examined them closely. "They *are* like mine," he decided with a huge grin.

"But not as bloodshot," Yerva said, coming in from downstairs.

I thought he was about to explode when he glanced over at her, but instead his grin grew even wider.

"A man must celebrate the birth of his son. The entire village must share our joy!"

With that he handed Sasha back to me, kissed me quickly on the cheek, and hurried back downstairs.

"Where is he going now?" Mama asked, her face painted in frustration.

"There are a dozen drunks waiting for a free drink downstairs," Yerva explained, turning to me. "Your husband promised."

"That will cost a fortune!" Mama said before she could stop herself. "And the two of you without a kopek to your names."

"It doesn't happen very often," I said, trying to justify the unjustifiable.

"Thank God for that," Yerva chimed-in, ignoring Mama's pointed look.

None of us said a word for several seconds. There was nothing else to say.

*****

Sasha was a good little boy, and Kateryna a loving and accepting big sister. That first month, however, was still difficult as we barely scraped together enough to feed ourselves and keep a roof over our heads. Just a few days after the birth, Bogdan's team leader created a temporary position that required experience more than strength, allowing him to work for three weeks with just one arm. The pay was less, but enough – just barely. From time to time I smelled beer on his breath, but decided to let it go unchallenged to give our marriage a chance to heal. In retrospect that might have been a mistake, but at the time I had too much to do and too much to think about to add an occasional beer to the mix.

I stayed at home for six months, nursing Sasha and taking care of Kateryna, until finally our need for money and my growing need to talk to an adult more often than once or twice a week prompted me to return to the fields. I should've known that 'our little secret' wouldn't remain a secret long in such a small village, but it was still a surprise when Dmitry questioned whether Bogdan and I could work together, even as members of different teams.

"Are you and your husband good now?" the field boss asked me the day I returned to work.

"Good? How do you mean?" I asked, even though I had a pretty good idea what he was referring to.

"Last time you worked here, before the baby, there was some… disturbance. Family quarrel or something."

"All marriages have rough spots."

"True. But they don't bring them to *my* field. At least not twice. Am I making myself clear?"

I nodded, afraid to speak.

"Good. Then I'm happy to have you back. As I'm sure your fellow workers will be as well."

They were. In fact, it was almost as if I'd never left. No one else asked me about the *disturbance* with my husband, though Alina wanted detailed information about Sasha and Kateryna both. No one asked me anything about Bogdan.

It was satisfying to return to work, so much so that I felt a bit guilty about enjoying it as much as I did. It wasn't that I didn't miss the kids; I did. But I missed talking with other adults even more. Bogdan didn't really count. Other than an occasional question about how the children were doing or what he or I had done in the fields, our conversations consisted of little more than grunted requests to pass food at the dinner table or complaints about the local government or the national Soviet. Increasingly, our time in bed consisted of nothing more than sleep. We were both usually too tired to even think about being passionate, and I – at least – had no interest in adding another mouth to our household budget. In fact, I went well beyond that.

One afternoon I feigned illness and went home early. Or not home, exactly. I went to the local midwife, the same woman who'd delivered both our children. In addition to delivering babies, Mrs. Marchuk was equally renowned for ensuring that women who did not want children did not become pregnant.

"Mrs. Kovalchuk, how are you doing this fine day?" she said when I came to her home clinic.

"Fine, fine. You?"

"Very well, thank you. What can I do for you? Are the children well?"

"They're fine." For a long moment we stared at each other.

"What, then, can I do for you?"

"I don't want another child, at least not yet," I blurted. It was a difficult thing for me to admit out loud, but she showed no sign of surprise or judgment. "We can't afford it, and two are all I can handle."

"I understand. And your husband? Is he of the same mind?"

In fact, he wasn't. We'd had several arguments already about his desire for more kids. It was one of the reasons we spent so little time in bed other than sleeping. He would've thrown a fit if he'd known I was visiting old Mrs. Marchuk. So I lied.

"Of course. You can only stretch a kopek so far…"

"Isn't that the truth. Wait here just a second."

She went into a back room and I heard the clink of glass bottles or jars. A few minutes later she returned, carrying a small brown paper bag.

"Make two cups of tea from this every time you have relations with your husband. Then drink half and flush his seed from your body with the other half."

My unspoken question must have shown on my face, for she got up and went to a drawer in the old cabinet behind her.

"Use this," she instructed, handing me a large black rubber bulb with a small hose attached to one end. I stared wide-eyed.

"You've never used one?" she asked.

I shook my head silently. I'd never even seen one. Wasn't entirely sure what it was.

"Okay then, let's start from the beginning." She explained what I was meant to do, and why, with the calming patience of someone who'd done so many times before. At first I felt embarrassed – as much from my ignorance as from the act itself. But as she explained, and demonstrated, I realized that this was exactly what I needed, exactly what could save our marriage.

"Just be sure your husband supports your decision," she said as she finished her explanation. From my expression she must've realized he wouldn't be party to my decision. "Or..." she continued, "at least make sure you keep it somewhere he's not likely to look, and use it only when he's nowhere to be found. Otherwise... there might be problems."

I didn't need any further coaching on that point. Bogdan would be furious. Of course, if our life up 'til that point was any indication, I'd be the one doing all the child-rearing. I needed time to learn whether I had any inclination to increase the size of our family.

My reticence spilled over into our bedroom. Where I'd often been the aggressor in our conjugal visits before the birth of our children, after Sasha I found myriad reasons for postponing the act, indefinitely. Bogdan wasn't happy, I knew, but I couldn't bring myself to chance another pregnancy. And, if truth be told, his drinking drove a wedge between us. It was a downward spiral: he'd drink; I'd be less accepting of his advances; he'd drink some more. It was almost as if it was happening to someone else. I saw it, but couldn't do anything about it. Maybe I didn't want to.

*****

The beginning of the end came when Sasha was four. We'd struggled to maintain some semblance of a family life, though with Bogdan spending more and more time downstairs in the tavern, it was increasingly difficult. I'd finally had enough.

"Bogdan, we have to talk," I said one night when he stumbled upstairs to our apartment. It was late, after ten, and the children had gone to bed – without his goodnights once again – hours earlier.

"Oh God, now what?" he answered, throwing off his coat and sitting by the stove to unlace his boots.

"I don't think this apartment is a good place for us. I think we need to move," I said with as much force as I thought I could muster without raising his ire.

He looked at me as if were crazy. "Move?! Do you have any idea how much that would cost?"

In fact, I did. I'd been putting money aside, secretly, for over a year, and by that time had enough of a nest-egg to make a down-payment on a little hut of our own. A place as far from any bar or tavern as I could find. When I explained that to him, instead of complimenting me on my financial good sense, he exploded.

"What?! We've been just scraping-by all these months and you've been taking money without telling me?"

He stood up, and I could tell he'd had more than enough to drink. His eyes always had a slightly crazy look when he'd had one too many.

"We needed money for a down-payment. Unless I put something aside, we'd never be able to move," I said softly. What I didn't say was that if I hadn't put money aside, he'd have drunk every penny of it.

"I'm the man in this home!" he bellowed.

"Keep your voice down! You'll wake the children!"

"The children! Always the children! What about me? When do I get what *I* want?"

Now I was getting angry. "And what is that, Bogdan," I said, getting up out of my seat myself. "To drink yourself to death?"

He stepped so close his beer breath was overpowering. "That's what you'd like, isn't it? Then you could do whatever you please."

"Don't be ridiculous," I muttered, tired of his constant self-pity.

I didn't expect the slap that slashed across my cheek. It caught me off-balance and I stumbled back, falling against the table, knocking a plate to the floor where it smashed.

"You bitch!" he screamed. "You can't even give me another kid and you're lecturing *me*!"

I put up my hands to protect myself, just as Kateryna staggered sleepy-eyed from the bedroom.

"Mama, what is it? I heard a crash…"

Bogdan glared at me, then at his daughter. Without a word he pulled on his coat and stomped out of the house.

"It's nothing, sweetheart, go back to bed," I cooed, moving to her side and turning her back toward the bedroom.

"Where did Papa go?"

"I don't know, honey. I don't know."

"When is he coming back?"

I felt like saying '*never*', but held my tongue.

*****

He did come back, in the early hours of the morning, reeking of smoke and beer and sweat. No apology. No explanation. I feigned sleep, hoping to avoid an argument. But arguments never really go away by themselves, they just sit and fester, growing more fetid by the day. Just as ours did.

We didn't move. With each passing day Bogdan spent more and more time in the tavern, and less and less with the children and me. At first I tried to dissuade him by gentle persuasion.

"Where are you off to?" I'd ask, for the umpteenth time.

"Out," he'd answer, as always.

"Wouldn't you like to help Kateryna with her math?" (or read to her, or stack blocks with Sasha, or even just talk to me.)

"Maybe some other time."

Of course, there was no other time. The education our children received before their formal schooling began came largely from Mama and Yerva, and what little I could squeeze in between eight to ten hours in the field, cooking, cleaning and ironing. Bogdan barely saw his children awake. The apartment became just a place to eat and sleep, and sometimes little enough of that: often he only grabbed a piece of toast or bowl of oatmeal before running out the door. For a time I consoled myself with the belief that at least he wasn't with another woman, that his distaste for family life carried over to everyone and everything. Until one July, when Kateryna was 5, Sasha 3.

I'd arrived at work after dropping the kids off at Mama's hut and was preparing for another day bagging grain under the hot summer sun. Alina, who'd become team leader when

Dmitry retired two years earlier, came over to where I was stacking burlap bags and stood watching, silently.

"What's up?" I asked after several minutes passed.

"It's not really any of my business," she began, and I knew immediately there was a problem.

"But...?" I prodded.

"But... she's back."

I stared, not understanding. "Who? Who is back?"

"That girl. Irina. The one your husband was... *friendly* with some years ago. She's back, working on his team."

I felt a tiny stab of pain somewhere in my chest. I should have been angry, should have raged against his infidelity, but the pain was minimal. Not unexpected.

"She's not a little girl anymore," Alina went on. "She's all grown up." The way she said it said more than her words.

"And what can I do about it?" I finally asked, more because I thought I should than because I wanted to.

Alina shook her head. "I don't know. Maybe I can talk with the field manager and get her assigned somewhere else..."

"There will always be another one," I said. "There's no shortage of young women with bad taste in men."

She looked at me askance.

"Including me," I added, and she smiled, a sad, knowing smile.

"Including most of us."

I decided I would address the situation at home, both because I didn't want our comrades to know any more about our private lives than they already did, and because I knew that if I were to have any chance of redirecting his amorous interests back toward me it would have to be one on one. The minute anyone else came into the equation, his ego wouldn't permit him to give up the girl, even if he had no particular interest in keeping her.

There was little chance he'd be at home when I returned from work, so I sent word to Mama that I'd be coming to get the kids later and went instead straight to the tavern. I fully expected he'd already be well on his way to oblivion, but what I didn't expect was that the girl would be there with him. I saw the two of them before they saw me, but I didn't hesitate. I went directly to where they were drinking with several other team members at the bar.

"Nina! Want a drink?" he asked when he noticed me approaching. He said it with good-natured drunken charm, but I saw the cold disregard in his eyes.

"We need to talk," was all I said. I tried to make it sound affable, but he was having no part of it.

"We're celebrating."

"Oh? What?"

"We finished field D," Irina said, seemingly oblivious to my anger.

"I was talking to my husband," I said, eliciting a hum of derisive commentary from the other men in the group.

"We can talk when I get home," Bogdan said, trying to ease out of the situation without a nasty argument. But I was well past civil conversation.

"By the time you get home, we'll all be asleep."

"All?"

"Me, your son and your daughter. You remember them, don't you?" The last was a low blow, but I didn't care.

More comments from his team members. Irina leaned over and whispered something in his ear. His lip curled in disgust and he pushed her away.

"Okay, fine," he said to me. "Let's talk."

"Outside," I said, and turned to leave before he could object.

"Your Mommy's waiting!" one of the guys yelled out drunkenly. Bogdan punched him so hard in the stomach that the man fell over, flat on his face. The others backed-off without further comment.

I stood outside in the cool evening air waiting for him to extricate himself. When he finally came through the tavern door, he looked chastened.

"So? What was so important?"

"I'm leaving," I said, surprising even myself.

"Where-to, your Mom's?" The full significance of my statement hadn't hit him.

"Probably. At first. Then the kids and I will get our own place."

He stared at me as if I'd been speaking a foreign language. "What do you mean, 'your own place'?"

"This isn't a family anymore. You spend most of your time down here with your 'friends', while the kids and I wait upstairs for a father and husband who never shows up. I've had enough."

The momentary shock turned quickly to anger. "You wanna leave?" he challenged, his face reddening. "Go ahead. Leave! But you're not taking my kids."

"Oh, what will you do? Leave them alone in the apartment every day?"

He stopped as if slapped. He obviously hadn't thought that far ahead.

"I… I'll get my mother to come out here. She'll look after them."

"While you sit downstairs and drink your paycheck every week? From what I know of your mother – and especially your father – that isn't going to happen."

"Then I'll take them there, to their house." He said it with such satisfaction, as if he'd solved the riddle of the ages.

"And do what for work? Your father has been complaining about the bad harvests for years now. How will you support the three of you?" I had no intention of letting him get out of my sight with our kids, but I still had a faint

hope that I could awaken something of the man I'd married.
"Don't tell me your father will pay the bills."

I saw realization slowly dawn on his face. "You think
you know everything, don't you?" he slurred, the coldness in
his eyes flaring into pure hatred.

I should have given him time to cool down. I should
have stepped back. But I was angry as well. "I know I know
more than you, that's for certain."

And then he hit me. The next thing I knew blood was
dripping from a swollen lip and I was looking up at him
from the gravel of the parking lot.

"You're not taking my kids," he said, his voice
quavering.

I almost said something stupid. Again. But, thank God,
I'd learned my lesson.

"I don't want to. I don't want to go at all. But if you're
going to spend all your time in the tavern…" I left the
statement unfinished, mainly because I had no idea what I'd
do if he refused to give me the kids.

His face held the grimace, but the fire in his eyes
dimmed.

"I don't spend *all* my time there."

"Most of it. And the little bit we get isn't enough. The
kids barely realize you're their father."

I saw his eyes narrow and I thought I was in for another
beating. What I didn't expect were the tears that streamed
down his cheek.

"I can't stand the crying," he said softly. "It makes me
crazy."

"Your son is three. He hasn't cried for nothing in a long
time."

I could tell he was taken aback. Perhaps he honestly
didn't realize so much time had passed. Perhaps he heard his
own words and realized how feeble they sounded.

Bogdan looked down at me and then looked away into the deepening gloom. "Where are they now?"

"At Mama's."

"We should probably go get them."

Now the tears flowed from *my* eyes. "The cart driver is waiting," I managed to squeak.

He reached his hand down to me and helped me to my feet. We stared into each other's eyes for so long I think I stopped breathing.

"I'll go get him," he finally said.

When he turned to leave my knees nearly folded up beneath me.

Chapter 8

When I look back at that time, I find it difficult to recognize me in my own remembrances. It's as if I'm seeing a foolish young girl who bears little semblance to the woman I've become. But then I realize that it was all those foolish choices, and the repercussions that arose from them, that have created the me that exists today. Would I change them if I could? Some. Maybe most. But I'm old enough to know that looking back rarely provides a roadmap for going forward, and more often than not only helps ensure that you'll walk into something while your thoughts are diverted. The past is passed. Nothing can undo what has been done. Or the pain it has caused.

*****

For a few weeks late that summer, life in our tiny apartment above the tavern improved. My husband avoided the bar, coming directly home from the fields most nights. He read to the children, played with them from time to time, and seemed to enjoy himself. I even heard encouraging words from Alina.

"What's happened with Bogdan?" she asked one lunchtime not long after our *discussion* in the tavern parking lot.

"How do you mean?" I asked, fearful he had gone off-track so quickly.

"My eyes and ears in his team say he's stopped eating lunch with Irina. From the look on her face, she's not happy about it."

I couldn't hide my relief. "Can't say I'm sorry to hear it."

"Didn't think you would be."

I gave her a brief reprise of our fight, leaving out any detail I wouldn't want *accidentally* passed on through the harvest grapevine to our co-workers. She nodded with understanding.

"Sometimes even a bunny must bite," she said.

I smiled at the image that appeared in my mind's eye. I only hoped the future brought smiles as well.

In fact, the improvement wasn't just with the kids. Bogdan began to treat me as he had when we'd first met: he held doors, gave me flowers, interacted willingly with the kids, and above all stopped visiting the tavern as if it were an alternate home. I was happy. The kids were happy. But I could never bring myself to lower my defenses completely. In the back of my mind I never forgot his deceit, never forgave his infidelity. Perhaps it isn't in me to forgive. I always marveled that Christ could forgive the people who'd killed him. I wondered if he'd've been so open if he didn't have a place in heaven already reserved.

It didn't take Bogdan long to return to his old ways. Two months after our showdown, he attended a workers' committee meeting, and came home smelling of beer.

"You were drinking," I said with as little rancor as I could manage.

"Just a beer," he said, continuing with his arrival routine.

"You should be careful," I added. He said nothing.

That one time became two, then three, and before long he was back to spending more time in the tavern than at home. When I told Mama, she was surprised at how unemotional I was about it all.

"It doesn't bother you?" she asked when I'd told her about his latest problems with the bottle.

"It should, I know. But I just can't find the energy to care. If he doesn't want to be part of our family, then maybe he shouldn't be."

"Are you going to leave him?" She wasn't nearly as emotional as I'd expected. Perhaps she was tired of all his excuses as well.

"I don't know. Maybe."

It was the first time I'd articulated the thought, even to myself. Oh, I'd complained plenty to Alina and my sisters, but I'd never crossed that invisible line between grumbling and action, and it made my skin tingle to even think about it. Leave him? The words echoed in my head. Could I? Would I? What about the kids? Kateryna was already 9, Sasha 7. They knew their father was *different* than many of their friends' dads, but they still loved him. At least I thought they did. It was hard enough to be certain how I felt about him, let alone them.

I decided to sit him down for a talk, to see where he stood and where we were headed. I wanted to talk when just the two of us were there so he wasn't tempted to act tougher than he already was for the benefit of an outside audience, and when he was sober, for obvious reasons. So I asked Mama (once again) to look after the kids and cooked Bogdan a nice varenyky dinner, hoping he'd be less confrontational if his stomach was full.

I hadn't expected a warm and loving encounter, yet the degree of his resentment took me by surprise.

"Varenyky?" he said as soon as he walked into the apartment after returning from the fields. "What's the occasion?" He said it with a tone that suggested I had an ulterior motive. Which I had.

"No occasion. I just wanted to talk."

"Right. About what?"

"Let's talk over dinner," I suggested, pulling out a chair and seating myself at the table.

"Uh oh. Trouble," he said as he walked past me to the bathroom, where he washed for dinner. I didn't smell alcohol as he passed, which gave me some small sliver of hope. "Where are the kids?"

"With Mama."

"Hmm." It wasn't so much an accusation as an unspoken doubt.

"How was your day?" I asked as he washed, hoping to defuse any pre-existing anger.

"Since when do you care?"

"Of course I care," I said, sounding defensive even to myself. "You're my husband."

He came into the kitchen wearing just a white t-shirt and baggy checkered undershorts, drying his hands on a towel. "Cut the crap. What's this all about?"

He sat heavily in the chair opposite me and immediately began shoveling varenyky onto his plate, followed by a heaping tablespoon of sour cream.

I had practiced an entire back-and-forth exchange, prepared to counter any argument he raised and put forth all my hard-reasoned explanations for what I planned. Instead, I said the first words that came to mind.

"Are you happy?"

He looked up at me, his mouth full of varenyky and cream, as if I'd lost my mind.

"Happy? Who in God's name is happy?"

"Don't you think we should be? Happy, I mean."

"Sure. And rich, handsome and talented as well. Tough luck." He didn't even smile, but went on eating.

"But at least the kids should be happy, right?"

Now he was staring. "Yeh. So what?"

"I don't think they can really be happy as long as *we're* not happy."

"Are you getting to a point, or do I have to listen to this philosophy nonsense all night?"

I bit back a snide remark and instead let loose. "What are we doing, Bogdan? You spend half your time in the tavern drinking with your buddies, I spend a lot of time talking to my mother and sisters, we hardly spend any time together. This isn't working."

I expected an argument. Maybe an explosion. What I didn't expect was resigned acceptance. "I can't argue with you," he said, his fork not missing a beat.

It stopped me cold. "You can't?"

"You can move out any time you want."

"Why don't you move out?" I didn't mean to sound snively, but I couldn't help it. Why should *I* leave?

"You don't want the kids to have to move, do you?"

"Of course not! That's why..." It wasn't until that moment that I realized what he was saying. I stopped and stared at him. He didn't even bother to look up from his plate. "You expect me to leave the kids with you?"

"I told you before – you're not taking the kids. But as for you – go on, get out. Be my guest. I'll miss the varenyky, but not much else."

I was struck speechless.

He went on eating his meal as if nothing had happened. It took a moment for blood to return to my head.

"*You* want to keep the kids? How? Who will look after them? We both know it won't be your family."

"There are a million women out there who'd love to have a boyfriend like me, with an apartment, a job, even a family. It wouldn't take me ten minutes to find a girl like that."

Perhaps I should've kept my mouth shut, but I couldn't believe what I was hearing. "You mean someone like Irina?"

He finally looked up from his varenyky. "If that's who I choose..."

The conversation was over. I stood up and began clearing my place. "You aren't the person I married. And I can't be part of this any longer."

Bogdan shrugged and didn't say a word.

*****

I felt as though a thousand pound weight had suddenly landed on my back, or perhaps I should say on my heart. As much as I'd thought about leaving my marriage, as many times as I'd complained about Bogdan's drinking and philandering, I still wasn't prepared for his cold-blooded announcement that he didn't care if I left.

He didn't care! We'd been married for a dozen years, had produced two wonderful children, had worked through some very tough times together – and now he didn't care if I left! I didn't know whether to cry or scream. What I did know is that I couldn't stand to be with him right then and there.

I threw on a light jacket and was halfway out the door when he called after me: "Have the kids back by breakfast, or I'll come get them." His tone was hard and cold. I didn't bother to respond.

I found a cart driver still out and about and paid him to take me to Mama's.

"So?" she asked as soon as I stepped through her door. She took one look at my tear-streaked face and knew. "Oh."

Yerva came out from the bedroom, where she'd just finished putting the kids to sleep, before I could even get my jacket off.

"What has that bastard done now?" she asked, drawing a rebuking look but no comment from Mama.

"He doesn't care if I leave, but I can't take the kids."

Yerva exploded. Mama sat silently.

"What will you do?" she finally asked.

I'd been thinking about a course of action all the way over in the cart. I'd been so uncommunicative that the driver finally gave up any attempt at drawing me into a conversation.

"I can't stay, and I won't leave my children with him," I said, sounding much more confident than I felt.

"Bravo!" my little sister cheered, but I understood she had no real grasp of what that would mean.

"Where will you go?" Mama asked, her voice so small and slight I thought she might cry.

I hesitated. There was only one way to be sure Bogdan didn't follow us – at least not right away. No one could tell him where we'd gone – on purpose or by mistake – unless they knew.

"I'm not sure yet," I equivocated. "Somewhere outside the oblast."

"So far!" Mama cried.

Yerva nodded in agreement. "Makes sense. No chance of accidentally running into him, or anyone who knows the two of you."

"Exactly," I said. "I've got a cart waiting outside. He'll take me as far as Khmil'nik. I'll find another driver there who'll take me further north."

"And your children?" Mama looked at me as if she feared my reply.

"Why they'll come with me, of course."

"And who will take care of them while you look for work?"

I had no answer. In truth, my thinking hadn't gotten that far. I'd been thinking any move would be weeks or months away.

"I'll go with you," Yerva said before I could find an answer. "I don't have school, so I can stay with you at least a couple of months until you get a job."

"You'll do no such thing!" Mama said. "It'll be bad enough to lose one daughter and two grandchildren…"

"She needs me, Mama," Yerva said calmly, putting a hand on Mama's arm. "She can't do it all on her own." She looked to me for confirmation.

"I… I'm sure I can get by," I stumbled, but Yerva was having none of it.

"Nonsense! You can't find work if you have to drag your kids with you, and you can't support your kids if you don't find work. It's a perfect solution."

I couldn't argue the logic. My heart swelled with thanks for such selflessness. I glanced at Mama, who stood suddenly and rushed into the bedroom.

"Mama!" I whispered after her, but she didn't stop.

Yerva restrained me with a touch. "Give her a minute. It's a lot for her to take in so quickly." As soon as she saw that I wasn't going to follow, she launched into a hundred questions, her excitement infectious.

I'd just begun to explain what little I'd finalized in my half-hour of planning, when the bedroom door opened and Mama reappeared. I expected a tongue-lashing, or perhaps tearful worrying, but instead she reached into her apron and pulled out a small wad of bills.

"Take this. It will help get you started," she said, thrusting the rubles into my hand.

My tears started flowing once again.

"Mama, no! You need this money yourself."

She gave me a big hug. "I'll be fine. What better thing do I have to spend my money on than my girls – and my grandchildren."

"It's just a loan," I said, knowing I was probably lying.

"If that's what you want it to be. Just make sure you're all taken care of."

I wanted to stay there with Mama, probably more than any time in the past few years. But I knew that Bogdan would be on alert, expecting some trick from me to get the kids away from him. That night might be my only chance to sneak them away without a terrible confrontation. We had to go – right then.

We packed enough clothes for the kids for a week, along with one special toy for both Kateryna and Sasha. Luckily I had kept a few old clothes at Mama's house just in case I needed to stay over for one reason or another, but I still had only a few days' wardrobe to pack away. It would have to do.

When we were done packing, the moon having already set in the early hours of the morning, we all kissed and hugged one last time. The two kids were only half-awake and grumpy.

"Why are we going out at night?" Sasha muttered.

"We've got a long trip and we need to get going early," I said, having decided to keep the reason and destination of our journey a secret, at least for a while.

"And Aunt Yerva is coming too?" Kateryna asked.

"I am," my little sister answered. She didn't seem so little right then. "We are all going on an adventure!"

I almost squawked at her, barely restraining myself. As it turned out, the kids caught the spirit of the moment and brightened noticeably.

"An adventure!" Sasha cried, his eyes opening wider.

"What fun!" his big sister agreed.

So with their grandmother struggling to control her tears, the four of us dragged our meager belongings out to the waiting cart and climbed aboard.

"You take good care of yourselves," Mama said in a low voice so as not to wake the nearby households.

The driver, our neighbor Vova, was only half-awake himself, but he nodded to her. "Don't you worry, Anna, we'll get them there safe and sound."

We all blew kisses to Mama as Vova shook the reins and his two old plow horses began the long slow journey north. All four of us stared intently behind the cart to watch Mama standing there in the darkness, her tiny hand waving goodbye. She grew smaller and smaller until she disappeared completely in the blackness of night.

For a long moment we sat in thoughtful silence, each lost in reverie.

"Who wants to sing a song?!" Yerva whispered eagerly, breaking the gloom of our leaving. We all joined in, our voices little more than a hopeful murmur in the vastness of the night. I doubt they all realized it at that moment, but a new phase in our lives had begun.

PART 2

Chapter 9

That night exists in my memory more as a feeling or a mash of emotions than an actual event. I remember exhilaration, relief, and yes, fear as well. We were leaving an impossible situation and arriving in an uncertain one. I had taken on not only the responsibility for my own indefinite future, but that of my children and sister as well. Not a small load to carry.

But I was optimistic, hopeful in the limited way of us Ukrainians. My fellow countrymen believed in a better future, just not for themselves, not just now. Sometime, for someone, life would be better. Perhaps by some stroke of cosmic good fortune that someone would be us, or at least the kids. Better to hope and be disappointed than live a life of hopelessness and despair.

We arrived in Khmil'nik in the late afternoon of the following day. The 200 kilometer trip was uneventful, but tedious and nerve-wracking. Both kids slept soundly until well after sunrise, while Yerva and I talked most of the night and leaned against each other for support the remainder of the day. Our driver said little but handled the team effortlessly as we passed through hilly terrain dotted with small lakes and stretches of glorious green forest. I couldn't help but sneak a peek behind us from time to time, more than anything to alleviate my worry that Bogdan had somehow discovered our flight and was hell-bent on bringing us home. At least the kids.

Despite the warm temperature during the day, at night it dropped down near ten degrees and we all snuggled close together to stay warm. I was so involved in my conversation with my sister, and then in keeping Kateryna and Sasha occupied, the endless ride passed with little notice. My head spun with thoughts of what would become of us, so I remember little of the places we passed or the few people we met.

When we arrived in Khmil'nik I was tempted to seek out another cart immediately so we could be on our way. But the kids were exhausted and both Yerva and I looked as though we hadn't slept in days, so I decided we'd chance a short stay at an inn on the outskirts of town. Vova knew of a place that wouldn't empty our purse and was far enough off the main road that anyone looking for two young women shepherding two young children would be unlikely to trip over them.

In a way I was sad to say goodbye to Vova, since he was our last link to our home and family. As we watched him drive off, tears welled in my eyes.

"What's wrong, Mama?" Kateryna asked when she saw me wipe them away.

"Nothing, darling," I said, but even a child could see it was more than that.

Luckily, Mrs. Pavlyuk – the innkeeper, was a happy, warm-hearted woman who liked people and loved children.

"Who are these two beauties?" the plump woman in her mid-50's called out when we entered the inn. She came out from behind her desk and pinched Sasha's cheek.

"This is Sasha," I introduced as he cowered behind my leg, attempting to ensure he wouldn't be attacked again, "and this is Kateryna." Mrs. Pavlyuk reached out to give her a little pinch as well, but Kateryna was too quick for her. The innkeeper pinched nothing but empty air.

"Looking for a couple of rooms, are you?" she asked as soon as she recovered from her aborted welcome.

"Actually, one room will suffice," I said, trying not to sound penurious.

Mrs. Pavlyuk eyed the four of us through narrowed eyes. "Then two beds, at least."

"If it's not too expensive…"

"I think we can find a room with two beds big enough so you needn't take turns sleeping," she said with a sly smile. She went back to her desk and rooted out a key. "Top of the stairs on the right."

As we struggled up the stairs with our packs and bundles, we were so tired that almost any room would've been a welcome sight. What greeted our eyes as I opened the door was more than welcomed, it was astonishing! The room was bigger than our apartment had been, with two large floor-to-ceiling windows that looked out on a lovely flower garden and manicured back yard. Rose bushes stood side-by-side with chrysanthemums and irises, intermingled with a host of flowers I didn't recognize and of course the ubiquitous sunflowers – an unexpected rainbow of color that lifted our spirits and made the strange inn feel almost like home. There were two beds, each wider by half than what we were accustomed to, and each with the springy mattresses I'd only heard about but never seen.

"Mama, can we live here?" Sasha asked with great expectations. For a moment I almost wished it were true.

"Just for tonight, my darling," I said, giving him a little hug. Despite Mrs. Pavlyuk's warm greeting and the hominess of our surroundings, I didn't stop worrying about Bogdan for a moment. Depending on his mood, and how much he'd been drinking, he'd either set out immediately to bring *his* children back, or he'd say "damn them all" and drown his sorrows. I didn't know which it would be, and couldn't take the chance.

Despite their exhaustion, or perhaps because of it, both my little darlings were too wound up to sleep. Yerva was wonderful with the children, in truth probably better than I at that moment. They played games, read, and drew pictures on old scraps of paper, while I met with Mrs. Pavlyuk and explained in broad outline the situation in which we found ourselves. As I'd hoped, she was understanding and sympathetic. Through her I met Dima, a nephew who regularly traveled the roads north and west for the delivery service he managed under his uncle's forbearance.

"I think we could find room for the four of you on tomorrow's run," he said when the two of us talked to him at his small, neat office not more than a kilometer from the inn. A picture of Mykola Mikhnovsky, the father of Ukrainian nationalism, looked down on us from the wall where it was surreptitiously hung behind a filing cabinet. If any Party members had seen the photo of the intense young man with massive walrus moustache – instead of the equally intense Stalin or the grandfatherly Khrushchev – he would find himself in a great deal of trouble. Yet somehow seeing it there made me feel more confident, not less. Dima's open, welcoming face helped as well.

"We don't have much money," I began, hoping I could negotiate a price that wouldn't leave us without a kopek to our name.

"Where, exactly, are you headed?"

The question made me take a deep breath. I could no longer put off the decision that would shape not only my future, but my children's, for years to come.

"I don't really know," I finally managed. "I'm not very familiar with this part of the country. Perhaps you could give us some advice?"

Dima looked to his aunt with ill-disguised consternation. "I… well, what are you looking for? As I'm sure you realize, there are many towns in Ukraine."

I did realize – all too well. "Well, a place where I might find work, where the children could get a good education. A place that's not too expensive…"

"Berdychiv!" Mrs. Pavlyuk suddenly shouted, nearly jumping up out of her chair. "My brother Anton lives there. He'll be able to help you get settled. He, and Aunt Marina."

She said the last to Dima as if challenging him to contradict her.

"Yes, I suppose it might serve as well as anywhere," her nephew said with a nod. "It *is* the administrative center of the Berdychiv Raion, and since it's on my route tomorrow, I wouldn't need to charge you anything to go there." He looked to his aunt for affirmation. He got it.

"Exactly! You are an angel, Dima."

He blushed. "It's on my route," he mumbled, looking to me for my reaction.

"I... I can't thank you enough," I said, and then moved by emotion I leaned forward and kissed him on the cheek. "My children and I are in your debt."

"Nonsense!" he said, his cheeks redder than ever. "It's on my route."

To avoid embarrassing him further, and with the place and time for our departure settled, we returned to the inn where we found Yerva and my two kids hard at work drawing their concepts of what our new house would look like.

"Mama, Mama, come see!" Sasha yelled as soon as I stepped in the door.

"It's our new house," Kateryna joined-in.

"House?" I said with intentional surprise. "That might be a bit much to hope for. Perhaps a room in a house..."

But they wouldn't hear of it.

"We'll find a house, I'm sure of it," Kateryna said.

"Come look, come look!" Sasha echoed.

Yerva stood behind them, looking at me with a wistful smile.

I went to them and praised their design, although I knew we couldn't afford a house that elegant if I worked a thousand years in the fields. By the time we all settled down it was late afternoon and the shadows had grown long in the yard behind the inn. Yerva and I pulled the curtains and persuaded the kids to climb into their shared bed. They protested and tried every trick at their disposal to delay the inevitable, but eventually they both surrendered; they were asleep in seconds.

Yerva and I went to the main room and sat with a cup of tea, discussing a future that refused to reveal itself to us.

"Berdychiv, eh?" she said between long sips.

"I think so. I don't know much about it, but..."

"Then why there? All I know of the town is that there used to be a lot of Jews there. Until the War, I think."

"It's the administrative center of the Raion," I said, realizing even as I said it how weak the reasoning seemed, "and perhaps more importantly we can get a ride there — free."

She raised her eyebrows. "Oh? Since when does anyone in this country give anything for free to a stranger?"

"The driver's a nephew of Mrs. Pavlyuk. Nice man. He runs a transport service that takes him up there, so we'd just hitch a ride."

She screwed up her face in thought. "I suppose it's no worse than anywhere else. At least it's big enough that there should be jobs."

"We can only hope."

My sister spit over her shoulder three times. "To God's ears."

*****

The next morning Mrs. Pavlyuk knocked on our door at 7:30, inviting us to come down for breakfast. When I hesitated, she would not take no for an answer.

"You need a hearty meal before you start out," she admonished. "Especially the children. It's included in the room rate."

I wasn't about to argue with her, even though the rate she'd charged us was probably less than normal for the room alone. We washed and dressed quickly, making our way downstairs in a silent, sleepy-eyed procession.

"Well don't we look rested!" Mrs. Pavlyuk said as we stepped into her dining room. On the table in front of us sat a platter of deruni and vareniki, with toasted bread, boiled eggs and a big pot of tea.

"Is that for us?" Sasha asked wide-eyed.

"All for you – but save some for your Mama and Aunt and sister."

He let out a whoop and ran to the table.

"Don't use your hands!" I said, but it was already too late. He grabbed one of everything and threw them on his plate.

"You're such a child," Kateryna said imperiously as she sidled up next to him to demonstrate the correct use of knife, fork and serving spoons.

He didn't bother to argue, but looked up at her with a mouth full of vareniki and sour cream, opening wide to demonstrate the extent of his gluttony.

"Uggh!" Kateryna cried out, turning to me. "Mama, do you see? Do you see what he's doing?"

I couldn't help but smile. Even in a strange new city there were some things that never changed.

An hour later Dima appeared with his cart, a fancy modern model with spring suspension and cushions on the front seat.

"Ready to go?" he asked, jumping down to help us load.

"We're ready!" the two kids called out, all the excitement and energy in the world reflected in their faces and voices.

I hugged Mrs. Pavlyuk while her nephew secured the last of our bags.

"Thank you so much," I said, kissing her on both cheeks. "You've saved our lives."

"Nothing quite so dramatic," she smiled. "But I'm happy I could help."

"Just remember," I added, dropping my voice, "as we discussed yesterday – we were never here. You didn't see us."

"See who?"

I hugged her again, with both kids and then Yerva crowding in around me. When we'd all bid her goodbye I climbed up onto the front seat, next to Yerva and Dima with the kids in back, and once again we set off toward an unknown destination, hope, fear and determination mixed in equal parts. Well, perhaps not equal parts...

There was little doubt that my mind veered toward the darker colors of my emotional palette, but not to the complete exclusion of the others. It was just that I *knew* Bogdan. I knew he considered his children to be his property, like so many Ukrainian men of the time. His ego might not survive losing them, especially not to an ex-wife. On the other hand, the bottle held a powerful influence over him, and it was just as likely he'd rant and rave to his drinking buddies, and the girl, but never quite make it out the door. I held my breath.

The trip to Berdychiv was less traumatic, less exhausting, but no less rewarding than our earlier journey. We drove through more rolling hills, past myriad lakes and streams, often in the shadow of vast forests or beside recently-cleared fields. The air smelled of pine and rich, dark earth, the sun shining down on us from cloudless blue skies the color of a robin's egg. I kept Dima talking much of the way, while Kateryna and Sasha played every game Yerva knew and a few she invented on the spot. We headed nearly due north for several hours before turning east on the old road to Berdychiv. To be honest I was taken a bit by surprise when we entered the outskirts of the town. Dima had been such a good story-teller the kilometers had melted away and were imprinted more on our tired backsides than in our memories.

The first building of any note we saw was the massive Carmelite fortress complex, with an immense red brick wall surrounding soaring domes nearly two hundred years old.

"My God, it's beautiful!" Yerva said as the fortress came slowly into view. The fortress seemed to rise magically out of the Hnylopiat River, a large but lethargic tributary of the mighty Dnieper.

"Mama, is this our new home?" Sasha called out from the back of the cart.

For the first time since I'd made the decision, I was pleased to say, "Yes, it is."

I was prepared to stay a night or two at a local inn, during which time I'd try to locate a room or apartment where we could live while I looked for work. Dima and his Aunt, on the other hand, had other ideas.

Mrs. Pavlyuk had called her brother and his wife to tell them to expect the new arrivals, and had instructed Dima to drive us straight to their house – an imposing two story structure with white clapboard walls and a sweeping porch that encircled fully half the house.

"Mama, look!" Kateryna yelled excitedly when the kids got their first glimpse of the towering mansion. "It's our house!" She dug out the drawing she and Sasha had made the night before, and sure enough, there was more than a passing resemblance to the house they had designed.

I remember thinking the coincidence was a good omen, and for once I was right.

Even before Dima stopped his cart in front of the house, we saw Anton and Marina Kravets come striding down the gray stone steps that led up to the front porch, big welcoming smiles on their faces. Anton looked to be a bit older than his sister and several years older than his wife. His hair was gray and thinning on top, but his watchful blue eyes enlivened a plump but powerful face partially hidden behind a bushy mustache that seemed slightly out of fashion now that Stalin was long gone. Marina was tiny, trim and elegant, her shiny black hair coiled atop her head, high cheekbones framing the blackest black eyes I'd ever seen. If I'd still had grandparents, the Kravets were just how I'd have wanted them to be.

"Well there you are!" Marina called out to us, hurrying straight to Kateryna and Sasha to help them from the cart. "Welcome to Berdychiv! You two little darlings must be exhausted. Come, come! The men will bring your things."

With a smile and a nod to me and Yerva, she shepherded the children up the stairs and into the house before we had a chance to say a word.

"Don't be upset, she's always like that," Anton apologized good-naturedly. "I think she might have been a mother hen in another life. I'm Anton," he said, holding out his hand.

"Nina," I replied. "And this is my sister Yerva."

As soon as he'd shaken our hands he hugged his nephew. "About time you found a few minutes to visit us," he complained. "Good thing these people needed a ride or we might not have seen you for another few months."

Dima shrugged. "I have to keep to my schedule, Uncle. You know that. No schedule, no job."

"Such a hard-working boy," Anton said to me. "We can't be too angry. Come in, come in. Let us help you with your bags."

He and Dima collected all our things and started up the stairs.

"Let us take some of those," I offered, but they were already on their way.

Yerva and I followed close behind, feeling a bit irresponsible for allowing Anton, at his age, to haul so many of our possessions into the house. But I can't deny it was also a pleasant surprise.

When we stepped through the front door it was if we'd stepped into another world altogether. If Mrs. Pavlyuk's inn seemed luxurious to us, the Kravets home was palatial. We walked directly into a huge living room with adjacent dining room, high-ceilinged spaces with cut glass chandeliers, multi-colored Middle-Eastern rugs, and fine dark wood furniture that would've cost me a year's salary. An oil portrait of the two of them hung over a massive stone fireplace two meters wide.

"It's beautiful!" Yerva exclaimed a half-second before I could say the same.

"It's a drafty old barn," Anton said as he continued up carpeted interior stairs. "But we're used to it. Come up – we'll get you all settled for the time being."

There was no sign of Marina and the two kids, but I assumed they were already upstairs or in one of the many other rooms that seemed to open off corridors running every which way. At the top of the stairs Anton led us to a large, colorfully painted bedroom with two full size beds and an antique chest of drawers that was nearly as tall as I was.

"This was our children's room," he explained as he lay some of our bags on the beds. "I hope your little ones feel right at home."

"They've never even seen a home like this one," I said. "But I'm certain they will be thrilled."

"We're so pleased. Shall we take a look at your room?"

"I don't know what to say," I began. "We don't want to impose…"

"Don't be silly. Marina would be angry if you didn't spend some time with us until you got your feet under you. She loves children."

Our room was even larger than the kids' and the one bed was the size of their two beds combined, hidden beneath a lovely hand-sewn quilt bedecked with brilliant yellow cloth sunflowers.

"It's the nicest bedroom I've ever seen, let alone stayed in," I admitted.

"I'm happy you like it."

No sooner had he and Dima dropped our bags than I heard peals of laughter rising up from somewhere below.

"I hope the kids aren't driving your wife crazy," I fussed.

"As I said, she loves children. You'd better hope she doesn't drive *them* crazy."

"I think we'd better go see."

We followed the laughter down to the kitchen, where we found Marina entertaining Kateryna and Sasha with stories of her own children's upbringing in Berdychiv while they gorged on homemade cookies and milk.

"Are you behaving yourselves?" I asked as we surprised them in mid-story.

"They are absolute angels!" Marina answered.

"Somehow I doubt that," Yerva interjected with a smile that let them know she was only kidding.

We all joined in on the conversation, until Dima excused himself to get on with his route.

"Will we see you again?" I asked, my interest only partly objective. After all, he was a pleasant, good-looking guy with a successful transport company – nothing to turn up your nose at during those difficult years.

"Never can tell. I sometimes swing by to see my Aunt and Uncle." From his grin I was fairly confident he might not object to seeing me as well.

Before the sun was even fully set, first Sasha and then Kateryna began to yawn surreptitiously, trying to hide their exhaustion from the adults surrounding them. They put up a spirited fight, but by 9 o'clock they were both tucked into their beds, their prayers said, one last story read.

"Mama, are we going to live here with Uncle Anton and Aunt Marina?" Sasha wondered even as he struggled to keep his eyelids open.

"Yes, Mama, can we?" Kateryna chimed-in. "They're ever so nice, and they seem to like us, and they have all this unused space in their house!"

Yerva guffawed. "I'm not sure they see it that way, Katya," she explained. "Some people like having empty space around them."

"But they have *so* much; they must get lonely rattling around in here just the two of them."

"We'll see," I said, more to tamp down the discussion than in any real hope the Kravets would invite us. Their kindness had already far surpassed anything I'd expected, even given the renowned Ukrainian generosity I'd seen so much of in our home village. It was one thing to help a friend or neighbor, quite another altogether to go out of one's way to help strangers. In a society where even children were taught to watch each other for any variation from the Party line, strangers were seldom given the benefit of the doubt.

As soon as we'd extricated ourselves from Sasha and his big sister, Yerva and I went downstairs where Marina and Anton sat in front of a small fire to banish the effects of a cool night breeze that already had begun to sweep in off the plains, sipping tea and conversing softly.

"Are we interrupting?" I asked.

"No, not at all!" Marina answered, standing to show us to the sofa.

"In fact, we were hoping we'd have an opportunity to chat. My sister has only told us the barest essentials of your situation, you see," Anton continued.

"Well, that's a bit of a long story," I said, wondering if they really wanted to hear all the sordid details.

"Perhaps the two of you would like some tea as well, then," Marina offered. "And a cookie?" The twinkle in her eye made me homesick for Mama. I couldn't help wonder what she was doing and whether Bogdan had paid her a visit yet.

When Marina returned I was persuaded to relate our story once again, omitting none of the sorry tale despite the painful feelings it still provoked. At first I found it difficult to give word to all the hurt and shame I felt, but with gentle prodding from Marina and the occasional interjection from Yerva, I not only overcame my reluctance but found my emotions running so high I barely noticed the passage of time as I shared details of my husband's betrayal and my youthful naiveté. So when the clock on the mantel chimed ten, I was not only surprised, but embarrassed.

"Oh my, it can't be ten already!" I said even as the chimes continued to sound.

"My sister is something of a chatterbox," Yerva announced to the Kravets with a sly grin.

"That's quite all right!" Marina said, reaching over to pat the back of my hand. "What are friends for, if not to share the hard times, as well as the good."

Friends. It didn't seem possible that such wealthy and influential people could think of us as *friends*. Charity cases, perhaps. Country bumpkins, almost certainly. But friends?

I didn't know whether to continue with our story or not. Thankfully, Marina made the choice for me.

"You two must be tired. Why don't we pick this up again tomorrow morning?"

"When we're awake enough to take it all in," Anton agreed with a stifled yawn.

I didn't need any additional urging. I was spent, and I could see Yerva's eyelids twitch from fatigue.

As I lay in bed awaiting the coming of sleep, I could hear Yerva lying next to me, tossing and turning restlessly.

"Can't sleep either?" I finally asked.

She sat up, wrapping herself in her covers to stay warm. "It's just so much to think about: new town, new people, new lives. It's almost like a dream."

"Except it's not," I said. I knew exactly how she felt. Two days earlier we'd been at home, talking with Mama. Now... now we were refugees of a failed relationship, on the run.

"Do you think he'll come after you and the kids?" Yerva said after a long silence.

The bluntness of the question helped, as if lancing a boil I'd been afraid to address. "I don't know. I hope not. But he's not predictable." I tried not to sound frightened, but even in my own ears the clipped sentences screamed anxiety. "I hope he'll go back to his friends in the tavern and let us live our lives in peace."

"I suppose he's very angry."

I tried not to picture him in my mind's eye, but the harder I tried the more he loomed there, a huge dark figure much like a storm cloud come to life. "I suppose he is."

Another long pause. I could almost hear the gears turn in her head. "What if he wants to talk?" she asked, her voice tiny and hopeful.

"I don't know," I answered honestly. "I don't know that I could trust him. Besides, with any luck he won't find us here."

"That's right!" she perked up, "He probably won't find us. I mean, he doesn't know where we went and doesn't know how we traveled. It would be hard to find us."

"That was the idea," I said, but even as I said it I knew it was wishful thinking, a white lie to ease her mind. Oh sure, Mrs. Pavlyuk, and Vova, and Dima would more than likely keep our secret, but there were only so many transports moving through the village that night, and only so many places they could go. If he wanted to find us, if he really wanted, he could do it.

As I lay there listening to Yerva finally fall off to sleep, her regular rhythmic breaths a reassuring sound in a dark, unfamiliar place, I found that storm cloud coming to mind once more, unbidden. It was to be a long, sleepless night.

*****

The next day, and the next, passed with nothing more threatening than a good, dousing rainstorm. We all settled into the Kravets' home with surprising ease. Kateryna and Sasha adjusted to their new surroundings with none of the traumatic upset I'd been expecting, owing for the most part to Marina's constant loving care. Anton was a good host as well, but he had responsibilities outside the home and was only there first thing each morning and for dinner each night.

It turned out that Anton was a prominent Party functionary in Berdychiv, and had been since the days of the Revolution. One afternoon Marina told us his story: as a young sailor he'd worked the shipping trade between Ukraine, Russia, Finland, and other countries of the north. In January 1905, as a young man of 19, Anton found himself in Saint Petersburg when the Bloody Sunday revolt was so savagely put down by the Czar's troops. Anton lost friends, lost confidence in the Czar, and made a fateful decision to seek a new way for not only Russia, but all the former Rus countries. As a Ukrainian he faced discrimination in the Bolshevik movement within Russia, but when he volunteered to organize cells in his native land, he was warmly supported.

After the 1917 revolution, Anton fought with the Bolshevik forces against German and Polish influence in his country, and in 1919 he was assigned a position in the fledgling Ukrainian Soviet Socialist Republic as an intermediary between the military and the political wings of the ruling junta. After two more years of bloodshed between the Socialists, the Whites and the UNR, in 1922 Anton became a member of the local Soviet; in the intervening decades he'd risen to the top of the regional Party organization. In 1955 his son, also Anton, then 30 years old, was given a position in the local Raion. By the time of our arrival in Berdychiv, Anton Jr. had become Director of the Raion Administrative Council, and his father was the senior Party official in the oblast.

I don't know if my face showed it, but I was awed. Anton was one of the most powerful government officials in the oblast! And his son was a power in his own right in the region. The most influential Party official I'd ever seen was the head of our village council. Anton was closer in influence to the Party heads in Moscow than to village officials.

Surprisingly, neither Anton nor his wife showed any sign of their influential status. They conversed with us as equals and treated even the children with a warmth and care that made me long for my own mother, now all by herself so very far away. It was this same feeling that brought Yerva to me on the fourth morning of our stay in Berdychiv.

We had just finished breakfast, and Sasha and Kateryna had been sent outside to play, when she followed me upstairs to our bedroom.

"Nina, I think it's time for me to go home," she said as soon as she'd closed the door behind her. "You and the kids are doing well, but I miss Mama, and our little hut." She hung her lower lip in a mock pout that brought a smile to my face and a stab of pain to my heart. I knew she was right, but I hated to see her leave. I gave her a big hug.

"Of course, my darling little sister! As much as I'll miss you, you must go home. You've been a life-saver. I'll never forget all you've done for us."

She waved off my words like so many buzzing insects. "Don't be silly. You're my sister! What is family if we don't help each other?"

And so we spoke to Marina and determined that Dima would be returning to the city in two days. She invited Yerva to stay on, promising her a place in an excellent local school and eventually in the regional university, but Yerva's mind was set.

"My Mama is all by herself," she explained, drawing an understanding nod from our hostess. "I need to be there for her – and for me."

Kateryna and Sasha were heartbroken to learn their favorite aunt was returning to our village, but when we explained to them that their Babusya was home all alone, they understood – at least Kateryna. Sasha was still too young and his tears flowed freely. But by the time of Yerva's departure he had found the courage to face the separation with a brave face, if not a happy heart. A big hug from Yerva helped.

"I will come whenever I can," she told us as she stood beside Dima's cart, her bag stuffed full of goodies provided by Marina despite both our objections.

"Just be careful," I warned, even though I had every confidence she would protect our secret conscientiously.

"And you," she whispered so the children couldn't hear. "Keep your eyes open, and call me if you need me."

I tried to smile through blurred eyes as the cart rolled slowly away that morning, for the sake of the kids if nothing else. They had been wonderfully brave and I didn't want my weakness to hurt their optimism. Our future would be bright, or so I hoped.

*****

As the summer had nearly run its course, one of the first tasks we faced was to find good schools for Kateryna and

Sasha, and then work for me. Marina was a godsend in the first instance, introducing us to the local Party primary and middle schools as "friends of the family."

"Of course, Mrs. Kravets," the headmistress of the primary school said when confronted with Marina's request to place Sasha in her school. "We would be honored to have the son of one of your friends attend Shevchenko Academy." Her smile seemed rigid but she was eager to please. She treated Marina like a visiting dignitary, though barely recognizing my presence and that of my children with a curt nod. She gave us a quick tour of the facility, and once again I was stunned. The school had an auditorium with a large stage, fully-equipped playing fields, and even a television set! I was aware that such luxuries existed, at least in theory, but I'd never actually visited a school with so many resources and as far as I knew no one in our village had yet purchased a TV. To see one in a primary school was... amazing. Ukraine was changing so fast I could scarcely believe it, but in the little villages like ours some of those changes had yet to be felt. It made me feel like a country bumpkin once again, visiting the big city to learn of changes the rest of the population already took for granted. At least some of them.

In other parts of the city, areas that once housed the majority Jewish population before the pogroms and the Great Patriotic War decimated their community, I saw poverty that made our simple lives back home seem absolutely idyllic: ramshackle houses with boarded windows and peeling, weathered clapboard siding; streets pockmarked with massive potholes – some big enough to swallow the few motorized vehicles that dared to zig-zag among them; main thoroughfares with scarce slivers of asphalt still clinging to islands of eroded earth; rats the size of small cats strolling unafraid past stores and apartments.

I couldn't believe it was the same city. And an Administrative Center at that! One night, at dinner, the children having already gone upstairs to finish their homework, I raised the subject with Anton and Marina.

"I was over on the west side today," I began innocently enough, "and was surprised by how run-down the area is. The houses, the roads – not at all like this neighborhood."

I saw Marina glance under her eyelashes at her husband. "It's a disgrace," she said, emotion rising in her voice. "That people should live like that in today's Ukraine..."

"What do you expect?" Anton interrupted, looking up from his glass of wine with what I thought was anger, but could just as easily have been disdain. "It's the old Jewish ghetto. The Germans destroyed it during the War, and it's never quite come back."

"The Council has not provided those people with the resources they need," his wife argued with a vehemence that surprised me.

"We've been through this before," he said, his tone restrained but adamant. "There are only so many resources at our disposal."

"To each according to their needs..."

"Don't quote Marx to me!" Anton growled. "We've done the best we can with what we have. It isn't *our* fault that the Jewish community was decimated and their neighborhoods destroyed. It was the Nazis."

"But you haven't gone out of your way to help them since then."

"We've done what we could do! Now, Marina, I don't think our guest wants to listen to political squabbles at the dinner table..."

She turned to me, clearly exasperated. "That's what he always says when he doesn't want to address an issue." She glowered at her husband. "Isn't that right, dear?"

Anton stood, folded his napkin and placed it next to his plate. He'd only eaten half his meal. "I have work to do," he said, before nodding to me. "Please excuse me, Nina."

As soon as he left the room, Marina leaned in and whispered conspiratorially. "The Party doesn't like the Jews. Never has. They make excuses but the simple fact is they like to think of themselves as a purely Slavic entity. They're embarrassed to admit how much Jews contributed to the Revolution, and even during the years afterwards. It's our little dark secret."

I felt out of my depth. I did well in school but our textbooks said little about the Jews in the Soviet Union. I knew from overhearing friends and neighbors that we Ukrainians – at least some of us – held them in low regard.

"I… I don't really know too much about it," I stammered.

"What *did* they teach you in school?" she asked rhetorically. She paused. "Did you study in university?"

I felt my face flush. "No. I… we, didn't have much money. I qualified, but I needed to work. And then the children came along…"

Marina waved the rest of the story off with one impatient swipe of her hand. "I've heard this story before. Too often. Too many of our women receive too little education. I have no qualms about a woman dedicating the greater part of her time to her family – I did so myself – but I cannot see the need to keep women ignorant and in the home. Tomorrow we will visit my friend Mira at the state university."

I was too surprised to object, or even acquiesce. I felt as if a giant wave had just swept me out to sea, where I would either learn to swim or sink beneath the surface. University! I had hoped, even dreamed, but to have it appear like that, from out of nowhere…

My sleep was restless, my thoughts colliding willy-nilly. How could I study and work at the same time? I wouldn't put my children in one of those State-run centers, not even for a chance at a real education. Perhaps I could go to school at night? Kateryna was nearly old enough to stay with her brother alone. I'd been even younger than she when both Mama and Julija went to work after Papa died and I was left to look after Yerva. Yes, it could be done.

*****

Just before breakfast the next morning as I helped the children set the table, I started to bring up our proposed visit to the university when Marina shushed me in no uncertain terms.

"Not here! Not now!" she said in a quiet but insistent voice. She nodded toward the stairs and I realized she hadn't told Anton of our visit and had no intention of doing so. I had no idea why she would be so secretive, but it was her decision so I kept silent as he came to the table. It was awkward sitting there with him while we kept the visit to ourselves. I admit I felt a bit uncomfortable, as if we were hiding something from Anton that he deserved to know. But it wasn't my decision. Or so I told myself.

As soon as the kids were off to school, Marina led me to their garage at the far end of the house and opened the left of two bay doors. I'd never been back there – I had no reason to go – and truth be told, I had precious little experience with motor vehicles. Of course I'd seen them, but in our village the vast majority of local transportation still revolved around horses and carts. So when Marina pulled out the keys to an impressive green sedan, I was taken aback, to say the least.

"You *drive?*" I asked, the thought almost beyond my comprehension. I did not know a single woman, and not many men, who could drive an automobile.

"Of course. You don't think *I* have a driver?"

In fact, I didn't know they had two automobiles. I'd seen Anton driven off to work each morning since we'd arrived, a uniformed driver opening the door for him to sit in the back seat. I assumed it was a benefit of his position with the Party. But two cars? As impressed as I'd been with their home and positions in the community, I'd have to admit that learning they owned two automobiles had an even greater impact.

I watched in awe as she backed the car out of the garage and put the shifter stick into gear. I probably gripped the edge of my seat with both hands, not because I doubted her ability to steer the thing but because I'd never been in a vehicle that moved so quickly. *'Quickly.'* Marina probably never exceeded 30 kilometers per hour, but to me it was heart-stopping. The way she wove in and out of the mix of horse-drawn carts and motor vehicles impressed me greatly. If women could do such a thing, what couldn't we do?

It only took fifteen minutes or so for us to reach the university. It sat on the outskirts of the city, not far from the great walled monastery. To me, then, it seemed like a legendary seat of learning, while in retrospect it was a modest campus with a half-dozen old, brick and concrete buildings set upon a small hill with fully one hundred meters of grass surrounding it. I was enchanted.

"It's nothing to compare to the big universities in Moscow or St. Petersburg, or even in Kyiv, but we are quite proud of our little school," Marina said as we pulled up to the largest and most impressive of the buildings. I could tell from her tone of voice she meant that personally, not just as a member of the community. Her influence became quickly evident as the door to the building opened before we'd even stopped moving and two women stepped out to greet us.

"Mrs. Kravets!" the elder of the two called out as she came around to open Marina's car door. She was perhaps fifty years old, with short auburn hair graying at the temples, dressed in a modest but elegant dark gray blazer and skirt. The other woman, thin and visibly anxious, probably no more than 25, trailed behind the older woman like a chick to its mother hen.

"Sveta! So good to see you," Marina greeted the first woman as they exchanged perfunctory cheek kisses.

"And you've met my assistant, Tanya Popovych," Sveta answered.

"Indeed! A pleasure," Marina said with just enough enthusiasm to make the statement plausible. "And this," she went on, indicating me as I climbed out of the auto, "is a good friend of ours, Nina Kovalchuk. She's the young woman I was telling you about."

Good friend? They'd been talking about me? My head literally spun.

"Nina, this is Sveta Vlasenko, an old friend and the Director of the State University, and Tanya, her assistant." We exchanged pleasantries with me in a daze, feeling as though they were inspecting my every word and action. Mrs. Vlasenko was warm and welcoming enough, with Tanya echoing her attitude right down to body language and hand movements. But it felt like an audition, one I was utterly unprepared for.

Sveta led us into the main university building, past a utilitarian staircase and through simple concrete block corridors, to her office at the rear of the structure.

"Can we get you anything?" she asked Marina, before turning to me. I mimicked Marina, asking for a cup of tea with one sugar. My heart was pounding. I was as out of my element as I'd ever been, and loath to embarrass Marina before her friend. After a few minutes of small talk, the Director got right down to business.

"So, you'd like to attend our university, is that right?" she asked, smiling the proud smile of a grandmother discussing her favorite grandchild.

"Yes, very much," I said, hoping the questions would not become much more trying than that. I was, of course, so very wrong.

"What department?"

I cursed Marina under my breath. Why didn't she warn me, give me a chance to study for the interview? But even as I felt my heart fall through my chest, Marina came to my rescue.

"We've been discussing that," she answered for me, and I tried not to show any sign of surprise, "and we thought she should play to her strengths. She's quite adept at writing, enjoys reading, and has a good grasp of history. But, of course, an important consideration is how she can use her studies to find fulfilling employment when she receives her diploma." She glanced over at me and smiled.

"Ah. That is always a catching point, isn't it?" Mrs. Vlasenko said as Tanya nodded enthusiastically behind her. She reached behind her to a desk neatly stacked with piles of paper and pulled out a catalog. "What do you say we take a look?"

An hour later, we bid our goodbyes at the front steps, kissed awkwardly cheek to cheek, and then Marina and I drove off, the Director and her lapdog waving regally as they watched us depart.

"Library sciences?" I asked after a suitable period of thoughtful silence.

"You like books, don't you?"

"I do, but I don't know much about libraries."

"You will learn! That's what universities are all about."

I pondered that sentiment. I did like books. And I'd always been a good learner...

"Sveta says there are openings going unfilled." Marina made a strong case, but still... I wondered.

"What did you study in university?" I asked.

"Me? Why I studied political ideologies for two years, almost three, but then I met Anton and I thought, 'why study politics when you can learn on the job,'"

"So you never got your diploma?"

"I have two honorary degrees. That's quite enough."

We sat quietly for quite some time, each of us lost in our own thoughts. I was excited about the possibility of attending, of course, but there were so many details to be worked out. And the costs!

Marina must've sensed my turmoil. "What are you thinking about?" she asked, glancing over at me with a curious expression.

"There are books, and supplies, and I'll need to find someone to watch the children while I'm in class, and how will I pay the rent..." The more I thought of it, the more impossible it became in my mind.

Marina was having none of it. "There are funds to help students, and we can help a bit as well. And as for the children, I'd be terribly insulted if you didn't let me look after them when you're off to school."

"Oh, I couldn't, Marina!" I objected, quite sincerely. "You've already done so much!"

"'To each according to their needs; from each according to their abilities.' Isn't that what Mr. Marx said?" She looked over at me and smiled, what I took to be a mischievous, almost devilish grin. I had a sense the saying meant more to her than just the regurgitation of an old Party chestnut by one of its favored few.

We talked non-stop all the way home, or what I'd come to think of as my home even though I knew full well it wasn't. Part of me dreaded the day, soon to come I was sure, when we'd have to leave. Kateryna and Sasha had become so completely comfortable there, both with their luxurious surroundings (not so difficult to do), and with the Pavlyuks, Marina in particular, that I feared their reaction when we left. But, for now we were their guests, and it was clear Marina had big plans for us, me in particular.

That night I was so eager to share my good news with Mama and Yerva that I asked Marina if I might call them instead of waiting for their once-a-week Saturday night call.

"Why of course, dear," she said. "That's what telephones are for."

Inwardly I shook my head in astonishment and made up my mind that one day I too would think of the telephone as just another home appliance, like a toaster, instead of the expensive and rarely-used electronic miracle that all my family considered it.

After I'd put the kids to bed, I carefully dialed Mama's new number – her phone a gift from Julija and her husband.

"Mama – I'm going to the university!" I said before she could say anything more than hello.

"What? How?" I could sense the disbelief in her voice.

"Marina – Mrs. Pavlyuk – has arranged it all with a friend of hers who's the Director of the university. I'm going to study Library Science and work part-time in the school library!"

I expected excited congratulations. I got a long moment of silence.

"Who will take care of the children? Kateryna isn't old enough to leave at home to take care of her brother. It wouldn't be fair..."

"Marina has volunteered to watch them," I interrupted. "They enjoy spending time with her."

Another long silence. "You really shouldn't be imposing on Mrs. Pavlyuk, Nina. She's already done so much for you."

"I don't think she sees it as an imposition, Mama."

"Well whether she does or not, perhaps I should travel there to Berdychiv and look after my little birds. I mean, who better than their grandmother?"

It was just then I realized she was jealous that another woman would be spending so much time with her grandchildren while she would see them only rarely.

"But what about Yerva?" I countered, trying to show her that her care and ministration was already needed and appreciated right there at home.

"Yerva is out most every night with her friends," Mama said, and I could hear the loneliness in her voice. "She doesn't need her old mother looking after her."

I wanted to reassure her, make her understand she hadn't been abandoned. But what could I say?

"Let's see how things go," was the best I could come up with. "I'm sure Mrs. Pavlyuk will tire of looking after my two wild animals before too long, and by then we'll have a place of our own where you can come visit."

"How long do you think that will take?"

"Not so long," I said, not lying so much as trying to stay optimistic.

"Okay then, if that's what you think will be best..." Her voice was small, defeated. I wanted to reach through the telephone lines and give her a hug. But even if I could, I feared disappointing my patron, Mrs. Pavlyuk, who seemed to truly enjoy her time spent with the kids. I felt torn: no matter what I decided, someone I cared for would be upset. I decided to stay the course and hope that Mama could soon come – at least for a short time.

*****

The university was like a dream. My secondary school had been large, at least for our oblast. But compared to the university, it was like our hut compared to the Pavlyuk's mansion. The classes were much larger than I was accustomed to and most of the students were younger than me, some more than ten years younger. It was difficult at first, both the academics and the adjustment to being a student once again, but after my first week I grew comfortable, if not fully acclimated.

It was just then, just as I'd begun to think that our new life had begun in earnest and our escape from Bogdan had been completely successful, that I received a phone call from Mama. She never called except on our agreed-upon night, so I was anxious before she said a word. Make that three words.

"He was here," she said and my blood ran cold. She didn't have to say who *he* was. I knew.

"When?"

Turns out he had stopped by Mama's hut just after dinner time, stinking of alcohol.

"Where are they?" he asked, pushing his way into the hut despite Mama's objections. "Where are my kids?"

"They aren't here, Bogdan," Mama said calmly.

"Then where are they? I don't care about that bitch daughter of yours, but I want my kids back!"

Mama said his eyes were bloodshot and rimmed with dark circles; his skin had the ghostly pallor of someone deathly ill.

"I don't know," Mama insisted.

"You know. She doesn't do anything without letting her *Mama* know."

"Not this time. All I know is she left and isn't coming back. If she contacts me, I'll contact you."

Bogdan stepped forward and grabbed Mama by the arm. "Don't lie to me!"

At that moment, Yerva appeared from the bedroom carrying a long kitchen knife they kept there for protection.

"Take your hands off her, Bogdan!" she yelled, wielding the knife in front of her. "Get out of our house!"

He flinched at her cry, but his expression quickly turned to derision. "Put that knife down before I stick it up your ass."

Mama said she was terrified, but Yerva didn't back down. "You might do that, but then again I might get lucky and cut your throat before you can take it away from me. You want to take that chance?"

He hesitated, then grabbed Mama with both hands and held her between himself and my sister. "And maybe I'll break your Mama's neck before you get the chance."

"You hurt her and I'll see you hang," Yerva said, so cold and confident that Mama felt goose bumps.

For a long moment the two of them stared at each other, neither moving a centimeter.

"Go home, Bogdan," Mama finally said softly. "Your children aren't here and we don't know where they are."

Bogdan spat on the floor. "You two aren't worth the effort." He started for the door, turning back just before stepping outside. "Tell the bitch I'm coming for my kids. If she thinks she can keep them away from me, she's badly mistaken."

As soon as the door closed, Yerva ran and locked it behind him; Mama collapsed into a chair.

"The man's crazy," she said. "What if he finds them?"

Yerva went to where she sat, knelt, and put her arms around her. "Let's pray he doesn't," she said. "Let's all pray."

*****

When I hung up the phone I must have looked frightful, as Marina hurried to my side with anxious concern.

"What is it?!" she asked, taking my hand instinctively.

"My husband just visited by mother and threatened her," I said, my voice shaking. "And now he's promising to come take his children back."

"Oh, really?" she said with an air of scorn. "I think he would do better to rethink that idea. My husband and I have a lot of friends here in Berdychiv. He might find himself in more trouble than he can handle."

"You don't know him. When he's been drinking…"

"You don't know Anton. You and the children will be safe with us. I promise you."

"But what about when they go to school? What about when *I* go to school?"

She thought for an instant. "I'll ask Anton to have the Militsiya provide a security guard for you – at least for the next few weeks."

"You can do that?"

She smiled. "We can, and we will. Don't worry," she added, giving my shoulders a squeeze.

Perhaps I was naïve, but I believed her. I didn't know the extent of Anton's connections in the Party and local government, but from what little I had seen they seemed extensive. Maybe they *could* protect us.

Marina wasted no time. She called her husband at his office and explained the situation. I could only hear her end of the conversation, but that was enough. He agreed with a vehemence I could hear through the earpiece from meters away. He sounded personally affronted that someone would threaten a guest of his.

"He's calling some people he knows in the Militsiya," she said to me, covering the receiver with her hand. Moments later she resumed the conversation, nodding and responding in short words and phrases. Then it was done.

"He'll have someone come by here tonight," she explained as she hung up. "And tomorrow morning a driver will take the children to their schools where a plainclothes officer will watch them throughout the day. Don't worry, dear, this man will not get ahold of the children."

I took a full breath of air for the first time since I'd heard Mama's words.

*****

Not long after we'd finished supper, a knock sounded on the Pavlyuk's front door. The maid answered. A tall, thin man wearing a dark blue business suit waited patiently by the door as the maid came into the dining room.

"Militsiya Officer Vann here to see you," she announced.

"Send him in, send him in!" Anton said.

Vann made his way to Anton's side before the maid could even relay the instructions. If he was intimidated by the big house or the influence of its owner, he didn't show it.

"Comrade Pavlyuk," he began, using the slightly out-of-fashion term of respect as he bobbed his head to both Anton and his wife, "Senior Sergeant Vann reporting."

He was an attractive man, if somewhat hard around the eyes and mouth. His thinning brown hair was cut short, making him look younger than the 35 or so I guessed he was.

"Sergeant, this is my wife," Anton introduced, motioning with his hand, "and this is Nina – the woman you will be protecting." Vann nodded to each of us in turn. "Have you been briefed on the situation?"

"Chief Boyko gave me the basics," Vann answered, his voice soft but assured. "Where would you like me to station myself?"

Anton looked over to his wife. "Marina? That's your province."

"What will you require?" she asked the Sergeant.

"Just a position where I can see the main entrance to the house," Vann said. "I'll make regular perimeter inspections to insure no one approaches from the rear or sides."

"The Sergeant will need a bathroom and someplace to get a glass of water from time to time," Anton interjected. I could see Vann's eyes widen a hair in appreciation.

"Well then, I'll have Dasha bring a chair out to the front porch, and you can use the bathroom by the rear door. If you need something to drink, Dasha will get it for you." She addressed the last to the maid, who nodded in agreement.

And so beginning that night, and for many nights to come, Sergeant Vann took up residence just outside (and from time to time inside) the Pavlyuk mansion. During the day one of several other Militsiyamen came and relieved him, but since the kids and I all went to school during the daytime hours, they were basically a faceless and interchangeable guard presence. Not so Sgt. Vann. I readily admit that I felt foolish having a member of the Militsiya sitting outside our front door, especially since he was there to protect us against a drunken husband I usually thought unlikely to drag himself off his barstool long enough to make any trouble for us. But I can't say I disliked having the Sergeant with us. Even if I truly believed his presence was unnecessary. Or so I thought.

Several days had passed and we'd all begun to adjust to the routine of having the militsiya looking after us. Every morning, at the end of Sergeant Vann's shift, he'd make sure the kids were picked up by their designated driver and then take me to the university on his way home. When he'd first offered to drive me, I'd felt... awkward accepting.

"It's really not very far out of my way at all," he'd argued as we stood at the front door, his expectant smile and pale blue eyes extremely distracting.

"But you and the other men are already doing so much for us," I countered. "And Mrs. Pavlyuk has volunteered to take me."

Behind him, Marina – who'd come out to start the car and was eavesdropping without shame – waved at me to get my attention and shook her head 'No!' vigorously. With all her hand motions and mouthed words, it was hard to keep my attention on what Sergeant Vann was saying.

"... and so it wouldn't really be fair to put Mrs. Pavlyuk in a position where she might have to confront your ex-husband," he was saying when I tuned back in to his words.

"Husband," I corrected a bit reluctantly. "Separated."

"Whatever," he said. "There's no question in my mind that you'd be better protected by me than Mrs. Pavlyuk, and she'd be a lot safer as well."

Marina nodded as vigorously as she'd shaken her head moments earlier. I wasn't sure if she meant she wouldn't feel safe driving me, or if she thought Sgt. Vann would be better able to protect me, which seemed self-evident (although Marina was a pretty tough and powerful woman in her own right.) Whichever it was, I can't say I was completely opposed to having the Sgt. drive me to my classes, particularly if he really wanted to...

So it was decided, and starting that very first morning I was driven to the university by the good Sergeant. It turned out that Vann was a warm and funny man, utterly in contrast with his tough, rugged exterior. True, his humor was often a bit *colorful*, but nothing so risqué that I didn't laugh. He'd worked with the Militsiya for eleven years, had worked his way up from the bottom, and now was in line for a captaincy in the near-future. Or so he hoped. One other piece of information caught my attention: he'd never been married.

Now I don't want to give the impression I was looking for a possible successor to my drunken bum of a husband, but I won't deny I felt a certain... *something* from the very first. Our conversations quickly evolved from slightly stilted, businesslike exchanges of information, to the more relaxed casual give and take of newfound friends. Simply put, I liked the man, and I thought he liked me. Perhaps that's why we'd become so relaxed ('lax' as Anton would later put it) that we were caught unawares.

It was the second day of the second week he'd been driving me to school. Viktor (for that was his name, Viktor Konstyantinovich Vann) had just dropped me off in front of the university administration building. We'd been chatting about one thing or another, and I remember very well I was laughing as I got out of the car. I watched his car pull away and turned to enter the building. I saw something move quickly from off to my right, from around the near corner of the building. Before I could grasp what it might be, a hand clamped down across my mouth while the other grabbed my shoulder in a grip that brought tears to my eyes.

"Did you really think you could hide from me?" my husband growled in my ear. His voice was cold, cutting. He jerked me back around the corner, out of sight from the entrance. "Who was the stud in the car? Your new boyfriend? Did you think he could protect you from me?"

He kept dragging me back toward a wooded area close behind the administration building, ignoring my struggles and muffled screams as if they didn't exist. I was so frightened I don't know what if anything I was thinking, other than the overwhelming certainty that if he got me into the woods I was in big trouble. I clawed at his hands and tried to break free, but he was too strong, much too strong! I dug my heels into the earth but he just continued dragging me ever closer to the trees. I heard my heart thundering and thought I might be sick. I struggled to keep my head clear.

Then, not three meters from the edge of the forest, I heard a loud grunt. Suddenly his grip loosened and I fell to the ground. I scrambled up out of his reach and started to run toward the administration building. I'd only take a few steps when the violent sounds behind me made me stop and turn back. There, rolling on the ground, Viktor held Bogdan

in a bear hug from behind, the muscles in his arms bulging
as both their faces shone bright red! I saw Bogdan bite down
hard on Viktor's wrist as he held it across my husband's
neck, and scream as he wriggled from Viktor's grasp and
flipped over on top of him. To my horror, Bogdan sat on
Viktor's chest and rained heavy blows down on his arms and
shoulders as he struggled to protect his face. Without
thinking, I ran forward and grabbed Bogdan's hair from
behind in both my fists and pulled with all my might.

"You **** bitch!" he screamed as he toppled over
backwards, his face an ugly bruised red, his eyes wild with
fury. He scrambled to his feet and I fell back in shocked
impotence. I remember thinking I was dead. *This is the end.* I
closed my eyes and awaited his revenge.

But Bogdan had miscalculated. Apparently Viktor was
not as hurt as he seemed, for when I opened my eyes
moments later he held Bogdan's ankle by one hand and was
dragging him back to where he knelt on the ground. Face to
face, Bogdan was no match for the bigger Militsiya Sergeant.
Viktor punched Bogdan several times in the head and
stomach and in moments my husband lay flat on the ground,
unmoving.

I rushed over to Viktor, shocked to see blood streaming
from a cut over one eye.

"Viktor, you're hurt!" I said as I held his face in my
hands.

"Just a little cut," he said between gasps of breath.
"Nothing to worry about."

I don't know what happened but the next thing I knew I
was holding him tight, my head laying against his chest, and I
was sobbing. I heard his heart pounding – or was it mine?

"If I'd known a little blood would bring this reaction, I
would've cut myself shaving," he joked, and we both
laughed awkwardly. Much too soon he pushed me gently

away from him and grabbed a pair of handcuffs from the back of his belt.

"Need to get him immobilized before he comes to," he explained. He'd barely snapped the cuffs shut when Bogdan began to moan and shake his head dazedly. Viktor grabbed him by the handcuffs and pulled him to his feet.

"Up you go," he directed. Bogdan looked like a beaten dog, his eyes unfocussed, his head lolling. Viktor half-led, half-dragged him across the lot to the front of the building, where Viktor's unmarked car sat still running, the driver's door wide open. He used the car radio to call in the incident, and less than five minutes later two blue and yellow Militsiya cars arrived, their sirens blaring. Bogdan had remained silent all that time, sitting on the front stairs to the building with head bent in dejection. As soon as the official cars arrived, however, he regained his tongue.

"You think this is over?!" he yelled at me as Victor pulled him to his feet. "You think you're safe with this ryvok!? I will get out, you wait and see! And when I do…" One of the newly arrived Militsiya grabbed him by the arms and virtually threw him into his vehicle. As the door slammed shut, I saw him stare at me with pure hatred in his face.

"You *married* that guy?" Viktor asked from so close behind me I jumped.

"He wasn't always like this," I tried to explain, but it had been so long since Bogdan had acted like a normal human being that I too wondered why in the world I'd married him. "I was young."

"I can't believe a loser like him has a wonderful woman like you. The world is a confusing and contradictory place."

"Had," I said.

He looked at me in utter confusion.

"He *had* a wonderful woman like me. No longer." I forced a smile through my still-trembling lips. He smiled effortlessly, a smile that said more than any words. At least to me.

"Happy to hear that. *Very* happy." We stood there like two teenagers, grinning at each other mindlessly. "So," he said after a time, "you still going to your classes, or would you like me to take you home?"

"Of course I'm going to my classes!" I answered, perhaps a little over-emphatically. I still felt adrenaline pulsing through my veins, but there was no way I was going to let Bogdan disrupt my studies. They were our future.

"Okay, okay," Viktor said, holding his hands up in front of him as if to ward off a blow. "Just asking. I'll see you at 3 then?"

My classes that day ended in mid-afternoon, but I had other duties I couldn't ignore. "Actually, I have my internship orientation in the library this afternoon. I'm afraid I probably won't be able to leave until 5 or so. I imagine you'll be on your way home by then…"

His grin returned. "I think I might be able to swing by on my way and pick you up. If you don't have other plans?" The grin disappeared for the last and he seemed genuinely concerned.

"None. So I'll see you at five?"

"I'll be the one scanning the shrubbery to ensure you don't have any other former lovers lurking nearby with the intention of causing harm." He said it with such sincerity I wasn't at all sure if he was kidding me or not, until he smiled.

"No other former lovers – in the shrubbery or elsewhere."

He bowed his head ever so slightly in my direction. "A beautiful woman like you? I find that hard to believe."

"As I said, I was young. Very young."

He nodded, and the grin widened. "Go – study. Learn. I'll be back at 5."

With that he winked and walked to his waiting auto with
a bounce in his step that belied the scrapes and cuts on his
face. I waved, he waved, and I went in to take my classes.

*****

On our way back to the Pavlyuk's home that night I told
him all about my classes, and in particular about my
introduction to my library duties.

"The head librarian walked me through everything – the
filing system, the check-out procedures, where to look for
research materials – everything!" I was *so* excited. "I've never
even *seen* a library so large, and well-resourced as well. They
have over 100,000 volumes!"

"You have."

I thought I misheard him. "What?"

"*You* have over 100,000 volumes. You're now one of
them."

It hadn't really dawned on me until that moment. I *was*
one of them. I was a member of the university staff, a library
assistant level 3! I basked in the glory of that realization for
quite a while as the green hills and upscale homes whizzed
past in the growing dusk.

"Do you have any interest in knowing what happened
with your *ex*-husband?" he asked after a long quiet spell,
emphasizing the prefix with apparent satisfaction.

His question shattered the reverie that had enveloped
me. "Oh! Of course, of course! Where did those Militsiya
take him? What happens now?"

"They took him down to the city headquarters, where he
will be processed-in and interviewed. Then he will spend the
night, and very likely several more, before he is brought
before a judge who will determine whether he can be
released until his trial."

"Released?" I tried to control my voice, but I'm afraid it broke from nerves.

"Don't worry. He probably won't get out, especially if Mr. Pavlyuk has anything to say about it, and even if he does he wouldn't be stupid enough to come after you or the children a second time, would he?"

I wanted to say no, to reassure Viktor as well as myself that there was no likelihood Bogdan would continue his vendetta. But I couldn't. Sober, perhaps. But if or when he got ahold of alcohol? There was no predicting what he might do. I knew how he changed when he drank, and the knowledge made me sick to my stomach.

"I... I'm not sure."

Now it was his turn to stay quiet. I saw his eyes narrow as he considered what I'd said. "Perhaps you should have a conversation with Mr. Pavlyuk, or would you like me to talk to him?" he offered after nearly a minute of silence.

For just an instant I considered his offer. "No, thank you, Viktor. I'm sure it would be better for all concerned if I spoke directly to Mrs. Pavlyuk. I think she will understand our situation and she has... great influence with her husband."

Viktor unexpectedly broke into a big smile. "You might be right. She's a force to be reckoned with."

I knew I was right, yet it was a difficult subject for me to broach with her. My parents, and particularly my Papa, raised us to believe that manipulating the system for your own ends was unethical. Wrong. My father would never appeal to a village council member outside official channels, not even if he were a personal friend. But I needed to protect my family. I needed help, and I decided to ask Marina.

I waited until later that night, after Anton had adjourned to his den to smoke a cigar and review the day's newspaper as he did most every night. I followed Marina out to the front porch, where we women sat and discussed the day's activities as the sun sank beneath the surrounding hills. With the children in bed, this was a daily routine I had grown to love. It was the one time we could relax, with no demands from anyone, and communicate person to person. At first I'd been afraid to speak my mind, but as the weeks went by I realized our little sessions were as important to Marina as they were to me. I wasn't entirely sure, but I thought she had few close friends she could talk to openly and without restraint. Perhaps it was because I was so much younger; perhaps she saw something of herself in me. I don't know. I only know that she said things to me I doubt she said to anyone else.

I waited patiently for her to share her complaints about the staff, and friends, and even Anton. She was soft-spoken in her comments, never raising her voice no matter how egregious the perceived slight or incompetent act. She spoke slowly, interweaving her family history with details and emotions. By the time she finished the sun sat just above the nearest hill, painting the countryside a pale orangish-pink. The first buzzings of mosquitoes sounded in our ears. We sat and listened to the sounds of the night for a short while before I worked up the courage to tell my tale. I'd already explained all that had occurred at the university as soon as I'd arrived home. Now I wanted to make her understand the danger I felt. "Marina, Sergeant Vann (I always called him Sergeant when I spoke with the Pavlyuks) tells me that my husband might be released by a judge until he is tried in court."

"Oh?" she said. She often reacted with such non-committal comments, at least until she'd heard the entire story.

I reiterated everything Viktor had told me, emphasizing the discretion that apparently lay with the judge in determining whether Bogdan stayed in jail until his trial, or not.

"That doesn't seem right," she said when I'd finished.

"No, it doesn't," I agreed. "And I can tell you, I'm afraid for the kids."

"And for you as well."

I shrugged. For a long second I held my breath, wondering if she would take the hint. She did.

"I think Anton should talk to Chief Boyko about all this. Or perhaps with the regional Prosecutor."

"Do you think he would?" I asked, trying to contain my relief.

"Of course he would! Your husband is obviously a dangerous man. Anton would be *happy* to help ensure your family's safety."

I wasn't entirely sure of that, but I was sure that if Marina was determined to have him talk to the Chief, talk he would.

"Thank you, Marina. How can we ever repay you?"

She dismissed my offer off with a casual brush of her hand. "Don't be silly. You're like part of the family now – all of you."

I stayed and chatted for a short while longer, but I was so drained from the episode with Bogdan that my eyes began to shut of their own accord not long after the sun set.

"You poor child. You should go upstairs and get some sleep," Marina urged when she noticed my head jerk forward as she was telling me some story about another friend Anton had helped.

"I'm sorry. It's been a very tiring day."

"I understand completely. Go. Go get some sleep. We can talk tomorrow."

I thanked her again, stumbled upstairs, took a quick look in at Kateryna and Sasha sleeping, and then was barely able to wash and put on my sleeping gown before my eyes closed for the night. For the first time since I'd learned from Mama that Bogdan might come after us, I slept all through the night, soundly.

The next morning I debated telling the kids about their father, but decided they'd had enough trauma from the nighttime escape and the move to Berdychiv so I chose to wait a short while to see what developed. That morning we were all in high spirits: Marina and I from our conviction that Bogdan was at long-last behind bars, the kids from activities they looked forward to at their schools with newly discovered friends. The Militsiya driver showed up and took the kids off to school, while I waited for Viktor chatting with Marina.

Not much later, Viktor's big government car pulled up and he climbed out to open the door for me, as he did every morning during the week. I was about to greet him with a big hug when I noticed the hard-set look on his face.

"What? Why the long face?" I asked.

"He's out," he said solemnly. "Your husband's out of jail."

"How can that be?!" I said, probably much too loudly. Marina came hurrying over.

"Anton hasn't had a chance to talk to anyone this morning," she said defensively. "Most of those people don't get into their offices until well after 10."

"Apparently Bogdan had a hearing late yesterday afternoon, at which he claimed that the 'incident' was nothing more than a little domestic misunderstanding. He claimed I over-reacted." I could see the anger smoldering in Viktor's eyes.

"And the judge believed him?" I was incredulous. How could they take my drunken husband's word over the Militsiya's?"

"I wasn't advised of the hearing, and the representative sent from the Central Office had only the very barest of notes about the attack. So yes, the judge believed him."

"So he's out walking around this very moment?" Marina interrupted. By her expression and voice I knew she was nervous.

"I'm afraid so. I'm sorry. We've let you down." He looked so sad and forlorn I felt bad for him. But I felt worse for myself and the kids.

"It isn't you fault, Sergeant," I consoled. "You did all you could do."

"That's right, Sergeant. You were heroic in your actions to protect Nina. That fool judge is the one to blame. I'll tell Anton. I'm sure he'll be able to..."

"I'll be able to do what?" her husband interrupted, appearing unexpectedly, newspaper in hand.

"Some fool judge let her husband out of jail!" Marina wailed.

"He what?!" Anton's face was hard, his eyes narrowed to slits. He turned to Viktor.

"Who did this? What was his name?"

"It was Judge Melnyk, sir. In the Central Oblast Court."

"Melnyk? He's that young fellow, just took his seat a few months ago?"

Viktor nodded. " I believe so, sir. I think his father holds a position on the Administrative Council."

"Anatoli Melnyk?!" Anton asked. "This young snip is Anatoli's son?"

"I believe so, sir. Yes."

"Do you know him, Anton?" Marina asked, hopefulness in her voice.

"Of course I know him! I'll give him a call as soon as I get to the office. I'm sure this little fiasco can be corrected." He turned to me and took hold of my arm. "Don't you worry, Nina. We'll find him before he can do any more harm."

"Do you think he might come *here*?" his wife asked, looking to both Anton and Viktor for reassurance.

Anton answered immediately. "I very much doubt that. But just in case, do you think you can ask Captain Boyko for a couple of men to watch this place during the day?" he asked Viktor. "Or should I give him a call?"

"I'll contact him, Mr. Pavlyuk."

"Good. If there's any problem, you have him call me. Understand?"

"Perfectly, sir. I don't think it will be a problem."

"I hope not. And Sergeant, well-done yesterday. I'll tell your Captain how much we appreciated your help the next time I talk to him."

Viktor nodded but showed no other reaction. "Thank you, sir."

Anton went back inside, with Marina right on his heels.

"When do you think you'll be coming home?" she asked at the doorway.

"Probably late afternoon. Around 4:30 or 5?" I looked to Viktor to make sure those times were acceptable to him.

"Good here."

"Then have a good day. And don't let this foolishness with your husband interfere with your studies." With that, she shut the door and left us on the porch.

"All ready?" Viktor asked.

"Yes, thank you. Let's be on our way."

As we drove down the Pavlyuk's long driveway and turned out into the roadway that ran next to their property, Viktor began to apologize once again; I cut him off in mid-sentence.

"Viktor, it wasn't your fault! You did everything you could do. More. If it wasn't for you, I don't like to think what he might have done to me."

"The man's an animal," he growled. "I don't know how you stayed with him so long."

I hadn't really discussed my time with Bogdan with anyone other than my mother, but for some reason it felt right discussing it with Viktor. Once I started, it just flowed out of me: the initial good times, then the drinking, and the cheating, then the violence, and finally our escape.

"You're a very strong woman, do you know that?" he said when I'd finished.

"I wouldn't say that. I just did what I had to do – as a mother, more than anything."

He looked over at me. "Strong."

I don't know why, after all we'd been through, that one word touched me as it did, but I leaned over and kissed him on the cheek. I'm not sure what reaction I expected, but a big smile probably wasn't it.

"What is that, my reward?" he said, eyes twinkling.

I found myself blushing, but not the least bit sorry for what I'd done.

"Do you *want* a reward?" I asked, my smile matching his even as my stomach filled with butterflies.

"No, of course not!" he said emphatically. "I was kidding."

Somehow I knew he wasn't. I put my hand on his knee and patted it gently. "You're a good man, Viktor."

The next thing I knew he'd pulled the car off to the side of the road and we were kissing, not some timid 'thank you' kiss, but something more, much more.

By the time I caught my breath, I wasn't sure what had just happened. But the look on Viktor's face puzzled me even more.

"I'm sorry," he said solemnly, "I shouldn't have done that."

I felt the blood rush to my cheeks, not from embarrassment but from anger.

"Sorry?!" I nearly shouted, "What are you sorry for? I'm not sorry!"

His eyes opened a fraction wider than normal. "You're not?"

"Do I seem sorry?"

The smile returned. "Well, no, but I'm supposed to be protecting you..."

I'd heard enough. "Then protect me," I said, throwing my arms around his neck and kissing him deeply. For the first time in years I felt completely alive as my heart pounded in my chest. I didn't know where this would lead, if anywhere, but I knew I wanted to find out.

Chapter 10

For the next three or four days we all lived in a state of suspended animation, wondering whether Bogdan would strike again. Captain Boyko responded to Anton's request by ordering a full alert throughout the oblast and as far away as our home village, rallying dozens of Militsiya to the task of finding the 'escaped prisoner.' The description wasn't entirely accurate, of course, but after the tongue-lashing I presume he received from Anton or one of the other Party leaders, neither Judge Melnyk nor anyone else was not about to argue the point.

I was extremely thankful to Anton for all he'd done, and to Marina for energizing her husband to take such rapid action. Yet I was also a little unnerved. I knew, of course, that Anton was a high-ranking Party member. I expected him to carry great influence in the oblast. However, to actually experience the impact of that influence was an experience I was not prepared for. With one word to the Militsiya Captain a full-fledged manhunt was put into motion, with Bogdan as its objective. I almost felt a little sympathy for him. More importantly, however, I felt nervous about existing so close to such power. It seemed like living next to a rumbling volcano: it might erupt at any time, and when it did it might bury anything in its vicinity under ash and burning lava. What if he found out about my budding relationship with Viktor? Would he be upset? It was clear he – and Marina – were people of strong opinions. Would he think me *loose* or at least not sufficiently reticent about starting in with another man while still married to Bogdan? What if he and Marina decided to discontinue their support once I had someone in my life? Would I still find myself working and studying at the University? Would Kateryna and Sasha still be able to attend their elite private schools? My stomach tied itself in knots and I found it difficult to interact with our hosts as easily as I had. And as much as I tried to keep my anxiety from affecting my relationship with Viktor, I know it did.

My feelings for Viktor had grown quickly, more quickly than I would have thought possible. Of course, I'd been unhappy for a long, long time, and like a plant exposed to the sun after too long in the darkness, I flourished. The fact that the kids seemed to really enjoy spending time with him, and he with them, certainly added to my feelings. But that's not to say there weren't misgivings. Misgivings I tried to hide from him, without success as I learned one morning about a week later.

He was driving me to the University, as he had every day since Bogdan's release, when he broke a long, uncomfortable silence between us with a single question:

"Are you feeling poorly?"

"No, I feel fine. Why?"

"You look... unwell. And you haven't said a word in the last ten minutes. That's unlike you."

I wanted to smile at his little joke, but I just couldn't. I was so worried that I'd begun to lose sleep; even my appetite was greatly diminished. I didn't want to burden Viktor with my problems, but who else?

"I'm worried," I blurted before I could lock it all inside me again. "Anton seems like a very principled person, from the old school. What if he sees our *friendship* in a negative light? What if he decides I don't need him anymore and cuts me and the children off from his support?"

"Why would he do such a thing? And even if he considered it, certainly Marina would come to your rescue."

He seemed so confident. So sure of himself. "I don't know why he'd do something like that. I guess I feel dishonest sneaking around right under his nose without letting him know."

"Know what?" Viktor prodded. He wasn't going to make it easy on me.

"You know. About us."

"Oh? Is there an *us*?"

I felt a cold chill sweep though my body. "Isn't there?" Had I inflated a few kisses into something more than it actually was?

"Well *I* think there is, but as you said, you've kept our friendship a secret from everyone. I thought maybe you were embarrassed about having a relationship with a simple Militsiya Sergeant, after living with the Pavlyuks I mean."

I couldn't tell if he was serious or not. "Embarrassed? Viktor Vann, are you out of your mind? If there's one thing I'm not, it's embarrassed."

"Then why? Why do we need to hide our feelings from everyone?" I was taken unawares. I'd had no hint he was so bothered by our secrecy.

"Well, you're on-duty, assigned to protect me. I thought it might be difficult for you if they knew of our relationship." My excuse sounded weak even to my ears.

He pulled the car to the side of the road. "Shouldn't I have a say in that decision? Am I such a weak little thing I need you to protect me?" He didn't seem angry, but he clearly wasn't happy.

"Of course not! But I didn't want to... presume too much. I mean, we've only known each other these past few weeks and I didn't want you to think I was *expecting* something." The words poured from my lips as I struggled to control my emotions, more concerned about the outcome of our conversation than I would've thought possible only minutes earlier.

"Aren't you? Because I am. I'm expecting the chance to find out if this friendship can become something more. Or am I the one presuming too much?" His expression was a cross between hopefulness and concern. I couldn't help myself – I threw my arms around his neck and kissed him.

"You big idiot!" I said, tears streaming down my face. "There is nothing I would want more."

We sat there in each other's arms for so long I got to the University a little late that morning. Not that it bothered me. It didn't.

*****

That night, when Viktor drove me home after my shift in the University library, we decided on a strategy to let the Pavlyuks know about our relationship. I was more than a little nervous. If they withdrew their support and Viktor and I didn't stay together, the kids and I would find ourselves in a very delicate situation. The money I was earning at the library would barely be sufficient to pay for a room and food – *if* I was still working there. Our circumstances would change very quickly and very completely. But I couldn't go on hiding my feelings from them. They were not only our benefactors, but our friends. At least Marina. I wasn't certain how Anton would react, but I would soon find out.

When we pulled up in front of the massive house, I hesitated in my seat for an instant, gathering my courage.

"Do you want me to come in with you?" Viktor asked.

"No, thank you Viktor. I think it would be better if I talk to Marina first – just the two of us."

"Have her take it to her husband, eh? Makes sense."

"I think she'd understand the situation better. From the perspective of a woman."

"As long as you know I'm here whenever you need me."

A warm glow encompassed me. "I know you are, and I love you for that."

To my surprise, he leaned over and kissed me. Not some quick, nervous peck on the cheek, but a serious *statement* kiss.

In the Pavlyuk's driveway! I was both excited and terrified. What if either one of them happened to be looking out a window?

Viktor smiled, fully aware of my worry. "Go then! Talk to her. I've had quite enough of sneaking around as though we're doing something wrong."

As I walked up the front steps to the house, my legs felt wooden and my heart fluttered uncontrollably. I only hoped Anton wasn't home. I feared I might faint if I bumped into him before I could speak to Marina. Luckily, she was just coming downstairs as I came in through the door. I must've looked nearly as nervous as I felt, for Marina noticed something immediately.

"Are you all right, dear? You look as if you've seen a ghost! That husband of yours hasn't turned up again, has he?" She said the last with obvious trepidation. Despite her fierce exterior, she was as worried about Bogdan as I was.

"No, no, nothing like that," I replied, glancing around to make sure her husband was nowhere close by. "Is Anton home yet?"

"Not yet. He called to say that his last meeting would run late and he'll be home around 7. Why, do you need to talk to him?"

I felt slightly ashamed. "Actually, I need to talk to you, Marina."

"Oh? Well then let's sit down in the living room. Would you like a cup of tea?"

"No, thank you."

"No? Then I won't either." She sat in her favorite easy chair and I sat directly across from her on the sofa.

"So, what is it then? Some problem with the children?" I could see the concern in her eyes and realized how lucky I was to have a friend like her.

"No, not the children," I equivocated. I caught myself rubbing my hands together nervously and forced myself to stop. "Actually, it's about Viktor."

"Has something happened to him?" Again, the concern was genuine.

"No, it's just…" I was so nervous I could hardly form the words. Fortunately, Marina said them for me.

"Has he asked you? Already?"

Her reply caught me completely off-guard. "Asked me? Asked me what?"

"Why to marry him, of course! I could tell the moment you laid eyes on each other that there was going to be more to your relationship than just *protection*." She smiled just like Mama had smiled when I told her about Bogdan and me all those years before, a Cheshire Cat smile that warmed me from the inside to the tips of my toes.

"You *know* about us?" I muttered, my ears burning and my head in a twirl.

"Of course! Everyone who's seen the two of you together these past few weeks have commented what a wonderful couple you'll make. We just didn't expect things to move quite this quickly…"

"It hasn't!" I blurted. "I mean, he hasn't asked me. It's too soon. I'm still married."

She shook her head dismissively. "A technicality. If a man has ever given sufficient cause for a divorce, it's your husband. And unless I'm mistaken, he'll soon be sitting in a jail cell. No judge in his right mind would fail to end your marriage if you petitioned. *At least not in this oblast*," she finished, saying the last under her breath.

There was one more question I had to ask, though part of me was afraid of her answer. "Does your husband know?"

Marina laughed, a jolly good-natured chuckle. "He's the one who first mentioned it! He was considering having

Viktor removed from your protection detail – something about a *conflict of interest* or some such nonsense – and I told him if he did he'd be sleeping on the living room sofa! Can you imagine? Men!"

I breathed a huge sigh of relief. I should have known I couldn't hide anything from Marina – or from Anton, for that matter. For the first time in ages I felt almost completely at ease. Almost. As long as Bogdan was still free, I could never feel completely comfortable. But with the entire oblast Militsiya looking for him, I truly believed it was only a matter of time before he was behind bars and the kids and I would be finally safe. I admit I had mixed feelings about my children's father going to jail. After all, he *was* their father. Yet I no longer held out any hope we might reconcile, or that he would defeat his demons and give up alcohol. We were done. But a father was never done with his children, or at least shouldn't be. I only wondered how they would react to his imprisonment and then, down the road, to his release. I hoped they would survive with a minimum of scars, none too deep or debilitating. Only time would tell.

*****

Each day that Fall I awoke hoping the Militsiya would re-capture Bogdan. And each day I was disappointed. I was becoming increasingly frustrated, and I wasn't the only one. I heard Anton fume over the telephone as he spoke to Captain Boyko.

"Are your people incompetent?! Are you telling me you can't find one drunken louse in your own oblast? Perhaps we need new leadership at the top."

I saw Marina grow progressively more restless. If it had been anyone else, I'd have said she was frightened. But Marina?

Even Viktor showed signs of tension, though they were hidden beneath his tough Militsiya exterior. He joked less often, and his eyes seemed to scan the surroundings whenever we traveled with a seriousness that spoke of his worry.

Me? I tried my best to keep my fears under control, and for the most part I succeeded. Perhaps too well.

It was a school day, mid-week. I'd come back from the University with Viktor, as I still did every night, and the kids and I had had a relaxed dinner with Marina and Anton. As I recall, Bogdan's name was never even mentioned during the meal. After all, it had been several weeks since his attack at the University. We all assumed he'd fled back to our village, or perhaps north to Kyiv to hide in the urban chaos. We were wrong.

I'd put Kateryna and Sasha to bed and had gone to my own room to get ready. As soon as I closed the door to the room I thought I smelled something, but I wrote it off to nerves. I'd just begun to unbutton my blouse when a hand clamped down hard across my mouth. The smell of alcohol was unmistakable.

"Did you think I would just run away?" Bogdan whispered in my ear. His voice sounded tense, on edge. "I will never leave my children with these people – never!" He tightened his grip on my arm, squeezing so tight it hurt. He began to ramble, telling me how he'd hidden in the woods for over a week, and how he'd made his way to a village just a few miles away where he'd worked on a farm. "Did you think you were through with me? Planning to start your new life with the militsioner? You know, I really don't give a damn. Go with him or someone else, or no one. Do whatever you want. But the kids stay with me. I'm their father!" His voice suddenly soared so loudly I was sure someone would hear. But no sounds came from the hallway outside.

"Enough of this," he said, his tone hardening. "You will show me where the children are sleeping and I will take them with me. Keep your damn voice quiet and no one will get hurt. But if you try to call for help, you'll get what you deserve. Understand?"

I nodded my head.

"Good. Now show me."

I didn't know what to do. I couldn't let him get his hands on the kids, I couldn't! But I couldn't put Marina and Anton at risk either. Looking back, I suppose I was paralyzed with fear, for I let him drag me to the door and then out into the hallway. I struggled, but his hands were too strong and cut into the flesh of my arm where he held me tightly. He pushed me forward, in the direction of the kids' room, and I felt a wave of fright and revulsion sweep over me. I had to do something!

Suddenly I heard a thump, like when you tap a melon to check its ripeness, only much louder. At the same moment, Bogdan's grip loosened and I felt him fall to the floor behind me. As soon as his hand slipped from my mouth I let out the loudest, most terrifying scream I could manage.

"It's alright, Nina, it's alright," a familiar voice reassured me, a hand resting on my shoulder. But for a moment I couldn't understand what had happened and I stood there, in shock. When the door to the kids' room opened and they came running out, sleep clouding their eyes, I finally came out of my trance.

"Daddy! Daddy! What have you done to him?!" they yelled as they came running toward me. I leaned down to give them a hug, but they ran past me without even pausing.

As I turned I saw Kateryna burst into tears and Sasha pull Bogdan by the arm to try to awaken him. When I looked down at my husband I saw blood trickling down the side of his face, and only then did I see Anton standing over him, a wooden club in his hand.

"You killed him!" Sasha screamed at Anton. "You killed
Papa!"

"He's not dead," I said, not at all sure if it was true.
"He's unconscious."

"Why did you do it?! Why did you hit him?!" Their
questions came in a torrent, barely intelligible through their
tears. I tried to pull Sasha to me, but he squirmed away. "We
need to take him to the hospital, Mama!" he cried. "He's
hurt!"

Just then, Marina appeared from their bedroom, her hair
as perfectly coiffed as if she'd just come in from a luncheon,
wearing a deep blue Oriental style robe with embroidered
birds and butterflies. I'll never forget that image. "I've
already called the authorities. They're on their way," she said
calmly. She walked over to where Kateryna lay crying and
gently helped her to her feet. "He'll be okay, darling; the
ambulance will be here shortly." She stroked my daughter's
hair and received a frightened hug in return. I reached for
Sasha, but he pushed his way into Marina's embrace and
held onto her with all his might. Marina motioned to me
with her head and then led them back to their room, her hug
augmented by calming words of comfort. Kateryna resisted
briefly, but Marina assured her that Anton and I would take
care of Bogdan, and eventually they both succumbed to her
gentle insistence.

"Are you okay?" Anton asked, and it was as if the words
came from far away.

"I... Yes, thank you," I stumbled, my mind beginning to
clear.

"Don't worry, they'll come around once they have time
to think it over. It's a shock, seeing their father like this."

I looked down at Bogdan again, and a tiny part of my
heart ached. "Are you sure he's still... alive?"

Anton bent down and put two fingers to the side of
Bogdan's neck. "He's alive. Probably going to have a terrible

headache in the morning, but that will be the least of his worries. He should have stayed away."

"He's not thinking right," I heard myself say. "The alcohol and our leaving have completely unhinged him."

"Well, he'll have plenty of time to ponder his mistakes. I'm going downstairs to meet the Militsiya when they arrive. If he regains consciousness, yell down to me."

As soon as he'd gone I went into a bathroom and brought a moistened facecloth back out to the hallway and began to clean some of the blood from Bogdan's face. As much as I loathed what he'd become, as much as I feared what he'd tried to do to the kids and me, I couldn't help but feel sympathy for the man, my husband, a man who once I'd loved. I tried to remember what it had been like, back then when we were both naïve teens, thinking the world would be ours for the taking.

A shudder passed through his body and for an instant I thought he'd died. But moments later his eyes fluttered open and he stared, glassy-eyed and lost, up at the hallway ceiling.

"Wha...?" he tried to speak, his tongue leaden and unable to form words.

I put my hand to his chest. "You've been hurt," I said. "The doctors are on their way."

He turned to look at me as if just then realizing I was there. His eyes had a blank, far-away look and I realized he didn't recognize me. As foolish as it sounds, it hurt to be seen as a stranger by a man with whom I had shared so much. Moments later, however, sirens began to scream and I knew the Militsiya had arrived. I only hoped the ambulance had arrived as well.

It didn't take long before uniformed officials stormed upstairs with weapons drawn, Anton shouting encouragement. Thankfully, the kids were in their room and didn't have to see their father hauled roughly to his feet, his hands handcuffed behind his back. He didn't resist, seeming utterly spent, or perhaps still dazed by the blow to his head. The ambulance attendants insisted he be strapped into a stretcher for transporting to the hospital, and after a bit of back and forth Anton intervened and ordered the officials to allow it to happen.

"Make sure he stays healthy enough to face his trial," he directed, and no one among the visitors showed any willingness to disagree.

As they wheeled the stretcher from the house, Bogdan turned his head back to look at me with an expression that combined confusion and fright. Again I felt a flicker of sympathy, but Anton quickly set me straight.

"No telling what he would've done to you if he'd had his way," he said. "People like that, they've lost their souls to the drink and what's left, well, is hardly human."

Part of me wanted to argue, to cry out that he was still Bogdan Kovalchuk, no matter what the alcohol had done to him. Another part, however, realized that Anton was right: he would have hurt me, maybe worse, if someone hadn't stopped him. The realization stung and tears formed in the corners of my eyes.

"Come now, he isn't worth it," Anton said, his arm encircling my shoulders protectively. I wanted to lean against him, to let myself relax completely for the first time since my husband had been released from jail, but my mind was aflame with conflicting thoughts and emotions. Taking a deep breath, I collected my wits and gently pushed him away.

"I'll be fine," I lied. "I just need a full night's sleep. Thank you, Anton. You saved me."

His smile showed pride, yes, but also an unexpected degree of concern. As tired as I was, I lay awake for quite some time before sleep finally took me.

Chapter 11

This time the judicial proceedings were swift and sure. It became clear to me that Anton had spoken to his Party associates, for Bogdan was found guilty and sentenced in just a few hours. A young defender had been provided by the oblast, but he was either out of his depth or had received *instructions* from the Party. In any case, from what I heard he barely made a peep while Bogdan was convicted and sent to a regional prison for three years. From what Viktor told me, Bogdan's defense was much the same as he'd used the first time he was arrested: his crazy wife had stolen his children and was trying to keep them from him. This time, however, Viktor, Anton and others testified against him. He didn't stand a chance. I was surprised at first that the Prosecutor didn't call me to testify, but then I learned "they were afraid you'd come across as too sympathetic to him." Perhaps they were right.

It was difficult explaining to the kids why their father had disappeared from their lives, more difficult still to explain why we would never be living together as a family again. There were tears – a good many of them, both from Kateryna and Sasha, but also from me once the two of them had been put to bed. I knew full well that Bogdan needed to be apart from us, but still...

Viktor was wonderful. He tread lightly, allowing me the time and space to recover from the shock of Bogdan's imprisonment. Marina sat with me each evening after the kids had gone to bed, talking me through the confusing feelings I experienced. She was adamant that I should divorce Bogdan, and after a few months I began to agree with her. But there was someone else I needed to confer with, the only person I fully trusted to understand my dilemma.

I traveled back to our village at the end of the Fall semester, bringing not only the two kids but bags full of food and presents for Mama and Yerva. I was terribly excited to visit our village again, so I was surprised when Kateryna voiced some mild complaints that she would miss her friends and all the Christmas festivities in Berdychiv. Even Sasha looked wistful when she talked about the colorful decorations that her friends had described in the central square and all around the castle.

Nonetheless, we set off on our journey much as we'd arrived: sharing Dima's cart with all the packages and foodstuffs he was transporting back home. I sat up front with him while the kids happily sat in back, looking out at the countryside as it slid gently by kilometer after kilometer. Dima looked much the same as he had less than a year earlier, but there was no doubt our interaction was very different on this trip. He had heard about our troubles from some clients in Berdychiv and was sympathetic yet strangely reserved, as if we were fine china that might break with too much jostling. I tried to joke with him as we had the last trip, but he never joined-in with the same enthusiasm he'd shown a year earlier.

Whether he had a client that required him to travel all the way to our home village or not I never learned, but he stopped in Khmil'nik just long enough for us to say hello to his aunt, and to sample some of her baked goods and freshly brewed tea. By mid-afternoon we were on our way south again, carrying a good-sized bundle of food, honey and two hand-sewn dolls, courtesy of Mrs. Pavlyuk. Dima seemed somewhat revitalized by our stop at his aunt's inn, as he talked more freely and told me of his plans to expand the business to include routes that would stretch all the way to Kyiv and beyond. I must admit I only half-listened to his excited jabbering, as my mind was focused on seeing Mama – and Yerva – again after so much time. I'd never been away from them so long, and felt an emptiness inside me I knew could only be filled by their touch.

As we pulled up outside Mama's hut, Yerva came running out to greet us, her long pigtails flapping wildly in the cool breeze of early evening.

"You've come, you've come!" she cried excitedly, almost as if she hadn't quite believed we'd return until she saw us herself. She barely waited until I'd climbed down from the cart to crush me in a frantic hug, soon shared by Kateryna and Sasha. In just seconds all four of us were laughing and crying at the same time.

"What is this?" Mama called out as she shuffled down the path from our hut. "Who are these strangers?" I glanced up and tried to disguise my surprise at the gray hair that now dominated her once dark tresses and the uneven gait that brought her toward us so slowly.

"Mama!" I cried, running to her with the kids close on my heels. We all hugged in one big tussle, everyone talking at once and laughing and crying as if we hadn't seen each other in decades.

"Let me look at you three," Mama said after a bit, stepping back to take us all in with one glance. "My goodness, you children are so big I'd hardly recognize you. And you, Nina, you look happier than I've seen you in...forever!"

"We are all happy Mama, happy to be with you and Yerva again."

A cleared throat behind us reminded me that Dima still waited to offload our belongings. I re-introduced him to Mama, who immediately invited him to stay for dinner. He tried to refuse, claiming he needed to be on his way to meet his delivery schedule, but none of us were taking no for an answer.

That night we all talked and ate and opened gifts until well past bedtime, the only topic studiously ignored being

Bogdan and his incarceration. Actually it was Dima who reminded us of the late hour, excusing himself with the explanation that he needed to be on his way at first light the next morning. The way Yerva fawned over him, making a place in one corner of the living room complete with straw mattress and freshly-ironed sheets, one would have thought she had an ulterior motive beyond merely thanking him for bringing us home, if only for a short visit. Perhaps she did. I was more concerned with making certain the kids were comfortable and secure, and with drinking in as much of my old life as I possibly could. I was amazed how quickly the tiny hut felt like home once again, and how quickly we all fell back into our familiar relationships. It wasn't until I'd laid down to sleep that I thought about Viktor, and Marina, and our life up north. It seemed almost like a dream, a reality existing in another world, another dimension. Yet as distant as it all seemed, I couldn't help admit that I missed it. Each place was home. Each called to me.

We spent five days there, relaxing, remembering. My favorite times were when the kids had gone to sleep and Yerva was out with her friends, leaving Mama and me alone to sit, and sip tea, and talk. I'd always taken such interludes for granted, never paid them much attention. But after a year of separation, I'd come to cherish the special bond between us. As much as I admired Marina and enjoyed our little chats, they could not compare to my conversations with Mama. It was if she understood what I wanted to say before I could even say it. She *knew* me. Not just the embattled wife, or the nervous University student, or the worried mother. She knew the entirety of me, dating back to a time before I ever knew myself.

We would sit in the kitchen, the sounds of restless children tossing and turning in bed just behind us, sipping our tea and talking about anything and everything. At one point, I don't remember exactly how we came to it, we even talked about Papa.

Perhaps I was feeling guilty about giving my heart to Viktor so soon after our separation. Perhaps it was something else. Mama had mentioned a photo she kept there in the kitchen, a grainy old black and white snapshot of the five of us just a year or two before he died. I think she was talking about how quickly time passes.

"Do you still miss him, Mama?" I asked, knowing the question was too broad. "I mean, do you still think of Papa every day, or has the memory faded?"

I wanted to believe that their love could never die, but I knew from personal experience that time brought many changes, not all of them welcomed.

She smiled at my question, a sad little grin barely moving her lips. "Every day, my darling girl, every single day," she said softly, a far-away look coming across her eyes. "It's not the same as just after he passed away, of course," she corrected herself, "but my feelings for your father have never faltered, never been usurped by anyone else." Then, realizing what she'd said, she added, "Of course if I ever met the right man, I would not hesitate to start anew. It's just, well, just that Papa and I had such a good life together. We weren't the same sort of people at all, don't misunderstand me. I was always the homebody, always making sure the family was taken care of, while he always handled the outside world, everything from money, to relations with the local government, to even arranging for delivery of coal for heat. Do you know that when he died I didn't even know how to pay our taxes? I had to ask our neighbor. But when it came to what counts, when it came to how we viewed our family and ourselves, then we were as one. We could finish each other's thoughts." She smiled again, shyly.

"How did you go on? After he died, I mean." I still ached so much over the failure of my marriage to Bogdan that I could barely entertain the thought of losing a man I'd loved for so many years.

She shrugged. "I had no choice. I had the three of you girls, and I had this house. I had to go on." She paused, as if debating whether or how to continue. "I cried a lot at night, after all of you were asleep. Cried myself to sleep more nights than I'd like to remember. But I was determined that you girls would have a full life, a happy life, and so I went on. It was really that simple."

When I listened to her talk, saw the proud light in her eyes, I realized that the problems that confronted me were insignificant compared to what she had already conquered. She gave me hope; she game me confidence. No matter what happened between Viktor and me in the weeks and months to come, no matter what challenges fate brought to our lives, we would survive. I was not only determined, but certain we would make our way. And when we had finally planted our roots, in Berdychiv or wherever the four winds would carry us, we'd bring Mama, and Yerva if she was still unmarried, to live with us.

I could see the path, could see a way to the future that would bring peace and happiness to a family that had had far too little of either.

But I'd forgotten how strong the winds of change could blow.

Chapter 12

When we first arrived back in Berdychiv I felt like a stranger, an outsider parading as a genuine member of the community. Oh, Marina and even Anton did their best to make us feel at home, but their world was not ours and no matter how hard I tried to make believe we were part of it, I knew deep in my heart we never would be.

Luckily the kids had lots of friends and tolerated school well enough, so they were content most of the time. I spent most of my time at the University, studying, working in the library, and doing homework until late at night. When I had free time, I spent almost all of it with Viktor, either just the two of us (when Marina volunteered to babysit) or as a family when all our schedules coincided. It was awkward at first, I must admit, as Kateryna and Sasha struggled to accept Viktor as part of the family. I remember one day in particular when Kateryna turned to him and said, "You're never going to take our father's place, you know." Out of the blue. I think we were cooking shashlik at a local park. Viktor barely blinked.

"I wouldn't even try," he said, turning the skewers before the meat burned. "Your father will always be your father. But I hope we can be friends." He glanced over at her casually, as if they were chatting about the weather.

Kateryna looked to Sasha, who shrugged. "I suppose," she said, and the subject was never again raised, at least not in my presence.

Aside from the lingering uncertainty about Bogdan, I'd have to say the four of us got along together as well as could be imagined. Of course there were the occasions when either Viktor, or I, had to enforce rules the kids chose to ignore. At those times there were discussions, occasionally arguments, and raised voices. Sometimes they earned a day or two in their bedroom or even a slapped bottom when they were young. But for the most part we respected each other and enjoyed our time together.

So when Viktor finally asked me to marry him, after the kids and I had lived nearly a year with the Pavlyuks, the transition was remarkably smooth. True, I had to finalize my divorce and move from the luxury of the Pavlyuk mansion to the relatively modest surroundings of the little house Viktor had rented. But we were content. No, more than content – we were happy.

The marriage ceremony wasn't a lavish affair, just a short official blessing at the town hall. But Mama, Yerva, even Julija and Marko (with their three kids) all came up to witness the event. Marina and Anton hosted the reception afterwards, and we invited not only members of the Militsiya and University staffs, but friends we'd made since moving to our own home. The contingent from down south was absolutely flabbergasted by the Pavlyuks' estate, nothing so grand standing within several hours drive from our village.

"They *live* here?" Yerva asked when Viktor drove us there after the wedding. "It's bigger than our secondary school!"

Mama wandered through the house like an awestruck tourist upon first setting foot in Kyiv, until Marina took her by the hand and led her from room to room with a running commentary about where the furniture was made and how she (for the house was her domain, and Anton merely a resident) had planned and ordered everything in a grand design to construct the most 'elegant home in all the oblast.' Mama and the rest all agreed that, at least in their limited experience, Marina had succeeded fabulously.

We ate, and drank (even I, despite misgivings that lingered from my time with Bogdan), and danced to a small band that Sveta had recruited from among University students. They played old kobzari tunes using the turban and bandura, as well as more modern music to please the younger members of the audience. Viktor was magnificent in his dress Militsiya uniform, and I wore a simple white floor-length dress that Marina had ordered for me as a wedding gift. Everyone said we made a dashing pair; when we took the dance floor for our first turn as husband and wife, I felt as if I'd stepped from the pages of a fairy tale!

But even fairy tales must come to an end, and so Mama and the rest of the family returned to the village after five wonderful days in Berdychiv. I went back to the University and the Library, Viktor returned to his job, and the kids resumed school after the New Year's break. For five glorious months we lived in our new little house (new to us, little only in comparison to the Pavlyuks' mansion) and got to know each other as only people living together day after day really can. It was an idyllic time, or at least that's how I remember it now after all these years. Viktor was *so* different from Bogdan, especially the Bogdan of the last few years of our marriage. Where Bogdan had become increasingly cold and distant, Viktor wanted to know everything the kids and I did and volunteered to help all of us whenever he could. He wasn't an outwardly jocular man, in fact he probably would have described himself as overly reserved, but when he laughed, he **laughed** and the entire house shook with his laughter. Most important of all, at least for me: he never gave me any reason to doubt him. I knew deep in my bones he loved me and the kids and would do anything to keep us safe and happy. (And although this might not be the place to bring it up, he was a terrific lover as well, gentle when he needed to be and strong when it counted.)

To my great delight, Marina remained a good friend. She invited us over to her house once or twice a month, and her pleasure from entertaining Kateryna and Sasha was every bit equal to that of a real grandmother. The two of them loved her and looked forward to our visits as much as if we were traveling south to see Mama and my sisters. It seemed as if we'd finally found our niche, our place in a community that valued us as much as we valued it.

It was early May, the most wonderful time of the year in central Ukraine, when most of the omnipresent snow and sleet and mud at last fades from sight and myriad flowers begin to bloom in every field and surround every house, no matter how small or humble. The air itself seems to glow with hope and promise, and the scents of blossoms and new growth bring a spring to the step of even the most cynical of Party stalwarts.

I was working at the University Library late one evening, as was often the case, when Sveta – the Director of the University, appeared unannounced at the checkout counter where I was placing volumes to be re-shelved on a metal cart. It was unusual for the Director to visit our hideaway, and even more unusual for her to spend more than a moment in conversation with me. When I saw her serious expression, and that of my Library Director scurrying along behind her, I knew something was wrong.

"Nina, we've received some news," she began, and my heart sank.

"The kids?" I asked in a panic.

She shook her head sadly. "Viktor. There's been an accident."

It seems impossible even now that four such mundane words can change a life so completely. I took a deep breath.

He'd been chasing a thief, a man who'd robbed a grocery store in downtown Berdychiv. The Militsiya report said the two cars had been traveling at up to 100 kph, much faster than the little country roads surrounding the city had been built for. But Viktor was a good driver. He probably would've succeeded in overtaking the thief, except for one little remnant of the winter just passed – a patch of snow and ice that had taken refuge in the shadows close-by the roadway and had melted enough to wet the otherwise bone dry pavement and throw Viktor's official car into a tailspin. The black Volga struck a big pine head-on. The thief drove off, to be captured a few hours later.

The day of the funeral seemed too warm, too sunny, too... alive for what we'd all gathered to witness in the old cemetery that spread out across a hill behind the Castle. Mama was there, and my sisters, and Marina and Anton, and all the local Militsiya who weren't on-duty that day. There were also dozens of people I'd never met, people Viktor had helped or befriended over his eight years enforcing the law in Berdychiv.

An Orthodox priest said some kind words, an honor guard fired several shots into the air to honor their fallen comrade, and I sat in my new black dress and cried. I don't remember my actual thoughts, if splinters of memories and emotions can truly be called thoughts, but I know the general direction: it was the end. Of everything. Nothing so awful, so unfair, so senseless could possibly occur unless it marked the end of days, the passing of God's grace from this empty sphere.

For weeks after Viktor's death I couldn't eat, couldn't sleep, couldn't move the dark cloud that had settled over my head. The kids bore the brunt of my despair, trying desperately to smile or cajole me back to my former self. But in my mind, that self had died with Viktor. Our mutual life was *mutual*, shared, symbiotic. Without him, the life we lived was still-born and no happy words, or smiling faces, or even angry demands – of the sort Anton apparently thought would be conducive to my recovery – had even the slightest chance of moving me past that simple fact.

Mama and Yerva stayed with us for two weeks after the funeral, but their best efforts were like a buzzing gnat set against a raging bull, doomed to failure. In fact, the constant cheering and encouragement by everyone I met actually made me feel worse, as if I were the only person on earth who couldn't just *get on with it*.

Get on with it. *With what?* My life, our lives, were entwined with his. Without him, there seemed no reason to live. Oh don't misunderstand me, I never seriously considered killing myself. I loved Kateryna and Sasha too much to ever put them through what I was feeling then. It would be worse than unkind, it would be inhuman. I imagined Mama's tears if I ever succumbed to my dark moments.

But for a long while it seemed to me that I would never feel alive again, never laugh, never feel the sun upon my face and be thankful for the light and warmth it brought. I was lost, so very, very lost.

It was Marina who found me, set me back on the path to recovery. She did it by using my pain as a gateway to a future I couldn't see, didn't want to see.

It wasn't only the future I refused to see, I quite simply didn't want to see anyone, or anything. I was satisfied, if self-imposed isolation can be considered satisfaction, to simply sit and stare, pondering what might have been. Marina would not accept that sad excuse. No matter how often I told her I wasn't ready for visitors, she came to visit anyway. The more I tried to shut down, the more she insisted I open up. I remember one of the first nights, among many, when we sat on the porch of our tiny house and talked of Viktor. Not directly. Not immediately. But eventually, we talked.

"How are you?" she asked, her voice not the sympathetic whine of well-meaning acquaintances that had come to grate upon my nerves, but a simple question between friends. It was the first question she always asked.

"Okay," I said, not because it was true but because I didn't want to provide a foothold for a hike into my psyche.

"Really?"

I shrugged.

"You look thin. Are you eating?"

"Some."

"And the kids? How's school?"

"They are doing well."

"Good, I'm glad to hear it. I'd like it if they could come visit next week. Think they'd like that?"

"I'm sure they would."

"I'll call to set up a time."

"Good. Thank you."

This was the place in most other conversations where the well-meaning acquaintance would realize I had no intention of baring my soul or experiencing an epiphany. And they would leave.

Marina would not leave.

We sat there in the growing darkness for what seemed like hours; might well have been. I was determined to maintain my silence, to preserve the protective shell I'd erected around me to prevent anyone or anything from touching the pain I held inside. She was just as determined to wait me out.

"So, how is work?" she began, and although I knew she was merely keeping the conversation alive, I wasn't so damaged that I couldn't play the game – for her sake, if not mine.

"Okay, I guess."

"Did I ever tell you about my first husband, how I coped when he died?"

I thought perhaps I'd misheard. I'd never heard a word about a husband other than Anton. "You were married before?"

"I don't talk about it much. No reason. But yes, I was married. To a wonderful man: Ivan." I sensed the hurt beneath her words. Her eyes creased at the corners as if it caused her physical pain to remember. But she didn't hesitate. "We were married young, quite young actually.

This was back home, in the countryside. Probably not all
that different a place than where you grew up. It was the
kind of place that when you finished with secondary school,
you went to work or you married. Those were pretty much
our only options back then. I wouldn't have minded
working, but I met Ivan in my last year of school and
decided then and there that he was *the one*." She smiled
wanly. "As you might imagine, I was quite strong-minded
even in my youth." I could indeed imagine. "My father was
very much in favor of the marriage; my mother begged me
to continue with my schooling. It didn't matter what they
thought; I'd already made up my mind, and so Ivan and I
were married two weeks after school ended. He went off to
work as a harvester in the fields, and I went home to prepare
our tiny apartment for the children I expected to arrive in
short order."

Her voice softened, a sad, wistful note creeping into her
words. "But as we both know all too well, life has a way of
ignoring our carefully laid plans. For whatever reason, I was
unable to get pregnant – though not for lack of trying." Her
smile was crooked, more of a grimace than a grin. "And so I
found a job at a local store and we lived our lives as best we
could. As I said, we were young, and very much in love, so it
wasn't so bad. Besides, we were certain the stork would visit
us sooner or later, it was only a matter of time. What we
didn't know then was that we didn't have all the time we
expected."

She took a deep breath and I saw more clearly the effort
it was taking for her to tell her story. "It was late in the Fall,
September 28th to be exact. A Militsiya vehicle pulled up in
front of the store and an officer got out and came inside. We
didn't think anything of it; after all we had all sorts of people
shopping with us every day. But... this officer didn't go to
the aisles. He came straight to the register where I was
working.

"I can still remember his face: strong jaw, blue eyes, determined expression but strangely tentative. I felt something, a premonition or intuition – whatever you'd call it. I thought he might be there to warn us about a criminal on the run – the Militsiya did that a lot back then. But that wasn't it at all." She bit her lower lip unconsciously.

"'Your husband has had an accident,' he said. He was so calm that I thought it must not have been too bad an accident. But it was. Ivan was driving one of the big harvesters when it hit a buried boulder. He was thrown from his seat... and fell into the blades." She looked down at her hands, and then back up at me. I saw tears in her eyes. "He didn't have a chance. They even sealed the casket." She drifted away for a moment, lost in thoughts of those terrible times. I wanted to say something, to console her, but the words would not come. They stuck in my throat, nearly gagging me.

"I thought I would die," she continued after a short while, "but I was wrong." Her voice became stronger, more like the woman I'd thought I knew. "My friends and family helped me get through that first day, then the next, and little by little I found myself back among the living. A few months later I moved up here to Berdychiv, met Anton, and gradually began a new life. But I think about Ivan nearly every day. The difference," she said, leaning toward me and taking my hands in hers to make her point, "is that now when I think of him I think how happy he'd be to see the direction my life has taken, and that makes *me* happy. Now I can think of him and smile." Her smile this time was broad and genuine. I *felt* Ivan's presence, the strength he gave her.

"I'm not going to say this is how it will happen for you. We're all different, all must deal with life as best we can. But you've got to give it a chance, give life a chance to heal the pain."

For the first time since Viktor's death I felt the gray blanket of melancholy lift a bit, just a bit. I glimpse a vision of my future that consisted of more than just survival, more than just continuing to exist to ensure that the kids reached adulthood without the scars of our past crippling their prospects. I'm not sure I fully realized the importance of that conversation until much later, but I know I recognized a change within me, a lessening of the weight that pressed down on my heart. For that, and for so much more, I owe Marina a huge debt of gratitude and affection. She was, in so many ways, a second mother to me.

*****

As with any life, mine had its requisite ups and downs, the inevitable little victories and failures that all of us endure. But most importantly the kids prospered, I regained the greater part of my self-identity, and the years passed.

Kateryna graduated from secondary school a few years after Viktor's death, and Sasha two years later. Both of them went on to study at the University, both under the sponsorship of their godparents, the Pavlyuks. Of course, it didn't hurt that I remained on staff at the University library after receiving my diploma, but Marina's influence and financial assistance made their University years so much easier on all of us. Kateryna graduated near the top of her class and received an offer from a company in Kyiv upon completing her schooling. For a short while she vacillated about accepting the offer, since it would require her to move to the big, foreign, capital city, but eventually my Mama, Marina and I all convinced her to expand her horizons, and she moved north. Anton's intercession with some Party friends in Kyiv ensured that she had a safe and comfortable room to rent from Day 1, as well as a small coterie of people who looked out for her and helped make the transition as painless as possible. She met Maxim, a young businessman who also lived in Kyiv, after just a few months in her new home. They dated for nearly a year before announcing their engagement.

Sasha, on the other hand, was not much of a student but was very talented as a football player. He left University after only two years to play with a semi-professional team that represented the oblast, and after a year or so was called up to one of the top League teams in Kharkov.

With both of my little birds having left the nest, I began to feel the tug of my old village and the need to be near my aged mother and both sisters – both married by then with five children between them. The only thing that kept me in Berdychiv at that point was my love for Marina. She continued to be a good and faithful friend to me and the kids alike for several years, until first Anton, and then she, died unexpectedly not seven months apart.

I was at work in the library when I received a call from a mutual friend.

"Nina, I have some bad news," she began when I answered the call.

"What is it?" I asked, my mind whirling to think what might have transpired.

"It's Marina – she's had a stroke."

I felt as if someone had punched me in the stomach. I learned where they'd taken her and immediately left work and drove to the regional hospital. It was a gray, overcast day in November, and the stark concrete building looked nothing like a seat of healing and hope. I made my way up to her room on the third floor, where I found her connected by a spider's web of tubes and wires to the machines that both monitored and maintained her flickering life-force. She lay there unmoving, her eyes closed, her skin as pale as death. A lump swelled in my throat and tears streamed down my face.

"Marina, Marina it's Nina. Can you hear me?" I whispered, afraid to raise my voice and yet equally afraid to learn she was unable to respond.

She showed no reaction whatsoever. I remember stroking her hand as if it were a talisman that would revive her and return her to full health. It did not. I stayed there until the nurses made me leave well after darkness had fallen, only to return the next day, and the next.

There was no change. She remained in a state of unconsciousness, balanced precariously between this world and the next, her face peaceful and yet nearly unrecognizable without the energy and vigor that had always marked her as a special person. She was like one of those wax statues of famous people they put in museums. It was her, yet it was not.

On the third day, just a short time before I knew the nurses would appear to order me from the room, Marina gasped as if she'd seen a ghost and her eyes fluttered open. I leapt to my feet, both excited and fearful of what the change signified.

"Marina, it's me, Nina!" I called out to her, my heart racing with anticipation.

She blinked several more times and turned her head slightly as if looking at me.

I called for a nurse and took her hand in mine as we waited. "Can you hear me?" I asked. "Can you understand what I'm saying?"

She nodded weakly and then her lips began to move as if she were attempting to form words. I leaned close, hoping I could make out what she was trying to say. At first it was unintelligible, just a buzzing of her vocal cords and a gentle puff of air that signified nothing to me. But then, concentrating with the courage and determination I'd always associated with her, she roused the strength to make herself understood.

"Live!" she ordered. "Don't let him win."

At that very moment a loud buzzer sounded and a nurse barged in with two assistants; they shooed me out of the room. As I made my way toward the waiting room I saw white-coated doctors and nurses rushing toward Marina's room, the steely look in their eyes telling me the situation was grave. I prayed.

I sat there for what seemed like forever but was probably only an hour or two. I began to think I'd been mistaken, that someone else in that same wing of the hospital had required special attention. Then an older man, his hair gray, his demeanor gentle to the point of near-invisibility, came out into the waiting area and scanned the handful of worried friends and relatives waiting for news of their loved ones.

"Mrs. Vann?" he said softly, glancing down at a clipboard he held with both hands.

I forced my legs to lift me from the chair and wobbled toward him. He met me half way.

"You were visiting Mrs. Pavlyuk?" he asked, his face devoid of expression.

I nodded dumbly, every cell of my body in a state of numb expectation.

"I'm so sorry," he began, but before he could say another word I heard myself cry out and fall to the floor, the weight of his words too much to bear.

Marina was dead. The words seemed incongruous. Someone so full of life could not be dead. How could it be?

But it was.

The burial was an enormous affair. It seemed as if half the city came to bid her farewell, if not half the oblast. People stood ten deep all around the gravesite, their wails of loss carried by the breeze to the far corners of the region. I expected to cry. I brought handkerchiefs and tissues to absorb the torrent. But I could not. Not a single tear fell from my eyes, not a single moan escaped my lips. It was as if every drop of moisture in my body had already been expelled and all that remained was a dried husk, a teetering shadow.

When they laid her in the ground, the Orthodox priest said some words and quoted from the Bible. I'm sure it was a fine eulogy. I don't remember a word. I think I'd fallen into some sort of trance, or psychotic state. I couldn't have hurt more if it had been my real mother.

When everyone else left, I stayed behind. I knelt by the grave to pray.

"I won't let him win," I said aloud to the cold earth when I'd finished my short prayer. "I won't."

Only the wind howled through the trees in reply.

PART THREE

Chapter 13

With Marina gone there was no one and nothing left to bind me to Berdychiv. I missed my family. I missed our little village. So I went home.

The move was accomplished with little fanfare: Sasha was still living in Kharkov and spending much of his time overseas playing football, Kateryna had her own family by then, having given me a glorious little granddaughter just over a year after she married, and despite having a job I loved and all the friends I'd made over the years I'd lived there, the chance to spend time with Mama before she left us far outweighed any friendship or employment opportunity.

When we'd come north so many years earlier, we'd left with scarcely more than the clothes on our backs. This time I had to pack-up an entire house, a house filled with belongings and memories that evoked all kinds of emotions. It took me longer than it should have, I suppose, owing to the time I spent looking at photographs, remembering when and where we bought this or that, and most difficult of all, deciding what I would bring with me and what I would leave behind. But gradually, painfully, I winnowed the pile down to a manageable size and called my old friend, Dima, who by that time had become something of a transport mogul in the oblast. His little company had grown exponentially over the years since I'd last traveled with him, with a little help from Anton, true, but mainly from all the hard work and personable service Dima provided to every one of his customers. I fully expected him to send one of his young drivers to move me, so I was both startled and pleased when Dima himself appeared at our front door in a big, new, blue and yellow truck. He'd brought two helpers to do the heavy lifting, two young men who I realized – with some chagrin – were both younger than my Sasha.

"It's been a while," he said when I answered the door, kissing me on both cheeks. "But you are still a beauty, Nina."

I'm sure I blushed, not only from his sweet words but from the embarrassment of seeing a man I'd remembered from so many years earlier as a skinny little cart driver, standing tall and handsome in a tailored leather jacket, his blue eyes flashing and his jet black hair peppered with streaks of gray.

"You are looking very well yourself," I recovered, before inviting him in for a cup of tea while his two assistants carried box after box out to the waiting truck.

Over tea I told him of my life since we'd last met, a tale I managed to convey without tears or obvious emotion. It felt strange relating all that had happened over the years, almost as if I were describing the life of someone else. When I'd finished, he gave me a short reprise of his life during the same period, a story not so very different than my own: many long hours building up his business, a whirlwind courtship of a woman he'd met through his work, followed by two wonderful years living together before a crushing blow brought it all to an end: she'd died giving birth to a baby son, who lived just three days before dying as well.

He spoke with sadness, a detached voice I recognized all too well.

"One moment I was on top of the world," he explained. "The next, I felt as if someone had ripped my heart out of my chest."

I gripped his hand and he returned the squeeze. Who would've thought all those years earlier that we would encounter so much pain in our lives? And yet there we were, both survivors, both ready for the next chapter, whatever it would bring.

We chatted non-stop all the way to my village, it somehow feeling easier to talk with someone I'd known from *before*. It turned out he was still living in Khmil'nik, having purchased the inn his aunt had run when she'd died a few years earlier. He paid an older woman to manage the place and kept his own apartment on the top floor where he stayed whenever he wasn't on the road.

"Aren't you tired of it yet?" I asked. "All the travel?"

He smiled. "You don't leave something you love unless you find something to take its place," he said. "Haven't found it yet."

The hours passed so quickly I was almost disappointed when we pulled up in front of Mama's house just past noon. But seeing my dear mother hobble from her thatch hut erased any such thoughts.

"Mama!" I cried, and ran to her with no thought of Dima, or my belongings, or anything else. It had been so long since we'd spent any real time together it took us a few minutes to get over the initial awkwardness. At least it did for me. Mama showed no such reticence, no holding back or over-thinking. A hug, a kiss, and that huge smile I'd missed so badly.

"My girl is home!" she called out, to no one in particular. It was only then I noticed the tears pooling in her eyes.

"Mama, are you crying?" I asked, my happiness so complete it precluded even the thought of tears.

"I'm just a silly old woman," she sniffed.

It was only then I realized she *was* an old woman. In my mind she was still the youthful centerpiece of our family, with the boundless energy and effortless smile I'd known my entire life. But as I looked at her objectively I saw a gray-haired little woman, with wrinkles spreading like cracks in ice from her eyes and corners of her mouth, her back slightly bent, using a cane when she walked to offset the swelling in her ankles. For an instant I almost cried myself. When had this happened? Where was I while my poor mother slipped from robust health into old age?

I knew all too well where I'd been, where the focus of my thoughts had kept me. I admit I felt guilty. Even though I knew I'd done what needed to be done, and that my two sisters had been nearby the entire time I'd been gone, I couldn't help but experience a pang of conscience: after all she'd done for me, I hadn't been there when she needed me. I took a deep breath, blinked the moisture from my eyes, and hugged her again even tighter. I was home now, and all that would change.

"Do you want us to put all your things inside?" Dima called out from the back of the truck, where he and his two helpers waited patiently.

"Yes, please!" I answered, now doubly embarrassed. "Dima, come say hi to my Mama."

He gave orders to his men and came to greet us with a shy yet endearing look I hadn't seen in a man for years in the bigger cities of the north. It made me recognize how much I'd missed not only my family, but the small village idiosyncrasies I'd nearly forgotten.

"You remember Dima, don't you Mama?" I asked.

She smiled. "You were younger then."

"And you are still as lovely as ever," he said, bowing his head in respect and to hide the subtle blushing in his cheeks.

"I like this one," Mama said, reaching out to pinch his cheek. "Will you have some tea?"

"I need to help get your daughter unpacked," he demurred.

"We'll keep a pot on the fire for you."

Dima glanced at me with an *'is this okay with you?'* look, which I answered affirmatively with a nod of the head.

"That's a good-looking young man," Mama said as I helped her walk back to the house.

I didn't say so then, but I thought the very same thing.

*****

I hadn't planned to stay with Mama for more than a short while, thinking of both her privacy in the tiny hut as well as my own independence. But somehow as one week became two and then a month, I never quite seemed to find a place of my own as she gave the unmistakable impression that she found my search "foolish." And so I stayed. The prospects for a university librarian were somewhat limited in the village, but to my great surprise I learned that the oblast had established a regional library located halfway between our village and the next along the main road to Uman. I fully expected the typical concrete block box with a handful of tattered, moldy books. I was wrong.

Somehow the powers-that-be had risen to the occasion and had constructed a small but well-designed space with shelf after shelf of new (or nearly new) books in a wide variety of topics. Soviet libraries at that time were heavily invested in works by and about the Communist regime, with emphasis on political theory as it related to every other walk of life. This library contained books previously banned (by authors such as Pasternak and Solzhenitsyn), as well as a remarkable section of 'International Authors' such as Walt Whitman, Upton Sinclair and Henry James. And of course, all the great Ukrainian authors from Gogol and Bulgakov to the *radical* views of Akhmatova. I decided that a Party aficionado must have been involved in the planning and construction, for in no other way could such volumes be seen on the shelves without someone paying the price.

I applied for a job at the library, expecting to be told to fill out an application and wait for a reply that would never come. Two weeks later, I was called in for an interview.

The interview committee consisted of the Head Librarian (a stern woman in her mid-fifties with graying hair pulled back into a tight bun), a representative from the Raion Administrative Council (a much younger woman, younger than me, with a ready smile and a pleasant, open face), and a well-dressed gentleman who appeared too sophisticated for our little village and was introduced to me as *Comrade* Kostyshyn. His smile was too white, his teeth too even, his suit too well-tailored. It was clear he was an outsider, but then again, after all those years so was I.

The interview was a standard affair, with the Head Librarian (Miss Nazarenko) introducing the committee and thanking me for my application. She asked straightforward questions about my background and experience, while the Council representative, (Mrs. Savaryn), was more interested in how well I was adjusting to my return to the village. Comrade Kostyshyn remained silent during the first part of the interview, though he watched my reactions with the attentive eye of a cart driver inspecting a new horse.

Miss Nazarenko glanced over at him from time to time as if offering to defer to his line of questioning, but until both women had mined the basic information about my recent and past experience, he refrained. The Head Librarian was about to launch into what sounded like a much more detailed examination of my library know-how, when suddenly Comrade K. interrupted.

"Excuse me, but may I ask a question or two?" he asked, but with a tone that suggested he was telling, not asking.

"Of course, of course Comrade!" Mrs. Nazarenko fawned, and then I knew that our Comrade was more than just another local bureaucrat.

"You moved here from Berdychiv, is that correct?" he asked, his voice so bland and unemotional a wave of nerves rushed through my chest.

"Moved back," I gently corrected, blushing from my effrontery. "I moved back here, to where I'd grown up, from Berdychiv, yes Comrade."

He nodded, showing no sign of irritation that I'd corrected him. "And in Berdychiv, you knew, I believe, Comrade Pavlyuk and his wife, Marina?"

I swallowed. Although I knew Anton had been well-regarded in the Party machinery, I also knew how quickly such regard changed. What if the Pavlyuks had fallen from grace in the short time since Marina's death?

I decided the truth was my only avenue of reply. "I did, Comrade. In fact, my children and I lived with them for several months when we first moved there."

"Exactly," he answered, as if he knew full-well what I was going to say before I said it. My nervousness redoubled. "And they were your sponsors at the regional university?"

I nodded, my tongue suddenly unwilling to cooperate.

"Comrade Pavlyuk and his wife must have been very impressed with your capabilities," he went on, and for the first time I realized he was talking as much, if not more, to his fellow Committee members, who listened attentively. "I'm impressed." He said the last as some kind of benediction. They understood.

After a brief recess while the Committee discussed my candidacy, I was called back into the small conference room where the three members sat with satisfied smiles on their faces.

Miss Nazarenko made the announcement. "Mrs. Vann, the Committee finds you not only qualified, but eminently suitable for the position of Assistant Head Librarian. Congratulations."

A weight fell from my chest. "Thank you," I said, my eyes meeting each member in turn, lingering a moment longer on Comrade K. I thought I saw him wink at me, but assumed I was just imagining things. Miss N. and I agreed to meet the following day to discuss the particulars of the position (i.e. how much I'd be paid and how many hours and days I'd work, as well as the details of the job itself.) With that completed, Mrs. Savaryn excused herself and left the building, Miss N. was called away to another meeting, and I was left with Comrade K.

"So, can I give you a ride anywhere?" he asked when I began to put on my jacket and scarf.

I hesitated before answering. Not only was I intimidated by his apparent link to the Party hierarchy, but there was something about the way he carried himself that made me think of a predator eying his prey. "I... I have a ride," I lied. "But thank you. And thank you for your support. Anton and Marina were wonderful people." I don't know why exactly I said the last, except maybe I hoped it might give him pause. It didn't.

"No need for your friends to bother since I'm already here with a big government car," he said, moving a step too close and putting his hand on my shoulder. "We can give them a call."

I tried not to shudder, but was only partly successful.

"I'm sure he's already on the way," I said, expanding my lie to include an imaginary 'he' who just might take umbrage with Comrade K's insistent offer.

"He? I understood you were a widow." His voice was calm but I detected a slight edge of irritation.

"Oh, I am," I continued, so committed to my lie I'm not sure I could've told the truth even if I wanted to. "It's my brother-in-law who's coming to pick me up. My sister's husband." I could've slapped myself for adding the obvious.

He didn't miss my discomfort. "Oh? Well then, perhaps some other time." He reached up and tucked a loose strand of hair into my scarf. I had to will myself to hold still. "I get down here fairly often, and I have a feeling I'll be spending a great deal more time here at the library." When he smiled all I could see were wolf-ish fangs dripping in anticipation of a fresh meal.

I tried to smile back, but I imagine my effort more closely resembled a trembling grimace. He took no notice.

"Until we meet again, *Miss* Vann," he said, stressing my matrimonial status even as he leaned over and kissed me on both cheeks. His lips seemed to linger a half-moment too long with each kiss.

I was trembling from head to foot as I watched him leave through the library's glass front doors and climb into a big black Soviet limo, a Militsiya officer serving as his driver. It was only when the car finally pulled away that I could suck in a full breath. I waited a full ten minutes before tiptoeing out to the edge of the building, where I peered down the road to be sure the limo was truly gone. Only then did I make my way to the bus stop and sit to await the next bus back to the village.

When I told Mama about the interview later that afternoon, her eyes narrowed and storm clouds hung above her brow.

"Those Party people – they think the world revolves around them," she spat. I don't think she ever got over the lack of help from the local apparatchiki after Papa died. She blamed the Party even more than the Raion bureaucrats for the difficult life we lived. She saw Papa as a hero. They had seen him as a troublemaker.

"Don't you ever let him get you alone in that building," she warned, even wagging a finger at me to make the point more forcefully. "You can't trust a man like that."

I had no intention of doing so.

*****

Once I was working again and bringing in money to help Mama make ends meet, life slipped naturally into a simple, satisfying rhythm. I awoke early each morning, fed the chickens and collected eggs before milking the cow, bathed and dressed, then ate whatever breakfast Mama had concocted that day and made my way – by bus – to the regional library. There I checked-out and re-shelved books, answered Information inquiries, monitored magazine and newspaper subscriptions, and basically did whatever Miss N. didn't want to do. I began to recognize many of the regular visitors and they certainly knew me. It gave me a warm, inclusive feeling, living amongst people who knew my parents, and their parents before them. For the first time in a long time I felt truly part of the community, not as an outsider come to escape my past, but – if you will – as the prodigal daughter returned.

With Yerva living on her own (and supporting a musician boyfriend who seemed better than most of his sort), I became the principal housekeeper in our little hut, as well as Mama's *helper*. The arthritis in her hands and ankles left her unable to handle many of the daily chores she had performed for so many years, but somehow she still cooked the nightly supper and kept the dust and cobwebs from completely overwhelming us. We became closer than ever before, perhaps because we shared the sadness of a husband lost and the joy of children grown. Each night after supper, when the dishes were scrubbed and the hot tea poured, we sat in the kitchen and chatted – about the past, the present, and the future, though mostly about days long gone by. Sitting there with her I couldn't help but remember all the evenings I'd sat on the front porch with Marina, our discussions focused more on a future we both felt confident imagining, though, as it turned out, we could not have predicted all the strange twists and turns that ensued. It was an odd sensation reliving those moments from Berdychiv, almost déjà vu but different enough to give me a feeling of dislocation, a sense of sameness in a completely different context.

I could detect the slightest of memory lapses in Mama's recollections, tiny hesitations and awkward gaps that reminded me she was older than the image I kept locked in my mind. When I thought of her I still imagined the woman who'd fought to keep our family together, and scraped and saved to put food on the dinner table. She was still that, of course, but increasingly encased in the web of years that ensnare us all, gradually binding her limbs and clouding her senses.

It was during one of our talks, quite late – at least by how we villagers defined it – when a moment of quiet reflection was interrupted by a sharp knock on the door.

"Who could that be at this late hour?" Mama said, her hand grabbing her cane – for protection more than help standing.

"I'll see," I said, getting up with more than a little apprehension myself.

Imagine my surprise when I pulled open the door and found Dima, carrying a large paper bag, standing on our top step, a hesitant smile on his face.

"It's not too late, is it?" he began before I could say a word.

In fact, I was very glad to see him. Perhaps more glad than I was willing to admit even to myself. It had been over a month since he'd brought me home, and in recent days I'd considered calling to invite him to visit us when he was next in our oblast.

"Of course not!" I said, impulsively hugging him and kissing him on each cheek. He blushed adorably. "I was wondering when you'd get around to visiting us."

"Who is it?!" Mama asked, her voice a mixture of excitement and nerves.

I pulled him into the kitchen. "You remember Dima, don't you Mama?"

She shook her head in good-natured disgust. "I'm old, not ancient. How could I forget a young man as handsome as he?"

Dima blushed an even deeper shade of red. "I... I brought you something," he stumbled, setting the bag on our table. "It's not much..."

"Don't be foolish!" Mama chastised. "A gift is always welcome."

He reached into the bag and pulled out a large leg of pork. Mama's eyes bulged.

"Not much?! We haven't had good pork in months!"

"Dima, you shouldn't have!" I said, even as I rejoiced.

"It's not so much, but we moved a large shipment yesterday and I thought of you two..." He looked directly at me as he said it. Whether it was his look or something else, I impulsively kissed him – on the lips!

"You are a dear, dear man!" I fussed, attempting to both thank him for his thoughtfulness and hide my shock at my boldness.

He looked as if he'd swallowed his tongue. Thankfully, Mama came to our rescue.

"You'll have to come to dinner tomorrow to help us eat all of that meat."

"Will you still be here?" I asked. I sounded eager even to myself.

He blinked, his senses gradually returning. "I *could* be," he said. "Yes, I will!"

We all laughed, shared tea, and listened to Dima's tales of life on the road. Mama and I could've listened for hours, so foreign and exciting it seemed compared to our quiet little corner of the world, but Dima was more interested in hearing my story, so I told him all about the library and my work there. Well, not everything, but all the stories he needed to hear.

It was quite late, by *anyone's* standards, when he finally left to stay at a nearby inn.

"That young man has more on his mind than a good pork dinner," Mama said as I watched his truck pull away.

I couldn't help but smile.

The following day I found myself thinking about my old acquaintance more than my job. I misshelved several books, answered a reference question that hadn't been asked, and generally floated through my day with my head bumping against the clouds. I was so distracted that I didn't notice a new arrival until his voice sent shivers down my spine.

"I understand from Mrs. Nazarenko that you've adapted to your new position without a problem," Comrade K. announced from just behind my back as I stood between stacks replacing returned books.

I jumped. "Comrade! I didn't see you come in!" I tried to modulate my voice, but I'm afraid my voice leapt despite my efforts.

"You look right at home," he went on, staring into my eyes with an energy that bordered on rudeness.

"I...I've been quite happy here, yes."

"The Pavlyuks would be so pleased." The tone was flat, as if he were reading yesterday's weather forecast.

"I hope so." I was beginning to regain my footing, my heart once again beating more or less normally.

"We should celebrate. Are you available for dinner tonight?"

I froze. Cold sweat dripped down my forehead. I had no interest in dining or doing anything else with the wolfish Comrade. I was fairly confident I knew his ultimate goal. But if I refused him, would he see to it that I was dismissed? I needed that job, both for myself and for Mama. I was caught in a dangerous place and didn't know which way to turn.

Then, in a heartbeat, I was saved. "There you are!" a voice I'd heard inside my head all morning suddenly announced from just a few feet away. "I've been looking all over for you." Dima gave me one of his beaming smiles and, without thinking or hesitation, I leapt into his arms.

"Dima! I was beginning to think you'd gotten lost!" My voice was much too loud for the sanctity of the library, but at that point I had no control over my body. I'm sure Dima could feel me shiver as I desperately clung to him.

When I glanced back at Comrade K., I saw for just an instant the furious disappointment in his eyes. In an instant, it was gone.

"Who is this young fellow?" he asked, showing no sign of the anger I knew boiled inside of him.

"Oh, I'm sorry Comrade!" I said, perhaps too apologetically. "This is my... good friend, Dima Zvyahilsky. Dima, Comrade Kostyshyn knew the Pavlyuks."

Dima reached out his hand. "Oh? They were very good people. I wish I'd had the chance to spend more time with them. They helped Nina a great deal."

Comrade K. shook his hand with little enthusiasm, as if shaking out a dirty washcloth. "Zvyahilsky – is that a Jewish name?" he asked without expression. However, it was Ukraine and Dima had lived there his entire life. We both knew what he was asking.

Dima laughed. "It sounds like it, doesn't it?" he said lightly. "But actually my grandfather was an Orthodox priest."

Comrade K. nodded absently. "Yes, well, I was just asking Mrs. Vann..."

"I'm so sorry, Comrade," I interrupted, my relief overcoming my fear. "Dima and I already have plans for tonight." Then a thought struck me. "But you are welcome to join us if you have no one to eat dinner with..."

For an instant the Party executive's lip curled in an unconscious sneer. "No, no, I couldn't intrude," he said with barely a hint of sincerity. "Besides, I should really be getting back up north."

We exchanged a few mock pleasantries and just like that, he stalked out of the library and was gone.

"Who was *that?*" Dima asked as soon as the Comrade left. The distasteful look on his face told me he'd correctly taken the measure of the Party boss.

"Just someone I met interviewing for this job. No one important."

He raised one eyebrow. "Oh? He certainly seemed to think he was important."

"An occupational hazard for Party officials," I joked.

"Ahh."

"By the way, what brings you to the library? You're not looking to borrow a book, are you?"

He smiled bashfully.

"I stopped by your house and your mother told me how to get here. I was hoping to take you to lunch?" The way he made his statement into a question endeared him to me even more than he already had.

"I don't get much time," I began, but he cut me off.

"*Any* time would be wonderful!"

"Well, perhaps it would be better if we went to dinner tonight." I had to struggle not to make my statement a question as well.

"Oh?" His face lit up. "Is that what all that was about with your Party boss?"

"Something like that. I'll explain tonight."

"Isn't you mother preparing the pork?" he asked, a hint of reservation creeping into his tone.

"I'll check with her," I said knowing full-well she would gladly postpone the dinner.

He tried to hide his happiness.

*****

It's funny how some events in our lives, no matter how small or seemingly insignificant at the time, stay with us over the years, while some *big* events fade or even disappear. That dinner with Dima was one of the former.

He picked me up at 7 pm as we had agreed. I was fretting that he'd show up in his huge transport truck, afraid to look foolish in a village where I knew nearly everyone.

"I don't care if he shows up in a garbage truck," Mama said as she helped me dress. "He's a good man and a good *catch*." I saw her expression in the mirror and cringed.

"I'm not going fishing!" I protested, my heart only half in my words. "This is just a dinner with an old friend."

She watched me struggle to tame one tiny wave of hair that refused to sit as it should. "If you say so," she answered with that incredibly dismissive tone mothers seem to develop as a matter of course.

When Dima arrived I was still tinkering with my outfit, so Mama answered his knock.

"Mrs. Levchenko!" he said, surprised to see her instead of me. He held a big bouquet and wore a blue suit that looked to be either very new or very seldom used.

"Don't worry, Dima, Nina will appear sooner or later!" Mama said, loud enough to ensure I'd overhear her. "She's been fussing with her clothes and hair for the last hour, at least. Come in."

"I have not!" I yelled from the bedroom, where I continued to do exactly that.

I strained to hear the conversation in the adjoining room until I finally decided that any further changes would accomplish little if anything, and with a deep breath marched out into the living room.

Dima sat at the kitchen table, his flowers balanced precariously in a glass jar that was much too small for the size of the bouquet, while Mama stood at the stove, a pot of water just beginning to heat up. Dima looked as nervous as I felt.

"Nina!" he said, jumping up as if shocked. "You look... wonderful!" The expression on his face said more than his words. I knew I looked better than usual (I should have, after all that effort), but with his wide eyes I could almost believe *wonderful* was possible.

We chatted politely, the three of us, and shared a pot of tea, before I excused Dima and me as soon as good manners would allow. I felt the slightest twinge of guilt leaving Mama all alone in her little hut, but I'd spent many a night talking with her since my return; this was something special. Of course, I didn't have to try too hard to convince her. She seemed as eager for us to leave as I was.

To my great relief, neither Dima's transport nor a garbage truck was parked on the road in front of the hut. In fact, in the fading twilight I thought it looked quite fashionable, even on the newer side.

"What a nice auto!" I said, hoping to motivate him to reveal how he'd acquired the large green sedan.

"It's not new," he said, softly. "But it's in quite good condition."

I agreed enthusiastically, and for my enthusiasm learned that he'd borrowed it from one of his clients, leaving his transport as collateral. I was impressed. I didn't think anything could come between Dima and his truck. Maybe I'd underestimated the man...

There were few restaurants of any description in our village, and fewer still that could be described as first-class. Probably none. So I was more than curious where he would take me. When we whizzed straight through town and onto the roadway east, I tried hard to suppress my curiosity, failing miserably.

"Are we going to Haisyn?" I asked after counting to ten, or at least nine. Haisyn was the biggest town in our part of the oblast, a virtual metropolis compared to our village.

"Could be," he said with a sly smile reminiscent of the Mona Lisa.

I attempted several non-dining conversations but found my mind constantly drifting back to the location of our first-ever night out. (If it isn't obvious by now, I hate secrets. The very idea of keeping information from someone – in particular from me – is anathema. I'm going to find out eventually anyway, so what's the point?) By the time we passed through Haisyn and continued east, I was squirming in my seat.

"Have you eaten at this restaurant before?" I finally asked, my lower lip scraped raw from where I'd been biting it to keep from any further restaurant questions.

"I haven't." His laconic responses, which once I'd found endearing, now seemed tortuous. I was on the verge of a breakdown.

And then he pulled off the main road onto a small dirt side road. I looked over at him, expecting an explanation, but received studious ignorance instead. By now my mind was whirling. *My god, where is he taking me? I mean, he's very cute, and seems like a good person, but what do I really know about him? What if he's not what he appears? What if…?* Thankfully, just then he pulled into a driveway so overgrown with shrubbery that it seemed for a second as if he'd driven straight into the woods. My heart nearly jumped from my mouth before I saw the elegant two-story white structure, with a parking lot crowded with expensive-looking cars.

"Here we are!" he announced grandly. "Suitable?" He looked over at me with that infuriating little smirk.

"It looks… fine," I muttered, my pulse slowly returning to normal.

Inside the білий голуб, for that was its name according to the gorgeous hand-painted sign hanging above the entrance, a well-dressed and surprisingly sophisticated looking clientele ate at two dozen small tables elegantly topped by starched white tablecloths. Fine china and crystal were illuminated by flickering candlelight. I was literally shocked: *this* restaurant in rural Ukraine?

"Where *are* we?" I whispered to Dima as we waited to be seated.

"I think it's called Babanka. At least that's what I've been told," he whispered back to me.

"But... how... I've never even heard of this place." Not that I was someone who frequented such spots, or any other, for that matter, but working in the library I spoke with dozens if not hundreds of people each day – surely one of them would have mentioned such a magnificent restaurant less than two hours from our village.

Dima leaned closer, his lips nearly brushing my earlobe. "It's a special place, for Party executives," he said so softly I could barely hear him.

"How did you ever get a reservation?" I must've spoken a bit too loud, for a he winced and motioned for me to lower my voice.

"Friends of friends," he explained. "It wasn't easy." I didn't know if he was trying to impress me or just telling the simple truth. As I glanced around, I recognized many people who would've fit in perfectly at any of the Pavlyuks' private parties. I felt conspicuous by my station in life, imaging that all the patrons who *belonged* there were looking at me and judging. Or at least all the women. From the leering looks and smiles coming from several of the men, however, they were not at all concerned by our clothes or financial standing. I had a sense of how an appetizer must feel before dinner.

Feigning a calmness I didn't feel, I followed our greeter to a table tucked off in the corner of the room. To some it probably would have been considered a snub to have been banished to a distant locale, but to me it was a great relief. Dima did not seem concerned about anything but me, which eased my embarrassment considerably. The look of pride in his eyes made me feel like the most beautiful woman in the room.

"Dima, this must be impossibly expensive," I told him to let him know that I understood full well that this was not just another night on the town.

"It's worth it," he answered, his look unwavering.

It took a while, but eventually we got over our unease and enjoyed a wonderful dinner. The service was impeccable and the food as good as I've ever eaten. It really must have cost a fortune!

We talked about our recent pasts briefly, neither of us intent on looking backwards for long. Then we moved on to our hopes and dreams for the future, a topic that concerned us both far more. I spoke of my plans to move up within the ranks of regional librarians until I had a library of my own, and perhaps eventually curate a large collection such as that in the library where I then worked. Dima wanted to expand his transportation business into a national enterprise, and eventually perhaps even to neighboring countries.

"You have big dreams," I said, envious of his ambition.

"I do. And not just in my work." He blushed.

"I have a feeling you're going to have a great deal of success."

"I hope so. But business success isn't everything. You can't build a big house on a weak foundation." I nodded, hoping he'd explain further.

He started talking about twelve-wheeler trucks and the need for a good dispatcher. I nodded again, hoping he wouldn't ask any relevant questions. I was interested, but my interests were more personal. Eventually he got the hint.

"I'm probably boring you to tears!" he said after I failed to fully stifle a yawn.

"No, of course not!" I lied, pinching the inside of my arm to keep my eyes open. "You've accomplished so much in the past few years!"

It was clear he was proud of his accomplishments, and prouder still that I recognized them. The time flew by, until we found ourselves sipping tea with our desserts in a half-empty room.

"What time is it?" I asked when I noticed all the empty tables.

"Not late."

"I have to work tomorrow."

"So do I. But tomorrow is too far off to worry about. All I want right now is to enjoy my time with you."

I don't know if it was the wine or his words, but my head spun. We finished the meal quickly, he paid – shielding the cost from me, and made our way outside to his parked sedan. By this time I was floating on air and his smile spread from ear to ear. I took his hand as we walked in silence to the car; he held on tightly until he had to let go to open my door.

He hesitated for an instant, and I braced for whatever came next. But his courage seemed to lag and eventually I climbed inside without comment.

It seemed we both were waiting for the other to begin a conversation, and the longer we waited the more uncomfortable our silence became. After several minutes he tuned in a music program on the radio to disguise our awkwardness.

"Good song!" I said enthusiastically, happy for any reason to break the unnatural stillness.

"Yeh, one of my favorites."

More silence. At first I assumed he was as nervous as I was. But then, as time went by, I began to worry that perhaps I'd said, or done, something to offend him. My mind began to spin out of control, formulating possible offenses that seem ridiculous in retrospect. Then, however, they seemed very real, painfully real. I didn't know what to say, how to broach the subject. So we listened to the radio and drove through the night in silence.

By the time we arrived back at Mama's house, I was a nervous wreck. I'd formulated and discarded a half-dozen apologies, for what I wasn't certain.

"Well, here we are," Dima said as he turned off the motor.

"It didn't seem as far coming back," I ventured, hoping to stimulate any discussion, no matter how insipid.

"It's always like that. Places always seem further until you've been there once."

I found my head nodding. "Yes, yes it does."

"So... You have work tomorrow?" he managed to ask after a long pause.

"I do. But it's not so bad. The people are nice enough." We'd already discussed the library over dinner. More seemed too much. "How about you? When are you on your way again?"

"Tomorrow, I'm afraid. Actually, I should've left today, but I think I can make up the time."

"Oh? Where are you going?" I thought he'd already told me, but it was the best I could do given the circumstances.

"Cherkasy, via Smila. Not so far. Pretty good roads." He sounded as lost as I felt.

I decided to push my luck. "Any plans to come back this way?"

His head snapped around in my direction. "We oftentimes get deliveries in this oblast. Every month or two at least."

"Oh? Maybe next time I could cook something..."

"Next time?!" It was hard to tell, sitting there in the dark, whether he was excited or skeptical. He changed direction immediately. "Are you a good cook?"

"I think so. It's not as though I cook a lot of fancy dishes, but if you like simple Ukrainian meals..."

"I *love* Ukrainian food!" he exploded. "There's nothing like good varenyky, after a steaming bowl of borsch!"

"Cabbage, minced meat, or cherry?"

"All of them!" I could feel the tension dissolve.

"Well, if you let me know when you're coming, I can whip up some of each, and maybe some mushroom and onion too."

"I will call as soon as I have my schedule!"

We sat there smiling at each other like foolish teenagers until the silence seeped into our bones and the awkward uncertainty returned.

"I guess I'd better get inside," I finally said, more to say something than because I really wanted to go.

"I... really enjoyed tonight," he stammered. In the gloom I couldn't tell for sure, but I was nearly certain he was blushing again.

"So did I. It's been a long time since I've had such a pleasant night."

"It has?"

"A *long* time."

Our faces were no more than a half-meter apart, so when the impulse to kiss him overwhelmed me it took just an instant to bring my lips to his. Even then I wasn't sure if he'd laugh, cry, or recoil in surprise. After an instant of shock, he slid across the seat to where I sat and continued what I'd started, but with a great deal more energy and emotion than I'd dreamt. My heart was pounding, but in a good way.

"О боже мій!" I managed to gasp when we finally separated. "Where did *that* come from?"

He smiled, not quite as bashfully as earlier. "I wasn't sure you wanted that kind of attention. You'd been... pretty quiet."

"You can give me *that* kind of attention any time."

His eyebrows shot up. "How about now?"

It was nearly an hour later when I finally pulled myself from his borrowed car and stumbled into our house. Not surprisingly, Mama was sitting in the kitchen, nursing a cup of black tea.

"I was about to go out there and see if you needed help," she said with just a hint of a grin.

"No, no need. But thank you for the thought."

"I take it your dinner went well?"

I looked to the stove. "Do you have any more tea?"

"Oh, so is this going to be a long story then?"

"It might be..."

It was. I rehashed the entire meal as well as the ride there and back. Two cups of tea worth. I probably would have gone on, except Mama began to yawn.

"Are you ready for bed already?" I asked, my energy rekindled in the retelling.

"I'm well past my bedtime. We can talk more tomorrow." She pushed herself painfully to her feet and kissed me on top of my head. "I'm happy for you."

I gave her a big hug and helped her hobble to her bed. I should've been tired as well, but I knew I wouldn't be able to sleep for hours to come. So I brewed another pot of tea.

Chapter 14

Time is an unpredictable commodity, moving much too fast one minute and much too slow the next. That was my sense of things for the next few months as Dima and I tried to carry on a budding long-distance relationship with each of us heavily involved in our jobs and other responsibilities. I saw him two or three times a month on average, enough to keep the romantic fires burning but not enough to fan them out of control. I think we both needed a relationship like that, for reasons as different as our personalities. I needed time to adjust to a new man in my life after swearing I'd never consider it again, as well as time to help Mama run the house and farm. Dima barely had time to handle all the complexities of an expanding business in a rapidly-changing society, let alone devote the hours necessary to encourage a full-fledged romance. But still, gradually, I found myself thinking of the two of us as an *us*, and wondering what if anything would come next.

I hadn't seen or heard from Comrade Kostyshyn in months, and truth be told I'd come to think of him as a distant shadow unworthy of my concern. Miss Nazarenko was making noises as if she were planning to retire, but none of us had been given any hint when – or if – it might occur. Mama was getting weaker, her health a major concern for me and my sisters. Yerva became pregnant, and even though she studiously ignored Mama's hints that she should marry, her boyfriend had become a live-in companion.

In short, life had slipped into a normal routine, busy but unremarkable. I should've known the equilibrium wouldn't last. It never did. But I was blissfully unaware of the turn my life would take in the first months of that winter, nearly thirty years ago.

I was at work, in the Library, when one of our staff members came to me with a look of worried consternation.

"Mrs. Vann, there is someone here to see you," she said, her voice guarded.

"Oh, who is it?" I saw dozens of people every day and so wasn't particularly surprised that someone was asking for me.

"I... it's no one I know. But he says he knows you." There was something about her tone and expression that gave me pause, but I decided to look for myself.

I think I expected to see Comrade Kostyshyn, or perhaps even Dima. The last person I expected to see was Bogdan, my ex-husband. He stood just inside the front door to the building, his head bowed. He wore shabby pants and a stained and patched work shirt beneath a jacket far too lightweight for the nippy nighttime temperatures we were already experiencing. His hair was long and filthy, his beard utterly unkempt. He looked twenty years older than when I'd last seen him.

My breath caught in my chest.

"Bogdan! What are you doing here?" My words were less than welcoming, but I was so taken aback I could only say what I was thinking.

He looked up at me, his eyes haunted like those of a trapped animal.

"I heard you were working here," he said, his words slow and methodical, but not – as far as I could tell – drunken.

"I am. I do," I babbled. "But..." I was baffled.

He nodded. "I know. It's taken me a long time, but I've finally been able to face what I was and what I did. I'm sorry. You didn't deserve what I did to you." He took a deep breath. I heard the wheeze in his chest. "The kids too." His voice was raspy, deeper than I'd remembered. "I was a drunk. A bad drunk. I'm sorry." He looked back down at his hands, wringing them unconsciously.

"Do you need... money?" I asked, my mind only just beginning to think rationally.

He held up a hand. "No! Nothing. I didn't come to ask for anything. Except, maybe, your forgiveness. What I did to you was…" He searched for words. "…bad."

I was struck dumb. I didn't know what to say, or what to feel. It was as if a ghost had come to me from the grave.

"Where are you living?" was the best I could do.

He shrugged. "Around."

"Do you have a job?"

"I do odds jobs now and then. More during the growing season."

Just then the staffer who'd told me of Bogdan's arrival came into the reception area. "Is everything okay, Mrs. Vann?" she asked. I could see she was worried about me.

I realized for the first time we were playing out our family tragedy in a public space.

"Yes, thank you, Vika. I'll be with you shortly."

She stared at Bogdan, then at me, before leaving us.

"I don't want to cause you any trouble…" he began.

"No, no, it's not that. She's just… concerned."

What might have been a smile cracked the dirt that caked his cheeks. "Can't really blame her. I'd probably scare myself if I had a mirror."

I smiled in spite of myself.

"What are your plans?" I found myself asking, not so much because I really wanted to know as because I had nothing else to ask.

"Plans?" He looked bewildered. "No plans, really. I might move up to Kyiv…" He trailed off.

"Oh? Well, that might be good."

He nodded. "Yes, well, I'm glad to see you doing well. Say hi to the kids." He gave a limp wave in my direction and turned to leave. At the doorway he stopped. "I really am sorry," he said. "For everything."

"Thank you. And good luck to you." I meant it. As much as he'd hurt me, as much as he'd hurt our family, I couldn't kick him when he was down. I've always believed in forgiveness and redemption. Who better to practice on?

I watched him shuffle away through the glass front door, wondering if what had just happened was real or some sort of vision. I was still wondering as I returned to work.

*****

"He came to the Library?!" Mama said when I told her about Bogdan's visit.

"I know. I was amazed too."

"I'm not sure if I'm amazed or horrified. How can you ever trust that man?"

Her question made me pause. *Did* I trust him? *Could* I? Of course, if he moved to Kyiv as he'd threatened, I most likely would never see him again. But if he found me, could he find the kids as well? "I don't know that I can," I finally answered. "But there's not much I can do about it. He served his time, and now he's a free man."

"Well I don't like it. Without Viktor or the Pavlyuks to protect you, I worry."

I tried to put up a brave front. "Don't worry, Mama. First of all, he's moving north."

"Or so he said."

"Or so he said. And second, I'm a big girl now. I know a lot of people here in the village."

"Not that you can always count on them in time of need." I could tell from her voice that she was thinking back to Papa's death. She'd never forgotten, nor forgiven.

"I don't know. Some of the people would help out if I needed it, I'm pretty sure."

"Well I'm not." Her pout almost made me smile.

"Don't worry so much. For all I know, he's a changed man."

Her grunt was not a sign of agreement.

"Perhaps you should talk to Comrade Kostyshyn," she suggested after a moment's consideration. "He could alert the Militsiya."

"No!" I said, my vehemence startling my mother. "I do not want to ask the Comrade for anything."

Mama stared at me. "Did you have a problem with him?"

I didn't want to worry her any more than I already had, but I didn't want to pretend everything was just fine between us either. "I don't like the man," I said. "He's only interested in himself."

"He has powerful friends in this oblast. They might be able to help."

"I don't want to ever owe Comrade K. anything."

Mama seemed to understand. "Ah. Well then, I guess we'll just hope for the best." She took a sip of tea. "What do you hear from Dima?"

Even as I told her, my mind strayed back to the Comrade's actions in the Library. I prayed I would never need to go to him for a favor.

*****

The fact was, during that time I had very conflicting feelings toward Dima. On the one hand, I very much enjoyed the time we spent together. He was a wonderful, simple man who treated me like a princess. He was handsome enough, quite successful in his own way, and after an initial shyness he opened up like a flower after the rain. But... it had been only a short time since Viktor's death. I still thought of him often, and when I did I felt as if I were... cheating on Dima. I know he wanted to be part of my life, and I wished the same, but I couldn't give him one hundred per cent of my attention. I tried. God knows I tried.

But vivid memories of Viktor lingered for quite some time. It wasn't fair to Dima.

And then too, I worried about him. With Comrade Kostyshyn on the one side, and Bogdan on the other, I didn't think it was fair to drag my dear sweet Dima into my crazy world. Perhaps I was being overly cautious. Perhaps Mama's concerns leached into my own. Whatever the case, Dima and I continued to see each other every two or three weeks but our relationship could only proceed so far before I backed away, leaving him frustrated and confused. Not that we didn't have our moments...

I remember one night in particular when we'd gone to see a local musical group play at a bar in Uman. We'd had a wonderful time, enjoying a tasty dinner, sipping some vodka, listening to a modern version of traditional Ukrainian folk music. We danced, laughed, and for a short time forgot all the worries of work and everyday life that tended to build up whenever we weren't together.

Not long after midnight Dima drove me home, or rather back to our village to the inn where he'd rented a room for the days he spent visiting me.

I hadn't been paying too much attention to his route, having imbibed my share of vodka at the bar. My eyes were heavy and I was enjoying the music blaring from his car radio. When I did realize we weren't headed to Mama's, I suddenly awoke from my warm, relaxed stupor.

"Where are we going?" I asked, not so much worried as confused.

"To my room," Dima said simply.

For a moment I wondered if we'd discussed the detour, but eventually concluded that we had not.

"Why?"

"It's too late to take you to your mother's house," he said. "We'd only wake her up."

I almost laughed aloud. Coming from anyone other than Dima I would've thought it was a come-on, but Dima rarely if ever tried typical male trickery.

"Oh? Won't it be crowded, the two of us in one little room?" I couldn't refrain from teasing him.

"I don't think so. It's a good-sized room."

I debated whether to argue the point, but whether it was my inebriated condition or the simple needs of a woman who hadn't been with a man for quite some time, I leaned back in the seat and closed my eyes. When next I opened them we were pulling into the parking space at his building.

"We're home," he announced. With some effort I forced my eyes open and we made our way up the outside stairs to his second floor room, a small but tidy space of perhaps 15 square meters. Of course he only stayed in that room when he was visiting me, but he'd become such a regular visitor that he reserved the room for his next visit at the conclusion of the current one. I'd never been inside, so I felt a bit like an outsider as I came into his personal space. I tried not to seem like I was snooping, but I *was* curious.

"Make yourself at home," he said before returning to the hallway, I assumed to use the toilet.

If Mama's house was tiny, Dima's room was less than half its size. A single bed, looking sad and lonely to my bleary eyes, sat in the exact middle of the room, a clean but worn blue bedspread pulled up neatly over a flat, square pillow. A small table with two straight-backed chairs huddled in front of the only windows, just beside a sink, small fridge and hotplate. The linoleum in the kitchenette was torn and yellowed, with one corner curled up like a snarled lip. The air smelled musty, as if a smoker had once spent time there. It was not a particularly *homey* space.

"So, what do you think?" Dima asked as he returned from the hall. "Not too bad, huh?"

"Cozy," I said. Anything else would be a lie or unflattering.

He must have heard the lack of enthusiasm in my voice. "It's not the Summer Palace, but for a few days every now and then, it's okay."

I nodded. We both looked around aimlessly, the tension of a first romantic encounter weighing on each of us. The quiet of the night seemed oppressive.

"I need to use the bathroom," I finally offered.

He seemed delighted to have a reason to speak. "Out in the hall. Second door on the left. The lock in the handle doesn't work too well – better to use the throw-bolt."

The hallway was, thankfully, empty. The hardwood floors warped precariously, requiring considerable concentration for someone of my condition to navigate them. I'm sure I looked quite the drunkard as I weaved my way to the bathroom, one hand constantly touching the wall to keep me upright. When I eventually made my way to the door marked simply 'Toilet', and double-checked the throw-bolt to ensure my privacy, I stood at the small, stained porcelain sink and looked at myself in what remained of a mirror. Between the dim, yellowish electric light and the partially de-silvered mirror, I looked even worse than my inebriation would have dictated. Drooping eyelids, wind-blown hair, lipstick smeared – I suddenly felt ill-prepared for what I expected – hoped? – to occur in Dima's little room.

After I'd done my business, I splashed some water on my face, used my hand to smooth down the fly-away hair, and traced my lips with a piece of toilet paper to wipe off the traces of cosmetics abused. A deep breath, a reassuring smile, and I headed back to Dima's room. The return voyage was even more problematic than the last, as I now had to deal with my pounding heart as well as my drunkenness. I say *drunkenness*, and it's true enough that my limbs didn't respond to mental commands as well as I might hope. But

my mind was reasonably clear. Clear enough that I knew
full-well what I was inviting by sharing his narrow bed.
Knew, and welcomed, or at least accepted. A woman has
needs.

When I stepped through the door I thought for just a
second I'd returned to the wrong room. In the short time I'd
been gone Dima had lit several candles in small glass bowls,
found a radio station with gentle, romantic music, and had
secreted himself under the covers of his bed, just his head
and sleeveless white t-shirt still visible above the blue
bedspread.

"Any problems finding the bathroom?" he asked, a note
of nervous excitement shaking his voice.

"No, none." I looked around the room evaluatively.
"Did I miss room service?"

I expected a laugh, or at least a groan. Instead Dima's
eyes grew large and round. "Did you want something? I can
run downstairs…"

"Don't you move!" I ordered, surprising both of us.

I suppose I could've pled drunkenness, but the truth is I
felt blood rush to my female parts and I wanted nothing
more than to jump into bed and ravage my dear Dima.
Instead, I forced myself to slowly, seductively, remove each
piece of clothing with a teasing smile that immediately
brought the desired reaction.

"Come to bed," he pleaded, his voice unnaturally high.

"In a minute," I said, waving my bra as I pumped my
hips, my back facing him.

"Now - come now!" he ordered, his voice scarcely more
than a strangled gasp.

"Almost done…" I began, but before I could finish he
threw off the covers, jumped up and literally threw me back
on the bed. I saw at a glance that he was fully prepared for
what would come next. As was I.

The rest is a blur of sensation. He tore my panties from my hips and threw them impatiently across the floor. I pulled him down on top of me as his hands slid across by belly and his tongue filled my mouth. I didn't think, didn't worry. I surrendered myself completely to his passion; as his hands grabbed and kneaded, his breath roared ferociously in my ears.

And then he entered me and I cried out, in pleasure and release, the surge of sensation nearly overwhelming me. I had hoped to rouse a bit of animal in Dima; I unleashed a lion. We moved together as if one, our cries and whispers filling the tiny room as a metallic hammering from somewhere nearby provided rhythmic support for our frenzied coupling.

A tidal wave of blood surged from my hips to my brain as his stomach pounded mine, faster, and faster, until I could no longer withhold the explosion building within me. My scream intertwined with his, and in a bucking spasm of utter release we collapsed in a heap under his twisted blue spread.

I listened to our gasping breaths and pounding hearts, numb, or should I say overwhelmed, to anything and everything beyond that bed. I felt his hand sweep gently across my drenched hair as he nuzzled my earlobe.

"Wow," he whispered.

I smiled. "A very big wow."

I rolled off to one side and we held each other, slowly settling back into the reality of the moment. The pulsing of blood, the caressing warmth: I could have lain there forever.

"Did you...?" he began, but I put my finger to his lips. There was no need for talk.

I found a nesting spot in the crook of his arm and held him close. The last thing I remembered was my own satisfied breaths, the heat of his skin against mine, a glow that enveloped and overpowered me.

*****

I expected awkward, even embarrassed interaction the next morning, so when I awoke very early to a beaming, confident Dima, I was somewhat taken aback.

"How'd you sleep?" he asked, kissing me before I could fully open my eyes.

"Wonderfully," I answered, stretching luxuriously. "You?"

"Great! Terrific!" He was like a little boy on Christmas day.

"You seem to have a lot of energy for so early in the morning."

"I feel like I could climb a mountain!" he crowed.

"Be a shame to waste all that energy."

A look of confusion warped to a sly grin. "It would, wouldn't it?"

It didn't go to waste.

Chapter 15

For quite some time my life fell into a routine of normalcy that brought much-needed stability and peace to a world that had seen precious little of each for far too long. Oh, I can't say I wouldn't have enjoyed visiting with Dima more than the once or twice a month his work schedule permitted, but each of us seemed to understand full-well that our intermittent visits were the best we could hope for given the competing demands on both our lives. He had his business and family up north; I had my job at the Library and both Mama and my newest niece to look after.

Mama had begun to weaken years earlier, but only after the trauma of Bogdan's attack against me did the pace quicken. Her hip, which she'd injured working the fields before I'd even been born, became so arthritic she could barely walk even with the help of a cane. Then her memory began to waver, names and events melting into an indistinguishable mash that frustrated and embarrassed her. By the time Dima and I got together, Mama was nearing 80 and her mind played the kinds of tricks that required constant supervision. Yerva, Julija, and I took turns spending time with her, with Yerva taking on the largest part of the burden. She'd bring my little niece, Yana, to our hut and babysit both the baby and Mama during the week. I'd take over when I returned from work, and Julija would spend most weekends with her. It wasn't a perfect system, by any means, but we all owed Mama much more than we could ever repay her and so complaints were few.

With Yerva committed to spending so much time with Mama, I volunteered to watch Yana whenever my sister wanted a break. In practice that meant one or two nights a week and an occasional weekend day. For me it wasn't problematic at all – I missed the sounds and smells of a little one, and even the repeated changings and occasional stubborn outbursts didn't diminish the warm, satisfied feeling I got whenever we were together. Plus, I remembered very well how much I'd appreciated the short *vacations* from mothering I'd enjoyed back when Kateryna and Sasha were little, vacations usually facilitated by Yerva and Mama.

In many ways, that was one of the happiest, calmest times of my life. Routine may breed contempt and boredom in the young, but for me, rapidly approaching 50, it brought only a sense of inner peace I'd never known in my younger days. Of course it saddened me to see Mama slowly moving toward the end of her time with us, but her constant good nature and indomitable spirit helped make those days more joyous than sad.

*****

It was in the springtime, early May, when Mama died. I'd gotten up to prepare for work as I did every morning, and as soon as the tea was hot and the porridge steaming I went to her bed to awaken her. I don't know how I knew, but before I even touched her I sensed she was gone. She looked so peaceful curled up under her covers, her features fully relaxed for the first time I could remember, that I almost wanted to just leave her there for all eternity. But reality rarely permits such whimsy, and so three days later we all found ourselves in the village cemetery, standing beneath a perfectly blue sky with a gentle breeze teasing the maples and oaks that surrounded a few dozen simple gravestones dating back hundreds of years. All of us except my two kids. Kateryna was pregnant again and had been confined to bed for the final three months of her pregnancy, while Sasha was in Germany for a big game with his football club. I missed them, but neither life nor death wait for any man. The local Orthodox priest said words of comfort and acceptance, and a small group of friends and family laid her to her final rest.

We had planned a simple meal after the ceremony at our – now my – house and so were directing the attendees to the available vehicles when my eldest sister, Julija, took my arm and turned me toward a figure standing in the shadows of one of the bigger trees some fifty meters from Mama's grave. I had to squint to make out the ragged figure, but even before my mind could decide who I was seeing, my heart skipped a beat.

"It's your ex-husband, isn't it?" Dima asked, having sidled up next to me when he saw my blank stare.

"I... I think so."

"Let me go talk to him," he said, and before I could protest or agree he was striding toward our uninvited guest. That was something I'd never expected from Dima until we'd been together for a time – his quiet, powerful protectiveness. He wasn't a big man, far from it. And his personality was more pussycat than wildcat. But he never shied away from putting himself between any potential problem and me. It's probably one of the main reasons I loved him.

I watched nervously as Dima approached Bogdan, a familiar, uncomfortable flutter aloose in my gut.

"Don't worry, I'm sure he won't make trouble," Julija soothed.

I wasn't so sure.

Dima stopped about two meters from my ex-husband, from where they had a quiet, non-confrontational discussion that lasted all of a minute.

"What do you think?" I asked Julija, the butterflies in my stomach flitting to and fro.

"Hard to say. But it doesn't look bad, if that's what you mean."

It was. Despite our meeting a few months earlier, I still wasn't convinced that Bogdan had no intentions of getting back at me for sending him to jail. As he saw it. I unconsciously took my big sister's hand as Dima walked slowly back toward where we stood.

"So? What's he doing here?" I asked before he'd gotten close enough to talk.

Dima waited until he didn't need to yell. "He came to pay his respects to the grandmother of his children," he said without emotion. "Doesn't seem drunk."

That was a relief. As difficult as it might have been to deal with him when he was sober, it was near impossible to do so when he'd been drinking. It was like arguing with a stone wall, an angry, nasty stone wall.

"Should I talk to him?" I asked, feeling like a lost little girl.

"Can't really hurt," Julija said.

"That's up to you," Dima added. "But he doesn't seem to be here to cause trouble."

I took a deep breath and started in his direction.

"Want me to come with you?" Dima offered.

"No, thank you, though. I think I can handle this." In reality, I wasn't sure, but I needed to try.

I tried to look nonchalant as I walked toward Bogdan, but it wasn't easy feeling his eyes upon me. I studiously watched where I placed my feet, both to make sure I didn't stumble and to avoid his intense gaze. It was a little like being onstage, like when I'd played a talking sheep in a grammar school play. I *was* playing a part. Was he?

By the time I'd martialed enough courage to lift my eyes, I was just a few short steps away from where he stood. His hair was still long and ill-combed, but looked a little cleaner than the last time I'd seen him. His beard was shorter, his hair a bit more gray than I remembered. But it was his eyes that caught my full attention. He stared at me with a longing, a hunger, not in a sexual way but almost as if begging for my forgiveness, or maybe just forbearance.

"Bogdan," I said, struggling to conceal the quiver I felt inside. "I thought you were in Kyiv."

"I... didn't make it," he began. "Look, I don't want to cause any trouble, I just wanted to pay my respects." His voice was weak and raspy, as if he'd been sick.

"I'm sure Mama would appreciate that," I said, though in fact I thought it unlikely.

"Are you okay?"

I was caught off-guard. I had to think for a second. "Me? Yes, I suppose I am. Mama had been getting weaker for quite some time, so it didn't come as a surprise."

"But it's hard anyway."

"It is. Very hard."

He nodded thoughtfully. "Well, I'll just wait over here until you're all done, and then I'll pay my respects."

I don't know why the words came to my lips, but before I could stop myself I said, "Oh, you needn't wait. Come. You can say goodbye now."

He looked at me quizzically, as if unsure whether I was serious or luring him into some kind of trap.

"Come!" I encouraged, finally reaching out and taking his arm to lead him back toward the grave site.

He didn't say a word as we walked, but I could feel him tremble like some frightened animal as we approached the other mourners. I saw Julija and Yerva look at me with questioning eyes; Dima seemed perfectly at ease.

Bogdan nodded anxiously to everyone he knew; no one said a word. It was as if we'd all been frozen in time, unable to move forward or back until the spell that held us was broken. We all watched as he shuffled to the gaping hole, black earth piled by its side, and fell roughly to his knees. He toppled to his side like a marionette with its strings cut; I took a step as if to go help him, but Dima laid his hand on my arm.

"Let him do it," he whispered.

All eyes rested on Bogdan as he struggled to right himself. Slowly, painfully, he pushed himself back up to his knees, bowed his head and began to pray. It hadn't been long, less than five minutes surely, when he began to tremble. Yerva looked to me, concerned, and I looked to Dima.

"Give him a second," Dima said.

It wasn't much more than that when the trembling increased to violent spasms, and my ex-husband collapsed on the ground, unconscious. I screamed and ran to where he lay motionless, the rest of our small party close on my heels.

"Get some help!" I yelled as I rolled him over and saw the telltale drooping of the left side of his face.

Someone ran for a phone and called the local hospital. I knelt beside him and placed his head in my lap while Dima covered him with his black mourning coat. The ambulance arrived after several long minutes and the two-member crew loaded him onto a stretcher and into the rusting white vehicle, an oxygen mask covering his pale face.

"Should we go with you?" I asked the attendants. I didn't realize it at the time, but tears were streaming down my face.

"Are you family?" one of the emergency personnel asked.

"I was married to him, a long time ago."

The man shrugged. "Up to you, but it's pretty crowded in there. I think it might be better if you met us at the hospital." To my look of concern he added, "Don't worry — we'll take good care of him."

Dima put his arm around my shoulders. "Come. We'll meet them there." Reluctantly, I nodded and let him lead me away.

It was several hours later, hours spent sitting in the small, crowded emergency room, when a lady doctor finally came out with news.

"I understand you're his ex-spouse," she began, glancing down at a clipboard.

"Yes, that's right."

"Does he have any immediate family?"

"Not here. We do have two children, and he might still have family back in his home village…"

"They should be notified." She looked up at me. "He's suffered a stroke, a blockage of the blood supply to his brain. It's impossible to tell at this stage, but he may suffer from permanent paralysis on his left side."

I'd tried to prepare myself for just such a diagnosis, but it still hit me hard.

"What can we do?" I asked, on the verge of tears once again.

"There are rehabilitation facilities," the doctor began, "but… they are overcrowded and understaffed. Do you think any of his family members could look after him?"

I tried to think. The kids were young, with their whole lives ahead of them. They didn't need that burden. As for his family, I'd have to check. We hadn't been in contact with any of them for many years.

"We'll keep him here for another week or two," the doctor went on as if reading my thoughts. "You don't really need to make up your minds until then."

I thanked her and promised to let the hospital know what the family determined.

"It's so sad," I said as Dima drove me back home late that night. A light rain had begun to fall in the deepening twilight.

"It's sad to see anyone in that condition."

I glanced over at him, wondering whether he was just saying what he thought I wanted to hear or whether he truly agreed with me.

"I'll try to contact his family. See if any of them will agree to take care of him while he recuperates."

"*If* he recuperates."

"Yes, *if* he recuperates," I said, understanding his unspoken message. From what the doctor told us, Bogdan might recover completely or might linger in his current condition indefinitely.

"What if the family says no?" Dima said. "What if none of them will take him?" It was a question that had been torturing me.

"I don't know. I suppose we'll have to find out what the government can do for him…"

"Have you ever been in one of those facilities?" The undercurrent of the question made me wince.

I hadn't, and I told him so.

"It's not a pretty picture. My uncle had to go to one when we couldn't take care of him anymore. Rows of beds in big open rooms with people groaning and crying out in pain and frustration; the smell of urine, and worse; a handful of nurses to care for dozens of patients. It'll give you nightmares, I can tell you."

I shuddered. "Then I hope his family will take him in." But even then I knew they'd never forgiven him for marrying me and *running off* to our village. The entire time we were married we'd never gone to visit his people, nor had they ever come to visit us.

"I won't let the kids do it," I said, my thoughts working their way to my lips unbidden.

"No, I suppose not."

"We'll just have to see."

"Time will tell."

*****

Part of me wanted to wash my hands of the whole affair. After all, he was my *ex*-husband, and hadn't been much of a partner even when we were together. Still, I couldn't forget the few good years we had at the beginning. Despite promising myself I wouldn't get involved, I felt compelled to visit him every few days to see how he was doing and what kind of treatment he was receiving. On both counts, I was pleased. After less than a week Bogdan could sit up on his own and the drooping muscles on the left side of his face seemed to be recovering nicely. The doctor and nurses were pleased.

"All the signs are good," the doctor told me one night when she came in while I was visiting. "I don't know if he'll make a complete recovery, but it looks like we'll be able to release him in less than a week."

I grimaced.

"What?" the doctor asked.

"I still haven't heard back from his family. I haven't been able to reach any of them by phone, and they didn't reply to the letter I sent."

"Well, we do have a recuperation facility in Uman."

I involuntarily made a face.

"Have you been there?" she asked.

"I've heard stories."

"The wards are clean, and the patients receive three meals a day."

"Faint praise."

Her eyebrows arched and fell back. "They do they best they can with what they have."

"I'm sure they do, Doctor. It's just that I would want more than that if it were me."

"There *are* private facilities..."

"But they are costly – am I correct?"

She nodded, her lips pressed tight. "I'm afraid so. Quite costly."

I didn't have an answer for that and I was sure the doctor had other things to do.

"We'll figure something out," I said.

"Good. I'm sure you will."

We looked at each other for a long moment. "How long do you think you will keep him here?" I'm sure my cheeks colored.

"As I said, five, maybe six days. A week at the most."

"Right. Then we have a few days to put something together."

"Please keep me informed."

I promised that I would, having gotten the sense she would do her best to keep Bogdan there as long as was possible. But I knew she didn't have the final word. The clock was clicking.

*****

Two days later I received a message from Bogdan's sister. Their parents had died several years earlier, but she and one brother – though "unable" to care for their brother because of their own responsibilities with jobs and families – were willing to send a small amount of money each month to help nurse Bogdan back to full health, or at least to self-sufficiency. The money would be helpful, of course, but it wasn't anywhere near enough to pay for the care he needed. I called Dima to explain the situation, hoping he'd have an answer I hadn't considered.

"You have to decide how important this is to you," he said, his voice seeming tense, perhaps upset? "The State won't do what you want done. That leaves either private care – which as you know is very expensive – or…"

"Doing it myself."

"I don't see any other choice. But I don't see how you can work at the library and take care of him too. Not sure I understand why you'd want to."

I had to admit, neither did I. I only knew I felt trapped between my past and my future. How could I move forward with that part of my life festering, unfinished? It wasn't until Yerva brought my niece over two nights later that a plan came into focus.

Yerva was complaining about how little money her boyfriend brought home and how she was thinking of looking for a part-time job to help pay the bills.

"We can't keep on like this," she said. "If I have to make another meal from cabbage and potatoes I'm going to scream."

"Why didn't you tell me?" I asked, feeling guilty – as though I'd failed my family obligations.

"You've had enough to deal with. Besides, it's not your problem."

"Maybe not, but I'm your sister. Maybe I could help."

She laughed, a half-hearted attempt that barely reached her lips. "How? Did you suddenly find a pot of money that Mama left buried in the kitchen?"

"No, but..." It was then the idea hit me: Yerva was already taking care of her daughter, was already housebound, and wanted to earn extra money.

"Would you consider taking care of Bogdan – just for a month or two until he begins to regain his strength? It wouldn't be all that much different than taking care of Mama." I didn't know if a month or two would solve the problem, but at least it would be a start.

I suppose I thought she would leap at the opportunity. I overlooked the ill-will that still festered between my family and my ex-.

"Bogdan? You want me to take care of the man who tried to steal your children and almost strangled you?!" Her words stung like a slap across the face.

"It was the vodka, Yerva," I explained as calmly as I could. "You remember how he was before he started drinking so heavily, don't you?"

"You mean when he was cheating on you with the teenager from his field team?"

I felt a small stab of pain. "Before then."

She tried to resist but eventually nodded resignedly. "I remember."

"I think *that* Bogdan is still in there. At least I hope so. Not only for his sake, but for the kids. I'd be good if they had a father again after all these years. And soon, a grandfather."

The face she made was less than agreeable. "He tried to *kill* you," she said, pronouncing each word distinctly as if talking to a child.

"That was a long time ago. He's changed."

"Yeh, now he needs you." She stared as if daring me to contradict her.

I was desperate. I decided to try one last argument. "If not for him, will you do it for me? His sister and brother will be sending enough money to buy some chicken or pork each week..."

"You're serious?"

"Just during the week while I'm at work. What do you say? Please."

She looked very uncomfortable, but I refused to look away. And then she sighed. "All right, fine. But just until he can take care of himself."

I hugged her and kissed her cheeks. "Thank you! Thank you! You are a good sister."

"I'm probably a fool, but at least I'm not alone." A tiny smile cracked her stern countenance.

A fool I might be, but that night I slept better than I had for days.

*****

I didn't want Dima to hear the news from anyone else, but I was terrified to tell him myself. What if he took it the wrong way? What if he decided that I was doing too much for my ex-husband and not enough for us? Terrified or not, I had to tell him. Bogdan would be coming out of the hospital in just two days. There was no time for waffling.

I called him around nine o'clock at night, late enough that I hoped he'd eaten his dinner and was relaxing in front of the television or with a good book.

"Nina!" he said when he heard my voice. The pleasure in his voice whenever I called always brought a smile to my face.

"Dima, I hope I'm not interrupting anything…"

"No, of course not!" he said, but from his tone I could tell he was on his guard. "What's going on?"

"Well, it's about Bogdan," I began, admittedly a bit shaky.

"Did he die?"

For a second I thought he sounded pleased, until I chalked it up to my usual paranoia. "No, no, he's recovering well, in fact. But, you remember our last conversation, about where he'd go once he was released from the hospital?"

"I do."

"Well, I talked to Yerva, and she's agreed to look after him for a month or two, until he gets back on his feet."

"Oh, that's wonderful of her! Was it unexpected?" *Was he relieved?*

"A bit, yes."

"So she'll take care of Bogdan and her little one at the same time – makes sense, I guess. What does her boyfriend think of having your ex- around the apartment?"

I tried to calm my pounding heart. "Well, that's the thing, you see. He'll be staying at Mama's house, with me."

A moment of silence that seemed to last much too long. "Ah. So Yerva takes care of him during the week, and you take nights and weekends."

"It'll only be for a month or two..."

"Until he gets back on his feet. Yes, you said."

"There's no one else, Dima. I can't just let him go to one of the State rehabilitation facilities." I knew I sounded more than a little anxious.

"No, no I suppose not." I could almost hear him turn the idea over in his mind. "Well, if that's the way it has to be, then he's a lucky man. How can I help?"

I was so relieved I almost started bawling. "I don't know. You don't have a spare bed hanging around anywhere, do you?"

He chuckled. "I don't. But my sister's last kid just moved out a few weeks ago. Maybe she can lend his old bed for a month or two."

"That would be very much appreciated." I didn't know what else to say.

"I'll talk to her. Let you know."

There was the pause that so often occurs in a conversation, particularly by phone, after a major piece of information is transmitted, or a decision made, as if anything that follows can't possible compare to what has gone before.

"So, how are you?" he asked.

And I fell apart. Sobbing, laughing, all my hopes and fears and all the confusion that Bogdan's reappearance had generated bubbled up out of me in a non-stop torrent. I rambled, I cajoled, but most of all I made clear how important he was in my life, the one pillar of certainty in my crazy world.

"When will I see you again?" I finished, my need for him laid bare in my heart and mind.

"Well, I don't have a shipment scheduled down there until..." I could almost see him checking his calendar, "...the first part of next month."

"Too long!" I cried. "Can't you come down earlier?"

"I might be able to arrange a long weekend," he teased. "If there's room at the inn."

"There's always room at *my* inn."

"Sounds like it might get crowded."

I couldn't argue the point. "Then I'll get your usual room at the village hotel. Please, come!"

"Is tomorrow too soon?"

"If I could drag you through this phone line, I would."

He chuckled. "Sounds like an emergency. I'll get one of my guys to take my next scheduled load and I'll get down there sometime tomorrow evening. Maybe around six?"

"We can have dinner."

"It's a date."

When I hung up the phone I felt drained, exhausted, but happily so. I lay down and fell asleep, my dreams so sensual I'm sure I was blushing.

Perhaps it would all work out after all.

Chapter 16

Dima volunteered to stay until Bogdan was released from the hospital; I didn't have to ask. His visit had unfolded as perfectly as I could've hoped, and if anything our relationship had grown stronger in the face of what could only be termed uncertainty. He was supportive, loving, and strong. I tried to emulate his example, but I'm afraid I couldn't quite manage the emotional strength required. Truth was, I was a mess. I didn't want anything to interfere with what we'd forged between us, but at the same time I couldn't let Bogdan languish in a State facility. Call me crazy, or as Julija put it: 'you give us women a bad name.'

I tried to examine my motives to determine why I would chance damaging or even losing what I had with Dima for someone who really didn't mean anything to me anymore, someone who'd tried to kill me, and the best I could come up with was "I'd want him to help if it was me who was ill." It made some sense to me, not so much to Julija.

"He's not your problem anymore!" she'd insisted when she learned – from Yerva – what I was planning.

"I know that. I do. But…"

"But what? Do you still have feelings for the man?"

"Of course not! Except, maybe sympathy."

"So send him flowers! You *don't* have him move in with you."

"He has nowhere else to go."

"Hundreds of people go to the State facility every year. Are you going to take all them in too?"

"Now you're being ridiculous."

"*I'm* being ridiculous! Me?! This is crazy!"

With those words echoing in my ears, Dima and I pulled up to the hospital on a gray, brisk Fall day to bring Bogdan home.

"You sure you're ready for this?" Dima asked as we sat in the hospital parking lot, the engine off, the silence stifling.

"No, but it's too late to turn back now. Here we go!"

I remember feeling so nervous I thought I might throw up as we entered the hospital. We found Bogdan dressed, showered and shaved, sitting up in a wheelchair, talking to one of his nurses. His words were slow, slurred, but the drooping muscles of his face were considerably improved from a week earlier.

Trying to seem as cheerful as possible, I asked him if he was "All set to go?"

"Yethhh," he answered, his lips laboring to form the word.

I turned to the nurse. "Anything special we need to do?" I'd already received a long list of care requirements from his doctor, but I wanted to be sure.

"Not really. Just help him with his normal daily activities and get him to his rehab sessions on Tuesdays and Thursdays. The rest is up to him and the man upstairs." She lifted her eyes to heaven.

I took her elbow and steered her a few steps away. "How long," I whispered. "How long 'til he can live on his own?" I felt embarrassed, dishonest in a way. The Doctor had given me her opinion, but I hoped for something shorter, less arduous.

"Impossible to say. I've seen people recover completely in two months, and I've seen others that never get better. Some get worse." My anxiety must have shown on my face. "Don't worry," she added, patting my arm, "you'll do fine."

I turned back to see Dima poised behind the wheelchair, drool sliding down from the corner of Bogdan's mouth.

"All ready!" Dima said, trying his best to keep the mood light.

I took a Kleenex and wiped my ex-husband's mouth.

"Then let's go."

*****

The first few days were the hardest. I couldn't – or wouldn't – turn his care over to Yerva on day one, so I took two days of vacation time from the library and stayed home to get him situated and to develop some kind of functional routine. Dima was there the entire time. I don't know if it was purely his support for me that motivated him, or whether he might have had just the slightest hint of jealousy to see me living in the same house with my ex-husband, but whatever the case it was wonderful to have him by my side.

Bogdan, I must admit, was a very different person than the man I'd sent to prison years earlier.

"Hey, I jus' wan' to tell ya how mush I 'preciate this," he said moments after Dima had dropped us off at the house and gone to buy a few things I'd forgotten to purchase from our local store. "I know it mus' be hard on yuh, an' your boyfrien', and I'll do my bes' to make it as easy as I can." His speech had improved quite a bit since the day of his stroke, but he still slurred some words and labored over others.

"Just get better," I told him. I had my doubts, but I wasn't about to share them with him.

Taking care of him was less taxing than babysitting Yana. He didn't run around the house in a leaky diaper, he rarely screamed at the top of his lungs over god-knew-what, and he fed and washed himself, for the most part. One of the most awkward moments of his stay came that first day. He'd mentioned that he needed to use the toilet, and so I'd helped him maneuver his wheelchair through the cramped quarters of the hut and half-lifted, half-dragged him into the bathroom where I left him perched precariously – fully dressed – on the toilet seat. (Dima had volunteered to help, but I wanted to be sure Yerva would be able to handle him all by herself, so I insisted on doing it myself.) I stood just outside the bathroom door, close enough so that I could respond quickly if he needed help. I tried to eavesdrop surreptitiously, both embarrassed to infringe upon his privacy and anxious to know he was okay. But I was glad I did when I heard a muffled thump and then muttered expletives.

"What is it?! Are you okay?!" I called through the door.

There was a moment of silence. "Can ya' give me a han' in here?" he finally asked, his voice resigned.

When I opened the door I wasn't prepared to see him lying on his side beside the bowl, his pants halfway to his ankles.

"Los' my balance," he said. "This damn arm is almos' useless."

I helped him push and pull himself back onto the toilet and then brought a bench from the kitchen so he had something to lean against if he lost his balance again.

"Thanks," he said, looking about as miserable as a person can look.

"Don't worry about it."

When I went back out to the kitchen I found Yerva sitting at the dinner table, Yana in her arms. She and Dima were in the midst of a serious conversation.

"Hey – I didn't expect you until day after tomorrow," I told her.

"Decided to stop by to re-introduce myself. So it's not so… uncomfortable when I step in."

"That seems like a good idea. He'll be out in a moment."

"Dima said he had some trouble in there?"

"Lost his balance."

She looked thoughtful, if not worried.

"I dragged a bench in there so he can lean against it," I explained. "Seems to help."

She sighed.

"Can someone help me with this wheelchair?" he called out moments later.

Yerva gave Yana to Dima and came with me to the bathroom.

"Hi, Bogdan," she said, sticking her head in through the door. "Thought I'd come by to say hello."

"Oh, hi. Not the bes' timing, I'm 'fraid."

Yerva shrugged. "It doesn't bother me, if it doesn't bother you." She's a good girl.

It turned out Bogdan was easily tired, and so after just a short conversation he excused himself and we got him into the bed Dima had scavenged. The three of us talked in the kitchen, keeping our voices low to allow both Yana and Bogdan to nap.

"I don't know," Yerva said. "I can't get the image of his fingers around your throat out of my mind."

"Give him a chance," I urged. "If I can forgive him, or at least see that he's changed, can't you?"

"What do you think, Dima? You're pretty quiet."

He tilted his head as if weighing his options. "My uncle was a drinker, and he was a mean s.o.b. to my aunt and cousins. But he was always good to me and my sister. Vodka's a poison, and people who drink too much of it lose themselves."

"He says he hasn't had a drop in years," I said.

"So, maybe he's not the monster he once was. Only way to find out is give him a chance, I suppose."

I looked at my sister. "What do you think? Can you do this?"

"I guess we'll find out."

*****

The first day I went to work leaving Yerva – and Yana – at home with Bogdan, I could barely concentrate on my job.

I kept expecting a call telling me that Bogdan had done, or said something unforgiveable, and Yerva was quitting. But the call never came. In fact, when I came home that evening after work, I found my sister and ex- sitting at the kitchen table playing cards, with my niece in the cradle next to her mother.

"Isn't this the homey scene!" I said as I walked in the door.

"He cheats," Yerva said.

"Ya' should try shufflin' with only one good han'. It's no' so easy."

After some studiously neutral conversation, I helped pack-up my sister and niece and walked them out to their car.

"So: how'd it go? Really."

"Not so bad. He's definitely not the snarling beast I remember from years ago. We actually had some good talks."

"About what?"

"He misses your kids. Asked me if I thought they might come down and visit him."

"What did you say?"

"I told him that would depend on them. They've got their own lives now."

I certainly knew that to be true. I hadn't seen Sasha in over a year, and I only spoke with Kateryna every few months. Not that I put all the blame for our distant relationship on them. After Viktor's death I'd dedicated most of my time and energy to taking care of Mama. They, as young people do, went off to find their own lives. After several years of living pretty much on their own, I didn't expect them to just drop the lives they'd created and return to our 'sleepy little village in the middle of nowhere' as Kateryna had described it. But they might come for a visit. Couldn't hurt to ask.

As it turned out, Kateryna was quite enthusiastic about seeing her father again. Sasha begged off, claiming his training schedule and travels made it extremely difficult to get away. I wasn't convinced, since I still remembered all too well how he'd borne the brunt of Bogdan's drunken rages at home and expected he did as well, but saw no advantage to pressing him to come. I thought he'd come around, eventually.

Kateryna was eight months pregnant, round as a watermelon when she came to visit. Her husband, Petro, and young son, Mykolo, came as well. Petro held an excellent job with an international agri-business company, and I was surprised they allowed him to take a full week on such short notice. He'd never come to see Mama and me in the three years they'd been married, and had not even attended her funeral. I soon found out why they'd all come this time.

"We're moving, Mama," Kateryna explained after dinner their first night visiting. "Petro has been offered a position in New York City!"

She seemed excited, enthusiastic about the move. It made me sad, but I hid my reaction.

"Isn't that wonderful! You must be thrilled, Petro."

"It's a very good opportunity," he said with the quiet reserve that was his trademark.

"Yes, I'm sure it is."

Kateryna must have seen the disappointment in my face for she immediately jumped in.

"We'll fly you out for a visit as soon as we get situated!" she said, ignoring the well-known fact that getting a visa to visit America for the average Ukrainian was nearly impossible. "We'll show you New York!"

I smiled bravely. "That will be fun."

"Oh, don't feel too bad, Mama," Kateryna soothed, rubbing my shoulder. "We'll talk every weekend by phone and we'll visit whenever we can."

Every weekend was more frequently than we'd talked while she lived in Kyiv, so I took her promise with a grain of salt. Still, it was nice to hear.

"Don't be sad, Grandma," Mykolo said, giving me a big hug.

"No, of course not."

When Bogdan awakened from his afternoon nap, Kateryna and he had their first face-to-face meeting in years. He blinked as if still dreaming when he found her sitting on the foot of his bed, Mykolo in her lap.

"Kateryna?" he asked. She tried to speak, but emotion closed her throat. She nodded mutely. To everyone's surprise, Bogdan began to cry. Not a simple sob, but a deep, gut-wrenching wail that brought Mykolo scrambling from his mother's arms.

"Grandpa!" he cried out, scurrying across the bed to hug his grandfather. "It will be okay."

The sight of the sweet young boy, not yet three, consoling the broken old man brought tears to all our eyes. Bogdan lay stunned for several seconds until finally he recovered enough to return the hug. That brought Kateryna to his side as well, and in moments we were one big sobbing, smiling family – for the first time in nearly twenty years.

*****

There was more of the same, of course, when Kateryna and her family left to return to Kyiv and pack-up for the move to New York City. But we all understood it was something Petro needed to do to continue advancing in his career. Still, it was bittersweet to see them leave like that, not knowing when, or if, we'd ever see them again. Especially Bogdan. I think the reality of his mortality hit him harder that day than ever before, and it was several days before he resumed his normal schedule.

As the weeks rolled by, Yerva more than adjusted to her role as Bogdan's nursemaid, coming to accept him for what he'd become, not what he'd been. It was Dima who most surprised me, however. It would've been very natural for him to project a sense of jealousy, or at least possessiveness, what with all the hours I spent alone with Bogdan in our little hut. But what he gave me instead was something I cherished: his trust and support. Whenever he was in our oblast, which was every other week for the most part, he spent virtually all his free time with us – that is, Bogdan and me. It took a little time, but after repeated invitations he stayed with us (or me, really) instead of the inn downtown. We played cards, cooked and ate, and after several weeks, when my ex- regained enough strength to be able to leave the house, albeit in his wheelchair, we three went on long walks throughout the farmland that surrounded the hut.

We must've seemed an odd trio to our confused neighbors: Bogdan, bundled from nose to toes in his chair; Dima, pushing the chair as if it were his brother or son he was helping; and me, walking and talking to each of them as if they were my closest friends. And, in a way, I suppose they were. For while Dima was the only person I could see myself spending the rest of my life with, Bogdan was the one with whom I'd spent most of my youth. It's odd how we remember our happy moments so much more vividly than our sad ones, or at least I do. I could never forgive what my ex- had done to me, to our family, but I never forgot all the good times we'd had before the vodka turned him into a different person. And with the endless hours we spent together, I came to know the *new* Bogdan and appreciate what he could bring to our lives.

Eventually, after three or four months, Bogdan grew strong enough to walk with the help of a cane. Our walks became much shorter in length but about the same in time as I, and Dima when he visited us, slowed our pace to match

Bogdan's. Looking back, I suppose I was busy making plans of where Dima and I would live once he moved his business down to our village, a move I'd hinted at several times but never insisted upon. We'd find Bogdan a small apartment nearby, and all of us would live out full and meaningful lives in blissful harmony. But it's always dangerous to tempt fate by such planning, and our moment of bliss was brief indeed.

Dima more than fulfilled his part of the plan, giving Bogdan a make-work position sweeping out his offices and warehouse so that my ex- could earn enough to pay his own way. It was a good thing he did. The stipend from his family dissipated little by little until it was barely enough to cover his ancillary expenses such as pharmacy medicines and snacks. Without the maintenance job, he would live a very stark life.

No, the problems arose from the least expected directions. First, I received a call from Sasha, maybe two years after Bogdan began working for Dima.

"Mama, I've left the team," was how the telephone conversation from him began very late one night.

"What do you mean?" I asked, dumbfounded. Sasha had been one of the team's best strikers, a goal-making weapon that had brought him, and the team, great success over the sixteen seasons he'd been with them. I knew his scoring had diminished as he'd moved into his mid-thirties, but not so much that the team would think about dismissing him! Or so I thought.

He explained, in a solemn, almost tearful voice, that he'd developed "a problem with alcohol. Like Papa."

I cringed to hear the words.

"Is there any hope that another team might pick up your contract?"

All football players drank. Heck, all athletes drank. Surely that wouldn't disqualify him from playing with another team, even if it meant a smaller contract.

"I... doubt it." He explained that he'd had the *problem* for a number of years, but as long as his goal production kept the team at or near the top of their division, the coach and team owners were willing to look the other way. Now that he was 35, the problem was a real *problem*. No one was likely to give another chance to a player whose fame demanded a higher salary than his faded talents justified. Plus, there had been... outbursts. Turned out my son, my beautiful little boy Sasha, had developed into a demanding, loud-mouthed drunk that no team wanted in their locker room.

"What are you going to do?" I asked. I tried not to think how a son emulated his father, but it was difficult.

"I was kind of hoping I might...stay with you and Papa for a while. Just until I get my feet under me."

With Bogdan and me and increasingly Dima living in the tiny hut, there would be little room for anyone else. But I couldn't really tell him no.

"It won't be quite as lavish as the places I'm sure you've grown accustomed to," I said, hoping he'd get the message and perhaps volunteer to lease a larger home.

"That's okay. Beggars can't be choosers."

I laughed. "Beggars? Surely a longtime football superstar can afford something a little more... spacious than the family home."

A long silence. "I blew it all, Mama. Friends, partying, some bad investments – I'm broke."

Part of me wanted to chastise him, to rant about the foolishness of such short-sightedness. But I was his mother, and always would be. I told him we'd make room for him.

Again, it was Dima who came to the rescue. He'd already moved the business to Uman, a major crossroads in the middle of the country just a handful of kilometers to the east of our village. Now he purchased a home.

"He can live with us at first," he offered. "Maybe I can find him a job."

As it turned out, Sasha accepted the job but not a bedroom in our much larger house on the outskirts of the village. It was a two-story cement block structure with three bedrooms on the top floor and a full apartment on the ground floor. But Sasha would have no part of it.

"I won't ruin your life," he insisted. "I'll find my own place."

It was Bogdan who suggested the two of them live in the family's little hut, and after a moment's surprised reflection, we happily agreed.

"They can look after each other," Dima said. "Bogdan could use a strong hand around the house, and with any luck Sasha can learn from his father something about how to recover from an addiction to alcohol. And maybe they can figure out how to act like father and son."

Sasha was less enthusiastic than his father.

"You want me to *live* with that bastard?" he asked when I first posed the possibility.

"He's not the same man we knew all those years ago. He's changed."

"What's the old saying about leopards changing their spots?"

"This leopard doesn't drink anymore," Dima explained. "He wants to get to know you better. And you might learn a thing or two about sobriety."

"I don't know…"

"Give it a try. Unless you have a better offer…"

The bluster went out of Sasha's argument. "Yeh, well, maybe for a week or two…"

"That's all. If it doesn't work, you can try something else."

I could see his mind racing. "Okay. Sure," he finally agreed.

So a few days later Dima's transport company moved Sasha from Kyiv down to our family home. It wasn't a very difficult move. Over the last couple of years he'd sold, given away or lost almost everything he'd owned. He arrived at the house with a suitcase and two small boxes. We'd spent the previous few days preparing Bogdan for his son's arrival, an event that both excited and worried him.

"Does he hate me?" was the first question from his lips.

"He... doesn't hate you," I said, none too sure I was speaking the truth. "But he knows what you did, and he knows you haven't been in his life for many years now."

"I'd hate me, if I were him."

"Maybe he's a better person than you are," Dima said, never one to put up with Bogdan's woe-is-me self-loathing.

"We can only hope," my ex- said, a small smile the only sign he understood the irony of the situation.

So when Sasha arrived that Spring evening, all of us – Sasha, Bogdan, Dima and myself – were all on-edge. For everyone's sake we needed the meeting to go well. Sasha was in no shape to take care of himself, and none of us had the time or energy to devote to full-time care. Bogdan needed something more than a minimum wage job sweeping floors to keep his spirits up. Dima and I needed some time to ourselves.

As the sound of the transport truck rumbled to a stop in front of the house, I saw the anxiety in Bogdan's eyes. He was frightened.

"Sasha!" I cried as the door swung open revealing our only son, his skin a sickly yellowish shade, his eyes sunken, his hair thinned to the point of balding on top. I gave him a big hug, which was returned tentatively.

"Mama," he muttered. I felt more than saw his head turn toward his father. "Papa," he said so softly I could barely hear him.

Bogdan limped over to where we stood, his cane tapping hesitantly on the hard tile floor.

"You look like hell," Bogdan said. "But I'm glad you're here."

With his one good arm he reached out to give Sasha a hug. For just an instant Sasha froze, and as he did everything around him froze as well. We all held our breath. Then, without conviction at first, the uncertainty evident in every move, he returned the hug.

"You look like a bull kicked you in the head," Sasha said, pulling back to examine his father more closely. "A big bull."

Bogdan laughed. "Stomped me half into the ground. But it'll take more than that to send me to my maker."

A collective sigh reflected the lower anxiety level. "Does anyone want tea?" I asked.

That first day was difficult, awkward. But it seemed even then that both of them wanted nothing more than to find the father-son relationship they'd never had. Dima and I had made a back-up plan to take Sasha to our house for the night if things had gone badly. It wasn't needed. I won't say they bonded right then and there, but at least they didn't kill each other. When Dima and I got into our car that night, having shown Sasha the basics of looking after his father, we were emotionally exhausted and still cautious.

"Not so bad," Dima said with his usual loquaciousness.

"What happens when they start reminiscing?" I wondered. "Will they reopen old wounds?"

He shrugged. "Time will tell."

*****

The reconciliation was not always easy, nor without twists and turns. About a month after Sasha moved in, I got a worried call from his father.

"I don't want to alarm you," he began, and of course I was instantly alarmed, "but I think we have a problem developing with Sasha."

Since I'd been under the impression that everything had been going reasonably well between the two of them, I was understandably surprised.

"What kind of problem?"

"Well, it seems that some of the local lads have recognized him around town as a football hero, and they've taken to treating him to drinks in the local taverns."

"Oh no." Until then Sasha had avoided alcohol religiously since he'd moved in with his father, perhaps because he saw what drink could do to destroy a life, perhaps because he didn't want to appear weak before his father. In either case, the honeymoon had apparently ended.

"I'll have a word with him."

"I've already tried, and he seems to think he's got it under control. He doesn't want to admit he could end up like me."

The thought gave me shivers. "Maybe he'll take advice from me. None of the man-to-man thing."

"Good luck."

We arranged it so I could catch Sasha at home alone, on a day when Bogdan was working for Dima.

"Mama, what are you doing here?" he asked when he answered my knock.

"A pleasant surprise, I hope?"

"Of course! Yes! Come in, come in." He seemed a bit skittish. Probably nervous, I decided.

I was happy to see the hut clean and organized. Like most mothers, I suppose, I had imagined the place gone to ruin, dirty dishes piled high, beds unmade, dirt piling up in corners. In fact, it was every bit as clean as when I'd lived there.

"You and your father are doing a good job," I said, glancing about appraisingly. "This place is spic and span."

He smiled. "Not what you expected?"

"What I hoped," I answered diplomatically. My turn to smile.

"So, what brings you by in the middle of the week? Don't you have work today?" I heard an unspoken question in his voice.

"I do. I just came by on my lunch hour."

"Ah," he said, nodding. "Checking up on your wayward menfolk?"

"I just realized it had been a while since I'd seen my favorite son."

"In the middle of a work-day? Come on, Mom, what's up?"

I felt uncomfortable snooping, but I couldn't put off my concerns any longer. "All right: how are you doing? I mean, is everything going okay?"

"I'm good, Mama. Taking care of Papa, reacquainting myself with the village…"

"I understand you're something of a celebrity around town."

His lips dropped into a frown. "Ah, so that's it. Papa has been talking to you about my *wild, irresponsible* lifestyle."

"He's concerned, Sasha. He said you've been drinking again."

He began to pace. "I have a drink or two every now and then. So what?"

"You know *so what*, Sash. You know you have a problem."

"Had. I *had* a problem. A sip or two of vodka isn't going to hurt anything. After all, it's not as if I were in training."

I was getting dizzy watching him stalk back and forth. "Sit. Please." He did as I asked, though clearly under protest.

"Sasha, your father wasn't always a bad man," I began and clearly caught him by surprise.

"I know that. Or at least I vaguely remember."

"Do you remember when he changed, when he stopped being a good person?"

"A little."

"It was when he started drinking." He started to protest. "No, wait, let me finish. At first it was just a drink or two with friends after a hard day in the fields. Everyone did it, so I didn't think anything of it. But then a drink or two became three or four, and then he started staying out all night."

"I'm not Papa, Mom!" he said defiantly. "I can keep it under control."

I raised my eyebrows. "That's exactly what he used to say. And for a while he did. But then…"

"I can handle it."

"Look, Sasha, the same blood that flows in his veins flows in yours. With the same strengths, and weaknesses. I don't know if could stand it if the same thing that happened to him happened to you." I didn't mean to, but I burst into tears.

He quickly moved to my side, comforting me. "Okay, Mama, it's okay. I hear what you're saying. I'll lay-off the vodka for a while. Straight and narrow," he said, crossing his heart.

"Promise?"

"Yes, I promise. Now wipe off those tears. Would you like a cup of tea?"

And just like that it was over. I, of course, was hopeful he'd keep his promise, but my experience thirty years earlier told me it wouldn't be easy for him.

We had a very nice talk. As he relaxed a bit it became clear he was getting impatient to get out into the world once more. But to do what?

"I don't know. All I've ever done is play football."

"You could learn to do something else. Look at me – I was even older than you are now, with two children, when I learned library work."

"I'm not so good with books," he said with a smile.

"You'll find something," I said. "Just give it some time."

As I excused myself to head back to the library, my head was spinning with possibilities. My only worry was whether any of them would appeal to him.

That night when I got home, I repeated the entire conversation to Dima, nearly verbatim.

He listened thoughtfully. "Can he drive a truck?" he asked.

"I'm sure he could learn, if he can't."

"Would he? I mean, it might seem like a big step down: star footballer to truck driver."

"I think he just wants something to get out of the house and earn a living."

"Do you want to ask him?"

"Why don't you?" I didn't want to get between them.

So he did. We decided to wait until the next time we were over at the hut, both to make it more personal, and to give me time to talk to his father, which I did the next day.

"Sasha would like to get a job," I said as we sat sipping tea. Sasha was out shopping for his father.

"He has a job," Bogdan said.

"You know what he means – a real job, out of the house."

He nodded. "I'm not surprised. He has way too much free time now, while I'm off at work. Makes it hard to stay away from the taverns."

"So, you'd be okay with it?"

He looked me right in the eyes. "I was a drunk for a long time, Nina. Anything that can help prevent my son from following in my footsteps, I'm okay with."

"I might not be able to get over here every time he's at work…"

He waved his hand to cut me off. "I'm not a cripple. I can walk with a cane, I can cook, I can clean – I appreciate all your help, all everyone's help, but it's time for all of us to get on with our lives."

What could I say? I kissed him on both cheeks. "You know, you grew up okay."

He laughed. "Took long enough, don't you think?"

"But you got there. You should take pride in that."

"I do, believe me. But I also remember all the pain I caused, to you, the kids – to a lot of people. I can't undo all that, but I can try to be a better person. And I am."

I left the house that day thinking my life had finally come around, that the family had finally exorcised its demons and was on its way to a brighter tomorrow.

Or so it seemed.

Chapter 17

In fairy tales everyone lives happily ever after. If only it worked that way in real life.

It did for a while. Sasha took the job with Dima's company, and after three or four months found his own apartment and moved out – with his father's blessings. Bogdan continued to improve physically until he could walk without a cane and his speech showed little signs of the stroke that had almost killed him. He still limped, and anyone who'd known him before the illness could tell he wasn't quite the man he'd been before, but nonetheless – it was a small miracle. Kateryna and her family relocated to New York, where they sent glowing letters of a new life in a new country. We talked by phone every other week or so, but I missed Yana and Volodymyr – her son, born an American in New York City. I feared Bogdan might take offense when he learned that Kateryna had named her first boy after her grandfather, instead of him, but I'd once again underestimated the change the man had made in his life.

"Volodymyr," he said when I informed him, rolling the name over in his mouth like a fine wine. "Good name. Good for them to remember your father as well." I didn't know if he was suggesting it might be a good idea for him too, and didn't ask.

Best of all, Dima and I lived together in the closest thing to complete harmony that I, at least, could possibly imagine. We rarely argued, and when we did we argued the point, not each other. With everything seemingly moving in the right direction, we even discussed getting married. Truth was, I had been the one who'd objected during the first years of our relationship, thinking that it wouldn't be fair to bind a man – especially a man as good as Dima – to a family with as many loose ends as mine. But now that they were finally tied…

We set a date: January 1, 1992. We thought the date would symbolize a new start, a fresh beginning not only for the two of us, but for our entire family. Some members of his family were not entirely supportive of our decision. His oldest brother, Yakiv, and his sister, Maryska – both of whom had worked in Dima's transport company for years and had helped it grow to one of the region's largest – saw the marriage as a threat to their control over the company, and maybe a step down for the successful businessman to marry a poor, twice-married farm girl from the south. There were arguments, none of which I witnessed but several described by Dima. I remember his description of one discussion very clearly. He'd gone back up north to meet with his siblings about the family business (a business he had founded and for which he was and always had been the President), and had decided to break the *happy* news.

"So, if we're pretty much all finished with the business part of this meeting, I have some other news," he'd begun. He told me that his family had looked somewhat askance, unsure what *other news* might signify.

"Nina and I are getting married!"

His enthusiasm was met by exchanged looks between Yakiv and Maryska. Only Danylo – his youngest brother, and several non-family employees gave their unconditional approval with shouted "Congratulations!" and laughter. His older brother and sister were conspicuous by their pale faces and utter silence.

"Is she pregnant?" Maryska finally asked.

Snickers were quickly suppressed. "Of course she's not pregnant!" Dima said. "We realized that our lives are much better together, and have decided to make it legal."

"You shouldn't rush into such weighty decisions, decisions that impact us all," Yakiv whined.

"Rush! We've lived together for years! It's long past time."

"But we haven't heard about it until now," his sister pressed. "I mean, this decision has ramifications well beyond your personal happiness."

Dima's smile disappeared. "Our decision isn't hasty or spur-of-the-moment. And if you're worried about the business, I can assure you it will continue to run as it always has."

The entire room was silent.

"Three cheers for Dima and Nina!" Danylo broke the tense atmosphere. All except Yakiv and Maryska joined-in.

Two days later Dima received legal documents by courier. His brother and sister were taking him to court to demand full one-third shares of the business.

"Have they lost their minds?" Dima asked me when the documents arrived. "I started the business – without them. I made the business grow for nearly three years on my own. I only hired them to give them something to do. Yakiv was working as a waiter, and Maryska had no job whatsoever. They're lucky to have salaries, let alone full shares in the company!" I'd never seen him so angry, and disappointed.

The battle over the company was neither quick nor simple. Maryska had cultivated a friendship with a high-ranking Party official, who used all his power to influence the outcome of the suit. Luckily, Dima was not without contacts of his own, and the court battle became a drawn-out chess match of moves and counter-moves. Dima was spending more time in courtrooms and talking with lawyers than dealing with the company. Worst of all, he felt betrayed by his family.

"They don't give a damn about me or the company," he told me one night about a month into the process. "All they care about is the money."

As weeks became months, the case dragged on and Dima fell into a profound depression. I begged him to visit a doctor, or at least the local priest. But he wouldn't listen. He pushed himself, too hard, too long. I could see the toll it was taking and did my best to help him get through it all. My best wasn't enough.

On December 25, 1991 the Soviet Union ended. Just like that, nearly 75 years of Communist rule disappeared, virtually overnight. We'd all known it was only a matter of time. The forces Gorbachev had unleashed could not be turned back. The old order no longer worked, not even for itself. We had seen protests, demonstrations and strikes for years as the old system had shuddered to a halt. We thought after our Declaration of Independence on August 24th that life would return to normal relatively quickly. On December 1st when we elected a new President, we were even more confident. As Ukrainians, we rejoiced. From an unwilling republic of the old Union we returned to the status of an independent nation. But changing the laws and changing the name of the country could not change decades of Communist rule.

What it did do was throw the bureaucracy of local government into chaos. Even the most mundane activities were accomplished with difficulty. At the Library, we worked for two months without being paid. The lawsuit against Dima and his company? It was caught in the changing legal system like an insect in amber.

We postponed the wedding.

"We shouldn't do this while the suit is still pending," Dima announced just before Christmas that year. "Let's wait for Spring. We should be able to celebrate more completely then." I told him I didn't care if the suit dragged on; it didn't change what we felt for each other. But he was adamant.

On February 17th, at 2:30 in the morning, Dima suffered a massive heart attack. He moaned, called my name once aloud, and was gone. I still think the lawsuit and the changes in the country contributed to his death: he couldn't accept the first, and couldn't navigate the second.

We held the burial on another cold, gray day, snow
drifting lazily from the overcast skies above. His brother
Danylo represented Dima's family, the only one of his clan
willing to spend that much time with *the enemy*, and to be
frank, the only one we had any interest in sharing our grief
with. The others were certain that their brother had made
provisions for me in his will and were equally certain I did
not deserve whatever he'd left me. It sounds naïve looking
back, but I had no idea what, if anything, he'd left me. We
never discussed death, or wills, or anything of the sort. Our
lives had been so complicated in the past, we cherished the
relative calm of his last few years, years in which we'd had
the time and peace of mind to understand how much we
meant to one another.

"The past is passed," Dima used to say. "We learn from
it and move on."

Easier said than done. Sometimes the past reaches out
and grabs ahold of the present, influencing not only our
current life but our future as well. The battle over Dima's
transportation company was just such a moment. When our
lawyer read the will in his office, with both Maryska and
Yakiv present and accompanied by *their* lawyers (three of
them!), the atmosphere was cool and barely civil from the
very first. When the lawyer announced that ownership in
Dima's company was to be transferred – in its entirety – to
me, the temperature in the room fell to positively polar.

"This is outrageous!" Maryska announced after a
moment to digest the news. "It is clear this woman
influenced his decision!"

"Of course she influenced his decision," countered
Sasha – who was there both to provide me with moral
support and to see if Dima had left him anything, "she was
his *wife*!"

"She turned our brother against us. We, who did as
much as he did to make the company a success…"

I probably should have kept my mouth shut, but I knew how vehemently my dead husband rejected that assertion. "Dima didn't see it that way. But I'm sure we can come to a reasonable compromise..."

"The courts will decide that," Maryska said, jumping to her feet in a huff. "Come, Yakiv." Like an obedient guard dog he came to heel as the siblings stalked out of our lawyer's office, followed closely by their gaggle of lawyers, all squawking and honking like the angry geese they so closely resembled.

"Let them go," Sasha said when I stood, thinking to try to defuse their anger. "Surely the courts will see the strength of our claim."

He was young and had no personal experience with the legal system. I looked to our lawyer for a more professional opinion. I could tell at once he was nowhere near as sanguine.

"I certainly hope that will be the case," he said quietly. "But it's very difficult to predict the outcome of these sorts of trials. After all, in the end it will depend on the decision of one man, or woman. And in the current state of affairs...." He shrugged.

We all held our breath.

The family wasted no time in pushing forward their claim on the company. They asserted that with the death of Dima the company's very future was at stake and so the courts needed to come to a decision sooner rather than later. Maryska's old Party friend had by that time used his influence and wealth to make the jump from fervent Communist to equally fervent capitalist. He used that influence to sway the Oblast Administration into assigning an old buddy of his as presiding judge.

"This could be a problem," our lawyer explained. "A very big problem."

"But can't we ask for a new judge? Isn't that part of the new law?" Sasha argued.

The lawyer looked as if he'd bitten into a bitter lemon. "We could. But the same bureaucrats who assigned this judge will only replace him with someone at least as bad, maybe worse."

"Dima had contacts," my son said, grabbing me by the shoulders with unalloyed hope glowing in his eyes. "Won't they help?"

I hated to see that glow diminished, but I couldn't lie to him either. "My husband is dead. People aren't likely to go out on thin ice for someone who can do nothing for them any longer."

"But we can try! We have to try!"

I tried. I contacted a half-dozen of Dima's friends and business associates. They were all duly sympathetic, and all voiced the appropriate condolences. But...

"Hordiyenko (Maryska's friend) wouldn't take kindly to any interference in the case. It would be much better to simply come to an out-of-court settlement with his family," one of Dima's closest business contacts advised. "I'm sorry." That was essentially the same reply I received from all of them. They were all *very* sorry.

The case plodded through the court system, every aspect taking weeks, sometimes a month or more. I was lost. Without Dima to share his thoughts of how to proceed, I was left with only Sasha and Bogdan, neither of whom inspired great confidence. Sasha advised plowing full speed ahead. Bogdan, however, had matured in recent years and was more thoughtful.

"Let's say you fight them to the very last," he advised. "They have some very powerful men on their side, including, I am certain, the judge. The odds of success are, in my opinion, not so good. You – and your children – will likely get little if anything of the company. If, on the other hand, you sit down with his family – and Maryska in particular – and can come to some kind of compromise, you may be able to negotiate at least some sort of positive outcome."

Our lawyer agreed with that evaluation, and eventually so did I. As time passed, it became increasingly clear we were not winning. Despite passionate objections from Sasha, I sent word directly to Maryska that I wanted to meet with her to discuss the claim. To my relief – and surprise – she agreed. One afternoon, I believe it was in May 1992, she came to the house I had shared with her brother until his death. I'd assumed she would demand I come to her, but she was quick to agree to make the journey.

I'd prepared varenyky, (cabbage, meat and cherry) and had brewed a strong pot of tea in anticipation of her arrival. I hoped food and drink would lessen the barriers that stood between us. When a large black car pulled into our driveway, I thought at first she had had one of the transport company employees drive her down for the meeting. But when the driver's door opened, out stepped Maryska, dressed all in black from head to toe. Suddenly my drab blue outfit seemed overly cheerful.

"Maryska. Thank you for coming all the way down here to meet with me," I welcomed her, trying to show I bore her no ill will. She was not so welcoming.

"Nina." She eyed my dress. "You no longer mourn?"

"I observed the traditional forty days. I see you do not."

"Forty days is a minimum. My grief cannot be limited."

I could see this would not be an easy discussion. I managed to get her into the house and seated comfortably. We exchanged simple pleasantries, though nothing that could be described as friendly or even sociable. When I offered her the tray of varenyky, she took one and brought it close to her face, as if to inspect it.

"That one is cherry," I explained, pointing out the different ways I'd crimped the dough for each different dumpling.

She took a tiny bite. "Very tasty," she said, putting it down as if it might explode. She sipped her tea in complete silence, her expression a cross between haughty disinterest and unadulterated dislike.

"So," she finally said when I sat down opposite her, "you want to talk. Here I am."

"Well, we all know from Dima's will what his wishes were," I began. I hoped my nervousness was not obvious.

"We know what Dima wrote in the will. Whether they were his wishes when he died, no one can say," she countered.

"But the will is very clear."

"Did you wish to make an offer?" she asked, without emotion.

"I… well, yes, I suppose I do. I recognize all the work you and your brother put into making the company what it is today…"

"No one will ever know how much we contributed."

"No, I'm sure they won't. But we can try to make certain you are… adequately compensated for your contributions."

"Yes? Go on."

"Well, I've been thinking: it won't help anyone, not your family and not mine, if we spend many years and many thousands of rubles fighting each other. Only the lawyers will get rich. Wouldn't it be better if all that money stayed with us?" I tried not to sound too eager.

She showed no response. Eerily, she reminded me of Dima as she sat there, silent but clearly alert. "I'm listening."

"Well, what if we divide the company 50-50, and you and your brother continue to run it?" It seemed eminently fair to me. They'd get fifty per cent more than Dima had left them, and I'd get a healthy share of a company run by people who felt good about the accommodation.

"That's only twenty-five percent each for Yakiv and me, while you keep fifty," she complained without missing a beat. "Why not one-third each?"

I'd been prepared for just such an offer, having discussed the upcoming negotiations with Bogdan a few days earlier. "If you can live with it, fine. Just don't give in too easily," he'd advised. "Make a show of fighting it."

So I did. "Dima left me one hundred per cent of the business," I began, trying to sound firm but not inflexible. "Giving you fifty per cent seems more than fair."

I didn't realize it when the words left my lips, but I'd opened a can of worms. "Give? You aren't giving us *anything,* Nina," Maryska said, her voice hard. "We worked for our share. It's we who are giving *you* a share you never earned."

I thought I could keep my temper in check, but something about the way she said it made me explode. "I may not have earned it, but my husband earned that and much more. You two were just employees, hired hands he gave jobs to because no one else would hire you!"

"Hired hands?!" Maryska stood abruptly and stared at me with cold hatred in her eyes. "I always thought you were a just a pretty fool, and now I can see I was right!"

She stormed out of the house without another word. I probably should have run after her, probably should have tried to repair the damage. But I have feelings as well. Dima *had* built that company and *had* given jobs to his siblings when no one else would. I'd be blasted if I was going to give them two-thirds of what he'd worked so hard to build!

Repercussions came quickly. Two days later our lawyer received a notification from the court to appear for a hearing. Sasha and Bogdan accompanied me for moral support.

The head judge, a man who'd held a similar post under the communists, was a fat, gray-haired sloth of a man who clearly liked to listen to his own voice and didn't much care for any testimony that ran contrary to the judgment he'd already made.

Maryska was their first witness. She told a convincing story – particularly if you didn't know the woman – about how she and Yakiv had sacrificed everything to found the transport company with Dima. When our lawyer tried to pin her down, to make her admit that the company was already firmly established by the time they came to work for it, the judge accused our lawyer of "making improper, unfounded assertions", and warned him that "slander will not be allowed in this courtroom."

The next witness was Yakiv. It was clear from the outset he was not anywhere near as bright or manipulative as his sister. He answered questions haltingly, as if trying to regurgitate stock lines he'd attempted to memorize. Our lawyer tried once again to poke holes in the testimony, and was threatened with a stint in jail unless he 'stopped trying to intimidate the witness.' At first he objected, argued with passion, but the threat of jail time quickly ended that.

Perhaps most damaging to our cause was the testimony of one of Dima's top executives, a vice-president who'd been with the company even longer than Maryska and her brother. He testified that Dima's two siblings had made "substantial and irreplaceable" contributions to the development of the company. When our lawyer asked exactly what these contributions were, the VP listed a number of accomplishments whose origins we could not prove. Worse yet, he claimed that he'd noticed "a real change" in Dima's deportment beginning when he'd moved in with me, an abandonment of most of the 'old-timers' resulting from a "near-hypnotic hold" I seemed to have over him. We suggested that my hold might have been love, but the suggestion was tossed aside as "self-serving justification." We tried to persuade other long-term employees to testify on our behalf, but it was clear they saw the lay of the land and refused. They wanted to keep their jobs as well as the generous bonuses several of them received (or so we were told) immediately after the case was closed.

We lost. The will was invalidated and the court split the company in exactly the way Maryska had suggested when we met (one-third each to her, Yakiv, and me), but with the proviso that I remain a silent partner, unable to offer any input into the running of the company.

I can't say I was surprised or overly disappointed. I'd already decided that one-third of a successful company was better than endless bickering and court battles, but it stung nonetheless. Most of all, I was saddened by his family's attitude. We'd never been close, but I'd never thought of them as adversaries. Obviously, the feeling was not mutual.

But if I was disappointed with the verdict, Sasha was beside himself. I'd warned him and his father – both of whom had come to the courtroom as a show of support, that they needed to keep their tempers under control. I wasn't particularly worried about Bogdan; as I've said, he'd become a much different man than he'd been twenty-five years earlier. But Sasha...

"You two are scum!" he screamed as soon as the verdict was announced. "Dima should've fired the two of you when he had the chance! My mother deserves this company much more than either of you!"

The judge screamed for him to be seated and keep quiet, but it was as if he'd lost his mind. He kept yelling until an armed guard grabbed him and dragged him from the courtroom, still spouting insults.

I had hoped to speak with Maryska before she left, to let her know that I accepted the Court decision and hoped we could get past all the squabbling and establish a less-adversarial relationship going forward. After Sasha's outburst, she brushed by me with what could only be described as a dismissive sneer.

"What were you thinking?!" I asked my son when we were reunited outside the courthouse.

"It isn't fair! Dima built the company, and he wanted you to have it. Those bloodsuckers don't care about their brother, only the money!"

"They've worked there for a long time," I said, trying to calm his anger. "They think they are owed more than just a few thousand rubles."

"But Dima didn't think so, or he would've given them a part of the company!"

Bogdan put a hand on his son's shoulder. "The Court has decided," he said calmly. "Let it go. There's nothing we can do about it."

"What's wrong with you two?!" he went on, his face a deepening purple. "You can't just give in to those two thieves!"

"Sasha, enough!" I said as people began to stare. "We can discuss this at home."

He shook his head in disgust, turned and stormed off.

"Sasha! Sasha come back here!" I called after him.

"Let him go," Bogdan said. "He needs some time to cool off. Football players live in their own world. He doesn't know how the system really works."

And neither did we.

Two days after the final Court decision, a messenger delivered another packet of official papers to me. There was a whole sheaf of papers relating to the decision and the reapportionment of company ownership. I flipped through the legal mumbo-jumbo and decided I needed my lawyer to look them over. Then I saw two other single page documents, each a virtual duplicate of the other.

They'd fired Sasha and Bogdan. Not that they described it as such – they called it "a necessary restructuring" – but the end result was the same. Bogdan wasn't surprised.

"They don't want us around eavesdropping on their conversations, spreading negative gossip."

"You wouldn't do that!"

"I know that, and you know that, but after Sasha's performance at the courthouse, I understand how they wouldn't be so sure about him."

I had to agree. Sasha had cut his own throat. I tried to get him on the phone, to be the one to break the bad news to him, but there was no answer. I hadn't spoken to him since the Court decision, following Bogdan's advice to give him a little space, but I really needed to get ahold of him then. I knew his temper and wanted to head-off any explosions that would only make things worse. I called the manager of the apartment where he'd moved – an old friend – but she hadn't seen him for several days. I called the one friend of his I knew, a co-worker at Dima's company, and it was immediately clear to me that something was wrong.

"I'm so sorry to bother you," I said, "but have you seen my son, Sasha?"

"I, ah… I haven't seen him today…" It was clear he was evading.

"This is important, Olek. I *need* to reach him." I tried to put as much urgency into my voice as possible. He got the message.

"You might try the Prancing Goat, in Haisyn. But don't tell him I told you."

"I won't. Thank you."

I was… confused. I'd never visited the tavern, but I knew of its reputation as a place where *nonconformist elements* hung out. Back in the Communist times it had been one of the few bars in the oblast to serve an all-male clientele. I could say I was taken aback to learn my son might frequent the place, but truth was I must have known something deep down in my heart long before that. Sasha had never brought home a girlfriend, never mentioned going out on a date. All his friends had been guys since his secondary school days, but I'd always assumed that was because he was an athlete. So I can't say I was shocked, but even if I had been I was determined to find him – wherever he might be.

I got in my car and drove to Haisyn. It was a small city, less than 20,000 inhabitants, the administrative center of its oblast. The downtown was tiny, really just a few blocks of stores, shops and restaurants. The Prancing Goat wasn't hard to find: its bright pink and purple sign announced its niche from quite a distance.

When I walked in, just after noon, it took a second for my eyes to adjust. The lighting was nearly non-existent and smoke made the dim interior even murkier. A murmuring of voices abruptly died down to a mere whisper. As soon as I could see, I realized nearly every eye in the moderately crowded tavern was looking my way. Of course, since I was the only woman in the place, that was not surprising. I scanned the tables and booths for my son, but saw only strange faces staring back at me.

"Mama! What are you doing here?" a familiar voice called out as Sasha appeared through the smoky haze like a ship through dense fog.

"I might ask you the same thing," I said, trying not to sound too much like the disappointed mother I was.

"I'm… just having lunch." I could smell the vodka on his breath. His eyes were already bloodshot.

I couldn't help myself. I hugged him tight. "Oh Sasha, you were doing so well…"

"It's no big thing," he said, pushing me gently away.

"We need to talk."

He realized that I wasn't just there to chastise him about his drinking. "About what?"

"I think it would be better if we talked in private."

He looked aggravated, but gave in to his curiosity. "Hold on. I'll be right back." I could barely see him through the tobacco haze go back to a booth in the rear of the pub where he talked with a young man about his age, nodding in my direction. The other man laughed and waved Sasha off dismissively.

His mood hadn't improved when he returned.

"Okay. Where to?"

"My car is parked just outside. We can talk there." I had to restrain myself from taking his hand and leading him out. He followed close behind me.

Despite knowing what I'd find there, I groped for the right words to put him at ease. The best I could do was ramble.

"It's very smoky in there."

"People like to smoke when they drink," he said sullenly. I could sense he expected a tongue-lashing.

"It doesn't smell very good."

"I didn't really notice."

Thankfully the car was close by. I got in and unlocked the passenger side for Sasha.

"So, what was so important you had to come down here?" he asked even as he closed his door.

I got straight to the point. "I just received some documents from Maryska and Yakiv's lawyer."

"What did those assholes want?"

I frowned but held my tongue. "They've decided to downsize the company."

"Ah. So Bogdan and I are expendable, is that it?"

"That's it, I'm afraid. You don't seem surprised."

"Wouldn't you do the same thing if you were them?"

I hadn't considered the possibility. "I don't know. Maybe I'd want to honor my brother's wishes."

"We already know that isn't the case."

"Yes, I suppose we do." I took a second to transition to the main reason for my visit. "Now Sasha, I don't want you running off and making trouble with them about this. Let's just let it lie as the Court has decided."

He laughed. "Me? Little old me, cause trouble? Why Mama, I'd almost think you didn't trust me." His smile was challenging.

"You've been drinking again."

"Aha. So that's the real reason for all this. You needn't worry. I can handle it."

"Sasha, it's barely noon and I can already smell the alcohol on your breath."

"I'm not a little kid anymore, Mama!" he exploded. He must have seen me recoil for he calmed down nearly at once. "Sorry. It hasn't been a good day."

I put my hand on his. "Sasha, don't do this. Don't go back down that road. You of all people know what alcohol can do. You saw what it did to your father."

"I'm not him."

"But you're his son. You need to learn from his mistakes, not repeat them."

He looked as if he was going to argue further, but then reconsidered. "Yeh, I'll... do what I can do."

It wasn't what I wanted to hear, but it was something. I decided to let it go, for then.

"Have you already had lunch?" I asked instead.

He smiled. "Do two vodkas count?"

"Sasha Levchenko! You come with me right now and get something decent to eat!" My mock anger didn't fool him. He knew I was more concerned than angry.

"We can go back inside."

"Isn't there some place a little more..."

"Respectable?" he asked, a hint of petulance in his voice.

"I was going to say *upscale*. Where you don't have to cut through the smoke to find your table?"

His look softened. "I think I know a place that might be more… acceptable."

He led me to a little restaurant on the next block, a traditional Ukrainian kitchen with about a dozen tables. The waitresses all wore customary national dress and the room stank of cabbage and onions. We were lucky enough to be seated nearly at once. I realized when we were at our table that I hadn't been *out* with just my son for ages, perhaps even before he went to Kharkov to play football. I ordered a pot of tea and we shared an order of varenyky, and we talked.

It was wonderful. With all that had happened in recent months, I had only rarely spoken to him and certainly not one on one. Talk of the lawsuit and Dima's death evolved into a much longer conversation about him and his life. About living with his father for so long, and about his hopes for the future. And eventually, as almost an afterthought, about his lifestyle.

"I suppose you know what kind of bar I was just drinking in," he said well into our conversation.

"I do," I said, keeping my voice as non-judgmental as possible.

"Did you know?"

I shook my head, afraid I might tear-up if I said anything.

"And? Were you… disappointed?"

Homosexuality isn't looked upon favorably in our country even now, but back then it was worse. People thought men who liked men were perverts, some kind of devilish offspring.

"I… I loved you before I walked in there, and I love you now."

"But you wanted more grandchildren, right?" He half-smiled.

I did my best to return his grin. "I wouldn't object, but I don't live my life thinking about what I don't have – including grandchildren."

I saw tears forming in his eyes and that was that. I couldn't stop the waterworks. He reached across the table and I took his hand in mine. I'm sure we looked quite the pair: the aging woman with the young stud, both bawling their eyes out.

After a few seconds, maybe a minute or two, we got ourselves back under control.

"I love you Mama," Sasha said, gripping my hand tightly.

"And I love you. Always have, and always will."

After that, everything went much better. It was as if his secret had stood between us, stopping the kind of exchange mothers and children should have. We talked more often, and were more open about our feelings. He told me about his *special friend*, and after a few weeks I actually met him. It was difficult, I won't lie. I didn't know how to act at first, what to say, even where to look when they touched, more like lovers than buddies. But slowly, little by little I came to accept his feelings without second thoughts. I won't say I never thought about the grandchildren I'd never see, but I didn't lose sleep over it.

If only all my life had run its course so smoothly.

*****

Despite my fear that Sasha would fall apart after losing his job, it was Bogdan who presented the biggest challenge going forward. I assumed that losing a menial part-time job would have little if any effect on him. I was wrong.

Oh, he hid his disappointment well enough.

"It's just a job," he said when I told him about it. But he was in his mid-fifties and had been fired. No one was looking to hire someone like him, and after months of going shop to shop, business to business, his mood darkened. When Sasha went to him (at my urging) to explain his sexual preferences, he put on a brave face. He hugged our son and told him he didn't care. But he was a Ukrainian man, and inside he hurt.

"Is it our fault?" he asked me by phone just hours after Sasha had left his house.

"It isn't anyone's fault," I tried to explain. I had read some studies in our library and thought I knew something about people like Sasha. "He is the way he is and probably would've been the same way no matter what we did, or didn't do."

He acted as though he understood, but time would show he did not. Or if he did, he could not believe that we were guiltless. Not three months after Sasha and I had had our conversation in the little restaurant in Haisyn, I received a call while at work at the library.

"Mrs. Vann, your ex-husband is passed out on a sidewalk in front of the tavern," one of the servers at the pub told me. I knew her from the library, not well, but enough so she knew my story. The village was small; probably half the people who lived there knew my story. "I think he's drunk."

My heart sank. After so many years, how could he? For just an instant I debated whether I should go. After all, he was my *ex*-husband. I owed him nothing. Legally. But in my heart I couldn't let him lie there. I got in my car and drove into the village. As I drove my thoughts bounced from past to present, a kaleidoscope of events and emotions that nearly overwhelmed me. I was lucky to get there without an accident.

I parked just down the street from the tavern, and got out of my car with a sense of dread. What if he was dead, or had had a stroke? What if the *old* Bogdan had come back? It didn't take long before I saw him, collapsed in a pile on the sidewalk, just as had been described to me. He hadn't shaved in several days and his body odor was evident from several feet away. I hesitated – my last chance to back out. But I couldn't abandon him.

I rolled him over and slapped him gently on the face. Memories of the bad old days rushed back to me.

"Bogdan, Bogdan wake up!" I whispered, loud enough for him to hear but not so loud as to attract attention from passersby. Several of them had already stopped across the street and were staring.

He groaned as his eyelids fluttered. "What the hell..."

"It's me, Nina. You passed out."

"I didn't pass out!" he growled, reminding me of just how nasty he could become when soused. "Had too much to drink."

"Well you're lying on the sidewalk. Let me get you home." I took his arm and tried to lift him to a seating position. He shook me off forcefully.

"Let me be, woman. I don't need any help from you."

"Bogdan, come on! You'll wind up in a jail cell!"

"Let 'em try!" he said, rolling back into a fetal position. "They can kiss my ass."

"You're making a scene!'

"*I'm* making a scene? Our son walks the streets with his faggot friends, and *I'm* making a scene?!"

He choked and I thought he might have vomited. But when I turned his face to check, I saw he was crying.

"Bogdan, it's not the end of the world," I tried to console.

"He likes men!" my ex- wailed, tears streaming down his face, snot dripping from his nose. "Our son likes *men!*"

There was nothing I could say that would undo that fact. So I didn't try.

"Come!" I ordered, pulling him up by the front of his shirt. "Enough feeling sorry for yourself! We're going home."

This time he didn't resist. It was as if all his energy had drained with his tears. "Why don't you just leave me here," he whimpered as I pulled and tugged. "Let me lie in my own piss."

"Because you are my ex-husband," I said with more conviction than I felt, "and the father of my children. I'll be damned if I'll have every gossipmonger in this town talking about me and mine for the next few weeks. Now are you going to help me here, or do I have to drag you?!" In reality I was feeling so weak I wasn't sure my knees would support *me*, let alone him as well. To my great relief he struggled to his feet, hanging onto me like a drowning man to a life-preserver.

He didn't say another word as we weaved our way back to the car. I propped him up while I unlocked the passenger door, and then slid him into the seat. He sat with his head thrown back against the headrest, as if he were staring through the roof of the car at God knew what.

For several minutes we drove in silence. Eventually I decided we needed to talk.

"It really isn't the end of the world, you know," I said, hoping to talk some sense into him. "There are a lot of homosexuals in Ukraine."

"Not in this village," he managed to mumble. "Maybe in Kyiv."

"He's still our son, Bogdan. He's going to need our support."

"Support? You expect me to support a faggot?"

"Stop it!" I yelled, swerving to the side of the road and slamming on the brakes. "When you were a cripple, could barely get out of bed to go to the bathroom, who was it who came to help you? Who was it that cooked your food and cleaned your house, and even wiped your butt when you couldn't do it! I don't want to hear a word against our son! Not a *word*!"

Bogdan's head slumped forward and he stared at the floor of the car. As usual, I could only sustain my anger for a few moments. I began to feel sorry for the wreck of a man I once loved, but sorrier for our son.

"Sasha is a good boy. Man," I corrected. "He can't control the way he feels, any more than you or I can. I know this is a shock. I know it's not what we might have wanted. But he is our son, and we will continue to love him and support him. Or at least I will."

Bogdan took a deep breath. "You're right, of course. It's just... Sasha!" He looked up at me with true despair in his face. "He was a star!"

The pain he felt made me wince, but didn't change my resolve in any way. "He's still a star. Our star." I waited a moment to gather my courage to say what I needed to say next. "If you can't see it that way, if you can't see him as our son, then I don't think I can be around you anymore. I think it would be better if you found another place to live."

He nodded absently. "Yes, I understand." He looked up at me as if waiting for a reaction. I remained silent. "I'll try. I'll really try," he finally said. "But maybe it *is* better for me to move. I've been there too long as it is."

Part of me wanted to argue with him, to remind him he had no other place to go. But part of me knew he was right. If he was ever going to live his life on his own, he needed to start doing it.

We drove the rest of the way back to the little house in silence.

Chapter 18

Bogdan moved out of Mama's little hut three weeks later. He didn't complain, didn't beg for me to let him stay. I don't know where he got the money for the move – he couldn't have made much working for Dima, and that was nearly a year earlier. But he moved. To a small apartment above the largest local granary office, downtown. He actually got a job with them, with the granary. The manager remembered him from years earlier, remembered the strong, dependable field-hand he had been, and was willing to let his recent work for Dima speak louder than the years of drunken madness that had preceded it.

Sasha got a job through one of his old football teammates. His reputation helped him in the new position, as an auto salesman in Uman. His reputation as a footballer, I mean. The other? It remained a secret, at least from the general public. I have a feeling his boss knew full-well his sexual preferences, but as long as he sold cars the rest didn't matter. And he did sell cars.

I continued on at the library, working my way up to Director when Marina – my longtime boss – finally retired. It was a good job, not only paying enough to meet my expenses, but enough so that I put aside a little each month. I was saving to be able to travel to America to visit Kateryna and her family. I hadn't seen my two grandchildren since they'd left years earlier, but it was a big expense. Kateryna and Petro had offered on more than one occasion to pay for my trip, but I imagined they were barely keeping their heads above water, what with all the expenses they had with two children. Kateryna had begun working soon after Mykolo and Ivanna started school, and although she earned a good salary compared to Ukrainian workers, they were constantly making-do in a land that was much more expensive than here in our village. Finally, after nearly three years of saving, I had enough to buy my ticket. But it wasn't so simple.

I had a difficult time getting my visa from the American Embassy. They claimed that my *ties* to Ukraine weren't enough to guarantee I wouldn't move to the U.S. They certainly didn't know me! Even if Sasha, and even Bogdan, and all my friends hadn't lived there, Ukraine was my home, the one place in all the world where I felt completely, utterly myself. Ironically, it was an intervention by Comrade Kostyshyn – my old tormenter at the library – that made it all possible. He had risen quite high in the post-Soviet Ukraine, a man of both means and influence. I rarely saw him at my work – I'd always assumed I'd gotten too old for his attentions – but one day, out of the blue, he appeared at the dedication of a costly renovation of the reading rooms.

"Mrs. Vann – Nina!" he greeted me as I waited with my staff for the arrival of the politicians and business people who wanted to take credit for the library building project. "It has been too long!" I saw many of my staffers looking at me with surprised confusion as Kostyshyn hugged me and kissed me affectionately on both cheeks.

"Comrade," I began, but he cut me off, holding up one finger.

"Comrade no longer," he said with a smile. "Just Fedir nowadays."

"Fedir, good of you to come."

"How could I not! My favorite librarian at my favorite library. I'm just sorry it took so long for improvements to come here."

"At least they came." What else could I say? My memories of him were less than warm.

But he would not be put off. He told me about his life, bragging with the ease of a man used to being envied.

"And you? You look well."

I thanked him and gave a short synopsis of the years since I'd seen him last. Then, in passing, I mentioned my travails trying to secure a visa to visit my daughter.

"The Americans are often quite prickly about their travel requirements," he said knowingly. "Would a word to the Ambassador help?"

I hesitated. On the one hand, I thought a word to the U.S. Ambassador almost certainly *would* help. On the other, what would I *owe* the good Comrade? I decided I was too old to worry about the harassment he had been known for years earlier. From the looks of him, he might be too old as well. "I couldn't ask for such a favor," I said with a smile that suggested the exact opposite.

"It's nothing," he said with a flip of his head. "I'm having lunch with him next week. I'll put in a good word."

I thanked him appropriately, thinking it was very likely he would do no such thing. But then again, what did I have to lose?

I went back to work, and as the routine of my daily life took over I forgot all about his grand promise. Until I received a phone call one afternoon, from the U.S. Embassy. An officious sounding woman explained that "new information" had come into the Embassy's possession regarding my application for a visa, and that although she couldn't promise anything, she strongly suggested that I reapply. It would cost me nearly half a week's wages, but I decided to take the chance.

Miracle of miracles, I got the visa. I suppose I'd always known that the wealthy people in Ukraine – and everywhere else, I imagine – live different lives than the rest of us. It's not just that they have bigger houses and cars, or nicer clothes and furs. No, they also get opportunities the rest of us can only dream of. Unless one of them decides to help someone like me. If there was a cost to be borne – I'd deal with that if and when it came up.

*****

I took a bus to Kyiv and stayed overnight in a small hotel in the eastern suburbs of the city. The morning of my flight, a taxi took me to Boryspil airport where I steeled myself to pass through the gantlet of ticket and passport officials that awaited me. Not that I wasn't worried. I'd never flown before; never even been in an airport. My heart was beating like a hummingbird's wings when I handed over my brand new passport to the airline representative behind the ticket counter. I just knew something was going to require explanation, or a khabar (a small bribe to see to it that someone does what they are supposed to do for free.) But, to my great surprise, the smiling woman handed my passport back, along with my boarding pass, and told me to "have a good flight." What kind of place was this, the United States, where people did their jobs without khabar, and smiled while doing it?

Even our own immigration officials were reasonably efficient, though without the smile. You'd have thought I was some kind of criminal element for all the stern looks and bored, disinterested comments I received. But they sent me on my way without a single hiccup.

The flight? What can I say? To fly for the first time is to step into a living dream! The surge of power as the huge plane rolls down the runway, the nervous sensation in your stomach as you wonder how a massive, heavy vehicle like that one can possible lift off the ground... it is incredible! I spent nearly the entire time looking out the tiny window next to me, at the ground below whenever possible but at the clouds whenever the ground was obscured. As amazing as it was to see the earth from the perspective of such altitude, I must admit the clouds held my attention much more. The way they shifted, transformed, broke apart and came together again – and so many kinds of clouds! It was more dreamlike than many of my actual dreams.

Kateryna and Petro met me at the airport in New York. My darling Ivanna was in her stroller, and Mykolo was already walking! I almost cried to realize how much of their young lives I'd already missed. Even Kateryna looked older, although I didn't tell her so.

"You look great!" I said instead. Her beaming smile was my reward.

They took me through the endless expanse of the airport as though it was nothing to them. Perhaps it wasn't. To me it was overwhelming, even a bit frightening. So many people! So much noise! I'd thought Kyiv and Boryspil were something to behold. And I hadn't seen anything yet.

They lived on the second floor of a tiny apartment in the East Village of Manhattan, a part of New York City. Petro drove us back across the George Washington Bridge so I could see the skyline of the city. Amazing! It made Kyiv look like a little village in comparison. Everything was so tall, so new, so loud!

The area where they lived was more reminiscent of Ukraine: the buildings were lower, older, and more run-down. I heard someone speaking Ukrainian even as we walked from where we parked back to their building.

"Of course, it's Little Ukraine!" Petro laughed when I told them. But there were many other languages as well, including some from Eastern Europe.

I can't remember all the new experiences from those two weeks, but there were many. New food, new people, new sights – it was as if I was visiting another planet, so different did it seem from my home. The most important time I spent, however, was not out in the streets of New York, but with Kateryna and her family in their tiny apartment. (It wasn't much bigger than Mama's little hut. When Kateryna told me how much they paid for rent, I almost swallowed my tongue!) Mykolo had already developed his own personality; in some ways he reminded me of Sasha at that age. (I didn't talk to my daughter about her brother's sexual preferences. I decided he'd tell her if he wanted to, and if not, then who was I to be making that decision.)

Ivanna was a little angel. Some children have a happy disposition from the very first. She was like that. Always smiling, always wanting to be held and played with. I still remember how happy I was with them.

But the longer I stayed in New York, the more I found myself longing to return to Ukraine. There was nothing really wrong with the city; I suppose it was fine for those who'd grown up there. But for me, it was just too foreign. Some people smiled too much – it made me nervous. What did they want? Others never smiled at all and acted as if they would just as soon knock you over as look at you. And when we walked in the streets, people almost did knock us over! Everyone rushed here and there as if they were late for an important appointment. They rarely looked where they were going, and almost never apologized if they bumped into you.

The food was... different. Kateryna and some of her friends cooked good Ukrainian meals, but they also ate the hamburgers and pizzas that were sold on every block. Then there were the people. In Ukraine, everyone looks, well, Ukrainian. In New York, you had people from seemingly everywhere: black, white, Spanish, Jewish – even Chinese! I felt uneasy, out of place. How could Kateryna and Petro live there? As my stay drew to a close, I decided to ask them.

"Have you decided yet when you'll move back to Ukraine?" I wondered as we sat drinking tea after dinner in their apartment one night.

Kateryna looked to Petro, who shrugged.

"I'm not sure we will," he said.

My daughter looked to me with concern. "It's not that we don't miss you, and Sasha, and everyone," she said. "It's just... Petro likes his job, and the kids *are* Americans..."

"And Ukrainians," I added.

She smiled, but it was a sad, thoughtful smile. "Yes, and Ukrainians. But this is our home now, Mama. I really don't know if we *could* move back there."

"Of course you could! We'd find you a nice house, near where I live. Or, I could move near you..." I struggled to find reasons that might convince them.

But there was no indecision in their expressions.

"Why don't you move here?" Petro asked after an awkward pause. "We could find a bigger place in Brooklyn, or maybe even the suburbs. You could live with us."

Now it was my turn to remain silent. Move there?! To that strange place where people spoke a strange language and ate strange food and wore strange clothes? "I don't think I could live here," I said after a painfully long wait. "And besides, I couldn't leave Sasha back home all alone."

"Mama, he's 35 years old!" Kateryna cried. "He can take care of himself!"

They tried. And I can honestly say I listened. But I was too set in my ways; I could only have one home in my heart, and that was Ukraine. So for the remainder of my stay we kept away from the topic of moving, and just enjoyed each other's company while we could. I can't say I didn't have a good time. I did. But as the two weeks came to an end, I was more than ready to go back. To go home.

Everyone came to the airport to see me off, and there was a lot of kissing and hugging and tears. But I couldn't help thinking they were – in a way – happy to see me go, and I knew I was – in a way – happy to be leaving. As I went past the agent who took my boarding pass, I turned and waved goodbye to my *American family*, as I called them. Petro held up Mykolo, so he could wave goodbye. Kateryna bent down over Ivanna's stroller to lift her hand in a close approximation of a wave. I waved back through my tears, and then turned and walked down the narrow hallway to the plane. I felt both drained and elated, disappointed and yet happy.

Sometimes there are no good alternatives, just some that are better than the rest.

Chapter 19

Life in Ukraine seemed a bit slow and somber when I first returned. Nobody seemed to be in a rush, few people smiled, and even the weather was more gray and cool than normal.

But it was home. The smells might not have been as heady and mysterious, but they were my smells. People I'd never met didn't wish me a *'good day'* every time I turned around, but my neighbors brought me mushrooms they'd picked in the forest, and invited me to eat varenyky and shashlik for no reason other than that the weather had turned nice. Nothing was as big, or as new, or as important, but everything was mine.

*****

The years pass more quickly now. At least they seem to. It is a strange sensation: the days pass slowly, at times painfully so, while the years pass in a blur of… living. I retired from the library many years ago. I would have worked longer, but with the economy the way it was they enforced the retirement age in government jobs very strictly. They were nice enough about it. They gave me a going-away party, and presented me with flowers and a beautiful embroidered shawl, something I still wear on cool fall nights. But it was still a little sad.

One quick story. There was quite a crowd at the retirement party: friends, co-workers, even Sasha and Bogdan managed to find clean clothes and made an appearance. I was kept running, saying hello, accepting thanks, that sort of thing. After all, I'd worked there for nearly 30 years, a good part of that as Director. I knew everyone in our village, and most everyone in the oblast. So when a little old man in a wheelchair was pushed into the library by a young woman attractive enough to turn heads, I wondered why I didn't recognize him. I went over to correct that oversight.

"Hello there," I said, smiling my best 'welcome to the library' smile refined over years of use.

"Hello, Nina," the old man said, staring at me with lively eyes that belied his shriveled body. I must have shown my confusion for he quickly added, "the years have been good to you. Better than me."

The voice. It was raspy, shaky, but I recognized that voice.

"Comrade Kostyshyn!" I cried out, a bit louder than I'd intended. "What... I mean, how are you?"

His lips moved in what might have been a smile. "I've been better. Cancer, of the pancreas. Not good, I'm afraid. But I'm being rude – Nina, this is my wife, Sofiya. Sofiya, the Director of our regional library, Nina Vann. It is still Vann, isn't it?"

I felt a recurrence of the same chill I'd always felt whenever he'd visited. "Yes, it is."

"Whatever happened to that nice young man, I believe he owned a transport company?"

"He died," I said, feeling as if I'd somehow debased Dima's memory by even discussing him with this man.

"Oh. I'm sorry. And you never remarried?"

"Fedir, you're being nosey!" his wife chastised lightly.

"Am I? Ah, perhaps so. As you get closer to the end manners don't matter quite so much. I hope I didn't upset you?"

"No, not at all," I lied, keeping my smile firmly in place. "Well, I need to keep circulating. Please, enjoy yourselves."

He nodded, she muttered some polite words, and I drifted back into the swirl of the party, my mind suddenly abuzz with memories and feelings I'd thought long gone. But then I met some friends who swept me back into the

present and I soon forgot all about Comrade K and his wife.
I never saw them leave that night, but I heard a few weeks
later that he had died. It was big news in our oblast; he'd
been a major power broker for decades. The Orthodox
Church hosted a special mass for his soul, and even
representatives from the national government in Kyiv came
to pay their respects. I try never to speak poorly about the
dead, but I very much doubt that any mass could have saved
that man's soul. Too many years working for the other side.

I only mention him because another man with a
checkered past also fell ill at about the same time: Bogdan.

It was no more than a month after Comrade K's death
that Sasha revealed to me his father had been feeling poorly.

"He's actually missed a few days of work," Sasha said.
"Went up to Kyiv to see a specialist."

That didn't sound good at all. "Oh? For what?"

"Not sure. You know, Papa. He likes to keep things to
himself."

That I did know. We rarely spoke by that time, maybe
once a week or even less by phone. The revelation about
Sasha had shaken him badly, and I'd made it clear I didn't
want to listen to his objections and disappointment. We kept
our distance for the most part, with the kids and grandkids
our only ongoing link. I did hear news from Sasha, who
despite knowing full-well that his father could never accept
his lifestyle kept in much closer touch with him than I did.
It's funny how a person can feel more upset about the way
someone else is treated than the person himself. Especially
when it's a child of yours. Somehow they maintained a truce
that allowed a weekly meal together and the occasional visit
to help with chores around the apartment. I have to say I
was happy they shared as much as they did, even if it was a
difficult and often uncomfortable relationship.

As soon as Sasha told me about his father's illness, I
called Bogdan.

"I hear you were up in Kyiv seeing a doctor," I said with little prelude. "What's going on?"

"Good news travels fast."

"This is a small village. All news travels fast. You know that. So, why were you up there?"

"Eh, been feeling a bit tired lately –more than usual. And my appetite's way down."

"You? You could always eat a horse!"

He chuckled. "Not any more. Lucky if I can choke down a couple of varenyky. And the whites of my eyes are looking a little yellow."

That didn't sound good. "What did he say – the doctor, I mean?"

"He examined me, took some blood. Should hear back in a few days."

"No guesses?"

"He was pretty tight-lipped."

That didn't sound good. "So how are you feeling now?"

"Same: tired, run-down. But hey, I'm not a kid anymore, right? What do I expect?"

I wanted to reassure him, tell him it was probably nothing. But I knew his history, knew how badly he'd abused his health over the years. "Yeh, probably so," I said. "You'll let me know when you hear from the doctor, right?"

"Yeh, sure. Or you could just wait to hear it in the daily gossip."

"Might get it faster that way."

He chuckled. "Maybe so."

We exchanged a little more idle chatter, though neither of us had anything of interest to say. When we finally hung up I realized I'd been gripping the phone so hard my knuckles were white.

*****

He called me three days later, just after I'd finished breakfast.

"Heard back from the doctor in Kyiv," he began without prelude.

From his matter-of-fact delivery I assumed the news was good, or at least not too bad.

"Oh? What's going on with you?"

"Cirrhosis of the liver, complicated by hepatitis. Seems he thinks I drank too much for too long."

I'd heard of both diseases, but didn't know much about them. "What's the treatment?"

This time his laugh sounded hollow. "Not much. He told me to stop drinking."

"You did that a long time ago, didn't you?"

"I have a sip every now and then, but nothing like the bad old days."

"Then how's that going to help you?"

"Good question. He gave me a couple of prescriptions, but said they're only about twenty per cent effective."

"Twenty per cent?! That's ridiculous!" I was shocked and outraged.

"Just think how I felt," he said, trying to sound more at ease than he could possibly be.

"We need to get you to another specialist," I said. "Maybe Moscow."

"Oh? And who's going to pay? Our insurance doesn't work there anymore, now that we're independent. And the guy in Kyiv is supposedly quite good. What will the Russians know that our own people don't?"

I'd forgotten that with the dissolution of the Soviet Union each new independent country had its own medical system, and its own programs to pay for them. I wasn't as sanguine about our Ukrainian doctors having every bit of know-how as their Russian counterparts, but I had no hard information to the contrary either. I decided to look into it further.

Once we hung up I went directly to my old library. I looked though every resource book and directory I could find and discovered that it was extremely difficult to determine whether one country's medical system is significantly better than another's, particularly if the two countries were part of the same country just a few years earlier. I did learn that liver transplants were much more common in Russia than in Ukraine, and the success rate was somewhat higher. Perhaps that was why Bogdan hadn't mentioned the procedure to me. Or perhaps he wasn't a good candidate.

I called a local physician I'd known for many years and asked him.

"Cirrhosis with Hepatitis B?" he repeated when I explained. "I'm afraid his prognosis is not so good. If you don't cure the hepatitis first, the transplant has little chance. And for someone as sick as he must be, curing the hepatitis will not be easy."

When I pressed, he agreed that a trip to Moscow, or even Poland – which I hadn't considered – might be worthwhile. What I also hadn't considered was Bogdan's stubbornness.

"No chance," he said when I broached the subject with him.

"Why not?!"

"I've lived all my life here in Ukraine, and I will die here in Ukraine."

"But what if you can live longer by spending a short while in another country that has more resources?"

"Not for me." He said it with such finality I wanted to slap him.

"You're too young to just give up!"

"I've lived long enough. I saw my daughter marry. I met my grandchildren. What else is there worth living for?"

"The sunrise! A perfect cherry varenyky. A whale breaching! There's *so* much!"

He smiled, a sad 'you don't get it, do you?' kind of smile. "I talked to the doctor. I'm not going to be watching a lot of perfect sunrises or stuffing my face with tasty pies. I'm going to get more and more confused, my stomach, ankles and legs are going to swell, and I'll feel even more exhausted than I do now. And then, thankfully, I'll be gone."

I started to interrupt, but he stopped me with by holding up his hand.

"It's my own fault. I drank too much for too long, I did terrible things to you and other people I knew... I basically wasted my life – if you believe in divine retribution, this is it."

He had never been particularly religious; I wondered whether he seriously believed he was being punished for past actions or if he was just saying something he thought would strike a chord with me.

I wasn't letting him off the hook so easily. "God would not punish a man who repents," I said, sounding more religious than I felt. "You've changed your life. Now you have to keep living! For the kids and grandkids, if nothing else!"

His smile became a frown. "Do you really think they would be better off with me slowly falling apart right before their eyes? Would you be better off? Of course not. And I won't be the selfish SOB who makes all of you suffer so I can stick around for another few months, or even years, eventually not knowing who you all are, or maybe even who *I* am. I've already lived that life. Didn't like it."

I began to panic. His arguments were good.

"But…" I began, not knowing where I was going but not willing to surrender to his pessimism. He put a single finger to my lips.

"You can't win this one," he said softly. "Because *I* can't win this one."

I began to cry and he put his arms around me and gave a big hug.

"It'll be okay, Nina. It'll all be okay."

*****

He didn't give up, despite all the visits to the hospital, all the treatments, the loss of memory and the loss of hope. But he never lost his sense of self and his firm belief that what he was doing was at least a partial payback for all the bad he'd caused so many years earlier. It gave him great satisfaction and made his last days a time of pride instead of a time of embarrassment and dread.

He died on a Friday. It was raining by the time I got to the hospital late in the afternoon. A nurse had called me at home to tell me I needed to get to the hospital quickly if I wanted to see him before he went. Kateryna and her family had had to go back to the States a week earlier, and neither Julia nor Yerva had forgiven my ex-husband for all his peccadillos in days gone by, but Sasha came with me.

When we entered his room, the only light came from the blinking indicators on all the equipment connected to his body. Even though I'd seen it all before, for some reason the cold, impersonal reality of the mechanical systems struck me hard that day and I struggled to keep from tearing it all away. Strangely enough, Bogdan looked utterly peaceful lying there amidst his electronic minders. Certainly more peaceful than I.

"He's in a better place," Sasha said, trying to console me.

"Perhaps. But he's not here."

For all his flaws, and I haven't forgotten them to this day, it seemed wrong he wouldn't see the grandkids grow, or give comfort and advice to Kateryna and Sasha. He'd been present in our lives for so long we'd assumed he'd always be there, and then he wasn't. It was as if the moon suddenly stopped rising: it might not cast much light on our world, but it *is* familiar and expected.

We buried him in a simple ceremony three days later. Only Sasha and I, and two old men I didn't recognize, attended. I thought Bogdan would have approved – nothing mawkish, just enough words to send him on his way. When the funeral was over, Sasha and I rode back to my house together.

"So, what now?" he asked me out of the blue.

"What do you mean?"

"I mean you were spending so much time and worry dealing with Papa's illness you barely had time enough for yourself. Now that he's gone that'll change."

"Will it? I hadn't really thought about it."

"Probably didn't have time. But now you'll have to."

"I suppose I will." I didn't want to think about anything just then, but I knew he was right. For the first time since I'd been a teenager, I didn't have a man in my life – if only to cause me grief and sorrow. What *would* I do next?

"Would you like to move in with Egor and me?" Sasha asked.

I couldn't hide my surprise. "Move in?! What, do you think I've suddenly become old and infirm just because my ex-husband died?" I was barely 60 and thought of myself as young and fit, though the mirror often contradicted me. Besides, Sasha had barely been with his new *special friend* for six months by that time. I wasn't about to introduce a 'mother-in-law' of sorts into such a newly-minted relationship. He had no such compunction.

"Why not? I'm not saying you *need* to move in with someone, but won't you be lonely? And we could help you with things about the house."

I took a deep breath. I knew he was trying to be helpful, but the entire conversation rubbed me the wrong way. "I appreciate the offer," I said calmly. "But I enjoy my independence and want to keep it as long as I can. Besides, you two can come visit me every now and then to keep me company."

He smiled. "We'll do that."

*****

It wasn't until some days later that the full impact of his question finally hit me. What *was* I going to do with my life now that I wasn't dealing with Bogdan, or someone else? After weeks of pondering and more than a little vacillation, I made up my mind. I'd always wanted to try to reconnect with the simpler farm life I'd experienced when I was younger. Why not then?

When I announced that I was moving from my long-time home to a one bedroom house in the country, I wasn't unaware I might stir controversy among my relatives. I just didn't know how much.

"Are you crazy?!" Yerva responded when she learned my plans. "Have you lost your mind? What happens if you fall and hurt yourself way out there? Or if a burglar or intruder breaks into the house? What will you do then?"

With her jaw stuck out and her eyes aflame, she reminded me of nothing more than a fire-breathing dragon from a childhood book of fairy tales.

"I suppose I'll deal with it, as I have for all these years now," I answered, trying not to smile. Perhaps she was only looking after my welfare, but it seemed ridiculous that everyone I knew believed I'd suddenly become enfeebled. Yes, she wasn't the only one.

"You know you're always welcome to move in with us," Sasha repeated when he heard. I knew he was only saying what he thought he must, and so I didn't feel at all bad with turning him down a second time.

"Mama, come to America!" Kateryna said.

"Thank you, but Ukraine is my home and I'm too old to change now," I said. No further arguments were forthcoming.

So as soon as the weather warmed up I got Sasha (and Egor) and a few local friends to help me move my few possessions out to my new home. It was a nice little place, reminiscent in some ways of the house of my childhood but with a bit more room and all the modern conveniences. It sat on a narrow dirt lane only a few kilometers from the old house, surrounded on all sides by endless fields of grain punctuated by the occasional vegetable patch or a cow or two. Beech, pine and oak trees bordered the fields, providing a windbreak and shade, with the occasional birch giving a picturesque look to the rolling farmland.

My house was set off on its own, the nearest neighbor living around a kilometer away. That was how it had been for years in the countryside: people living close enough to help each other in an emergency, but not so close as to infringe upon the independence – or was it misanthropy – of the Ukrainian farmer. The decades under Soviet rule had made many people reluctant to trust folks they didn't know well, and just barely accepting of those they did. I won't put myself in that group, but I won't deny that I wasn't looking for uninvited social interaction. I'd had my fill of human drama and was quite content to share my days with the sun and the wind and the animals I kept on my little slice of farmland.

I began with a small collie dog, to keep me company and warn me of approaching visitors. Then I *inherited* a cow from a neighbor who was getting too old to tend her, in exchange for a few liters of milk each week – a deal I was happy to accept. After a while I decided that a small herd of sheep would keep my dog, Volga, busy herding the few animals I could afford so they didn't wander into the surrounding fields. They munched the grass in my yard down to height so I didn't need to mow, and provided wool and meat I used or sold, depending on my needs and demand. Besides, they rarely talked back or caused me unexpected pain or heartache.

As time went by, I suppose I became something of a recluse. Sasha and Yerva visited fairly often, at least twice a month, and I saw Julija and her family nearly that often, but when they weren't visiting I kept pretty much to myself. I did go into the village once a week or so to buy those items I couldn't grow or trade for, but I certainly didn't spend much time in the local restaurants or bars. I was comfortable, reasonably happy, and enjoying my *silver* years in relative isolation.

But new times bring new changes, and we have to change with them. About three or four years after I moved to my little farmhouse, Sasha came to see me on one of his regular visits 'out to the country.' As soon as I kissed him hello I knew he had something to tell me. Ever since he was a little boy he always fidgeted whenever he had news. He was fidgeting that day.

"We got the visa," he said, apparently thinking I'd understand his shorthand.

"A visa for what? For where?" I asked.

"To move to the States!" he answered, his face alight with the prospect. "Egor and I have been waiting for over a year now, filing paperwork and paying fees, and they finally said yes!"

"You're *moving* to the States?"

His smile faded when he realized I wasn't as pleased for him as he'd hoped I'd be. "Kateryna has been after me for a long time now. You know that. With the way people here in Ukraine look at... people like me, and the bad job prospects, it'll be a good change. And then you'll have *two* reasons to visit – or maybe move there!"

I couldn't pretend I was pleased. I just couldn't. "Not for me, I'm afraid. This is my home, and always will be."

"Mama, don't be so old-fashioned! Ukraine isn't what it once was. You should come with us, to the States!" The way he said it sounded like a TV commercial.

"I'm sure you'll do wonderfully there," I said, without having to exaggerate. The U.S. seemed like just the place for my Sasha. Over there they have people of all nationalities and lifestyles, so he and his friend would fit in much better than here in our older, more tradition-bound Ukraine.

He dropped the hard-sell but continued with a more subtle approach for nearly all the conversation. Eventually he realized he had no possibility of changing my mind and we moved on to more mundane matters. But I could tell he wasn't done trying to convert me. Every time we talked over the next few weeks he put in a gentle reminder that I was welcome to come to the States with them. I wasn't tempted.

I suppose I held out the slightest hope he might change his mind, just as I'd always hoped that Kateryna and Petro would eventually see the error of their ways and move back home. It was not to be.

A little under two months later, I went to Boryspil Airport to see the boys off. I tried to put on a happy face to make it easier for them, but it wasn't at all easy for me.

"You must come for a visit as soon as we're settled," Egor said as we stood by the entrance to the Security line. "We'll have a room all made up for you."

I smiled at his optimism as well as his sweet disposition. I could understand what Sasha saw in him, or at least some of it. Some would always be beyond me.

Sasha gave me a big hug and kiss.

"It's not so far," he said, his smile bittersweet. "Just a seven hour flight. And I'll call every week."

I nodded, afraid to speak for fear my voice would crack. I could already feel tears beginning to well up.

He kissed me on both cheeks and headed down the corridor toward the Security checkpoint. At the last bend in the route he turned back and waved with a sad grin. I returned his wave, my own grin cock-eyed and brittle. And then he was gone.

And I was alone.

Or so it seemed for several days after he left. I was relieved when he called to let me know they'd arrived safely and were 'crashing' with Kateryna and her family. Relieved, yet saddened. Somehow it hadn't quite seemed real until I learned he was there with his sister. Both of them an ocean away in a world so different from mine…

*****

As I said, it took a while for me to adjust to both children having *abandoned* me. Not really. Or maybe a little. I think I was angry with them at first for leaving their homeland – and me. But as the days passed I began to think more about the future than the past, more about what I *had* than what I'd lost. Why? I don't really know. Perhaps because I *had* to. To sit at home crying about my losses would do nothing other than diminish my current life. And besides, I had a menagerie of farm creatures to take care of. I couldn't just sit and stew.

The feeling of emptiness that had threatened to paralyze me eventually blew away like a dark cloud. I found the rhythm of living alone seductive. No one to answer to. No one to lose.

My animals and I became a family of sorts. I fed them and talked to them, shorn them and milked them. They gave me simple affection and unconditional love. As best they could. It was enough for me.

And has been for nearly two decades now.

Mykolo and Ivanna have both graduated from college and have found good jobs in the United States. Neither has come to Ukraine for a visit for many, many years, but I understand. They are young. They think time will last forever. Petro is now a bigshot with his company, and Kateryna works part-time with some charity – in the U.S., of course. Something about helping refugees. I don't understand it all that well, actually. Sasha stayed with his friend Egor for five or six years, and then lived alone for quite some time. He met an American, Robert, while vacationing in Mexico. Strange, isn't it, that people travel to other countries only to meet people from back home? But I'm happy. They've lived together for quite a while now, and seem to get along as well as ever. They were here for a visit last year. Sasha tried to persuade me to go back to the States with them once again, but I haven't changed my mind.

"Home is where the heart is," I told him. "I don't need a big house and car. I just need Ukraine."

He wasn't satisfied, but he knows better than to push the argument. I've always been stubborn, but more so now that I'm older. Why not? If you can't do what you want when you're my age, when can you?

I live here in my little house, on my little road, with all my animals, and I can honestly say I'm happy. Or at least happy enough. I do think about the past now and then – who doesn't? – but many of the details are fading; that's why I wrote this down. I don't remember like I once did, and soon all those years will be a gray mash of shifting vagaries.

But that's how it should be. The past is a canvas already painted, a field already sown. Today is the only day that matters, the only day we can still influence. So I get up each morning, lift my face to the rising sun and take a deep breath.

It is good to be alive. Still.